Over **400** of your favorite games and puzzles!

Nelson's GIANT BOOK of Bible Activities for Kids

W. B. FREEMAN

OLIVER NELSON

THOMAS NELSON PUBLISHERS
Nashville

Copyright © 1992, 1993 by W. B. Freeman

All rights reserved. Puzzles may be photocopied for individual or group use.

Published in Nashville, Tennessee, by Oliver-Nelson Books, a division of Thomas Nelson, Inc., Publishers, and distributed in Canada by Word Communications, Ltd., Richmond, British Columbia.

The puzzles in this special edition were originally published in *Nelson's Super Book of Bible Activities for Kids: Book 1* and *Nelson's Super Book of Bible Activities for Kids: Book 2*.

Unless otherwise noted, the Bible version used in puzzles 1–167 is the King James Version of the Holy Bible. Scripture noted NKJV is from THE NEW KING JAMES VERSION. Copyright © 1979, 1980, 1982, Thomas Nelson, Inc., Publishers.

Unless otherwise noted, the Bible version used in puzzles 168–322 is THE NEW KING JAMES VERSION. Copyright © 1979, 1980, 1982, Thomas Nelson, Inc., Publishers. Scripture noted KJV is from the King James Version of the Holy Bible.

Printed in the United States of America.

ISBN 0-8407-9258-1

Introduction

This puzzle book has a wide variety of puzzles about the Bible designed especially for children 4–11 years old.

The degree of difficulty for the puzzles is identified with one, two, or three stars at the top of each puzzle.

⭐ = puzzles for children 4–6 years old. These puzzles are for nonreaders and are mostly maze, matching, hidden element, hidden picture, identification, and dot-to-dot puzzles that require NO reading skills.

⭐⭐ = puzzles for children 6–8 years old. These puzzles require some reading and spelling skills — generally for words of one or two syllables, and generally for words that are concrete nouns and simple verbs common in first-, second-, and third-grade schoolwork. The puzzles for this age include some crosswords, hidden words, secret codes, and jumbled letters puzzles.

⭐⭐⭐ = puzzles for children 9–11 years old. These puzzles are for children grades four to six. The puzzles require an ability to read and spell at the intermediate level, as well as to recall words, letters, and concepts. The child is asked in some cases to look up Bible references and to read them for comprehension or to use a simplified concordance. The puzzles include crosswords, hidden words, anagrams, secret codes, rebuses, and number puzzles. (The number puzzles require an ability to add, subtract, multiply, and divide.)

 = Puzzles with this symbol require the use of a Bible for completion. Unless otherwise specified, the King James Bible is used for puzzles 1–167, and the New King James Bible is used for puzzles 168–322.

 = Puzzles with this symbol require the use of a Bible concordance, such as the type found in a children's Bible.

Encourage young children to look for puzzles with one star, so as not to become discouraged at their inability to work all of the puzzles. Encourage children first grade and older to try puzzles that are slightly ahead of their level. Puzzles provide good motivation for learning new skills!

Friendly competition is possible using the puzzles in this book. Organize groups of students into teams; some of the puzzles lend themselves readily to group problem-solving, such as anagrams and crosswords.

Christian school teachers and home-schooling parents will find many of these puzzles useful in reinforcing Bible lessons.

Certificates are available for rewarding puzzle work.

The Created

Find the names of God's creations hidden in the square by going across (both left and right), up, down, and diagonally. We found one word for you. Cross each word off the word pool as you find it.

O	M	A	U	P	F	A	F	M
M	A	N	Q	R	O	N	U	C
T	T	Z	X	A	W	T	I	R
L	R	W	H	A	L	E	S	F
Y	E	A	O	H	F	I	S	H
A	E	T	L	M	L	E	T	L
U	T	E	T	U	A	X	A	R
E	A	R	A	E	H	N	R	B
V	M	I	O	T	D	T	S	C

Word Pool

~~WATER~~   FOWL
LAND   FISH
SEA   MAN
STARS   WOMAN
WHALES   TREE

See answer on puzzle answer page 1.

All Aboard, Matey

Noah took animals into the ark two-by-two and seven-by-seven (Genesis 7:1-16). Help the duck below find her mate, already inside the ark, before the door is shut!

Banners of Praise

Praise is an expression of our love and thanks to God, and of our trust in Him. Another reason we praise God is because the Bible tells us to — when we praise Him we are obedient to what God tells us in His Word.

Use the secret code to fill in the letters in the banners of praise.

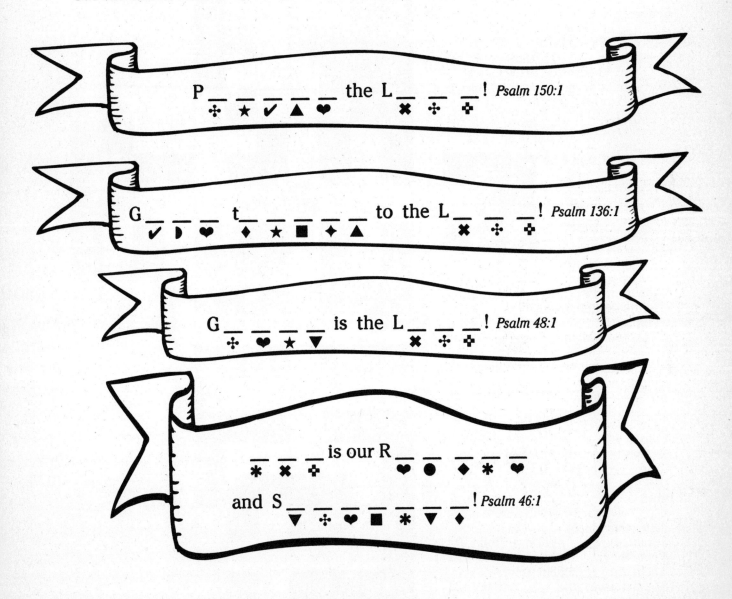

P _ _ _ _ _ the L _ _ _ ! *Psalm 150:1*

G _ - _ t _ _ _ _ _ _ to the L _ _ _ ! *Psalm 136:1*

G _ _ _ _ is the L _ _ _ ! *Psalm 48:1*

_ _ _ is our R _ _ _ _ _

and S _ _ _ _ _ _ _ ! *Psalm 46:1*

Secret Code

♦ = H   ■ = N   ✛ = R   ✜ = D   ◗ = V   ● = F   ★ = A

✦ = K   ♥ = E   ✔ = I   ▼ = T   ◆ = U   ✖ = O   ▲ = S   ✳ = G

See answer on puzzle answer page 1.

Knowing His Name

There are many names for Jesus in the Bible, each one telling us something about who Jesus is. Fill in the crossword grid with the names of Jesus. Use your New King James Bible if necessary.

Across

1 _____ of the valleys (Song of Solomon 2:1)
3 #4 Across of _____ (Matthew 27:54)
4 ____ of #3 Across (Matthew 27:54)
6 ____ of God, who takes away the sin of the world! (John 1:29)
9 Every tongue confess that Jesus Christ is _____ (Philippians 2:11)
11 Thou shalt call his name _____ (Luke 1:31)
12 Thou art the _____, the Son of the living God (Matthew 16:16)
15 In the beginning was the ____ (John 1:1)
16 This is Jesus, the _____ of Nazareth of Galilee (Matthew 21:11)
17 A high _____ forever according to the order of Melchizedek (Hebrews 6:20)
18 Behold, the #2 Down of the tribe of _____ (Revelation 5:5)
21 Christ, the _____ of the world (John 4:42)
22 I am the way, the #8 Down and the_____ (John 14:6)

Down

2 ____ of the tribe of #18 Across (Revelation 5:5)
3 I am the _____ #14 Down (John 10:11)
5 I am the ____ of the sheep (John 10:7)
7 I am the _____ of life (John 6:48)
8 I am the way, the _____, and the #22 Across (John 14:6)
10 Bright and morning _____ (Revelation 22:16)
13 Before Abraham was, ____ (John 8:58)
14 I am the #3 Down _____ (John 10:11)
18 Jesus of Nazareth the King of the _____ (John 19:19)
19 I am the #20 Down _____, and My Father is the vinedresser (John 15:1)
20 I am the _____#19 Down, and My Father is the vinedresser (John 15:1)

See answer on puzzle answer page 1.

All Tuned Up

How many musical instruments mentioned in the Bible can you find in this puzzle? You may read about these musical instruments in Genesis 31:27; Psalm 81:2; Isaiah 5:12; Ezekiel 28:13; Daniel 3:5.

```
S  Q  C  L  D  M  Z  K  P  F
P  B  X  H  O  R  N  I  O  E
N  H  U  T  J  C  P  R  N  W
D  V  A  F  U  E  H  I  Y  L
Y  E  K  R  S  Q  R  B  R  D
G  M  T  M  P  U  H  W  E  S
I  X  O  A  O  T  A  R  T  J
L  E  R  B  M  I  T  O  L  E
P  I  M  X  F  O  I  Y  A  W
J  A  V  E  C  G  R  M  S  E
T  U  R  P  L  E  X  U  P  L
```

Word Pool

HARP   TIMBREL   TAMBOURINE   HORN
LYRE   PSALTERY   PIPES

See answer on puzzle answer page 1.

Fruit Basket Upset

Galatians 5:22-23 lists the fruit of the Spirit. See how many you can unscramble before you look them up in the Bible.

Rearrange these scrambled letters to find the fruit of the Spirit.

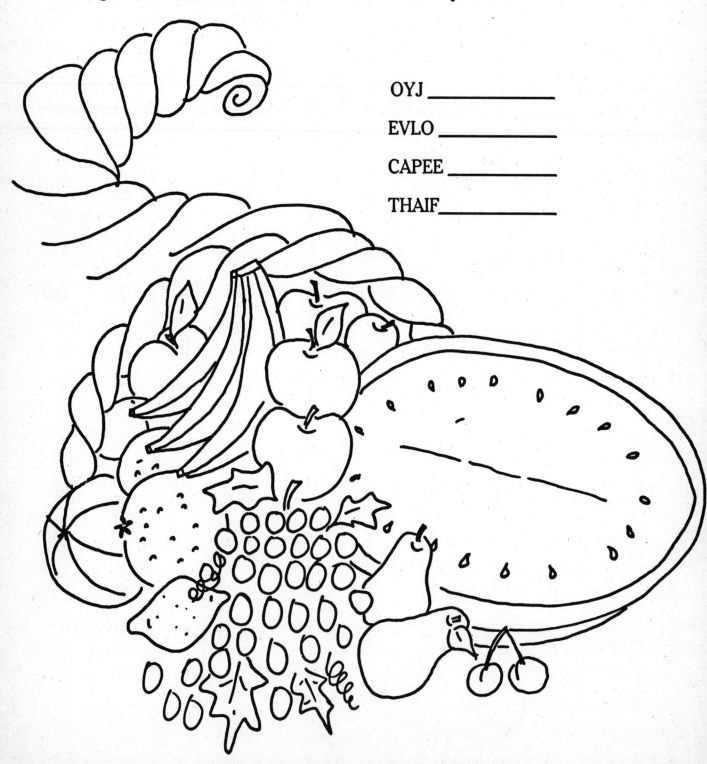

OYJ _____

EVLO _____

CAPEE _____

THAIF_____

See answer on puzzle answer page 1.

The Blessed Ones

In the Sermon on the Mount, Jesus tells about the blessings in store for the citizens of the Kingdom of Heaven. Fill in the answers to these clues to complete the crossword puzzle. If you need help, turn to Matthew 5:3-12 to find the answers.

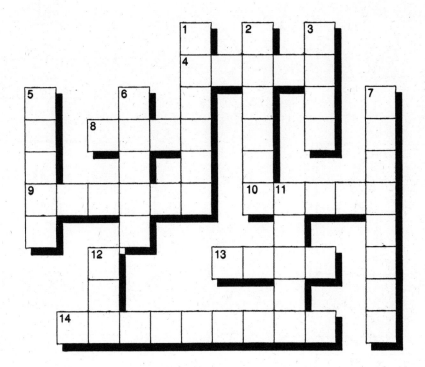

Across

4 The ones who make this will be called the children of God

8 Theirs is the Kingdom of Heaven

9 Hunger and _____ after righteousness

10 They _____ be filled

13 Rejoice, and be exceeding _____

14 Blessed are ye when men shall revile you and _____ you

Down

1 Blessed are the poor in _____

2 Blessed are the peace-_____

3 They will inherit the earth

5 What the meek inherit

6 Those who do this will be comforted

7 What the peacemakers will be called

11 Blessed are the pure in _____

12 The pure in heart will _____ God

See answer on puzzle answer page 1.

Bible Trees

First unscramble the names of the trees below. Then match the trees with their fallen leaves and the verse in the Bible that tells about this type of Bible tree.

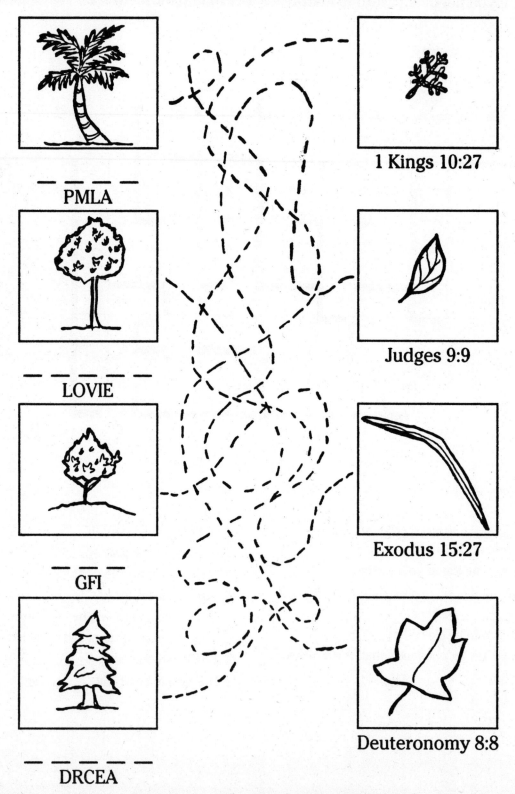

1 Kings 10:27

PMLA

LOVIE

Judges 9:9

GFI

Exodus 15:27

DRCEA

Deuteronomy 8:8

See answer on puzzle answer page 1.

Our Place

Use the secret code to fill in the vowels to reveal the message of the psalm.

BL__SS__D   __S   TH__   M__N   TH__T
  ☆   ☆   ▲   ☆   ■   ■

W__LK__TH   N__T   __N   TH__   C__ __NS__L
  ■   ☆   ♥   ▲   ☆   ♥   ✱   ☆

__F   TH__   __NG__DLY,   N__R   ST__ND__TH
♥   ☆   ✱   ♥   ♥   ■   ☆

__N   TH__   W__Y   __F   S__NN__RS,   N__R
▲   ☆   ■   ♥   ▲   ☆   ♥

S__TT__TH   __N   TH__   S__ __T   __F
 ▲   ☆   ▲   ☆   ☆   ■   ♥

TH__   SC__RNF__L.
 ☆   ♥   ✱

Secret Code

■ = A   ☆ = E   ▲ = I   ♥ = O   ✱ = U

See answer on puzzle answer page 1.

Christmas Story

Fill in the blanks in the Christmas story from the word pool on the next page and then use those words to complete the crossword puzzle. The Christmas story is found in Luke 2:7-14.

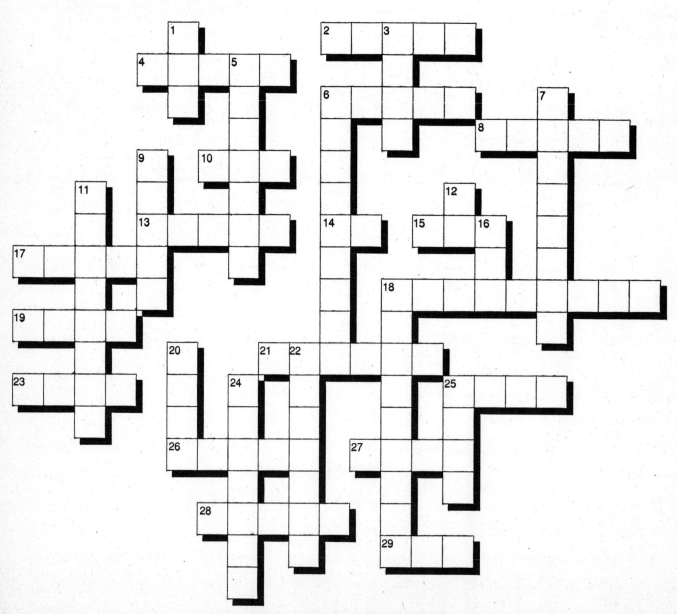

See answer on puzzle answer page 1.

And she brought forth her _____ _____, and wrapped him in
6 Down   29 Across

_____ clothes and laid him in a _____; because there was no
18 Across   21 Across

_____ for them in the _____. And there were in the same _____
3 Down   10 Across   5 Down

_____ _____ in the _____, keeping _____ over their _____
18 Down   22 Down   8 Across   4 Across   6 Across

by night. And, _____, the _____ of the _____ came upon them, and
12 Down   9 Down   20 Down

the glory of the Lord shone _____ about them; and they were sore
28 Across

afraid. And the angel said unto them, _____ not: for behold, I bring
27 Across

you good tidings of great joy, which shall be to all people. For unto you is

_____ this _____ in the city of _____ a _____ which is
25 Down   1 Down   26 Across   24 Down

Christ the Lord. And this shall be a sign unto you; Ye shall _____ the
23 Across

_____ wrapped in swaddling clothes, lying in a _____. And
25 Across   21 Across

suddenly there was with the angel a multitude of the _____ _____
7 Down   19 Across

_____ God, the Father (another name for father is _____) and
11 Down   16 Down

saying, _____ _____ _____ in the highest, and on _____
13 Across 14 Across 15 Across   2 Across

_____, good will toward men.
17 Across

Word Pool

HOST   DAY   FIRSTBORN   MANGER   ROOM   SHEPHERDS   LO   SWADDLING
LORD   INN   PRAISING   FEAR   FIELD   EARTH   BORN   SAVIOUR   COUNTRY
SON   FIND   ABIDING   DAD   DAVID   WATCH   ROUND   HEAVENLY   FLOCK
GLORY TO GOD   PEACE   BABE   ANGEL

Reward

Connect the dots below to reveal what one of our rewards will be when we get to Heaven (Revelation 2:10 and 3:11).

Bible Garb

Find the items of clothing worn in Bible times in the box of letters below. The words can be found up, down, across and diagonally.

```
P  L  R  S  W  I  A  S  H  O  E  R  X  U  M
T  R  H  E  A  D  B  A  N  D  A  N  A  S  K
J  E  L  D  I  F  F  Y  O  L  W  R  K  B  A
A  S  W  E  S  D  C  I  P  M  E  A  C  N  L
H  E  P  Y  T  B  O  H  G  R  O  V  A  E  S
V  E  I  L  C  D  E  R  F  L  R  T  S  C  F
K  L  I  C  L  P  A  J  C  E  E  N  C  I  G
S  P  A  O  O  R  E  C  A  L  L  A  H  N  M
N  M  E  A  T  V  B  D  A  I  O  U  F  Y  B
R  I  N  G  H  B  M  A  N  T  L  E  R  F  T
S  W  U  T  C  B  I  H  Y  R  N  O  P  E  W
M  N  E  A  I  E  B  L  P  I  D  S  N  C  S
S  W  D  O  H  P  E  M  N  H  R  N  E  O  M
O  S  R  C  H  P  O  W  E  S  O  F  A  P  I
I  R  K  P  F  A  E  N  M  B  A  E  W  T  H
```

Word Pool

COAT   SHOE   VEIL   RING   EPHOD   WIMPLE   BONNET
FIG LEAF   HEADBAND   MANTLE   CLOAK   SHIRT   WAISTCLOTH

See answer on puzzle answer page 1.

A Blessing

Follow the instructions below, line by line, to reveal what Jesus said about children. Write the letters on the blank lines.

1. Cross out all of the X, Y, and Z letters

XZLYEXTYZZTHZYEXCXYHIXZLYZDRXZEXZYN

— — — —   — — —   — — — — — — — —

2. Circle every third letter

UYCPLOBXMWTEZJTPMOHGMDSE

— — — —   — —   — —

3. Cross out all of the S, L, and U letters

UALSNUSDLDOULNLOSTUUFLOSRSULBLUISDLTSHUEM

— — —   — —   — — —

— — — — —   — — — —

4. Cross out every other letter (beginning with the second letter)

FXOTRVOBFOSQUNCMHXITSKTRHVEB

— — — —   — —   — — — —   — —   — — —

5. Cross out all of the R, E, and V letters

REKVIRNRRGEDVEORVMEOVVFERGRORVED

— — — — — — — —   — —   — — —

See answer on puzzle answer page 1.

Let's Pray

Connect the dots to reveal what we are called as Christians to do for one another.
(See James 5:16.)

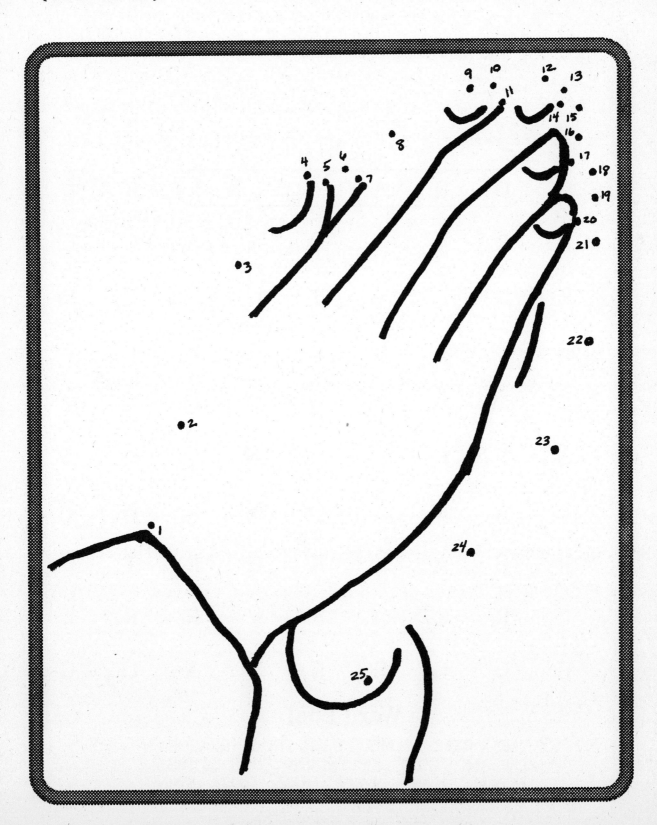

All Creatures Great and Small

Find the names of animals listed in the Bible. All the clues are listed in the word pool. Search for the animal names by going left, right, up, down, and diagonally, circling each word as you find it. Cross off words in the word pool as you find them. We found LIZARD to get you started.

```
O  O  G  D  R  A  Z  I  L  E  L

X  D  R  A  G  O  N  A  L  E  E

E  E  N  I  W  S  L  D  E  M

N  E  Z  U  I  E  I  O  P  A

D  R  M  G  O  D  O  N  H  C

G  A  T  P  U  H  N  R  A  A

R  L  A  M  B  O  Y  A  N  P

O  R  U  A  E  R  G  E  T  E

D  L  R  Z  A  S  V  R  R  E

E  E  D  G  R  E  T  A  O  G
```

Word Pool

APE BEAR CAMEL DEER DOG DRAGON
ELEPHANT GOAT GREYHOUND HORSE LAMB
LEOPARD LION ~~LIZARD~~ MULE OXEN SWINE

See answer on puzzle answer page 2.

The Way Home

The Prodigal Son left home to find a good time. But instead, he ended up eating with the pigs. He then decided to return home to be hired as his father's servant. His father, though, welcomed his long-awaited son home — not as a servant, but as part of the family. Mark the way taken by the Prodigal Son in the maze below. (Note: The Prodigal Son returned home a different route than when he left.)

Jesus' Call

Jesus wants to live in each one of our hearts. In Luke 19:1-10 we read about a man who received Jesus into his heart. By decoding Jesus' message to Zacchaeus, you will find out what Jesus said to him when He saw him sitting in the tree. Then decode Zacchaeus' response to Jesus. To read the hidden messages, cross out all the letter B's and write the remaining letters on the blanks below.

1. Jesus' message to Zacchaeus:

Zacchaeus, B H B U B R R B Y B A B N D B C B O B B M B E
D B B O B W B N, F B O R T B O D B B A B Y I B M B U B S T
B S T B A B Y B A T Y O B B U R H B O B U S B E.

Zacchaeus, _ _ _ _ _ _ _ _ _ _ _ _ _

_ _ _ _ , _ _ _ _ _ _ _ _ _ _ _ _

_ _ _ _ _ _ _ _ _ _ _ _ _.

2. Zacchaeus' response to Jesus:

Zacchaeus R B B E B C E B I B B V E B D B B J B E B S U B S B
J B B O Y B F B U B L L B Y B.

Zacchaeus _ _ _ _ _ _ _ _ _ _ _ _ _

_ _ _ _ _ _ _.

See answer on puzzle answer page 2.

Moses' Church

To find the Bible name for Moses' church, write the names of the picture clues and add or subtract the letters as shown. Write the letters that are left in the answer blanks below.

− − − − − − − − − −

Carpenter's Shop

Some of the tools from Joseph's carpentry shop were left outside by mistake. Find them before the storm hits!

SAW HAMMER AX BOLT FILE CHISEL NAIL

Great Rescues

The Bible has many daring stories of brave people whom God rescued from impossible circumstances and dangerous situations. Some of those great rescues are described below.

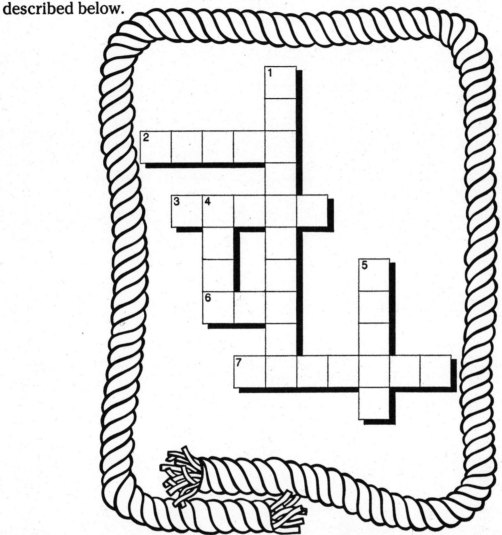

Across

2 While chained in a prison, this man was freed by an angel of the Lord (Acts 12:6-11)

3 Rahab let them hide in her house until it was safe to escape (Joshua 2)

6 Angels were sent to save this man's family before God destroyed the wicked city where they were living (Genesis 19:15-29)

7 In the desert without water, this person and #5 Down were provided a well of water for their survival (Genesis 21:15-21)

Down

1 God opened up the Red Sea so they could cross safely to the other side (Exodus 14:21-31)

4 After being saved from a shipwreck at sea, he gathered up a bundle of wood to warm himself by the fire. A poisonous shake fastened to his hand. He shook the snake off and threw it into the fire and suffered no harm (Acts 28:1-6)

5 In the desert without water, #7 Across and this person were provided a well of water for their survival (Genesis 21:15-21)

Word Pool

ISHMAEL   LOT   SPIES   HAGAR   ISRAELITES   PETER   PAUL

See answer on puzzle answer page 2.

God's Love

Decode the message to find out how much God loves us!

_____ ✚   _____ ◯   _____ ▢

_____ ◉   _____ ◑

_____ ⊕   _____ ▲

_____ ★   _____ 🦅   _____ ❄

_____ ◆   _____ ⊡

_____ 🚶

Secret Code

▲ = THAT ▢ = SO ◯ = GOD ★ = HE ◆ = ONLY ❄ = HIS
🦅 = GAVE 🚶 = SON ◉ = LOVED ⊡ = BEGOTTEN ✚ = FOR
⊕ = WORLD ◑ = THE

See answer on puzzle answer page 2.

Which Angel?

These angels form a host of angels, but one is the angel Gabriel who had a special message for Jesus' mother Mary. Find the angel Gabriel who is different from the rest.

1

2

3

4

5

6

See answer on puzzle answer page 2.

The Reluctant King

The Bible says that when the prophet Samuel called the children of Israel together to reveal to them the one God had chosen to be their first king, the new king was found "hidden among the equipment" (1 Samuel 10:22). Can you find Saul, the new king, in the scene below?

Leaning Not

The Book of Proverbs contains a great promise for those who put their faith in God and not in their own resources. Unscramble the letters below to find out what it is that God wants to do for you.

STRUT NI HET ROLD HIWT LAL UROY REATH, NAD NALE
TON NO UROY WON ANNNDDTUIGRSE; NI LAL UROY SWAY
WALKEDGONCE MIH, NAD EH LASHL TRICED UROY STAPH.
(Proverbs 3:5-6, NKJ)

— — — — — — — — — — —

— — — — — — — — —

— — — — — — — — , — — —

— — — — — — — — — — —

— — — — — — — — — — — — ;

— — — — — — — — —

— — — — — — — — —

— — — — — — — — — — —

— — — — — — — — — — — .

Fire Tested

The missing words in the story below are also the clues for this crossword puzzle!
You can read this entire story in your Bible, Daniel 3.

Nebuchadnezzar the king, the _____ of the Babylonian empire, made an _____ of himself out of

25 Across ... 2 Down

_____. The image was very large — about _____ cubits high and _____ cubits wide, and

6 Down ... 29 Down ... 31 Across

he set it up on the plain of _____ in the province of _____. Then the _____ issued a

13 Across ... 23 Across ... 1 Across

decree to all of the _____ in all the provinces to come together for the dedication of the image,

28 Across

with instructions, "When you _____ the _____ of _____ — the sounds made by the

12 Down ... 7 Across ... 17 Across

psaltery, the _____, the flute, the harp, and the lyre — you shall fall down and _____ the

20 Down ... 30 Across

image of King _____, and whoever does not follow this decree will be cast into a burning fiery

10 Down

_____. All of the people did as King Nebuchadnezzar had ruled, except for three young

27 Across

_____ men named Shadrach, Meshach, and Abednego. Word came to the king, "_____,

32 Across ... 19 Across

_____, and _____ refuse to follow the _____ you have issued." King Nebuchadnezzar

14 Down ... 8 Across ... 26 Across

flew into a _____ and said, "Bring these _____ men to me." When they came and stood before the

24 Across ... 11 Across

king, Nebuchadnezzar said, "Is it true you refuse to _____ before the golden image or to serve my

9 Down

god? I will give you another chance. If you do not bow before my image, I will throw you into this

burning, _____ furnace." Shadrach, Meshach, and Abednego knew the Lord God had commanded

27 Down

them never to serve _____ and so they said to the king, "The God we _____ is able to _____ us

16 Down ... 21 Down ... 26 Down

from this burning, fiery furnace, but even if He doesn't _____ us, we will not bow." King

21 Across

Nebuchadnezzar then ordered that the furnace be heated _____ times hotter, and he called

7 Down

mighty men of _____ from his army to tie up Shadrach, Meshach, and Abednego with strong

22 Down

_____ and throw them into the very _____ furnace. The three young men fell down bound with

15 Across ... 5 Across

cords in the midst of the fire but in a few moments, King Nebuchadnezzar rose and said, "Didn't we

cast three men into the fire? I see _____ men, and one of them looks like the Son of God.

4 Down

I _____ them loose and walking around in the furnace!" He called for Shadrach, Meshach, and

18 Down

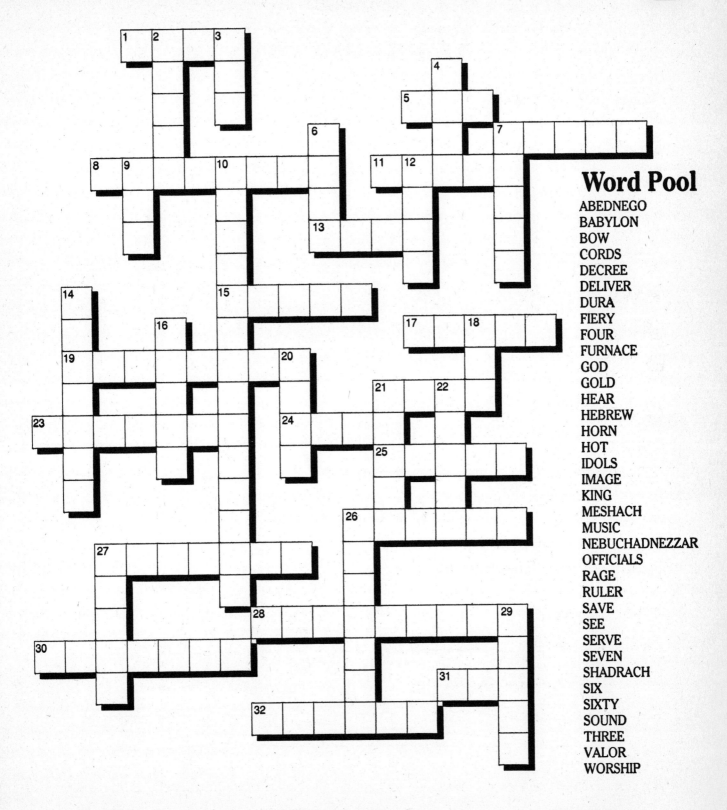

Word Pool

ABEDNEGO
BABYLON
BOW
CORDS
DECREE
DELIVER
DURA
FIERY
FOUR
FURNACE
GOD
GOLD
HEAR
HEBREW
HORN
HOT
IDOLS
IMAGE
KING
MESHACH
MUSIC
NEBUCHADNEZZAR
OFFICIALS
RAGE
RULER
SAVE
SEE
SERVE
SEVEN
SHADRACH
SIX
SIXTY
SOUND
THREE
VALOR
WORSHIP

Abednego to come out of furnace and when they did he said, "No other _____ can deliver like

3 Down

this!" Then the king issued a new decree that all the people should serve the Lord God of Shadrach,

Meshach, and Abednego!

See answer on puzzle answer page 2.

When to Pray

Cross out all of the non-letter symbols to discover when Jesus said that we are to pray:

7 % P ^ R * (A ^ ! Y 8 2) A % * T @ 2 A ; " L > L < 8 % T & # I 7 % 3 ! M , ? E * 5 S

_ _ _ _ _   _ _ _   _ _ _ _ _

See answer on puzzle answer page 2.

Good Food

Unscramble the label on each container to discover what kind of food is inside. All these foods are mentioned in the Bible.

ROLUF _ _ _ _ _   ONYHE _ _ _ _ _

NROC _ _ _ _   STRUIF _ _ _ _ _ _   SFIH _ _ _ _

See answer on puzzle answer page 2.

The Twelve

Find the names of the twelve disciples by searching left to right, right to left, up, down, or diagonally on the grid. Remember, there were two apostles named James. Cross the names off the word pool as you find each name and circle it on the grid of letters.

```
O   P   P   R   J   A   M   E   S   M   W
T   L   D   M   O   O   C   L   I   E   A
H   T   W   E   H   T   T   A   M   D   A
O   R   H   Q   N   O   N   O   O   C   B
M   W   A   A   E   E   L   F   N   R   T
A   E   M   P   D   O   C   O   F   A   R
S   R   A   E   H   D   J   A   M   E   S
R   D   D   T   D   I   A   M   E   Y   C
Q   N   R   E   D   T   L   E   E   L   Z
C   A   A   R   A   L   A   I   U   L   Q
B   L   T   J   U   D   A   S   P   S   M
```

Word Pool

PETER	JOHN	MATTHEW
JAMES	PHILIP	THADDAEUS
ANDREW	BARTHOLOMEW	SIMON
JAMES	THOMAS	JUDAS

See answer on puzzle answer page 2.

Bible Queens

All of the clues for the puzzle below relate to queens, and especially to queens mentioned in the Bible.

Across

3 Headpiece worn by a queen

5 Bright gemstones owned by a queen, often referred to as the "crown _____"

7 The prophet Jeremiah spoke out against those who made offerings to a false god, the "queen of _____" (Jeremiah 7:18)

8 The son of a queen

11 Jesus referred to the Queen of Sheba as the "queen of the _____" (Matthew 12:42)

12 A wicked queen, she reigned over Israel for six years (2 Kings 11:3)

14 The Queen of Sheba said about Solomon's court, "I did not believe [it] until I came and saw with my own _____[singular]" (1 Kings 10:7)

15 Although she wasn't called a queen, she regarded herself as one when she appeared with Agrippa (Acts 25:23)

16 She was named queen in the place of #10 Down (Esther 2:17)

17 When entering the presence of a queen, it is proper to _____one's knee

19 She was Pharaoh's wife (1 Kings 11:19)

20 Husband of a queen with equal ruling power

22 Members of a queen's family are often called the "_____ house"

23 It was a _____of the court of #3 Down who was baptized by Philip (Acts 8:26-38)

25 The sphere on top of a scepter or crown

26 The time during which a queen rules is called her _____

28 The children of a queen are known as royal _____

30 The land in which #19 Across was queen

31 A queen holds "_____" when she receives important visitors

32 He was the arch enemy of #16 Across

33 Esther asked her uncle Mordecai to fast and _____ while she prepared to approach her husband, the king (Esther 4:16)

34 Daughter of a queen

Down

1 "_____ Highness": the way to address a queen

2 Esther saved her people, the ____, through her courageous acts as queen

3 She was queen of the Ethiopians during the first century A.D. (Acts 8:27)

4 The apostle John had a vision of _____ sitting as a proud queen, without sorrow for her sins (Revelation 18:1-7)

6 The name for those ruled by a queen

8 The official residence of a queen

9 A good queen will seek to _____ her people fairly

10 She was dethroned for refusing to obey a commandment from her husband, King Ahasuerus (Esther 1)

11 The queen of this land came to test Solomon with hard questions (1 Kings 10:1-13)

13 She was the wicked wife of King Ahab (1 Kings 16:31)

18 Queen Jezebel had this man put to death to obtain his vineyard (1 Kings 21)

19 "Chair" on which a queen sits while in court

21 The staff that is the sign of royal authority

24 A feminine "bow" before a queen

27 Bernice was known for her _____ and circumstance (Acts 25:23)

29 When she discovered that her only _____ was dead, #12 Across had all other heirs to the throne murdered so she could be queen (2 Kings 11:1)

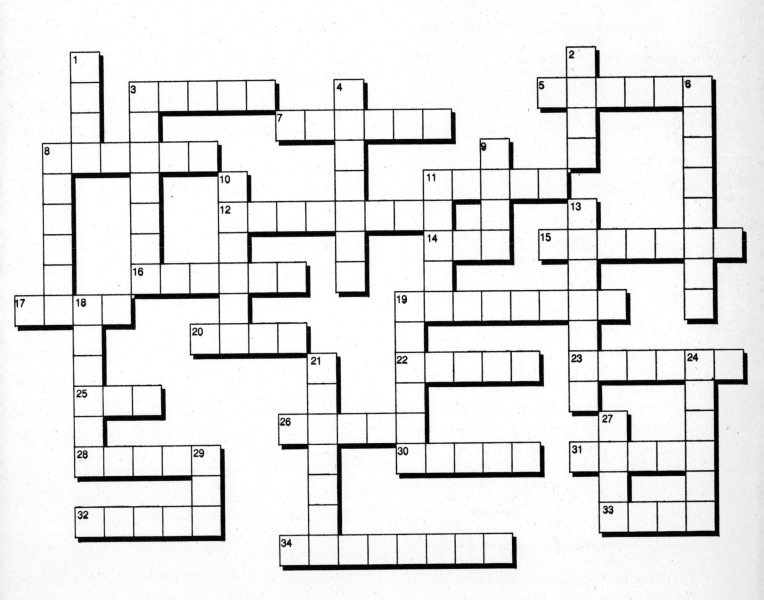

See answer on puzzle answer page 2.

Animalgram

Rearrange the letters in each clue to spell the name of a Bible animal.
When you have unscrambled all the clues, read down the circled letters
to reveal God's highest and best creatures.

MABL __ __ ◯ __

PAE ◯ __ __

INOL __ __ ◯

TOAG __ __ ◯ __

KNASE __ ◯ __ __ __

GDO ◯ __ __

OCW __ __ ◯

XOF __ ◯ __

SEOUM ◯ __ __ __ __

BABRIT __ ◯ __ __ __ __

ONEX __ __ __ ◯

__ __ __ __ __ __ __ __ __ __ __

See answer on puzzle answer page 2.

Divine Nourishment

Jesus taught that it isn't just the physical body that needs nourishment, but our soul as well. How do we nourish our soul? To find out what Jesus said, match the symbols in the secret code with those under the blanks, then write in the word represented by the symbol to discover the answer.

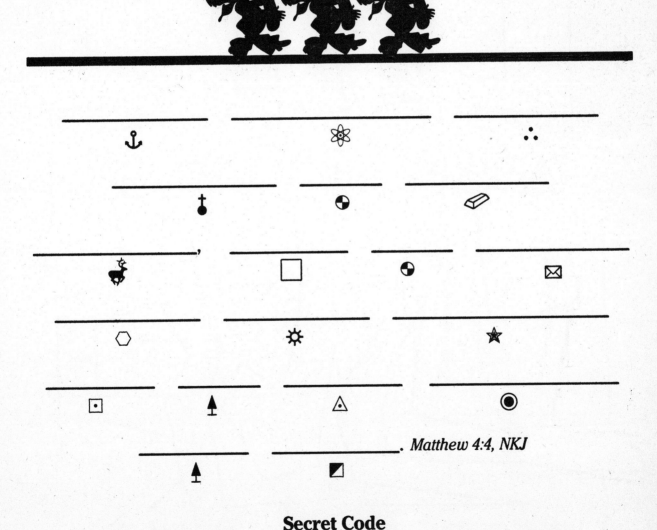

Matthew 4:4, NKJ

Secret Code

⚓ =OF	◉ =MOUTH	□ =BUT	✉ =EVERY	◪ =GOD	♘ =ALONE
⬡ =WORD	∴ =NOT	⊡ =OUT	◓ =BY	⚓ =MAN	✳ =SHALL
✺ =THAT	⬄ =BREAD	★ =PROCEEDS	△ =THE	⚕ =LIVE	

See answer on puzzle answer page 2.

Found!

The Good Shepherd is looking to find the one sheep that got away from the rest of the fold. Find His way to the lost sheep.

God's Command

Find the special command that God gives in John 15:12 by using the secret code to unscramble the message.

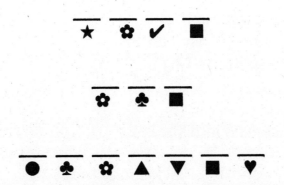

Secret Code

♥=R ✿=O ■=E ♣=N ✔=V ★=L ▲=T ●=A ▼=H

See answer on puzzle answer page 2.

Numbers in Exodus

The number of tablets of commandments
God gave to Moses (Exodus 31:18)

       _____

Multiplied by the number of years that
Israel ate manna in the wilderness
(Exodus 16:35)

x   _____

Multiplied by the number of curtains
in the tabernacle (Exodus 26:1)

x   _____

Divided by the number of omers of
manna to be gathered the day before
the sabbath (Exodus 16:22)

÷   _____

Plus the number of shekels of cinnamon
to be used in making the holy oil
(Exodus 30:23)

+   _____

Minus the number of chariots that
Pharaoh used in pursuing Moses and
the children of Israel (Exodus 14:7)

-       _____

Plus the number of gerahs in a shekel
(Exodus 30:13)

+   _____

Equals the number of elders of Israel
(Exodus 24:1), which is the same
number of disciples sent out by Jesus
(Luke 10:1-17)

=   _____

See answer on puzzle answer page 2.

Call of Comfort

Shade in all of the segments with a /./ to reveal what Jesus said that His followers should do when they have a need.

See answer on puzzle answer page 2.

Peter's Vision

The words that belong in the blanks are also clues for the crossword puzzle! You can read this entire story in Acts 10.

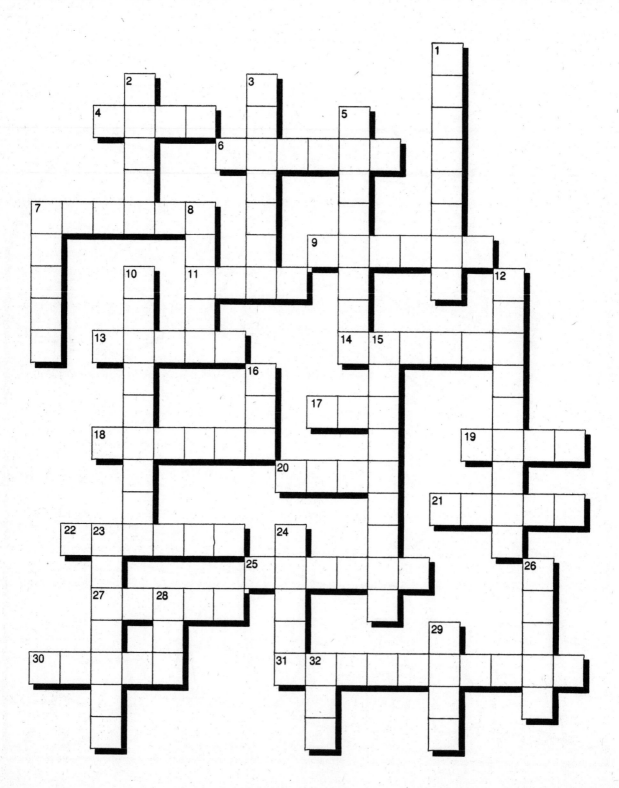

One day, when the Apostle Peter went up on the _____ of Simon to pray, he became very _____ , and then
                                                5 Down   22 Across

fell into a trance and experienced a vision. He saw _____ opened and an object like a great _____ was
                                                     9 Across   30 Across

lowered to earth. In the sheet were many types of four-footed _____ and birds — both "_____" and
                                                                3 Down   27 Across

"unclean" creatures. A voice called to Peter, "_____up and_____." _____ replied, "Oh no, Lord. I've never
                                                   11 Across 28 Down   2 Down

eaten anything _____in my life." The voice said, "What God has cleansed you must not call common." This
                23 Down

happened _____times. While Peter was wondering about the meaning of the _____, three men arrived at
          8 Down   6 Across

the place where he was staying and they asked for Peter. Peter went down to meet the men and he asked, "Why

have you come?" They said, "_____, a just man and a _____ of the Italian Regiment, was told by an
                            12 Down   10 Down

_____ to invite you to his house. Cornelius is a man who is well-known for giving _____ to the poor. He is a
13 Across   19 Across

man of much _____ who fears _____. Four days ago while he was on a _____, as he _____during the ninth
             14 Across   16 Down   20 Across   18 Across

hour, an angel stood before him and told him that he was to send us immediately to Joppa, to the house of a man

named _____, a tanner who lives by the _____, and that we would find you there." Peter agreed to go with
       7 Down   32 Down

the men, along with some other brethren from _____. When they arrived at Cornelius' _____, they found him
                                             24 Down   21 Across

waiting for them, along with his _____and close friends. Peter said, "You know how it is unlawful for the
                                 15 Down

_____to keep company with those of other nations, but God has shown me that I should not call any man
4 Across

unclean." Then Peter said, "I perceive that God is showing no partiality, but that Jesus Christ is Lord of

_____." Peter preached to them the _____of Jesus Christ, and as he did, the Holy Spirit fell on them. All of
17 Across   25 Across

the Jews who had traveled with Peter were _____ that the Gentiles had received the _____ of the Holy Spirit.
                                           31 Across   29 Down

Peter asked, "Who can forbid _____, that these should not be _____ who have received the Holy _____as
                             26 Down   1 Down   7 Across

we have?" Cornelius and all those in his house were baptized that day in the name of the Lord. They were the

first Gentiles to whom the Gospel was preached.

Word Pool

ALL   ALMS   ANGEL   ANIMALS   ASTONISHED   BAPTIZED   CENTURION   CLEAN
CORNELIUS   EAT   FAST   GIFT   GOD   GOSPEL   HEAVEN   HOUSE   HOUSETOP   HUNGRY
JEWS   JOPPA   PETER   PRAYED   PRAYER   RELATIVES   RISE   SEA   SHEET   SIMON
SPIRIT   THREE   UNCLEAN   VISION   WATER

See answer on puzzle answer page 3.

The Betrayer

Can you tell which of the disciples below is Judas? (Look up John 13:29 for an important clue!)

Buried Treasure

Connect the dots to find the treasure and unscramble the words from the word pool to identify the the precious stones in the Bible.

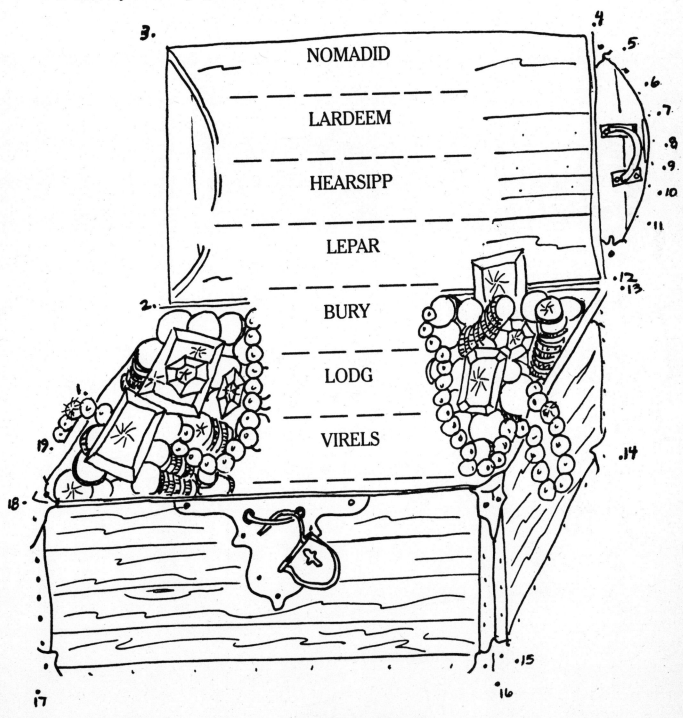

NOMADID

LARDEEM

HEARSIPP

LEPAR

BURY

LODG

VIRELS

Word Pool

SAPPHIRE   PEARL   RUBY   EMERALD   GOLD   SILVER   DIAMOND

See answer on puzzle answer page 3.

Pots

A widow came to Elisha one day and told him that men were coming to take away her sons as slaves because she could not pay her bills. Elisha told her to gather together all of the empty pots and jars she had — and even to borrow some from her friends — and then to pour from her one jar of oil into the other jars. As she poured out the oil, it multiplied and filled all of the jars, giving her plenty of oil to sell so she could pay her bills. (You can read this story in 2 Kings 4:1-7.) Help this woman by finding all of the pots and jars in the scene below:

Look for items such as these:

Pharisee Mystery

The Pharisees couldn't understand what Jesus meant when He said He would do these things in three days' time. Use the secret code to unscramble what Jesus said He would do.

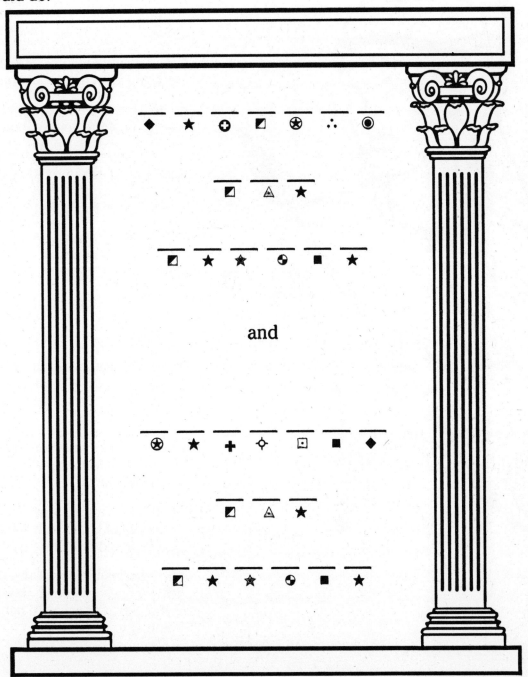

and

Secret Code

★=M ✚=B ✧=U ⊕=S △=H ⊡=I

★=E ◉=Y ■=L ◆=D ∴=O ◪=T ⊙=P ✪=R

See answer on puzzle answer page 3.

Well-Armed

All of the clues for the puzzle relate to types of weaponry and armor mentioned in the Bible.

Across

2 Described in Ephesians 6:16 as coming from the wicked one

4 The Apostle Paul described the weapon of the devil as being like this in Ephesians 6:16

6 Jehu drew one of these "with full strength" to defeat the wicked Jehoram (2 Kings 9:24)

8 The giant Goliath wore one of these made of brass (1 Samuel 17:5)

9 Dinah's brothers used this weapon to avenge the wrong done to her (Genesis 34:25)

10 The strongest weapons and chariots in Old Testament days were made of this material (Joshua 17:16)

11 Abner, Saul's son, used one of these to defeat Asahel (2 Samuel 2:23)

13 Pharaoh pursued Moses and the children of Israel with 600 of these (Exodus 14:7)

14 Another name for spear — Saul threw one of these at David, who narrowly escaped being pinned to the wall (1 Samuel 19:10)

See answer on puzzle answer page 3.

Down

1 Frequently used as a symbol of punishment or destruction in the Old Testament (Psalm 2:9)

3 The prophet Jeremiah said the tongue is like this when it speaks deceit (Jeremiah 9:8)

5 The tower of David was adorned with a thousand of these (Song of Solomon 4:4)

6 Revelation 9:9 describes beasts that wear these made of iron

7 Used to hold #3 Down (Genesis 27:3)

9 David used one of these to defeat Goliath (1 Samuel 17:40)

12 Leg coverings, such as those worn by Goliath (1 Samuel 17:6)

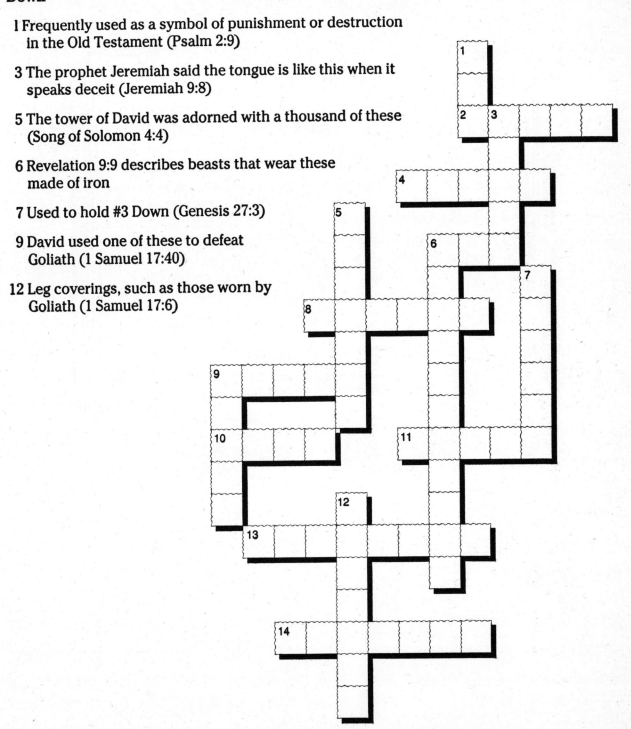

Word Pool

ARROW	DARTS	IRON	SHIELDS
BOW	FIERY	JAVELIN	SLING
BREASTPLATE	HELMET	QUIVER	SPEAR
CHARIOTS	GREAVES	ROD	SWORD

Author! Author!

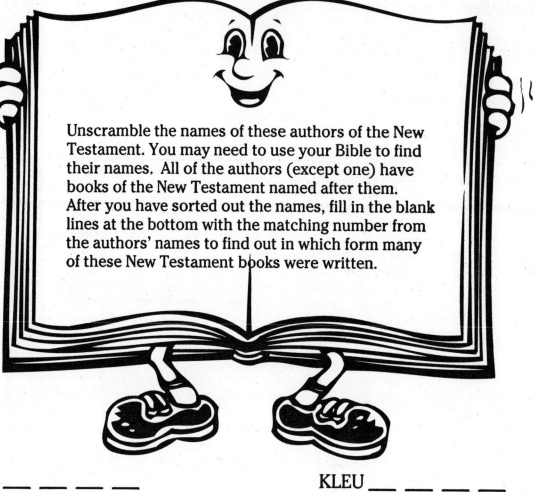

Unscramble the names of these authors of the New Testament. You may need to use your Bible to find their names. All of the authors (except one) have books of the New Testament named after them. After you have sorted out the names, fill in the blank lines at the bottom with the matching number from the authors' names to find out in which form many of these New Testament books were written.

NOJH __ __ __ __

KLEU __ __ __ __
                        5

WHATEMT __ __ __ __ __ __ __
              3

EUJD __ __ __ __

ARMK __ __ __ __

TREPE __ __ __ __ __
                  4   6

ALUP __ __ __ __
             1

MASEJ __ __ __ __ __
                  2

__ __ __ __ __ __
1 2 3 4 5 6

See answer on puzzle answer page 3.

Our Goal

Solve the puzzle below to reveal what Jesus said we should always seek first in our lives.

__ ITE = ________

R __ __ __ = ________

__ __ G = ________

__ OUSE = ________

__ __ F = ________

__ __ LF CLUB = ________

__ EER = ________

Write out your complete three-word answer here:

_ _ _ _ _ _ _ _   _ _   _ _ _

(See Matthew 6:33.)

See answer on puzzle answer page 3.

Potential

Jesus promised those who believe in Him that they would have eternal life —
unlimited time that holds unlimited potential! How many words (with two or more
letters) can you find in the phrase EVERLASTING LIFE? Write your answers here:

More than 20 words — FAIR   More than 40 words — GOOD   More than 60 words — VERY GOOD
More than 80 words — OUTSTANDING   More than 100 words — TRULY SUPERIOR

See answer on puzzle answer page 3.

Lot's House

The Lord sent angels to warn a man named Lot and his family of coming danger. Can you help the angels find their way to Lot's house?

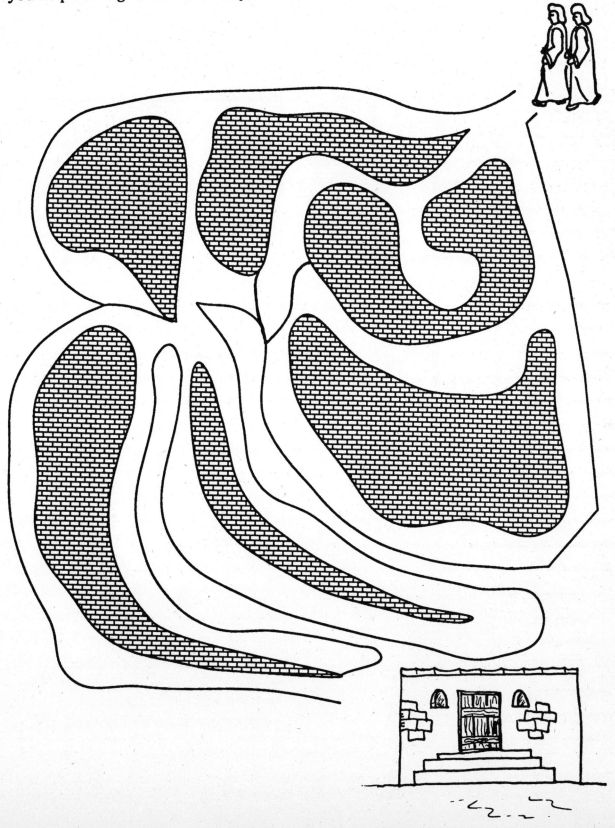

Praise Him!

Psalm 150 (NKJ) tells us where and how to praise the Lord, and what to praise Him *for.* Use your Bible to fill in the blanks.

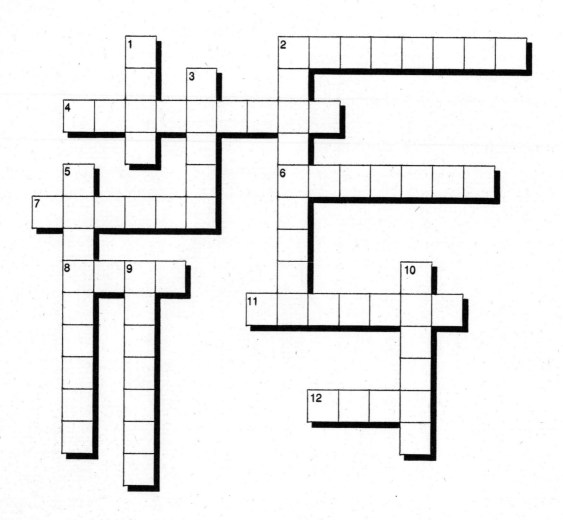

Across

2 Praise Him with _____ instruments

4 Praise God in His mighty _____

6 Praise Him with the sound of the _____

7 Let everything that has breath _____ the Lord!

8 Praise Him for His mighty _____

11 Praise Him with loud _____

12 Praise Him with the _____

Down

1 Praise Him with the #12 Across and _____

2 Praise God in His _____

3 Praise Him with the #9 Down and _____

5 Praise Him according to His excellent _____

9 Praise Him with the _____

10 Praise Him with #2 Across instruments and _____

See answer on puzzle answer page 3.

The Chosen

The names of some of God's chosen prophets are scrambled below. Unscramble the letters and fill in the blanks with the correct names. Use your Bible to check your answers; all of the names are also the names of books in the Old Testament.

SHEAO __ __ __ __ __

AAIISH __ __ __ __ __ __

DABOHIA __ __ __ __ __ __ __

MANUH __ __ __ __ __

SMOA __ __ __ __

HJNOA __ __ __ __ __

See answer on puzzle answer page 3.

Food Delivery

After Elijah had spoken God's words that it would not rain in Israel, God commanded Elijah to flee to a brook named Cherith. God said to Elijah, "I have commanded the ravens to feed thee there" (1 Kings 17:4). Every day, the ravens brought Elijah bread and meat in the morning and in the evening. Can you help the raven below find its way to Elijah?

Noble Burden

Simon, a man of Cyrene, is remembered by Christians throughout history for helping Jesus in a way unlike anyone else. Complete the dot-to-dot to find out just what it is that Simon did for Jesus.

Bible Heroes' Hometowns

The home cities or lands of some famous Bible heroes are listed below beside their names. See if you can find these places in the puzzle square by going across (forward and backward), up, down, or diagonally. One example is circled to help you begin.

```
E  B  H  R  O  N  E  L  H  T  E  S  J
J  E  R  U  S  A  L  E  M  H  S  U  A
S  T  O  S  A  Z  T  R  O  U  R  Y  R
U  H  E  M  O  A  R  T  S  Y  L  N  I
R  L  E  M  O  R  E  S  U  S  R  A  T
P  E  U  I  H  E  B  H  S  I  T  H  A
Y  H  A  R  H  T  V  A  W  S  I  T  Y
C  E  B  E  T  H  S  A  I  D  A  E  H
Y  M  A  G  D  A  L  A  A  C  H  B  T
```

HOMETOWN

BETHLEHEM (David)   UR (Abraham)   TARSUS (Paul's birthplace)
ROME (Paul's citizenship)   NAZARETH (Jesus)   LYSTRA (Timothy)
CYPRUS (Barnabas)   BETHSAIDA (Simon Peter)   JERUSALEM (Daniel)
THYATIRA (Lydia)   MAGDALA (Mary)   TISHBE (Elijah)
BETHANY (Lazarus)

See answer on puzzle answer page 3.

Associations

Many people in the Bible are associated with a certain item that was important in some way in their life as it is recorded in the Scripture. With a pencil, connect the item with the correct Bible character by going through the maze.

See answer on puzzle answer page 3.

Bible J's

All of the clues in the puzzle below begin with the letter "J." We've given you one name as a headstart!

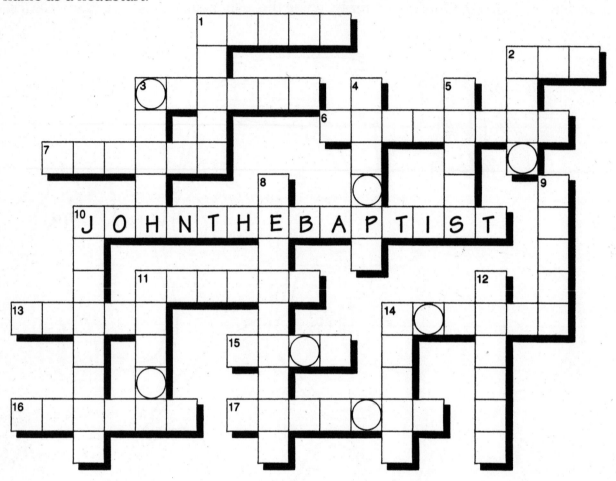

Across

1 He was the father of the twelve tribes of Israel

2 He suffered a great deal; one of the books of the Old Testament is named for him

3 He became king when he was only eight years old; he called his people back to God and is considered one of the greatest kings in Jewish history (2 Kings 22:1)

6 The mother of Miriam, Aaron, and Moses (Exodus 6:20)

7 A great river in Israel; it connects the Sea of Galilee and the Dead Sea

10 He was considered the "forerunner" of Jesus — the prophet who cried, "Make straight the way of the Lord"

11 He led the people in their battle against Jericho

13 The mother of one of the "sons of Solomon's servants" listed in Ezra 2:56

14 Wife of Esau, daughter of Beeri the Hittite (Genesis 26:34)

15 She was skilled in driving tent pegs and is credited with bringing down the mighty general Sisera, an enemy of Israel (Judges 4:17-22)

16 She was a follower of Jesus and the wife of an officer in Herod's household (Luke 8:3)

17 She was the wicked wife of King Ahab (1 Kings 16:31)

Down

1 He was a believer in Thessalonica who was a friend to Paul and Silas (Acts 17:5-9)

2 He was a prophet; one of the books of the Old Testament is named for him

3 The oldest son of #1 Across, he founded one of the twelve tribes of Israel; Jesus descended from him and is called the "Lion of the tribe of _____"

4 Jesus' earthly father

5 The Son of God

8 Jesus wept over this city (Matthew 23:37)

9 He spent three days in the belly of a great fish

10 He was a great friend to King David

11 An enemy of Israel, his army was defeated by Deborah and Barak (Judges 4:2)

12 One of the sons of Tola named in 1 Chronicles 7:2

14 He wrote the twentieth book in the New Testament and is called the "brother of the Lord"

Word Pool

~~JOHN THE BAPTIST~~ JAALA JABIN JACOB JAEL JAMES JASON
JERUSALEM JESUS JEZEBEL JIBSAM JOANNA JOB JOCHEBED JOEL
JONAH JONATHAN JORDAN JOSEPH JOSHUA JOSIAH JUDAH JUDITH

See answer on puzzle answer page 3.

Bonus "J"

Write down the letters that are circled in the crossword grid of Puzzle 54. Unscramble them to form yet another "J" word. Clue: It's celebrated every fifty years in Jewish history.

The circled letters from Puzzle 54:   Unscrambled:

___ ___ ___ ___ ___ ___ ___   ___ ___ ___ ___ ___ ___ ___

See answer on puzzle answer page 3.

Jesus' Challenge

Circle every third letter in the following box of letters and put the circled letters on the lines below. Break the letters into words to reveal what Jesus said to Simon Peter and Andrew while they were casting their fishing nets into the Sea of Galilee one day.

A M F B V O K E L O P L X

W O K L W H R M G D E U Y

A Q S N L Z D D O I C L W

J T I O S L R M L X F M G

O A U I K E R E J K Y P A

O D E U C X F I J I A H S T

Y H T B E D K R B N S A L

O Q I F Y P M X J E T I N

_ _ _ _ _   _ _

_ _   _   _ _ _   _ _ _ _

_ _   _ _ _ _ _ _

_ _   _ _ _

See answer on puzzle answer page 4.

Missing Son

Jesus was a boy of 12 when He traveled with His parents from their home in Nazareth to the synagogue in Jerusalem. Jesus spent much time in the Temple listening to the great teachers and rabbis. When the celebration was over, Mary and Joseph began the journey home traveling together with their friends and neighbors. Thinking that Jesus was in their travel caravan, Mary and Joseph did not worry that they had not seen Him — until that evening when they realized that no one had seen Him all day. They traveled the day's journey back to Jerusalem in search of Jesus. Connect the dots to discover where Mary and Joseph found Jesus.

Resurrection Morning

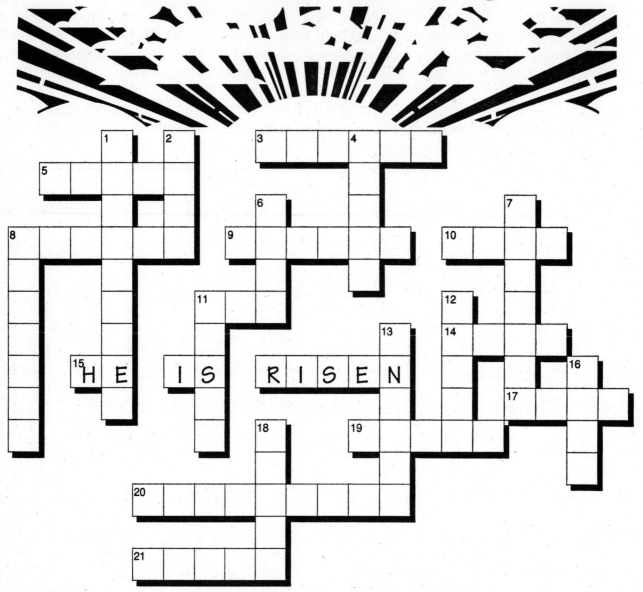

15 H E I S R I S E N

Very early in the morning, when the Sabbath was past, _____ Magdalene
6 Down

and Mary the mother of James, and some other women went to the _____
14 Across

where _____ had been buried, to take more _____ to put on His body. On
11 Down   8 Across

their way to the tomb, they asked among themselves, "Who will _____
10 Across

away the _____ from the _____ of the tomb for us?" They knew the stone
12 Down   17 Across

was too _____ for them to move by themselves. But when they arrived,
5 Across

they saw that the stone had already been rolled away, and they saw two

_____ in _____ _____. They were _____. One of the angels said, "Do
13 Down   8 Down   18 Down   7 Down

not be afraid. You seek Jesus of Nazareth, who was ____. __ __ ____!
                                                    1 Down   15 Across

He is not here. Go and tell this to the _____. Tell them that Jesus has
                                          20 Across

gone to Galilee and will meet them there."

   So they ran quickly to tell the disciples what they had seen and heard.

When _____ and John heard the _____, they set out running for the tomb.
     19 Across   2 Down

John reached the tomb first and saw the _____ cloth in which Jesus' body
                                        4 Down

had been wrapped. When Peter arrived, he went inside the tomb and

found also the cloth that had been around Jesus' head. Then Peter and

John left to their own homes.

   Mary Magdalene had returned to the tomb alone to look again for

Jesus' _____ that she feared had been _____. She stood crying when
       16 Down   3 Across

Jesus Himself stood by her. "Mary," He said quietly. When she turned to

look to see who was speaking, she exclaimed, "_____!" Her tears
                                                  9 Across

turned to ____ as she ran into the city to tell the disciples that she had
          11 Across

seen their Lord _____.
                21 Across

Word Pool

CRUCIFIED   LINEN   SHINING   LARGE   MARY   MASTER   ROLL   ALARMED
SPICES   JOY   JESUS   ANGELS   STONE   TOMB   PETER   DISCIPLES   WHITE
     ALIVE   NEWS   DOOR   BODY   STOLEN   ~~HE IS RISEN~~

See answer on puzzle answer page 4.

Holy Birth

The significance of Jesus' birth has been revealed to all the world. But it's up to each individual to seek the Lord Jesus to live in his or her own heart. Find the words in the word pool that are hidden in the letter box below that are associated with the birth of Jesus.

```
S  O  P  T  M  S  E  R  Z  M  N
P  O  I  L  S  T  Q  W  E  A  G
M  X  W  O  A  A  R  H  E  N  B
A  S  I  B  A  B  E  K  L  G  F
R  T  S  W  E  L  U  O  P  E  R
Y  E  E  D  H  E  S  T  A  R  V
B  G  M  T  H  P  E  S  N  N  I
S  H  E  P  H  E  R  D  S  L  O
B  B  N  I  U  R  T  C  S  E  W
```

Word Pool

STAR   WISE MEN
MANGER   BETHLEHEM
STABLE   SHEPHERDS
MARY   INN
BABE

See answer on puzzle answer page 4.

Bible Children

Across

1. _____ was a Jewish orphan girl who became queen of Persia

4. The child _____ was an answer to his mother's prayers, he heard the Lord call his name

7. As a shepherd boy, _____ killed a bear and a lion to protect his flock

8. Mary's son was named _____, which means, "the Lord saves"

11. God promised Abraham and Sarah a son, his name was _____

12. As a young girl, #6 Down saved the life of her baby brother _____ by hiding him in a basket in a river

Down

2. The birth of _____ was announced to his mother by an angel, he later became known for his incredible strength

3. _____ was the first-born twin son of Isaac and Rebekah

5. A young boy gave his five _____ and two #10 Down to Jesus to provide lunch to 5,000 people

6. As a young girl, _____ saved the life of her baby brother #12 Across by hiding him in a basket in a river

8. _____ was the second-born twin of Isaac and Rebekah

9. _____ grew up as the son of King David; he eventually became king himself

10. A young boy gave his five #5 Down and two _____ to Jesus to provide lunch for 5,000 people

Word Pool
SAMUEL   SOLOMON   MOSES   LOAVES
SAMSON   DAVID   FISHES   ISAAC   ESTHER
JESUS   ESAU   JACOB   MIRIAM

See answer on puzzle answer page 4.

Little Ones

Unscramble the names of the Bible children below, then fill in the blank with the letter from the matching number.

IIMMRA __ __ __ __ __ __
                    3

EAULMS __ __ __ __ __ __

IVDDA __ __ __ __ __
              4

SSEOM __ __ __ __ __
             2

ESJSU __ __ __ __ __
         8

CAISA __ __ __ __ __

UASE __ __ __ __

SHGRMOE __ __ __ __ __ __ __
        7

BCJOA __ __ __ __ __
        6

THREES __ __ __ __ __ __
             5 1

NMASOS __ __ __ __ __ __

Children are a __ __ __ __ __ __ __ __ from the Lord.
               1 2 3 4 5 6 7 8

(Psalm 127:3, NKJ)

Word Pool

DAVID   ESAU   ISAAC   ESTHER   JACOB   MOSES   MIRIAM
SAMSON   JESUS   SAMUEL   GERSHOM

See answer on puzzle answer page 4.

Free Access

In Hebrew, the original language of much of the Old Testament, words were written without vowels. The vowels have been left out of the words in this verse, add them to find out what Jesus had to say about what kind of people will be in Heaven. (See Matthew 19:14, NKJ.)

LT TH LTTL
CHLDRN CM
T M ND D NT
FRBD THM FR
F SCH S TH
KNGDM F
HVN.

—— —— —— —— —— —— ——

—— —— —— —— —— —— ——

—— —— —— —— —— —— ——

—— —— —— —— —— —— ——

—— —— —— —— ——

—— —— —— ——

These are the letters and the number of times that each is missing:

A - 2   E - 10   I - 5   O - 9   U - 1

See answer on puzzle answer page 4.

Shipwrecked!

Using the words from the word pool, fill in the blanks of this account of Paul's shipwreck from Acts 26–28, then transfer the words to the crossword puzzle.

Paul's preaching in _____ so angered the _____ leaders that _____ broke out among the
          7 Across   7 Down   20 Down

people. Finally, government authorities took Paul _____. Paul knew that he had not broken any laws
              1 Down

and asked to be tried by _____ in Rome.
          5 Across

Paul made the long trip to _____ by boat. They set sail in late fall, before the _____ storms that
          13 Down   15 Down

made travel dangerous for the sailing ships.

Over halfway to Rome, they ran into fierce storms that blew the ship about. For days the _____
                                                             22 Across

raged. _____ was thrown _____, and the crew and _____ gave up _____ for their safety.
      2 Across   12 Across   26 Across   11 Down

One night, an _____ of the Lord told _____ not to _____, that they would be shipwrecked, but
             3 Down   6 Across   16 Across

that everyone on board would be safe. It happened just that way. The ship broke apart in the strong

waves and everyone had to _____ to safety. Miraculously, everyone got _____ to the island of
                     25 Across   24 Across

_____.
18 Down

As Paul warmed himself by a _____, a poisonous _____ fastened itself to his _____ . The
                      23 Down   4 Down   8 Down

people were superstitious and assumed that Paul was an _____ , and that he would die from the snake
                                            19 Across

bite. However, Paul shook off the snake and was not harmed. The people then changed their minds

and decided instead that Paul was a god.

After that, Paul was invited to the home of the chief official of the island. The official's _____ was
                                                              9 Across

very _____, so Paul prayed for him and the man was _____ . Many more _____ people came to Paul
21 Across   10 Down   4 Across

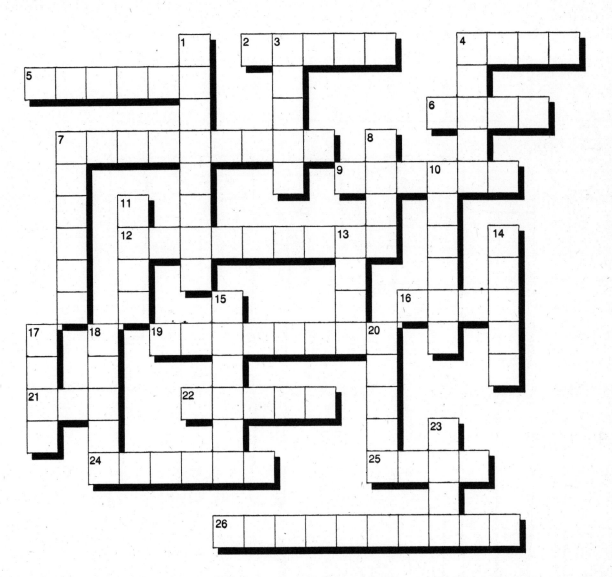

then for prayer and got well. _____ months later, after winter was over, they set _____ again and
14 Down · 17 Down

finally arrived in Rome.

Word Pool
ROME   JERUSALEM   ILL   PAUL   SWIM   MALTA
PASSENGERS   PRISONER   FIRE   SAIL   JEWISH   HAND
STORM   FATHER   OVERBOARD   RIOTS   ASHORE   HEALED
CARGO   SNAKE   HOPE   THREE   ANGEL   SICK
WINTER   CAESAR   EVILDOER   FEAR

See answer on puzzle answer page 4.

Dry Land!

When the rain stopped and the flood waters began to recede, Noah sent a dove from the ark to see if the ground was dry enough to open the door of the ark. The dove returned with nothing in its mouth. Seven days later, Noah sent out the dove again. This time, the dove came back with an olive leaf in its mouth. Help the dove below find its way back to the ark!

How to Pray

The Bible has a message telling us how to pray so our prayers will be answered. To find out what the Bible says, start with the first letter, then select every other letter. Then go back through the Bible passage a second time and start with the *second* letter and take every other letter. Use every letter one time. Write the letters on the blank lines to help you discover the hidden message.

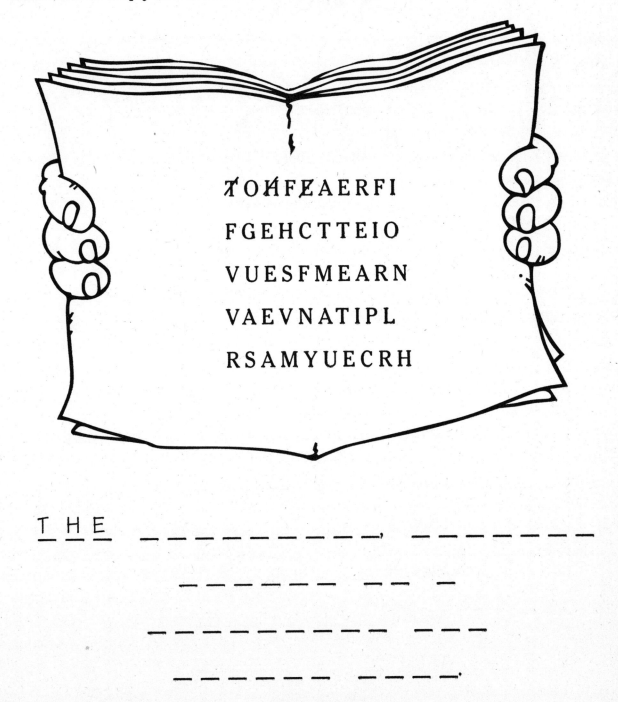

TOHFEARFI

FGEHCTTEIO

VUESFMEARN

VAEVNATIPL

RSAMYUECRH

T H E _ _ _ _ _ _ _ _ , _ _ _ _ _ _ _

_ _ _ _ _ _ _ _ _

_ _ _ _ _ _ _ _ _ _ _ _ _

_ _ _ _ _ _ _ _ _ _ .

James 5:16

See answer on puzzle answer page 4.

Islands of the Sea

These five islands are found in the Bible:

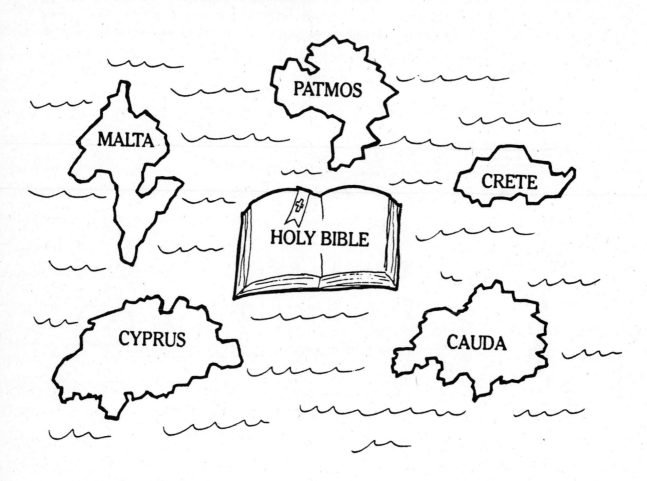

Unscramble the words below to reveal each one of these islands.

SMAPOT __ __ __ __ __ __

LAATM __ __ __ __ __

YRSUPC __ __ __ __ __ __

AAUDC __ __ __ __ __

TREEC __ __ __ __ __

See answer on puzzle answer page 4.

The Healed

Below is a list of some of the people in the Bible who were <u>healed</u> by Jesus.

The centurion's <u>servant</u>
Jairus' <u>daughter</u>
Two <u>blind</u> men
The demon-possessed <u>dumb</u> man
The <u>woman</u> with the issue of <u>blood</u>
Blind <u>Bartimaeus</u>
Ten <u>lepers</u>
<u>Lazarus</u> raised from the <u>dead</u>

Can you find the underlined words in the square? Search left, right, up, down, and diagonally. As an example, "healed" is already circled for you.

```
H  O  B  M  U  D  T  S  R  U  T  Y
R  E  L  B  U  A  M  A  U  D  M  B
E  B  A  R  T  I  M  A  E  U  S  L
T  L  L  L  A  Z  A  R  U  S  D  W
H  I  A  E  E  O  T  R  A  B  O  N
G  N  Z  P  A  D  E  A  D  M  O  D
U  D  T  E  V  E  A  O  A  L  L  B
A  A  R  R  R  A  I  N  B  O  B  L
D  E  O  S  E  R  V  A  N  T  L  O
E  A  D  E  S  R  A  T  N  O  T  O
```

See answer on puzzle answer page 4.

Praise Branches

People lined the streets to welcome Jesus back to Jerusalem. As Jesus rode toward the city on the back of a donkey, the people shouted "Hosanna." Some took off their coats and put them in the road. Connect the dots below to show what some of the people waved in the air as a celebration of greeting and praise.

His Joy

Shade in the sections below that have a /./ in them to reveal what Jesus "endured," even though it was painful and embarrassing. The Bible says that He endured this because of the joy that He had in anticipating the resurrection, His ascension back to Heaven, and our salvation (Hebrews 12:2).

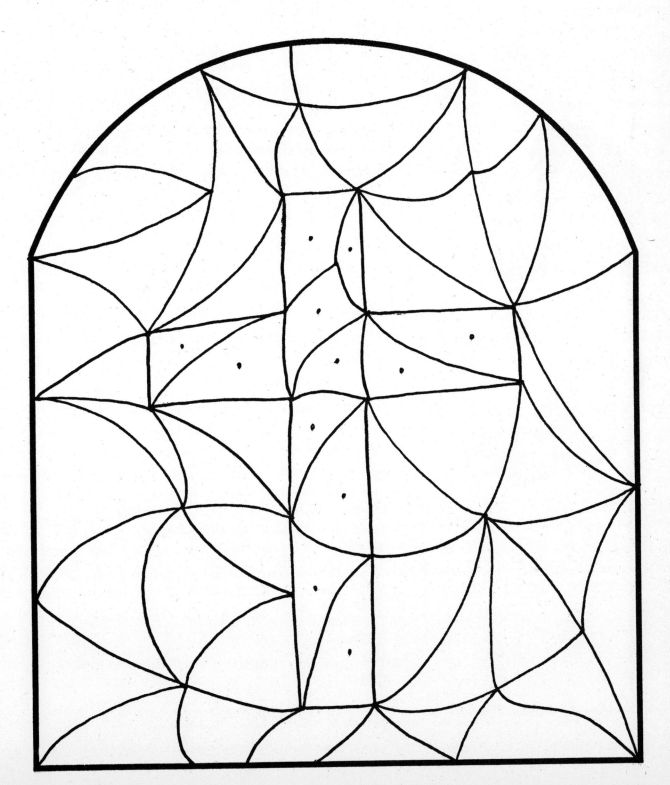

Bible H's

Hallelujah! and Hosanna! are just two of the Bible words that start with the letter "H." From the clues below, fill in the crossword grid with words starting with the letter "H."

Across

2 A priest and one of the two sons of Eli, his name means "tadpole" (1 Samuel 2:34)

4 God answered this mother's prayer with a son named Samuel (1 Samuel 1)

6 Jesus said the greatest commandment is to love the Lord your God with all your _____, with all your soul, and with all your mind (Matthew 22:37)

7 A book of the Old Testament written by a prophet with the same name

8 A heavenly _____ appeared at the birth of Jesus and sang praises saying, "Glory to God in the highest" (Luke 2:13)

9 Other names for the _____ (two words) are Paraclete and Comforter

11 The Old Testament was originally written in this language; Jews living in Israel speak this language today

12 King of Tyre and an admirer of David and Solomon, he sent supplies to help build the Temple (1 Kings 5)

13 This woman was a handmaid to Sarah and the mother of Ishmael (Genesis 16)

14 The Promised Land was described as a land flowing with milk and _____ (Exodus 3:8)

15 Jesus healed a man with a withered _____ (Mark 3:1-5)

Down

1 The name of one of the sons of Noah (Genesis 5:32)

3 The place where Christians will live forever with God

5 A powerful king of Syria and oppressor of the people of Israel (2 Kings 8:7-15)

6 Uriah, one of David's best warriors, was from this empire (2 Samuel 11)

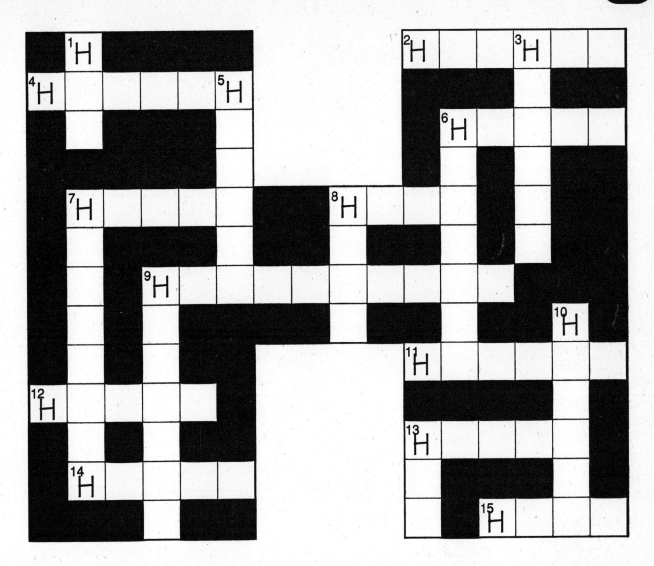

7 A devout king of Judah who restored true worship in the Temple (2 Chronicles 29)

8 One of the three Christian virtues, the other two are faith and love (1 Corinthians 13:13)

9 This Hebrew expression (which means "Save us!") greeted Jesus on His triumphal entry into Jerusalem

10 One of the most important cities in the Old Testament. This is where Abram's name was changed to Abraham and he received God's promise of a son (Genesis 13:18)

13 An Israelite, this man held up the arms of Moses with Aaron in the battle against Amalek (Exodus 17:10,12)

Word Pool

HAND   HEBREW   HITTITE   HAZAEL   HANNAH   HEART   HEAVEN
HOSEA   HOST   HOLY SPIRIT   HOPHNI   HEZEKIAH   HOSANNA   HOPE
HUR   HIRAM   HEBRON   HAGAR   HONEY   HAM

See answer on puzzle answer page 4.

Following Jesus

Matthew 16:24 tells us what we must do to follow Jesus. Use the code at the bottom of the page to finish this Scripture verse.

If any man will _____ after me, let him _____
                 ✪   ⊡

_____, and _____ up his _____
        ◨   ✛   ✖

and _____me.
          ▲

John 14:6 also tells us something about following Jesus.

Jesus saith unto him, I am the _____,
                                    ★

the _____, and the _____:
         🐟   ✪

no _____ cometh unto
        ◉

the _____, but by _____.
        ▲   ∴

Secret Code

▲= FOLLOW   ✖= CROSS   ✪= COME   ◨= HIMSELF
✛= TAKE   ⊡= DENY   ◉ = MAN   ▲ = FATHER   ✪ = LIFE
🐟 = TRUTH   ★ = WAY   ∴ = ME

See answer on puzzle answer page 4.

Old Books

The clues for this crossword puzzle contain a well-known Bible verse (from New King James version), and the chapter and verse number in the Old Testament book in which the verse is found. Identify the Old Testament book that contains the verse and fill in the crossword grid with the name of that book. If the name of a book has a number in it (like 2 Kings), leave out the number.

Across

3 The silver is Mine, and the gold is Mine, says the Lord of hosts. Ch. 2, vs. 8

4 I will put My law in their minds, and write it on their hearts; and I will be their God, and they shall be My people. Ch. 31, vs. 33

5 He has shown you, O man, what is good; and what does the Lord require of you but to do justly, to love mercy, and to walk humbly with your God? Ch. 6, vs. 8

6 The kingdom shall be the Lord's. Vs. 21

8 I will give you a new heart and put a new spirit within you; I will take the heart of stone out of your flesh and give you a heart of flesh. Ch. 36, vs. 26

10 Be strong and of good courage; do not be afraid, nor be dismayed, for the Lord your God is with you wherever you go. Ch. 1, vs. 9

11 Yet who knows whether you have come to the kingdom for such a time as this? Ch. 4, vs. 14

12 The hand of our God is upon all those for good who seek Him, but His power and His wrath are against all those who forsake Him. Ch. 8, vs. 22

16 The Lord is my shepherd; I shall not want. Ch. 23, vs. 1

17 For the joy of the Lord is your strength. Ch. 8, vs. 10

18 Entreat me not to leave you, or to turn back from following after you; for wherever you go, I will go; and wherever you lodge, I will lodge; your people shall be my people, and your God, my God. Ch. 1, vs. 16

19 The Lord is good, a stronghold in the day of trouble; and He knows those who trust in Him. Ch. 1, vs. 7

20 In the beginning God created the heavens and the earth. Ch. 1, vs. 1

24 If My people who are called by My name will humble themselves, and pray and seek My face, and turn from their wicked ways, then I will hear from heaven, and will forgive their sin and heal their land. Ch. 7, vs. 14

26 You shall be holy; for I am holy. Ch. 11, vs. 44

31 We were like grasshoppers in our own sight. Ch. 13, vs. 33

32 But let justice run down like water, and righteousness like a mighty stream. Ch. 5, vs. 24

33 But to you who fear My name the Sun of Righteousness shall arise with healing in His wings. Ch. 4, vs. 2

34 He brought me to the banqueting house, and his banner over me was love. Ch. 2, vs. 4

Down

1 Not by might nor by power, but by My Spirit, says the Lord of hosts. Ch. 4, vs. 6

2 Though the fig tree may not blossom, nor fruit be on the vines; though the labor of the olive may fail, and the fields yield no food; though the flock may be cut off from the fold, and there be no herd in the stalls — Yet I will rejoice in the Lord, I will joy in the God of my salvation. Ch. 3, vss. 17-18

4 Though He slay me, yet will I trust Him. Ch. 13, vs. 15

7 You shall love the Lord your God with all your heart, with all your soul, and with all your strength. Ch. 6, vs. 5

9 Through the Lord's mercies we are not consumed, because His compassions fail not. They are new every morning; great is Your faithfulness. Ch. 3, vss. 22-23

10 I will pour out My Spirit on all flesh; your sons and your daughters shall prophesy, your old men shall dream dreams, your young men shall see visions. Ch. 2, vs. 28

13 The Lord your God in your midst, the Mighty One, will save; He will rejoice over you with gladness. Ch. 3, vs. 17

14 Behold, to obey is better than sacrifice, and to heed than the fat of rams. Ch. 15, vs. 22

15 Arise, go to Nineveh, that great city, and cry out against it; for their wickedness has come up before Me. Ch. 1, vs. 2

21 You shall have no other gods before Me. Ch. 20, vs. 3

22 Vanity of vanities, all is vanity. Ch. 1, vs. 2

23 There is a way that seems right to a man, but its end is the way of death. Ch. 14, vs. 12

25 How long will you falter between two opinions? If the Lord is God, follow Him; but if Baal, follow him. Ch. 18, vs. 21

27 For I desire mercy and not sacrifice. Ch. 6, vs. 6

28 For unto us a Child is born, unto us a Son is given; and the government will be upon His shoulder. And His name will be called Wonderful, Counselor, Mighty God, Everlasting Father, Prince of Peace. Ch. 9, vs. 6

29 In those days there was no king in Israel;
everyone did what was right in his own eyes.
Ch. 21, vs. 25

30 Our God whom we serve is able to deliver us
from the burning fiery furnace, and He will
deliver us from your hand, O king. Ch. 3, vs. 17

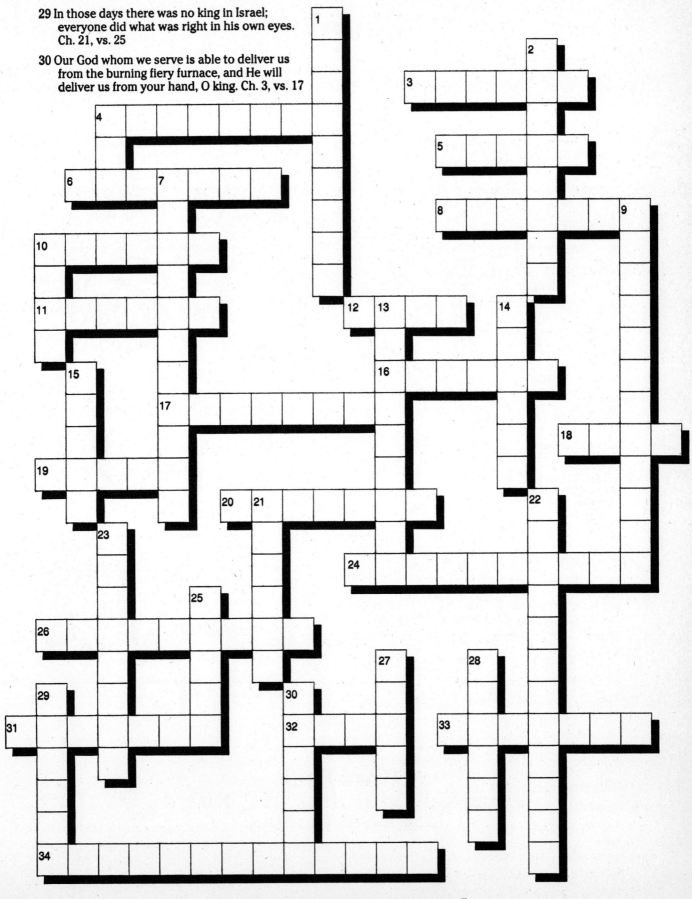

See answer on puzzle answer page 5.

Couples

The Bible tells us the stories of many famous couples. In the puzzle below, first unscramble the names of the four men and four women. Then mark or color over the line that matches each man and woman as husband and wife.

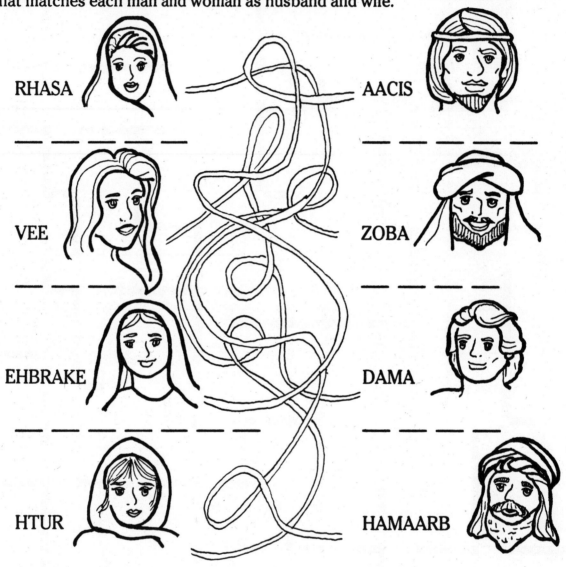

RHASA

AACIS

VEE

ZOBA

EHBRAKE

DAMA

HTUR

HAMAARB

Word Pool

ABRAHAM   ADAM   BOAZ   EVE   ISAAC
REBEKAH   RUTH   SARAH

See answer on puzzle answer page 5.

Holy Day

The Day of Atonement is the most sacred, holy day of the year for the Jewish people. By decoding the message below, you will find out what happens on this special day.

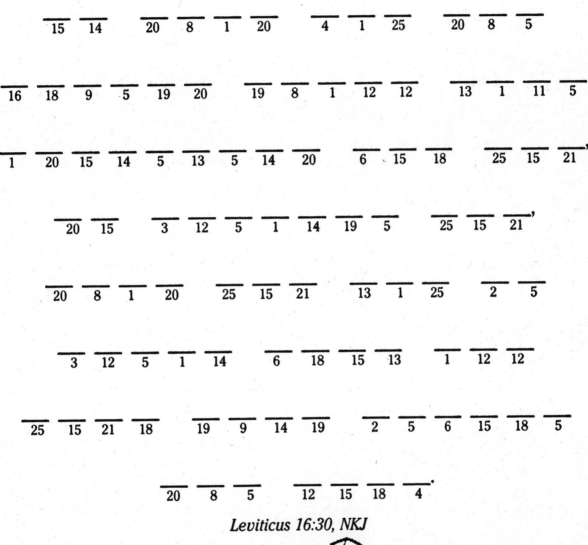

$$\overline{15}\ \overline{14}\quad \overline{20}\ \overline{8}\ \overline{1}\ \overline{20}\quad \overline{4}\ \overline{1}\ \overline{25}\quad \overline{20}\ \overline{8}\ \overline{5}$$

$$\overline{16}\ \overline{18}\ \overline{9}\ \overline{5}\ \overline{19}\ \overline{20}\quad \overline{19}\ \overline{8}\ \overline{1}\ \overline{12}\ \overline{12}\quad \overline{13}\ \overline{1}\ \overline{11}\ \overline{5}$$

$$\overline{1}\ \overline{20}\ \overline{15}\ \overline{14}\ \overline{5}\ \overline{13}\ \overline{5}\ \overline{14}\ \overline{20}\quad \overline{6}\ \overline{15}\ \overline{18}\quad \overline{25}\ \overline{15}\ \overline{21},$$

$$\overline{20}\ \overline{15}\quad \overline{3}\ \overline{12}\ \overline{5}\ \overline{1}\ \overline{14}\ \overline{19}\ \overline{5}\quad \overline{25}\ \overline{15}\ \overline{21},$$

$$\overline{20}\ \overline{8}\ \overline{1}\ \overline{20}\quad \overline{25}\ \overline{15}\ \overline{21}\quad \overline{13}\ \overline{1}\ \overline{25}\quad \overline{2}\ \overline{5}$$

$$\overline{3}\ \overline{12}\ \overline{5}\ \overline{1}\ \overline{14}\quad \overline{6}\ \overline{18}\ \overline{15}\ \overline{13}\quad \overline{1}\ \overline{12}\ \overline{12}$$

$$\overline{25}\ \overline{15}\ \overline{21}\ \overline{18}\quad \overline{19}\ \overline{9}\ \overline{14}\ \overline{19}\quad \overline{2}\ \overline{5}\ \overline{6}\ \overline{15}\ \overline{18}\ \overline{5}$$

$$\overline{20}\ \overline{8}\ \overline{5}\quad \overline{12}\ \overline{15}\ \overline{18}\ \overline{4}.$$

Leviticus 16:30, NKJ

Secret Code
1=A, 2=B, 3=C
and so forth.

See answer on puzzle answer page 5.

Commitment

The Bible contains a promise for people who commit their lives to the Lord. To find out the promise, put the words together from the two lists of letters. Each word of the Bible promise has been divided into two parts. Finish the first part of each word in List 1 with the second part of the word found in List 2. There may be more than one way to complete the words, but there is only one right way that will reveal God's promise. The first one is done for you.

List 1	List 2	Completed Word
COM	ND	_____
YOU	RD	_____
WO	E	_____
T	R	_____
TH	RKS	_____
LO	LL	_____
A	GHTS	_____
YO	MIT	COMMIT
THOU	LISHED	_____
WI	E	_____
B	UR	_____
ESTAB	O	_____

COMMIT _____

_____

_____

_____ *(Proverbs 16:3, NKJ)*

See answer on puzzle answer page 5.

Secret Mission

As the children of Israel traveled closer and closer to the Promised Land, Moses sent twelve men ahead to spy out the land. Help the spies find their way back to Moses. (You can read about this story in Numbers 13.)

Naomi's Journey

One of the most beautiful stories in the Bible is the story of Ruth and Naomi in the Old Testament. Fill in the blanks in the story with words from the word pool and then use them to complete the crossword grid. You may want to use your Bible. The story is found in the Old Testament, in the book of Ruth.

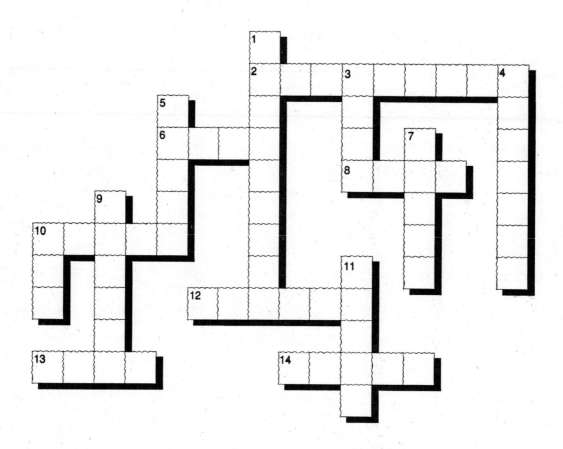

A time of _____ in the land of Judah forced _____ and his wife _____ and
    12 Across   2 Across   7 Down

their two sons to move to a faraway country. They left their home in _____ and
        1 Down

went to _____ where they heard they could find work and food. While they were
   3 Down

away from their country, Naomi's _____ died. She brought up her two sons alone.
       4 Down

When her sons had grown up, they both married. But, sadly, both of the sons also

died and their wives, _____ and Orpah, also became widows.
   6 Across

Naomi told her two daughters-in-law that she was going to return to her homeland, Judah, because the famine was over. She told them to stay with their families in their own country of Moab and that she would go alone back to her country. But Ruth told her mother-in-law that she wanted to go with her and remain with her. She said, "Entreat me not to _____ you or quit following you. I want to go where you go and
\ \ \ \ \ \ \ \ \ \ 11 Down

live where you live. Your _____ will become my people and your _____, my God."
\ \ \ \ \ \ \ \ \ \ \ \ \ \ 9 Down \ \ \ \ \ \ \ \ \ \ \ \ \ \ \ \ \ 10 Down

Naomi could not convince Ruth to stay behind.

So Ruth and Naomi began their journey and returned to Bethlehem at the time of the harvest season. In Judah it was a custom for the harvesters to leave some of the _____ in the field for the poor people to _____. Ruth gathered grain in a field
5 Down \ 10 Across

owned by a man named _____ so she and Naomi would have food to eat.
\ \ \ \ \ \ \ \ \ \ \ \ \ \ \ \ 8 Across

Boaz told the reapers to leave extra grain in the field so Ruth could gather it. It turned out that Boaz was related to Ruth's mother-in-law, Naomi. By the end of the harvest, Boaz had come to love Ruth and he asked for permission to marry her. So Ruth and Boaz were married. They later had a son named _____. He became the
\ 13 Across

father of Jesse, who became the father of _____, the great king of Israel and founder
\ \ \ \ \ \ \ \ \ \ \ \ \ \ \ \ \ \ 14 Across

of the royal line of which Jesus Christ was a descendant.

Word Pool

RUTH BOAZ GRAIN NAOMI BETHLEHEM ELIMELECH FAMINE
HUSBAND PEOPLE GOD GLEAN MOAB OBED DAVID LEAVE

See answer on puzzle answer page 5.

Pilate's Sign

Luke 23:38 says that a sign was placed over Jesus as He hung on the cross. The sign was written in three languages. Use the secret code below to find out what the sign said.

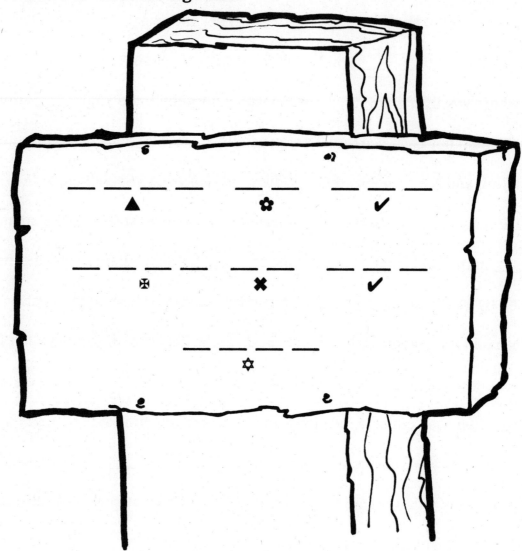

Secret Code

▲ = THIS   ✿ = JEWS   ✠ = KING
✔ = THE   ❀ = IS   ✖ = OF

See answer on puzzle answer page 5.

Shepherds

In Bible times in Israel, the work of a shepherd was very important. A shepherd had to find food for his sheep as well as protect them from wild animals. Jesus called himself the Good Shepherd (John 10:11) because of His great care for His people. Listed in the word pool below are the names of some people who were shepherds in the Old Testament. See if you can find their names hidden in the puzzle.

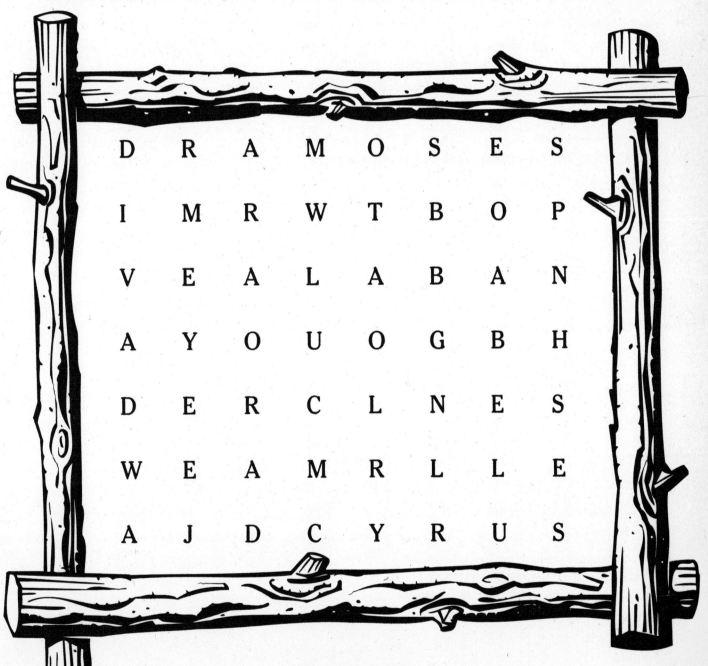

```
D R A M O S E S
I M R W T B O P
V E A L A B A N
A Y O U O G B H
D E R C L N E S
W E A M R L L E
A J D C Y R U S
```

Word Pool

MOSES   DAVID   ABEL   AMOS   JACOB   LABAN   CYRUS

See answer on puzzle answer page 5.

Numbers and Kings

The number of years that it took Solomon to build his palace (1 Kings 7:1)

_____

The age of Josiah when he became king (2 Kings 22:1)

\-   _____

The number of years that Solomon had reigned as king before he began to build the Temple (1 Kings 6:1)

x   _____

The number of years that Asa ruled in Jerusalem (1 Kings 15:10)

+   _____

The number of years that Ahaziah reigned over Israel (1 Kings 22:51)

+   _____

The number of months it took for Joab and his men to conduct a census for King David (2 Samuel 24:8)

÷   _____

The number of years that it took Solomon to build the Temple (1 Kings 6:38)

=   _____

See answer on puzzle answer page 5.

What Was Moses Carrying?

When Moses came down from Mount Sinai after spending time there with the Lord God, he brought with him something that he didn't have before he climbed the mountain. Connect the dots to find out what it was.

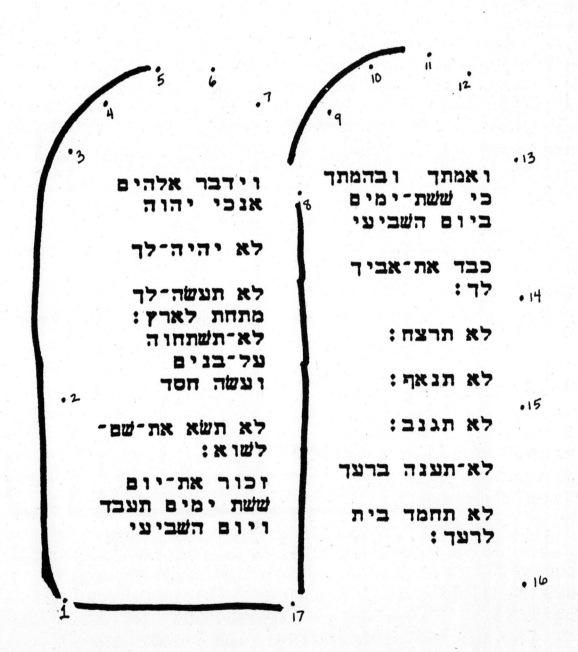

Dear Romans

The Book of Romans is one of the most important books in the Bible. It has been called a "manifesto" of the Gospel of salvation in Jesus Christ. The words in the word pool all relate to the new life of the Christian — life in the Spirit — as described in Romans chapter 8. Use the words in the word pool to answer the clues and complete the crossword grid.

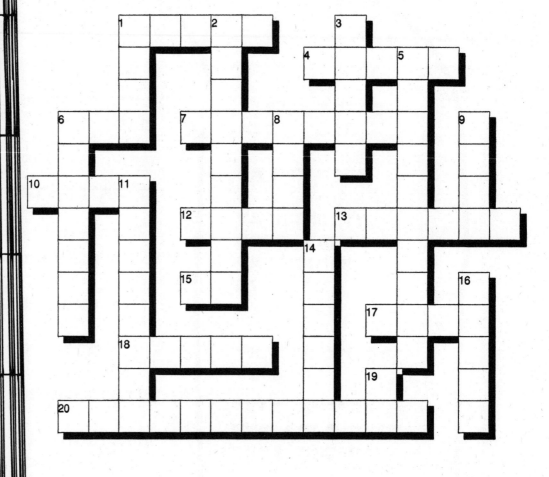

Word Pool

WILL   LOVE   GLORY   GOOD   LED
CHILDREN   RIGHTEOUS   HEIRS   PEACE
CONQUERORS   FREE   HELPS   ABBA   LIBERTY
ADOPTION   IMAGE   NO   CONDEMNATION
DWELLS   LIFE   SPIRIT   US

Across

1 The _____ which shall be revealed (vs. 18)

4 To be spiritually minded is #8 Down and _____ (vs. 6)

6 Those who are _____ by the Spirit are sons of God (vs. 14)

7 The Spirit gives witness that we are _____ of God (vs. 16)

10 As God's children we can call Him "_____, Father" (vs. 15)

12 Nothing shall separate us from the _____ of God (vs. 39)

13 If the #14 Down of God _____ in you, you belong to Him (vs. 9)

15 If God be for _____, who can be against us? (vs. 31)

17 The law of the Spirit of life makes us ____ from the law of sin and death (vs. 2)

18 God's purpose is for us to become the ___ of His Son (vs. 29)

20 For those who are in Christ Jesus there is #19 Down _____ (vs. 1)

Down

1 All things work together for _____ to those who are called according to His purpose (vs. 28)

2 God sent His Son that the ____ requirement of the law might be fulfilled in us (vs. 4)

3 As children of God we are His _____ (vs. 17)

5 We are more than _____ through Him who loved us (vs. 37)

6 Creation will be delivered from bondage to obtain _____ (vs. 21)

8 To be spiritually minded is _____ and #4 Across (vs. 6)

9 The Spirit prays for us according to the _____ of God (vs. 27)

11 As God's children we have received the Spirit of ____, not the spirit of bondage (vs. 15)

14 If the _____ of God #13 Across in you, you belong to Him (vs. 9)

16 The Spirit _____ us in our weaknesses (vs. 26)

19 For those who are in Christ Jesus there is _____ #20 Across (vs. 1)

See answer on puzzle answer page 5.

The Multitudes

The Israelites were God's chosen people — the "people of promise" and also the "promised people" — the descendants of Abraham to whom the promise was given that his heirs would be as numerous as the stars in the sky and the grains of sand on the seashore. How many words with two or more letters can you find in the word ISRAELITES?

More than 20 — Good   More than 40 — Excellent   More than 60 — Superior!

See answers on puzzle answer page 5.

A Scattered Lunch

On his way to hear Jesus speak, this little boy lost the contents of his lunch basket. The cart in which he was riding overturned accidentally. Can you help him find his lunch of five loaves and two fish?

Clue: Bread in Bible times was flat and round — like the "pita bread" in stores today.

Jesus' Plea

Jesus tells us two things in Matthew 26:41 (NKJ) that we must do to keep from sinning. To find out what He said, find His message hidden in this box of letters. Begin at the arrow and draw a line to connect the letters that make up the verse. Draw a diagonal line from the letter to the correct connecting letter to make up all 18 words in the verse. Go down one column, then up the next column until you reach the end. We've connected the first five letters for you.

Begin
↓

End
↑

```
W  U  P  R  T  V  B  M  D  P  K  O
R  A  M  N  P  O  Y  E  M  I  T  A
T  G  I  N  P  O  E  C  S  W  E  L
V  C  D  R  A  E  S  D  O  W  E  W
H  R  E  B  M  Z  N  O  I  E  S  I
P  A  R  T  O  P  R  I  B  L  W  I
N  U  N  Y  T  E  T  A  L  C  H  D
W  D  R  E  S  A  O  I  H  I  N  S
P  O  U  R  T  S  R  C  N  L  E  Y
L  R  M  O  U  I  S  I  J  G  B  L
A  W  Y  B  O  L  P  S  B  E  F  N
E  Y  O  T  U  N  P  S  W  U  R  E
L  A  S  R  T  W  E  K  T  O  H  P
A  E  R  M  O  H  P  K  E  T  S  A
```

W A T C H ___ ___ ___ ___ ___ ___ ___

___ ___ ___ ___ ___ ___ ___ ___ ___

___ ___ ___ ___ ___ ___ ___ ___

___ ___ ___ ___ ___ ___ ___

___ ___ ___ ___ ___ ___ ___

___ ___ ___ ___ ___ ___ ___ ___ ___

___ ___ ___ ___ ___ ___ ___

See answer on puzzle answer page 5.

Shout of Praise

When Jesus entered Jerusalem one day, crowds lined the street to greet Him. They waved giant palm fronds and cried praises to God. Unscramble the letters in the palm fronds below to spell one of the words that the people shouted. The word means "save, we pray."

_ _ _ _ _ _ _ _

See answer on puzzle answer page 5.

Temptations

Samson is a great hero in the Old Testament. He had great physical strength, but he became weak by giving in to temptations. Complete the story of Samson and Delilah with words from the word pool and then use them to fill in the crossword grid. This story is found in Judges 13-16.

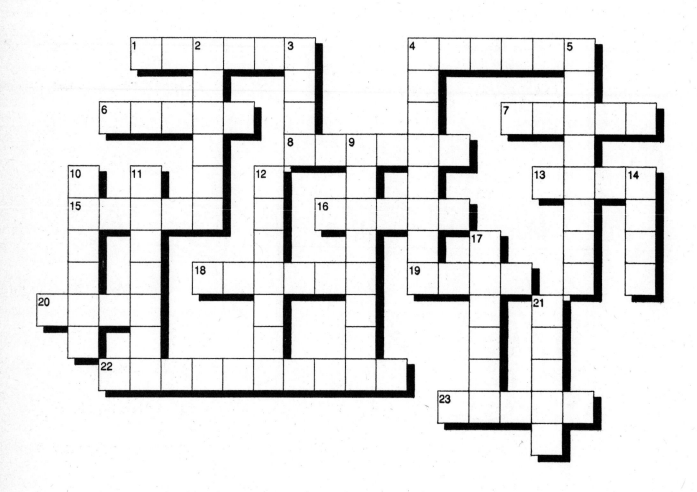

_____ was a _____ and _____ of Israel. He had superhuman _____ because he
4 Across   9 Down   6 Across   4 Down

obeyed the _____ law that he would never take a _____ to his _____ . He was strong
            5 Down   7 Across   19 Across

as long as he kept this vow.

Samson fell in love with a _____ woman named _____ . The Philistines were the
                          22 Across   11 Down

_____ of Israel, and when they found out about Samson and Delilah, they convinced her to
15 Across

_____ him. Each official would give her 1,100 pieces of _____ if she found out the
10 Down   17 Down

_____ of Samson's great strength so they could destroy him. Day after day Delilah begged
8 Across

Samson to tell her the reason for his strength. But Samson never told her the right answer.

Delilah was persistent and one day she asked him again. By this time he had grown tired of

her questioning. He finally gave in and he told her that he would lose his strength and

become _____ if his hair was cut off. So that night she called in a man to _____ Samson's
14 Down   21 Down

head while he was _____ . When Samson awoke his extraordinary strength had left him and
18 Across

he was just like any other man.

The Philistines captured the weakened Samson, put out his _____ , and took him to
3 Down

_____ . There he was put to work pulling a millstone to grind wheat. While Samson was in
20 Across

jail, his hair started to _____ back.
13 Across

One day the Philistines held a celebration over their capture of Samson. They asked for

Samson to be brought out of prison so they could see him and _____ at him. He was put
16 Across

between the _____ of the _____ . As he stood there, Samson prayed that God would
12 Down   1 Across

restore his strength, just one more time, so he could repay the Philistines for what they had

done to him. He braced himself between two pillars, and with a _____ push he cracked the
2 Down

pillars and the temple fell in on all the Philistines who were in it. Samson died along with

them. He was a _____ man and in his death he killed more Philistines than he had killed in
23 Across

his lifetime.

Word Pool

ASLEEP BETRAY BRAVE CHAMPION DELILAH ENEMY EYES GROW
HAIR JAIL JUDGE LAUGH MIGHTY NAZIRITE PHILISTINE PILLARS
RAZOR SAMSON SECRET SHAVE SILVER STRENGTH TEMPLE WEAK

See answer on puzzle answer page 5.

Extra Baggage

Each of these Bible characters is associated with three of the four items pictured next to their names. Circle the "extra baggage," the item that does not belong with that person.

DAVID

MOSES

NOAH

ADAM AND EVE

JONAH

See answer on puzzle answer page 5.

Relatively Speaking

Unscramble these words to discover the names of just a few of Jesus' distant relatives. (Hint: You can find Jesus' "family tree" in chapter 1 of Matthew NKJ.)

BAHMARA __ __ __ __ __ __ __

CASIA __ __ __ __ __

BAOCJ ⃝ __ __ __

HAUDJ __ __ __ __ __

RPEEZ ⃝ __ __ __ __

NEHOZR __ ⃝ __ __ __ __

AMR __ __ __

MABANAIMD __ __ __ __ __ __ __ __

HAOSHNN __ __ ⃝ __ __ __ __

LANMOS __ __ __ __ __ __

OBZA __ __ __ __

BEDO ⃝ __ __ __

SEJES __ __ ⃝ __ __

VAIDD __ __ __ __ __

Now unscramble the circled letters to find the name of Jesus' earthly father:

__ __ __ __ __ __

See answer on puzzle answer page 5.

The Holy Spirit

Jesus told His disciples that it was good that He go away to His Heavenly Father so He could send the Holy Spirit to us. The crossword and all the clues below relate to the work and person of the Holy Spirit.

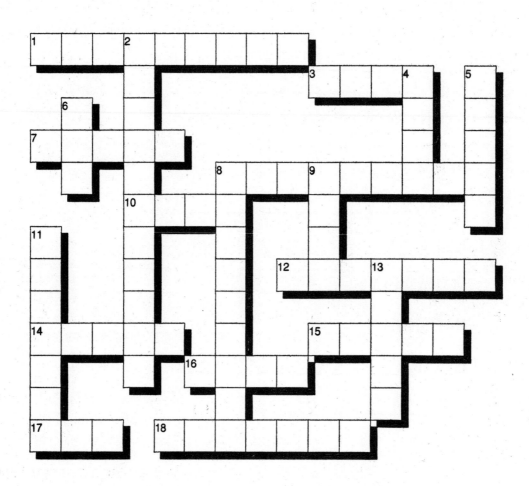

Across

1 Jesus promised that when He went away He would send the _____ (John 16:7)

3 The sound from Heaven that accompanied the coming of the Holy Spirit was of a rushing, mighty _____ (Acts 2:2)

7 The prophet Joel told of a day when God's Spirit would be poured out on #6 Down _____ (Joel 2:28)

8 Another name for the Holy Spirit is the _____, from the Greek word *parakletos,* and means helper or counselor.

10 When the Holy Spirit descended on Pentecost, tongues as of _____ appeared on each person (Acts 2:3)

12 John the Baptist testified that Jesus was the One who came to _____ with the Holy Spirit (John 1:33)

14 The Holy Spirit gives _____ such as the word of wisdom, word of knowledge, working of miracles, and prophecy, to equip Christians for ministry and service (1 Corinthians 12:8-10)

15 The _____ of the Spirit is love, joy, peace, longsuffering, kindness, goodness, faithfulness, gentleness, self-control (Galatians 5:22-23)

16 The _____ of God is poured into our hearts by the Holy Spirit (Romans 5:5)

17 The Holy Spirit convicts of _____ (John 16:8-11)

18 The Holy Spirit gives us power to tell others, or _____ about Jesus Christ (Acts 1:8)

Down

2 The Spirit present in our lives as Christians is the _____ of the promised full harvest of our redemption (Romans 8:23)

4 At Jesus' baptism, the Holy Spirit descended on Him from Heaven as a _____ (Luke 3:22)

5 Mighty signs and wonders are accomplished by the _____ of the Holy Spirit (Romans 15:19)

6 The Holy Spirit was given to _____ #7 Across in fulfillment of prophecy (Joel 2:28)

8 On the Day of _____, the Holy Spirit was poured out on the disciples as they gathered in Jerusalem (Acts 2:1-4)

9 If we live by the Spirit, we are God's sons and daughters, and we call Him "_____, Father" (Romans 8:15)

11 When the disciples were filled with the Holy Spirit, they began to speak with other _____ (Acts 2:4)

13 Another name for the Holy Spirit is the Spirit of _____, because He will guide believers into right believing about Jesus (John 16:13)

Word Pool

ABBA ALL BAPTIZE COMFORTER DOVE FIRE FIRSTFRUITS FLESH
FRUIT GIFTS LOVE PARACLETE PENTECOST POWER SIN TONGUES
TRUTH WIND WITNESS

See answer on puzzle answer page 5.

Highways and Byways

Travel was difficult in Bible days. But as roads were built it became easier for people to get around and take the Gospel from city to city. The names of some of the major roads of Bible days are listed in the word pool below. Try to find the underlined words in the letter box.

```
R T O P U E M C O S E
S T R A I G H T H O N
U D T E H N I O C A R
A R E W S A M O I Y E
M O P G O T S P R L Y
M X N T R I P I E W Z
E I S R O A N L J P R
K E R O P N S A F E N
```

Word Pool

STREET CALLED <u>STRAIGHT</u>   <u>JERICHO</u> ROAD

ROAD TO <u>EMMAUS</u>   <u>KING'S</u> HIGHWAY   <u>EGNATIAN</u> WAY

<u>APPIAN</u> WAY

See answer on puzzle answer page 6.

Peter's Denial

Peter was one of Jesus' closest disciples. Peter, however, was not always bold in his witness. Before Jesus' crucifixion, Peter denied Jesus. Fill in the blanks with the words from the word pool. Then put the words in the grid to complete the crossword puzzle.

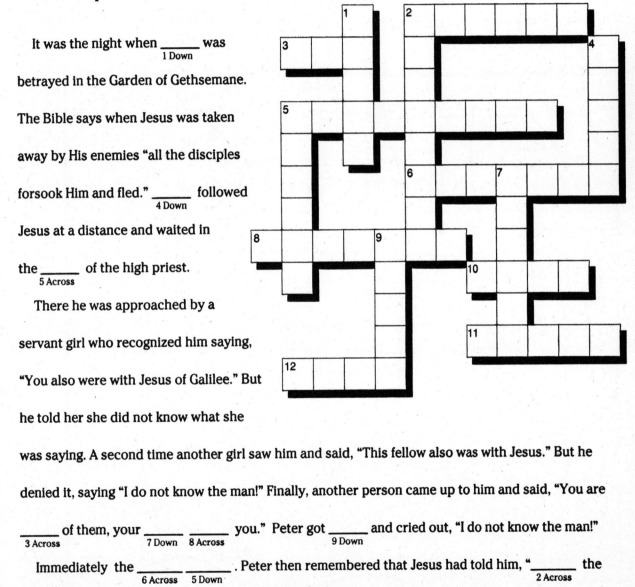

It was the night when _____ was
                        1 Down

betrayed in the Garden of Gethsemane.

The Bible says when Jesus was taken

away by His enemies "all the disciples

forsook Him and fled." _____ followed
                         4 Down

Jesus at a distance and waited in

the _____ of the high priest.
    5 Across

There he was approached by a

servant girl who recognized him saying,

"You also were with Jesus of Galilee." But

he told her she did not know what she

was saying. A second time another girl saw him and said, "This fellow also was with Jesus." But he

denied it, saying "I do not know the man!" Finally, another person came up to him and said, "You are

_____ of them, your _____ _____ you." Peter got _____ and cried out, "I do not know the man!"
3 Across   7 Down 8 Across   9 Down

Immediately the _____ _____ . Peter then remembered that Jesus had told him, "_____ the
                6 Across 5 Down   2 Across

rooster crows, you will _____ Me _____ times." Peter went out of the courtyard and _____ _____ .
                        12 Across   11 Across   10 Across 2 Down

Word Pool

ANGRY   BEFORE   BETRAYS   BITTERLY   COURTYARD   CROWED   DENY
JESUS   ONE   PETER   ROOSTER   SPEECH   THREE   WEPT

See answer on puzzle answer page 6.

"I *Sea* It!"

There's a picture hidden among these boxes. To find it, color in every box that has a black dot in it. When you're done, you'll be able to see a vessel that saved a famous Old Testament man and his family!

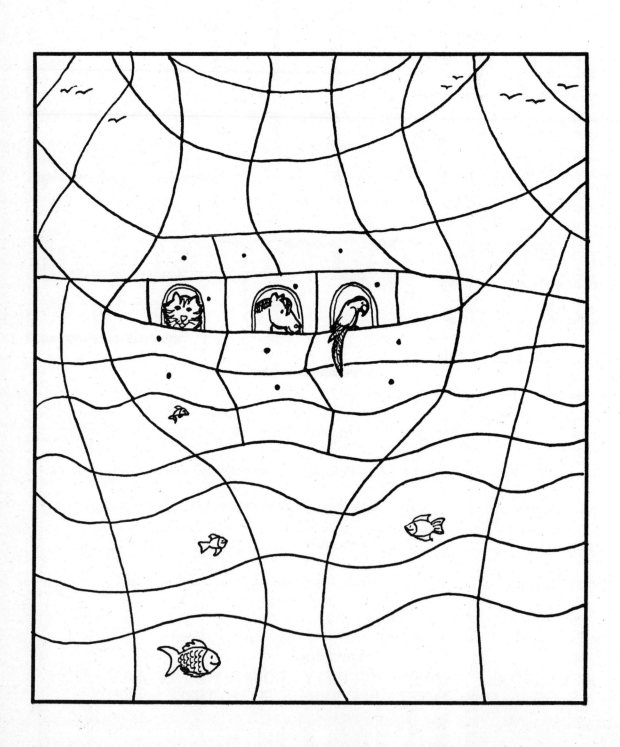

A Place with Room

The inn in Bethlehem had no room for Mary and Joseph on the night that Jesus was born. Connect the dots below to find a place that had room.

Elijah's Mission

In the Old Testament book of 1 Kings, chapters 17-19, you can read the story of Elijah, one of God's prophets. The words in this puzzle all have something to do with Elijah's mission: events in his life, and people that he knew. Using the word pool and the clues, can you fill in the squares? (And don't forget to read about Elijah in your Bible!)

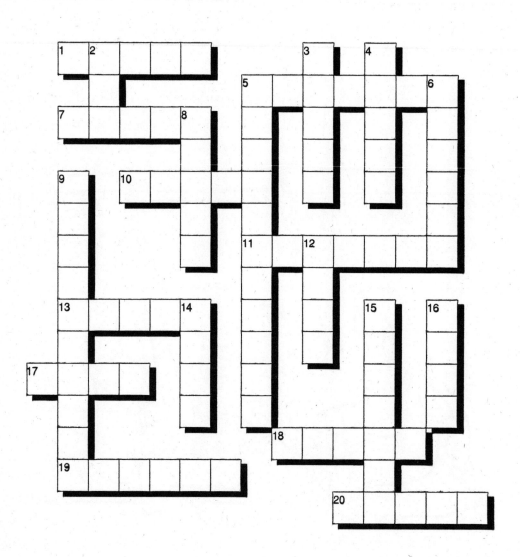

Across

1 The number of days and nights that Elijah survived in the wilderness after eating just two meals

5 Elijah placed this on Elisha; it meant that Elisha was the new prophet. (Use the plural form of this word.)

7 You use this white powder in baking

10 How many times Elijah sent his servant to check for rainclouds

11 The vehicle that the king rode in to escape the rainstorms

13 The mountain known as the "mountain of God"

17 The kind of animal used in the sacrifice

18 The weapon that the queen used to kill some of God's prophets

19 The prophet who took Elijah's place

20 How many times water was poured on Elijah's sacrifice before God consumed it with fire

Down

2 Use this liquid in a skillet to fry food

3 The opposite of "devil"

4 Sacrifices were placed on these

5 The place where Elijah met with the 850 false prophets (two words)

6 Elisha wanted a "double portion" of this from Elijah (2 Kings 2:9)

8 The bird that fed Elijah during the drought

9 When the earth shakes, it's called an

_____

12 The king of Israel during most of Elijah's lifetime

14 The false god worshiped by Israel's king

15 The false goddess worshiped by the king's wife

16 Where Elijah stayed while he was on Mount Horeb: in a _____

Word Pool

AHAB   ALTAR   ANGEL   ASHERAH
BAAL   BULL   CARRIAGE   CAVE   CHARIOT
COLLARS   DANIEL   EARTHQUAKE
EIGHT   ELISHA   FIFTY   FLOUR
FORTY   GOAT   HOREB   HURRICANE
KNIFE   MANTLES   MOUNT CARMEL   OIL
RAVEN   SEVEN   SINAI   SOUL
SPIRIT   SWORD   THREE

See answer on puzzle answer page 6.

Flight to Egypt

God warned Joseph to flee from Bethlehem with Mary and the young child Jesus, in order to escape wicked King Herod. Joseph led his family south, across the desert, to Egypt. They stayed there until after King Herod died a few years later. Help Jesus' family get to Egypt without meeting any of King Herod's soldiers.

EGYPT

The Right Path

Shade in the marked segments of the stained glass window below to reveal one of the things that Jesus said He is for us.

They'll Last Forever

Use the secret code to decode the verse and find out what it is that lasts forever. (Write the decoded letters above the code letters.)

—— —— —— —— —— ——   —— —— ——
P   T   L   D   T   V   L   V   O

—— —— —— —— ——   —— —— —— —— ——
T   L   K   U   P   Q   P   L   N   N

—— —— —— ——   —— —— —— —— —— :   —— —— ——
I   L   Q   Q   L   G   L   X   H   F   U

—— ——   —— —— —— ——   —— —— —— —— ——
S   X   G   C   K   O   Q   P   L   N   N

—— —— —— —— —— —— ——   —— —— —— —— .
V   C   U   I   L   Q   Q   L   G   L   X

Mark 13:31

Secret Code

A=I B=J C=O D=V E=C F=Y G=W H=B I=P
J=K K=R L=A M=Q N=L O=D P=H Q=S R=F
S=M T=E U=T V=N W=G X=Y Y=Z Z=X

See answer on puzzle answer page 6.

The next 16 puzzles can be played as a game — either by yourself, or with friends.

Each puzzle has 7 clues about a PERSON, a PLACE, or a THING in the Bible.

You will need to unscramble letters or solve a secret code to get each clue. Work the clues one at a time. As soon as you have solved enough clues so that you think you know the answer — be fairly sure, now! — say, "I'm going to take a Risk!"

If you get the answer correct with this many clues	Then give yourself this many points
1 Clue	40 Points
2 Clues	35 Points
3 Clues	30 Points
4 Clues	25 Points
5 Clues	20 Points
6 Clues	15 Points
7 Clues	10 Points

If you still don't know . . . solve the answer names at the end of each puzzle, and give yourself 5 points.

However, if you don't get the answer right, you must go ahead and solve all the other clues and then take a second Risk. If you get the answer correct, give yourself 10 points.

If you still miss the answer, solve the answer clue name at the end of each puzzle and give yourself 5 points.

The goal of the game is to see how many points you can earn.

(To make the game more difficult, give yourself a time limit of five minutes for each puzzle. At the end of five minutes, you need to take a Risk.)

To play this game with friends:

Have each person work on a separate piece of paper to solve one or more of the clues until he thinks he knows the answer. Then he must write down the answer that he is willing to Risk. For each of the puzzles, each person who is playing must wait until all other members are willing to take a Risk. Then reveal your answer! If you don't have the correct answer, you don't get any points for that puzzle. The person with the highest number of points at the end of the 16 puzzles is the winner.

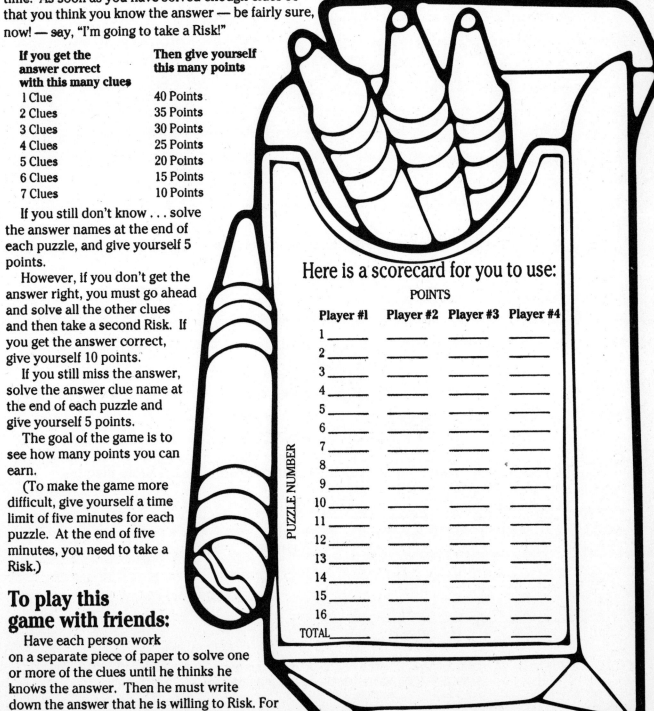

Here is a scorecard for you to use:

POINTS

PUZZLE NUMBER	Player #1	Player #2	Player #3	Player #4
1				
2				
3				
4				
5				
6				
7				
8				
9				
10				
11				
12				
13				
14				
15				
16				
TOTAL				

Who Is It?

Unscramble the clue words below to discover the name of a well-known Bible person.

40 points   N U G O Y ◯ __ __ __ __

35 points   D I M A __ ◯ __ __

30 points   H E E T R T O D B __ __ __ __ __ __ __ __ __

25 points   R E O H M T ◯ __ __ __ __ __ __

20 points   Z R T H E A A N __ __ __ __ ◯ __ __ __

15 points   S S U E J __ __ __ __ __

10 points   G N I R V I __ __ __ __ __ __

To get the answer, unscramble the letters circled above: Give yourself 5 points.

Letters __ __ __ __   Unscrambled __ __ __ __

See answer on puzzle answer page 6.

Where Is It?

Decode the clue words below to discover the name of a well-known Bible place.

40 points __ __ __ __ __ __ __ __
      D S F B U J P O

35 points __ __ __ __ __
      G S V J U

30 points __ __ __ __
      U S F F

25 points __ __ __ __ __ __ __
      T F S Q F O U

20 points __ __ __ __ __ __
      H B S E F O

15 points __ __ __ __
      B E B N

10 points __ __ __
      F W F

CODE: A in the code = Z in the answer, B in the code = A in the answer, C in the code = B in the answer . . . and so forth. **SUGGESTION:** Write out the entire alphabet for easier reference.

To get the answer, decode the word below: Give yourself 5 points.

__ __ __ __
F E F O

See answer on puzzle answer page 6.

Who Is It?

Unscramble the clue words below to discover the name of a well-known Bible person.

40 points   D N I E L D B   __ __ __ __ __ __ __

35 points   E S C T R P R E U O   __ __ __ __ __ __ __ ⃝ __ __ __

30 points   S U C M A D S A   __ __ __ __ __ __ __

25 points   S O N P I R R E ⃝ __ __ __ __ __ __

20 points   S S O N R Y M I I A   __ __ __ __ __ __ ⃝ __ __

15 points   S R E E L T T ⃝ __ __ __ __ __ __

10 points   U A L S   __ __ __ __

To get the answer, unscramble the letters circled above: Give yourself 5 points.

Letters __ __ __ __   Unscrambled __ __ __ __

See answer on puzzle answer page 6.

Where Is It?

Decode the clue words below to discover the name of a well-known Bible place.

40 points __ __ __ __ / __ __ __ __ __ __ (two words)
    8   15   12   25   6   1   13   9   12   25

35 points __ __ __ __ __ __
   10   15   19   5   16   8

20 points __ __ __ __ __ __
   14   1   20   9   15   14

30 points __ __ __ __ __
   13   15   19   5   19

15 points __ __ __ __ __ __ __
   16   12   1   7   21   5   19

25 points __ __ __ __ __ __ __ __
   16   1   19   19   15   22   5   18

10 points __ __ __ __ __ __ __
   16   8   1   18   1   15   8

CODE: 1=A, 2=B, 3=C and so forth. **SUGGESTION:** Write out the entire alphabet and put a number under each letter for easier reference.

To get the answer, decode the word below: Give yourself 5 points.

__ __ __ __ __
5   7   25   16   20

See answer on puzzle answer page 6.

Who Is It?

Unscramble the clue words below to discover the name of a well-known Bible person.

40 points   A D N E O T I N __ __ __ __ __ __ ◯

35 points   R H E S D E P H __ __ __ __ __ __ ◯

30 points   N I G K __ ◯ __ __

25 points   C R I O Y V T ◯ __ __ __ __ __ __

20 points   P S S M L A __ __ ◯ __ __ __

15 points   G N I L S __ __ __ __ __

10 points   G T O H L A I __ __ __ __ __ __ __

To get the answer, unscramble the letters circled above: Give yourself 5 points.

Letters __ __ __ __ __   Unscrambled __ __ __ __ __

See answer on puzzle answer page 6.

Where Is It?

Decode the clue words below to discover the name of a well-known Bible place.

40 points __ __ __ __ __
    C Z U H C

35 points __ __ __ __ __ __ __ __
   R K Z T F G S D Q

30 points __ __ __ __ __
   B D M R T R

25 points __ __ __ __
   R S Z Q

20 points __ __ __ __/__ __ __ (two words)
   V H R D L D M

15 points __ __ __
   H M M

10 points __ __ __ __ __
   A H Q S G

CODE: Z in the code = A in the answer, A in the code = B in the answer, B in the code = C in the answer . . . and so forth. **SUGGESTION:** Write out the entire alphabet for easier reference.

To get the answer, decode the word below: Give yourself 5 points.

__ __ __ __ __ __ __ __ __
A D S G K D G D L

See answer on puzzle answer page 6.

Puzzle 106
★★★

What Is It?

Unscramble the clue words below to discover the name of a well-known THING in the Bible.

40 points	P C U	__ __ __
35 points	R V R I E	__ __ __ __ ⊙
30 points	S S A E	__ ⊙ __ __
25 points	H S A W	⊙ __ __ __
20 points	N A I R	__ ⊙ __ __
15 points	A T S B P I M	__ __ __ ⊙ __ __ __
10 points	B T O A S	__ __ __ __ __

To get the answer, unscramble the letters circled above: Give yourself 5 points.

Letters __ __ __ __ __   Unscrambled __ __ __ __ __

See answer on puzzle answer page 6.

Puzzle 107
★★★

Who Is It?

Unscramble the clue words below to discover the name of a well-known person in the Old Testament.

40 points	L V R Y E A S	⊙ __ __ __ __ __ __
35 points	H P O H A R A	⊙ __ __ __ __ __ ⊙
30 points	C A B J O	⊙ __ __ __ __
25 points	T R V F E I O A	__ __ __ __ __ __ __
20 points	S D M R A E	__ __ ⊙ __ __ __
15 points	S R O L O C	__ __ __ ⊙ __ __
10 points	T A O C	__ __ __ __

To get the answer, unscramble the letters circled above: Give yourself 5 points.

Letters __ __ __ __ __ __   Unscrambled __ __ __ __ __ __ __

See answer on puzzle answer page 6.

Where Is It?

Decode the clue words below to discover the name of a well-known Bible place.

40 points ___ ___ ___
)   [≥

20 points ___ ___ ___ ___ ___ ___ ___ ___ ___ ___ ___
            #   > | #   (^   (≤   ([}

35 points ___ ___ ___ ___ ___ ___
        ^   %   !   ?   /   ?

15 points ___ ___ ___ ___
          #   (/   ≥

30 points ___ ___ ___ ___ ___ ___
        /   %   {   ]   =   %

10 points ___ ___ ___ ___
          +   ([}

25 points ___ ___ ___ ___ ___
        *   (=   =   ?

CODE: !=A   @=B   #=C $=D   %=E   ^=F   &=G   *=H   (=I   )=J   +=K   ==L   {=M   }=N   [=O
       ]=P   <=Q   >=R   ?=S   /=T |=U   \=V   •=W   ≤=X   ≥=Y   +=Z

To get the answer, decode the word below: Give yourself 5 points.

___ ___ ___ ___ ___ ___ ___ ___ ___
)   %   > | ?   !   =   %   {

See answer on puzzle answer page 6.

Who Is It?

Unscramble the clue words below to discover the name of a well-known Bible person.

40 points   A B B Y ___ ___ ___ ___

35 points   I M I R A M ⃝ ___ ___ ___ ___ ___

30 points   S K A E T B ___ ___ ⃝ ___ ___ ___

25 points   L A T O F ___ ___ ⃝ ___ ___

20 points   V E R I R ___ ___ ___ ⃝ ___

15 points   C E D U S E R ___ ___ ⃝ ___ ___ ___ ___

10 points   D A R E E L ___ ___ ___ ___ ___ ___

To get the answer, unscramble the letters circled above: Give yourself 5 points.

Letters ___ ___ ___ ___ ___   Unscrambled ___ ___ ___ ___ ___

See answer on puzzle answer page 6.

Where Is It?

Unscramble the clue words below to discover the name of a well-known Bible place.

40 points   L B E L S ⭕ __ __ ⭕ __

35 points   H L Y O / P C A L E __ __ __ __ / __ __ ⭕ __ __

30 points   A R F C S E I I C S __ ⭕ __ __ __ __ __ ⭕ __

25 points   P S I R T E S __ __ __ ⭕ __ __ __

20 points   R O W P H I S __ __ __ __ __ __ __

15 points   S W I S E D E N R L __ __ __ ⭕ ⭕ __ __ __ __

10 points   E T N T ⭕ __ ⭕ __

To get the answer, unscramble the letters circled above: Give yourself 5 points.

Letters __ __ __ __ __ __ __ __ __

Unscrambled __ __ __ __ __ __ __ __ __ __

See answer on puzzle answer page 7.

Where Is It?

Decode the clue words below to discover the name of a well-known Bible place.

40 points __ __ __ __ __ __
            U C K P V U

35 points __ __ __ __ __
            I N Q T A

30 points __ __ __ __ __ __
            R G T H G E V

25 points __ __ __ __ __ __
            H Q T G X G T

20 points __ __ __ __ __ __
            C P I G N U

15 points __ __ __ __ __
            V J T Q P G

10 points __ __ __ / __ __ __ __ __ __ __
            P G Y   L G T W U C N G O

CODE: C in the code = A in the answer, D in the code = B in the answer, E in the code = C in the answer . . . and so forth. **SUGGESTION:** Write out the entire alphabet for easier reference.

To get the answer, decode the word below: Give yourself 5 points.

__ __ __ __ __ __
J G C X G P

See answer on puzzle answer page 7.

Who Is It?

Unscramble the clue words below to discover the name of a well-known Bible person.

40 points   P G A Q __ __ __

35 points   T A L E T B __ __ __ __ __ __

30 points   D A N E S M I I T I __ __ ○ __ __ ○ __ __ __ __

25 points   H U O S T __ __ ○ __ __

20 points   P A M S L __ __ __ __ __

15 points   I C H E T R P S __ ○ __ __ __ __ __ __

10 points   F E C E L E S __ __ ○ __ __ __ __

To get the answer, unscramble the letters circled above: Give yourself 5 points.

Letters __ __ __ __ __ __   Unscrambled __ __ __ __ __ __

See answer on puzzle answer page 7.

Where Is It?

Decode the clue words below to discover the name of a well-known Bible place.

40 points __ __ __ __ __ __
     •   !   /   %   >

35 points __ __ __ __ __ __ __ __
     {   (>   !   #   ¤   %   ?

30 points __ __ __ __ __
     ?   /   (¤   ¤

25 points __ __ __ __
     }   %   /   ?

20 points __ __ __ __ __ __ __
     ^   (?   *   (}   &

15 points __ __ __ __ __
     ?   /   [>   {

10 points __ __ __
     ?   %   !

CODE: !=A   @=B   #=C $=D   %=E   ^=F   &=G   *=H   (=I   )=J   +=K   ==L   {=M   }=N   [=O
     ]=P   <=Q   >=R   ?=S   /=T |=U   \=V   •=W   ≤=X   ≥=Y   +=Z

To get the answer, decode the word below: Give yourself 5 points.

__ __ __ __ __ __ __
&   !   ¤   (¤   %   %

See answer on puzzle answer page 7.

What Is It?

Decode the clue words below to discover the name of a well-known THING in the Bible.

40 points __ __ __ __ __
         K F T V T

20 points __ __ __ __ __ __ __ __
         C S B O D I F T

35 points __ __ __ __ __ __
         G B S N F S

15 points __ __ __ __ __
         Q S V O F

30 points __ __ __ __ __
         G S V J U

10 points __ __ __ __ __ __
         H S B Q F T

25 points __ __ __ __ __
         B C J E F

CODE: A in the code = Z in the answer, B in the code = A in the answer, C in the code = B in the answer . . . and so forth. **SUGGESTION:** Write out the entire alphabet for easier reference.

To get the answer, decode the word below: Give yourself 5 points.

__ __ __ __
W J O F

See answer on puzzle answer page 7.

What Is It?

Unscramble the clue words below to discover the name of a well-known THING in the Bible.

40 points   LUFITUAEB __ __ ⃝ __ __ __ __ __ __

35 points   ESRENTA __ __ __ ⃝ __ __ __

30 points   RALYEP __ ⃝ __ __ __ __

25 points   TICY __ __ __ __

20 points   GRADU ⃝ __ __ __ __

15 points   LOESDC __ __ __ __ __ __

10 points   TENRY __ __ __ __ __

To get the answer, unscramble the letters circled above: Give yourself 5 points.

Letters __ __ __ __   Unscrambled __ __ __ __

See answer on puzzle answer page 7.

New Books

Well-known Bible verses from the New Testament (New King James Version) are the clues for this crossword puzzle. Each clue contains the chapter and verse number in the New Testament book in which the verse is found. Identify the New Testament book that contains the verse and fill in the crossword grid.

Across

1 Pray without ceasing. Ch. 5. vs. 17

5 Behold, I stand at the door and knock. If any one hears My voice and opens the door, I will come in to him and dine with him, and he with me. Ch. 3, vs. 20

6 But without faith it is impossible to please Him, for he who comes to God must believe that He is, and that He is a rewarder of those who diligently seek Him. Ch. 11, vs. 6

8 But seek first the kingdom of God and His righteousness, and all these things shall be added to you. Ch. 6, vs. 33

10 For God so loved the world that He gave His only begotten Son, that whoever believes in Him should not perish but have everlasting life. Ch. 3, vs. 16.

12 The effective, fervent prayer of a righteous man avails much. Ch. 5, vs. 16

13 But you shall receive power when the Holy Spirit has come upon you; and you shall be witnesses to Me in Jerusalem, and in all Judea and Samaria, and to the end of the earth. Ch. 1, vs. 8

15 For by grace you have been saved through faith, and that not of yourselves; it is the gift of God, not of works, lest any one should boast. Ch. 2, vss. 8,9

16 I can do all things through Christ who strengthens me. Ch. 4, vs. 13

17 And whatever you do, do it heartily, as to the Lord and not to men. Ch. 3, vs. 23

Down

1 Be diligent to show yourself approved to God, a worker who does not need to be ashamed, rightly dividing the word of truth. Ch. 2, vs. 15

2 And she brought forth her firstborn Son, and wrapped Him in swaddling cloths, and laid Him in a manger, because there was no room for them in the inn. Ch. 2, vs. 7

3 For what shall it profit a man if he gains the whole world, and loses his own soul? Ch. 8, vs. 36

4 And now abide faith, hope, love, these three; but the greatest of these is love. Ch. 13, vs. 13

7 For the wages of sin is death, but the gift of God is eternal life in Christ Jesus our Lord. Ch. 6, vs. 23

9 Not by works of righteousness which we have done, but according to His mercy He saved us. Ch. 3, vs. 5

10 Now to Him who is able to keep you from stumbling, and to present you faultless before the presence of His glory with exceeding joy, to God our Savior, who alone is wise, be glory and majesty, dominion and power, both now and forever. Amen. Ch. 1, vss. 24–25

11 Bear one another's burdens, and so fulfil the law of Christ. Ch. 6, vs. 2

14 That the sharing of your faith may become effective by the acknowledgment of every good thing which is in you in Christ Jesus. Ch. 1, vs. 6

16 Casting all your care upon Him, for He cares for you. Ch. 5, vs. 7

Answer on puzzle answer page 7.

The Religious Court

The Jewish high court tried civil, criminal, and religious cases. This court looked for evidence against Jesus to condemn Him to death — but they couldn't find any (Mark 14:55). They charged Peter and John with teaching false doctrine (Acts 4) and they charged Paul with breaking the Mosaic law (Acts 23). To find out the name of this high court, solve the puzzle below:

   - DAL = __ __ __

+ 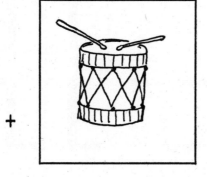   - EL = __ __

+ 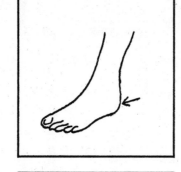   - UM + IN = __ __ __ __

Answer: __ __ __ __ __ __ __ __

See answer on puzzle answer page 7.

Noah's Numbers

Lots of numbers are in the story of Noah and the Great Flood (Genesis 5:32 to Genesis 9:29). Here is a number puzzle based on some of those numbers.

The number of every clean animal that God told Noah to take into the ark (Genesis 7:2) _____

The number of every unclean animal that God told Noah to take into the ark (Genesis 7:2) x _____

The month of the year that the rain began to fall (Genesis 7:11) x _____

The day of the month that the rain began to fall (Genesis 7:11) x _____

The number of days that "the waters prevailed upon the earth" (Genesis 7:24) + _____

The number of days and nights that the rain was on the earth (Genesis 7:12) - _____

The number of the month when the tops of the mountains could be seen (Genesis 8:5) + _____

The number of sons that Noah and his wife had (Genesis 7:13) + _____

The number of times Noah sent out birds to see how dry the earth was (Genesis 8:7,8,10-12) + _____

The number of stories (or decks) in the ark (Genesis 6:16) - _____

Noah's age when he entered the ark (Genesis 7:11) = _____

See answer on puzzle answer page 7.

I'll Fly Away

See if you can find and circle all ten of the Bible birds listed. Search the word list left, right, up, down, and diagonally. Cross the clues off the list when you find them. We found one for you as an example.

```
I  E  H  A  H  Q  U  L  P  W
T  P  S  W  A  T  S  I  E  O
S  E  P  R  W  L  P  A  L  L
T  L  A  I  K  M  A  U  I  L
O  I  U  Q  G  S  R  Q  C  A
R  C  I  R  R  E  R  D  T  W
K  A  L  A  L  W  O  S  D  S
T  N  V  M  T  V  W  N  O  L
P  O  A  E  E  Q  S  A  V  A
P  I  E  R  N  X  M  K  R  W
```

Word Pool

DOVE   HAWK   OWL   PELICAN   PIGEON   QUAIL   RAVEN   SPARROW
STORK   ~~SWALLOW~~

See answer on puzzle answer page 7.

Entering His Gates

The closer we are to Jesus, the more we will want to praise Him for who He is and how much He loves us. The psalmist tells us to enter into the gates and courts of His Temple with thanksgiving. (See Psalm 100:4.) On the lines below, write down all the words with two or more letters that you can make from the word THANKSGIVING.

More than 20 — Good   More than 40 — Exellent   More than 60 — Superior!

See answer on puzzle answer page 7.

Mothers and Daughters

Unscramble the names of the Bible mothers and daughters and then connect the mother with her daughter through the maze. Use the Scripture references in the verse pool below to help make the match.

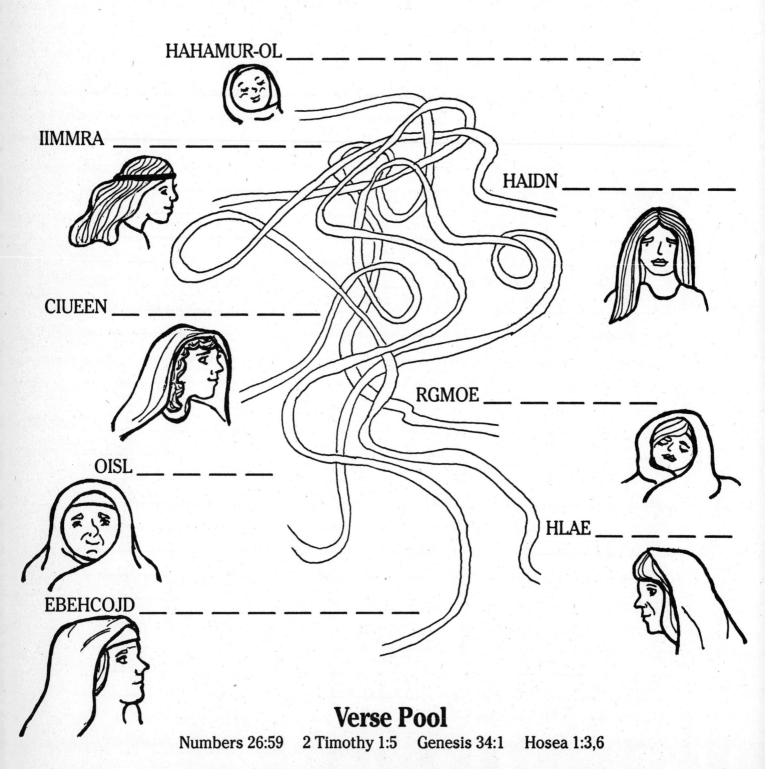

HAHAMUR-OL _ _ _ _ _ _ _ _ _ _

IIMMRA _ _ _ _ _ _

HAIDN _ _ _ _ _

CIUEEN _ _ _ _ _

RGMOE _ _ _ _ _

OISL _ _ _ _

HLAE _ _ _ _

EBEHCOJD _ _ _ _ _ _ _ _

Verse Pool

Numbers 26:59   2 Timothy 1:5   Genesis 34:1   Hosea 1:3,6

See answer on puzzle answer page 7.

Reciprocity

Jesus taught about being forgiven of our sins and forgiving other people. Follow the instructions to decode the hidden message and find out what He had to say.

1. Cross out the vowels A and U

AAFOURUIFAYEUFOARGUIUVEAMUEAN

2. Cross out every third letter

THSEINRTAREPSPSASHSEBS,

3. Cross out the letters S, I, and M

SYIOMUSRIHMESAIVMESNILMYSFIAMTSHIEMRS

4. Cross out all the numbers

3W32IL1LA4L7S8OF2OR6G9I2VEY5O8U.

Matthew 6:14

See answer on puzzle answer page 7.

Peter's Sermon

All the words in this puzzle can be found in Peter's sermon on the Day of Pentecost in Acts 2:14-40. The clues may not have anything to do with the sermon, but if you need help, the verse where you can find the word (New King James Version) is in parentheses at the end of the clue.

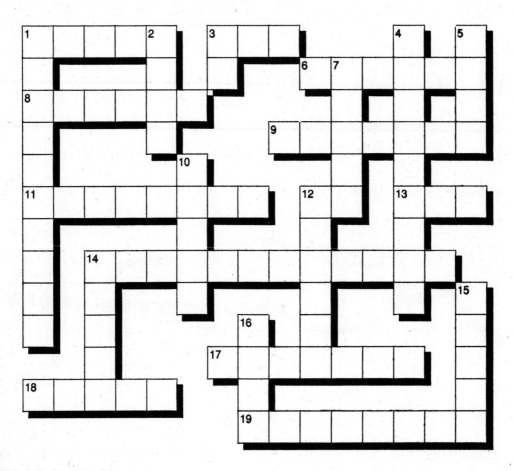

Across

1 Petitions or prays (v. 21)
3 "_____ of Israel, hear these words" (v. 22)
6 King's chair (v. 30)
8 Change your will (v. 38)
9 Lifted up (v. 33)
11 Foretell the future (v. 18)
12 "... He is _____ my right hand" (v. 25)
13 "But Peter, standing up with ____ eleven" (v. 14)
14 To raise up again (v. 31)
17 "... miracles, _____, and signs ..." (v. 22)
18 This sermon's preacher (v. 14)
19 John the Baptist did this (v. 38)

Down

1 Decay or destruction (v. 31)
2 What we have before salvation (v. 38)
3 Personal pronoun (v. 26)
4 Place to put your feet (v. 35)
5 Not alive (v. 29)
7 Valentine symbol (v. 26)
10 The Savior's name (v. 36)
12 Go up (v. 34)
14 Not wrong (v. 25)
15 He killed Goliath (v. 29)
16 Above-ground grave (v. 29)

See answer on puzzle answer page 7.

Rebekah's Service

When Abraham's servant came to Rebekah's home, she did a great favor for him.
Connect the dots below to show where Rebekah gave this service.

From the Heart

Jesus taught that there is something we are to do with our WHOLE heart, soul, and mind. Shade in the segments marked with a ♥ in the stained glass window below to reveal what it is.

See Matthew 22:37.

Sisters

Mary and Martha were two sisters who lived in Bethany. Jesus was often a guest in their home. One day Jesus came to visit and Martha was very busy making dinner for Him, but Mary sat at the feet of Jesus to listen to what He had to say. Martha became quite upset and asked Jesus to tell Mary to help her, but Jesus said, "Martha, you are worried about many things. Mary has chosen the good part." (You can read this story in Luke 10:38-42.) Circle the differences you can find between Mary and Martha.

Give Me A Hand

The Bible talks about hands in many different ways — as a symbol of power or honor, to communicate blessing, to extend or withhold fellowship, to express praise to God — and many more. The clues below all have to do with hands. Using your Bible, find the answers to the clues and fill in the crossword grid.

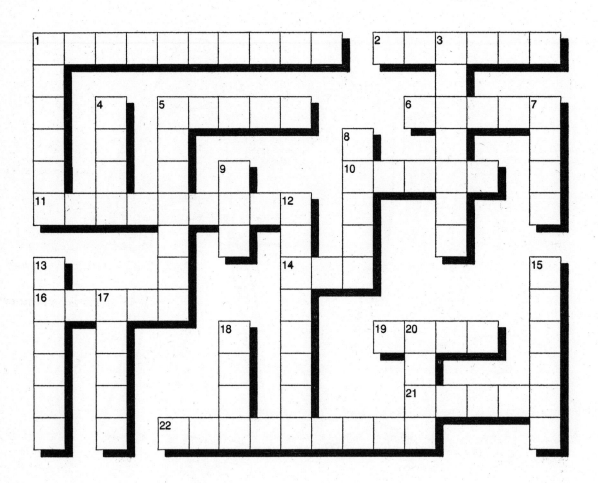

See answer on puzzle answer page 8.

Across

1 The right hand of _____ (Galatians 2:9)

2 _____ my hands and my feet, that it is I myself (Luke 24:39)

5 Esau's hands were _____ (Genesis 27:23)

6 An _____ stretched out his hand on Jerusalem to destroy it (2 Samuel 24:16)

10 _____ were driven through Jesus' hands (John 20:25)

11 The animals of the earth were _____ into Noah's hand (Genesis 9:2)

14 Jesus said those who believe will _____ hands on the sick and they will recover (Mark 16:18)

16 Another word for the circumstances and events of life that are in God's hand (Psalm 31:15)

19 To applaud (Psalm 47:1)

21 Cut off the _____ hand if it offends you (Matthew 5:30)

22 When Jesus _____ forth His hand, the wind stopped (Matthew 14:31)

Down

1 With His hands, God _____ the dry land (Psalm 95:5)

3 John and the disciples _____ the Word of life become flesh (1 John 1:1)

4 To make well (Mark 5:23)

5 The _____ are the work of God's hands (Psalm 102:25)

7 _____ up your hands to bless God (Psalm 63:4)

8 Deliver us from the hand of our _____ (singular)(1 Samuel 12:10)

9 Uzza was struck dead when he put his hand on the _____ to steady it (1 Chronicles 13:9,10)

12 The hand of the _____ makes rich (Proverbs 10:4)

13 Aaron and Hur _____ Moses' hands during the battle between Israel and Amalek (Exodus 17:12)

15 One of the works of God's hands (Psalm 111:7)

17 In God's hand are power and _____ (1 Chronicles 29:12)

18 The Lord stands at the right hand of the _____ (Psalm 109:31)

20 The hand of the _____ is not shortened, that it cannot save (Isaiah 59:1)

Escape from the King

As a shepherd boy, David was anointed by Samuel to succeed Saul as king of Israel. David had slain the Philistine giant Goliath and was a mighty warrior. He was a very popular hero among the people. That made King Saul jealous, and he plotted to kill David. To save his life, David had to run away and hide from Saul's pursuit. Begin in the center of the maze and help David escape from the jealous King Saul.

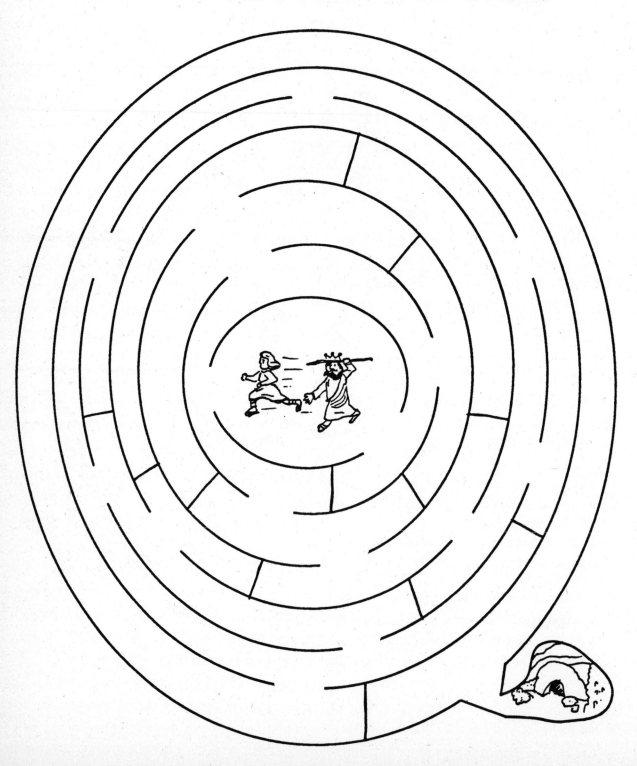

Unforeseen Helper

Jesus instructed Peter to go throw a fish hook into the sea and He said the first fish he caught would have a shekel in its mouth. This was the amount of money Jesus and Peter needed to pay the temple taxes. In the picture below, find the fish with the money that is about to get caught on Peter's hook.

Feelings

Anger, joy, thanksgiving, vengeance are just some of the feelings expressed in the Book of Psalms in the Old Testament. This book is unique in the Bible. It is a collection of songs and poems expressing the whole gamut of emotion based on human experience. You will probably need your Bible to answer the clues to fill in the crossword grid. The Scripture references are given at the end of each clue.

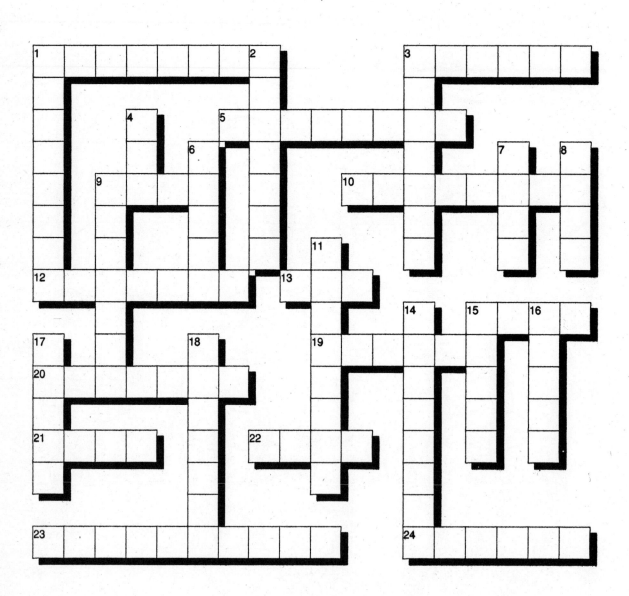

See answer on puzzle answer page 8.

Across

1 In my _____ I called on the Lord (18:6)

3 The Lord is near to those with a _____ heart (34:18)

5 The children of Israel made God angry, they _____ Him (78:40)

9 _____ was on every side (31:13)

10 My soul is _____ _____ (two words) within me (42:6)

12 God's testimonies are the psalmist's _____ (119:24)

13 _____ cometh in the morning (30:5)

15 I will be _____ in God (9:2)

19 The wicked are consumed with _____ (singular) (73:19)

20 Let me not be _____ (25:2)

21 My heart is in _____ within me (55:4)

22 I _____ those who _____ thee (139:21)

23 The Lord is gracious and full of _____ (111:4)

24 The psalmist's _____ is to dwell in the house of the Lord (27:4)

Down

1 I am . . . _____ of the people (22:6)

2 The _____ of death encompassed me (18:4)

3 _____ is the people that know the joyful sound (89:15)

4 My heart stands in _____ of thy word (119:161)

6 The _____ of God came upon them (78:31)

7 Ye that _____ the Lord, hate evil (97:10)

8 The psalmist was filled with _____ toward the foolish when he saw the prosperity of the wicked (73:3)

9 So _____ was I, and ignorant (73:22)

11 A broken and a _____ heart, O God, thou wilt not despise (51:17)

14 By thy wrath are we _____ (90:7)

15 My life is spent with _____ (31:10)

16 The Lord is slow to _____ (103:8)

17 _____ is that people, whose God is the Lord (144:15)

18 God became _____ when the children of Israel made graven images (78:58)

Smash!

The pictures below are of things in the Bible that were broken. The names of the picture clues are hidden in the square. Circle each word going across, down, or diagonally.

```
H  W  H  E  E  L  M
E  H  E  G  L  I  T
A  A  E  G  P  O  T
R  F  I  S  H  N  R
T  E  E  T  H  R  E
W  T  A  R  M  S  E
```

See answer on puzzle answer page 8.

God's Blessing

God gave a blessing to Adam and Eve. To reveal the blessing, use the secret code to
fill in the missing letters.

Be __ __ __it__ul and mul__ __ply;
　　♥　●　♥　　　　★

__ill the __ __rth and subdue it; have domin __ __ __
♥　　　■　　　　　　　　　　　　　　　　　　　◗

__ __ __ the __ish of the s__ __, __ __ __ __
✳　✔　　♥　　　　　■　　✳　✔

the b__ __ds of the a__ __, and __ __ __
　▼　　　　　▼　　　　✳　✔

ev__ __y liv__ __ __ th__ __ __ that m__ __es
✔　　　　◆　　　◆　　　　✳

on the __ __rth.
■

Secret Code
♥=F　●=RU　▼=IR　■=EA　★=TI
✔=ER　✳=OV　◆=ING　◗=ION

See answer on puzzle answer page 8.

Esther's Choice

After each clue, you will find the chapter and verse in the Book of Esther where the answer may be found. Use the New King James Version of the Bible to locate the answers to fill in the crossword.

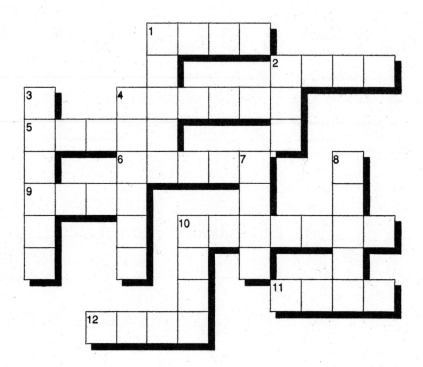

Across

1 What Esther asked all the Jews to do for her (4:16)

2 Mordecai's father (2:5)

4 King's house (1:5)

5 What Mordecai wore: Sackcloth and _____ (4:1)

6 Each drinking vessel was unique, different from the _____ (1:7)

9 All the officials gave ____ to the Jews (9:3)

10 What Esther invited the king and Haman to attend (5:8)

11 King Xerxes' response to Harbona, "_____ him on it!" (7:9)

12 Goes with ashes: _____ cloth (4:1)

Down

1 Another word for banquet or celebration with lots of food

2 Mordecai's nationality; he was a _____ (2:5)

3 King Xerxes' first queen (1:9)

4 Esther asked the king to spare her _____ (7:3)

7 Official documents were sealed with the king's _____ (8:8)

8 What Esther became (2:17)

10 The king called for a _____ to be read to him when he couldn't sleep (6:1)

See answer on puzzle answer page 8.

Glorious Entrance

Jesus made a glorious entrance into Jerusalem on His last visit there before the crucifixion. The city was crowded with people because it was the time of the Passover. As Jesus entered the city, His disciples and followers waved branches and cheered His arrival. Using the word pool, unscramble the words associated with Jesus' triumphal entry. Then put the letters that are circled on the lines below. Unscramble that word to find out what it was that the people shouted.

MULESARJE __ __ __ __ __ ◯ __ __ __ __

MERGANTS __ __ __ ◯ __ __ __ __

LAMP __ ◯ __ __

SCHERNAB __ __ __ __ ◯ __ __ __

YONKED __ ◯ __ __ __ __

SSJUE __ ◯ __ __ __

GINK __ ◯ __ __

Scrambled: __ __ __ __ __ __ __

Unscrambled: __ __ __ __ __ __ __

Word Pool
KING   GARMENTS   JERUSALEM   JESUS
BRANCHES   DONKEY   PALM

See answer on puzzle answer page 8.

Shout of Hope

As the Apostle Paul ended his first letter to the church in Corinth, he used a special word. Solve the puzzle below to discover the word.

 _____ - N = ____    _____ - BBIT = ____

 _____ - PKIN = ____

 _____ - IMBLE = ____    _____ - CT = __

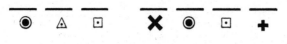

Decode the three-word message below to show the meaning of the special Bible word in puzzle 135 above.

◉ △ ⊡ ✖ ◉ ⊡ +

∴ ◉ ▲ ☉ ✪ ◪

Secret Code
∴=C   ◪=H   ◉=O   +=D   ✖=L   ⊡=R   ☉=E   ▲=M   ✪=T   △=U

See answers for puzzles 135 and 136 on puzzle answer page 8.

White on White

The Bible tells of many things that relate to the color white. See how many of those things you can find in the box of letters below. The words run in all directions — even backwards and upside down! Mark off the words in the word pool as you find them in the box of letters. (We've circled one of the words for you as a head start!)

```
B   X   U   Z   R   O   B   E   S   P
H   J   G   F   O   R   I   N   W   E
T   O   S   D   L   E   I   F   C   M
I   E   S   F   K   S   L   A   J   H
B   T   E   X   M   Y   B   O   H   G
Q   H   S   T   N   E   M   R   A   G
U   R   N   I   H   K   U   L   C   E
W   O   O   L   Y   N   J   S   W   E
A   N   W   O   P   O   B   X   L   Q
G   E   L   K   M   D   U   O   L   C
```

Word Pool
TEETH   ROBES   HAIR   SINS   ~~DONKEYS~~   EGG   SNOW
GARMENTS   WOOL   FIELDS   CLOUD   THRONE

See answer on puzzle answer page 8.

Rainy Days

God is the One who makes it rain, or keeps it from raining. In the Bible stories, God sometimes withheld rain to get people to seek Him, at other times there was too much rain as judgment against sin. And sometimes He sent just the right amount of rain to bless people with abundant crops. Using your Bible, answer the clues below to fill in the crossword grid. You will find that it wasn't just rain that God sent from Heaven.

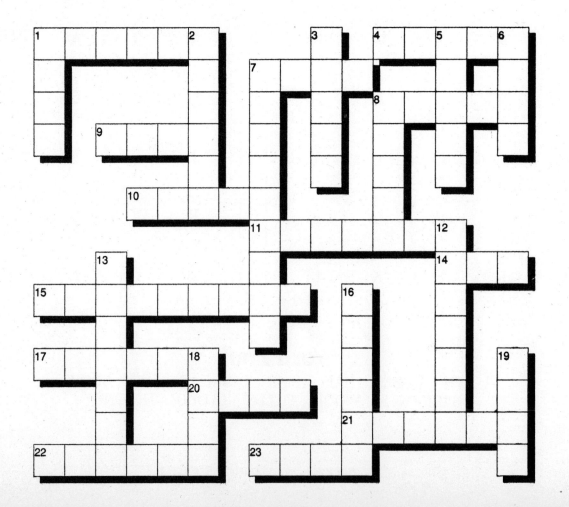

Across

1 The windows of _____ were opened causing the #8 Down that covered the #5 Down (Genesis 7:11)

4 I will rain _____ from Heaven for you (Exodus 16:4)

7 Elijah challenged the prophets of _____ to see whose God could bring fire and rain (1 Kings 18:21)

8 Rain fell on the earth _____ #6 Down and #2 Down (Genesis 7:12)

9 _____ found favor with God and he and his family were spared from the flood (Genesis 6:8)

10 When _____ stretched forth his rod, the Lord rained #1 Down from Heaven (Exodus 9:23)

11 The people of Israel turned to the Lord when God sent _____ and rain (1 Samuel 12:18)

14 God told Noah to build an _____ of gopher wood (Genesis 6:14)

15 The _____(two words) drives away rain (Proverbs 25:23)

17 When Heaven is _____ (two words), there is no rain (1 Kings 8:35)

20 The Lord promised to send rain if the people would hearken diligently, or _____ His commandments (Deuteronomy 11:13,14)

21 God said in His anger He would send a stormy wind, hail, and an overflowing _____ (Ezekiel 13:13)

22 The king's favor is like a cloud of the _____ rain (Proverbs 16:15)

23 Rain falls on the _____ and the #16 Down (Matthew 5:45)

Down

1 God rained _____ from Heaven to persuade Pharaoh to free the children of Israel (Exodus 9:18)

2 Rain fell on the earth #8 Across #6 Down and _____ (Genesis 7:12)

3 God rained _____ down from Heaven for the children of Israel to eat in the desert (Psalm 78:24)

5 Waters prevailed on the _____ 150 days (Genesis 7:24)

6 It rained #8 Across _____ and #2 Down (Genesis 7:12)

7 _____ and fire rained on Sodom and Gomorrah (Genesis 19:24)

8 God brought the _____ because of the wickedness of humanity (Genesis 6)

12 The _____ is a sign of the covenant God made with Noah that He would not destroy the earth by a flood again (Genesis 9:11-13)

13 When there is no rain, there is _____(Haggai 1:11)

16 Rain falls on the #23 Across and the _____ (Matthew 5:45)

18 The clouds _____ (present tense) out water (Psalms 77:17)

19 The _____ God causes rain (Jeremiah 14:22)

See answer on puzzle answer page 8.

Creation

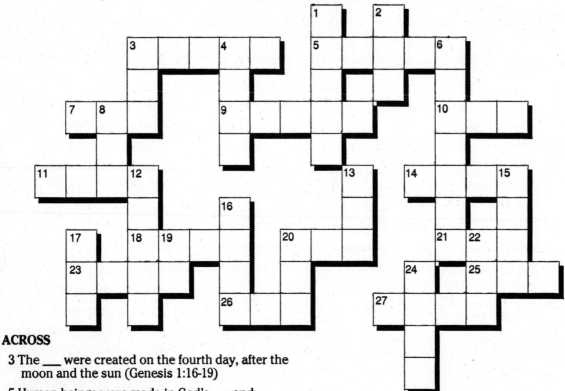

ACROSS

3 The ___ were created on the fourth day, after the moon and the sun (Genesis 1:16-19)

5 Human beings were made in God's ___ and likeness (Genesis 1:26-27)

7 Short for Thomas

9 God first said, "Let there be ___!" (Genesis 1:3)

10 God made ___ to be a companion for Adam (Genesis 3:20)

11 The birds ___ up into the sky (Genesis 1:20)

14 ___ were created to swim in all the seas (Genesis 1:20-21)

18 God ___ Adam out of the dust of the earth (Genesis 2:7)

20 The ___ was called the "greater light to govern the day" (Genesis 1:16)

21 "In the beginning, ___ created the heavens and the earth" (Genesis 1:1)

23 God brought all the animals to ___ so he could name them (Genesis 2:19)

25 God said, "___ there be an expanse between the waters" (Genesis 1:6)

26 On the third day, God caused ___ ground to rise up out of the waters (Genesis 1:9)

27 God saw that His creation was ___ !

DOWN

1 God called the darkness ___ (Genesis 1:5)

2 God formed a ___ from the dust (Genesis 2:7)

3 Short for Samuel

4 The sun was made to ___ over the daytime (Genesis 1:16)

6 The ___ and the morning were the first day (Genesis 1:5)

8 It only took God ___ day to make all of the animals (Genesis 24-25)

12 Adam was the first man in the Garden of Eden and Eve was the first ___

13 Adam and Eve were sent out of the Garden of Eden because of their ___

15 Adam and Eve tried to ___ from God after they had sinned (Genesis 3:8)

16 God made plants and trees bearing fruit with ___ in it (Genesis 1:12)

17 Evening and morning together were called a ___

19 Short for morning: ___ — the opposite of PM

20 On the fourth day, God put lights in the ___ (Genesis 1:14)

22 The creation story is told in Genesis, the first book of the ___ Testament

24 The ___ was called the "lesser light to govern the night" (Genesis 1:16)

See answer on puzzle answer page 8.

 140

Which Ones?

Circle the creatures below that are mentioned in the Bible.

See answer on puzzle answer page 8.

Lost Tribes

Find the lost tribes of Israel (the northern kingdom) in the puzzle below. The names run in all directions.

Word Pool

(Note: The word pool includes ALL twelve tribes of Israel, including the "half tribes" of Ephraim and Manasseh! Only the ten "lost" tribes are included in the puzzle.)

ASHER   BENJAMIN   DAN   EPHRAIM   GAD   ISSACHAR   JUDAH   REUBEN
MANASSEH   NAPHTALI   SIMEON   ZEBULUN

```
X  R  O  Z  B  A  M  I  A  R  H  P  E
J  O  P  Q  L  T  A  M  Y  E  R  L  I
Z  E  B  U  L  U  N  O  C  S  W  K  L
S  H  X  N  Z  D  A  S  R  L  D  I  A
R  A  H  C  A  S  S  I  I  J  Q  R  T
E  K  C  H  E  B  S  B  R  M  F  O  H
U  Y  S  G  G  L  E  E  N  S  E  W  P
B  R  I  A  F  O  H  J  C  F  H  O  A
E  S  D  T  P  S  W  S  C  N  A  P  N
N  T  I  D  A  N  L  T  C  J  O  E  T
```

Found Tribes

Unscramble the words below to get the names of the two tribes of Israel that formed the Kingdom of Judah — the tribes that were not lost in the great dispersion of the Jewish people.

HDJUA _ _ _ _ _   IMBJAENN _ _ _ _ _ _ _ _

See answer on puzzle answer page 8.

A Queen's Journey

The Queen of Sheba traveled more than 1,500 miles on camel to get to Jerusalem so she could experience for herself the riches, wisdom, and power of King Solomon. Help her find her way through the maze below.

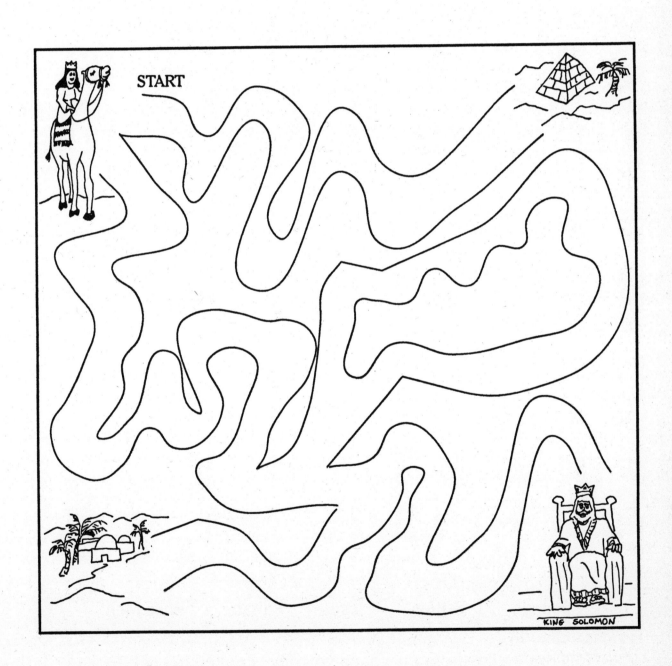

Star-Struck

1. Connect the dots below. What do you see? The Apostle Peter said that this is a symbol of what happens when the Lord Jesus comes into a person's heart (2 Peter 1:19).

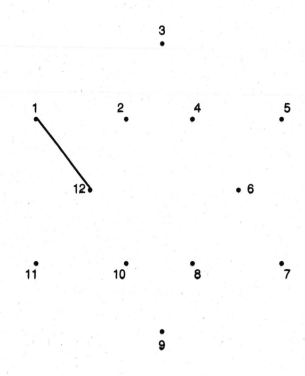

Noah   Paul   Abraham   John

Joseph   Esther   Jesus   Rahab   Wise Men

2. Now draw a line from the shape you have created to each person who is associated with this item (by what God said to them, showed them, or by what they said to others).

See answer on puzzle answer page 8.

The King Lion

Which lion below is not like the others? Circle it.

The Bible says that Jesus is the "Lion of the tribe of Judah" (Revelation 5:5). He alone
has the authority of a King to rule over ALL the earth!

Seasons

When God put the first rainbow in the sky, He made a great promise to Noah about the seasons.

1. Fill in the missing letters to the words below and you'll discover that promise. It's found in Genesis 8:22.

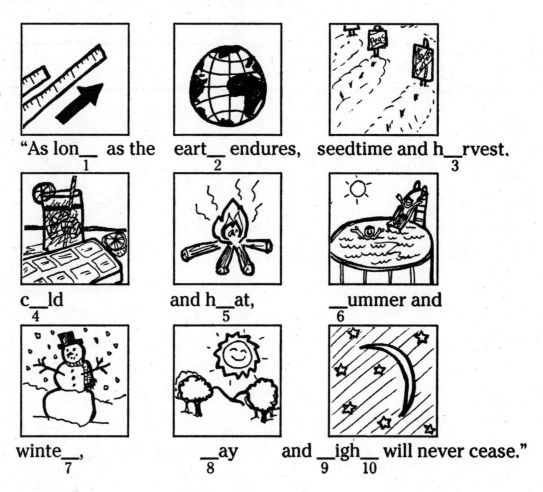

"As lon__ as the   eart__ endures,   seedtime and h__rvest,
    1   2   3

c__ld   and h__at,   __ummer and
4   5   6

winte__,   __ay   and __igh__ will never cease."
7   8   9   10

2. Now match the numbers with the blanks below for another message about the seasons.

__ __ __   __ __ __   __   __ __ __ __ __ __
1 4 8   2 3 6   3   7 5 3 6 4 9

F__ __   __ __ __   __ __ __ __ __ __ __ .
  4 7   10 2 5   6 5 3 6 4 9 6

God has a special reason for creating YOU, too!

See answer on puzzle answer page 8.

Transformations

Each of the people whose name is "scrambled" below was changed or affected in **a** significant way by Jesus.

1. Unscramble their names, just as Jesus unscrambled their lives or the lives of their loved ones — and gave them wholeness, purpose, and fulfillment!

LAPU   _ _ _ _

RYAM   _ _ _ _

PREEL   _ _ _ _ _

EPRET   _ _ _ _ _

HJNO   _ _ _ _

ASTDULERSE   _ _ _ _ _ _ _ _ _ _

BTAMIARSUE   _ _ _ _ _ _ _ _ _ _

TROUNNCIE   _ _ _ _ _ _ _ _ _

OEMNDICA   _ _ _ _ _ _ _ _

WOANMTALLEW   _ _ _ _ _ _ _ _ _ _ _

2. Pick out the scrambled letters and list them here:

_ _ _ _ _ _ _ _ _ _ _

3. Now unscramble the letters to reveal what Jesus desires for each one of US!

_ _ _ _ _ _ _ _ _ _ _

Word Pool: The answers are among these words: Antiochian, Bartimaeus, Martha, Peter, Gadarene, Woman with Tears, Herod, Adulteress, Mary, Samaritan, Magdalene, John, Woman at Well, Nobleman, Centurion, Blind Man, Deaf Man, Paul, Leper, Bethlehem, Priest, Demoniac, Pilate

See answer on puzzle answer page 9.

How Did They Feel?

Jesus told a story about ten young women in Matthew 25:1-13. Read the story and then draw the expressions you think that these women had on their faces!

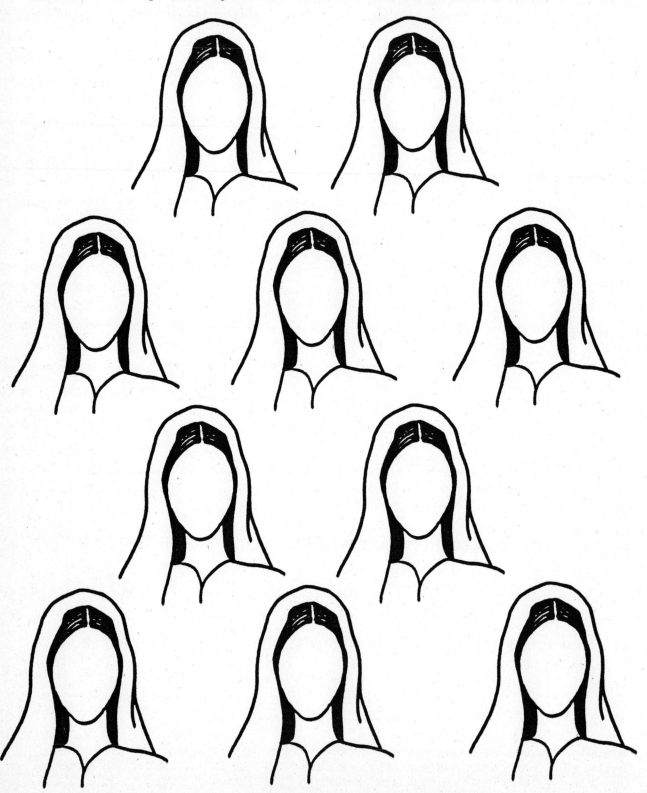

See answer on puzzle answer page 9.

Where'd He Go?

Jonah tried to run away from God, rather than obey God and go to Nineveh to preach. Can you find Jonah in the picture below?

Blowin' in the Wind

The Bible has many examples about wind. Many times wind is associated with miracles. Decipher the message below that describes what happened on the fiftieth day after Jesus ascended into Heaven.

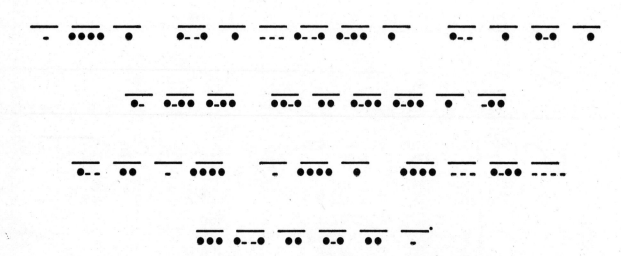

See answer on puzzle answer page 9.

In the Tabernacle

More than 100 words (two letters or longer) can be made out of the word
TABERNACLE! How many of these words can *you* find? (Note: Do *not* use a letter
more times than it appears in the word; for example, you may create a word with two
"A's" but *not* two "T's.")

T A B E R N A C L E

_____ _____ _____

_____ _____ _____

_____ _____ _____

_____ _____ _____

_____ _____ _____

_____ _____ _____

_____ _____ _____

_____ _____ _____

_____ _____ _____

_____ _____ _____

_____ _____ _____

_____ _____ _____

_____ _____ _____

_____ _____ _____

_____ _____ _____

Under 30 Words — KEEP LOOKING, 31-40 Words — GOOD, 41-50 Words — VERY GOOD,
51-60 Words — EXCELLENT, More than 60 Words — SUPERIOR

See answer on puzzle answer page 9.

How Many Times?

Write down the number of Jesus' apostles
(Matthew 10:1)   _____

Add the number of the tribes of Israel   +   _____
(Exodus 28:21)

Subtract the number of times Peter thought   -   _____
he should forgive those who had wronged him
(Matthew 18:21)

Subtract the number of times Peter denied Jesus   -   _____
(Matthew 26:75)

Add the number of sheep the shepherd had   +   _____
before he lost one (Matthew 18:12)

Subtract the number of books in the Bible   -   _____

Divide by the number of times Jesus was tempted
in the wilderness (Matthew 4:1-11)   ÷   _____

Add together the two digits in your answer   _____

AND . . .

You'll have the number of times a rich man named   =   _____
Naaman dipped in the Jordan River! (2 Kings 5)

See answer on puzzle answer page 9.

Wolf or Sheep?

Jesus taught that we should be aware of people who teach us bad things, while claiming that they are teaching us the truth. He called them "wolves in sheep's clothing" (Matthew 10:16). Can you find three wolves in the flock of sheep below?

God's Candelabra

When God gave Moses instructions for building the tabernacle, He asked Moses to include a special candlestand, called a menorah (me-nor-a). Today, many Jewish families still have a menorah in their homes.

1. Connect the dots below to create an example of "God's candelabra."

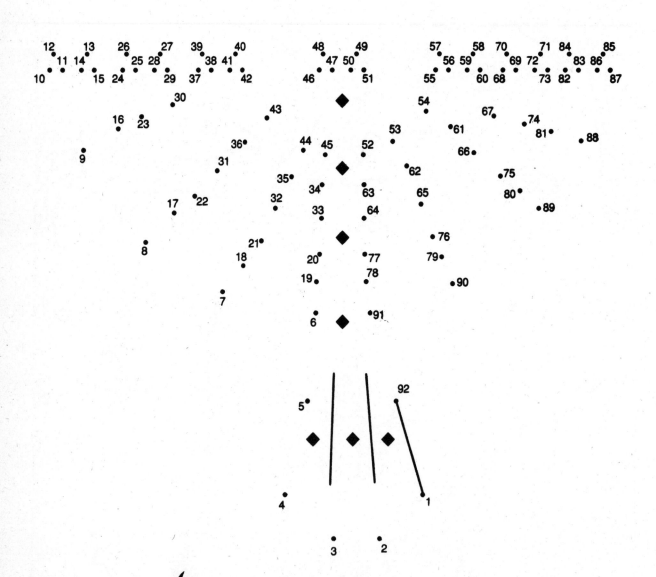

2. Now draw a flame atop each of the seven branches of the candlestand to light your menorah!

Read Exodus 25:31-40 for a full description of "God's candelabra."

Message to Moses

Moses was very afraid that the children of Israel would not believe that God had sent him to rescue them. "What if I tell them that the God of their fathers has sent me, and then they ask me His name?" asked Moses. Use the secret code to find out what the Lord said to Moses.

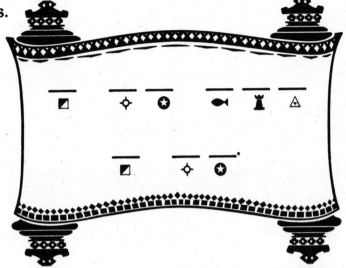

Then the Lord told Moses to say this to the Israelites:

Secret Code

◇=A ∴=E ♟=H ◪=I ✪=M ⊕=N △=O
■=S ★=T ○=U ◂=W →=Y

See answer on puzzle answer page 9.

Roots

All the clues for this puzzle have to do with the word "root" as it is found throughout Scripture. Use your Bible to "root out" the answers and complete the crossword grid. You may be surprised to find how many kinds of roots there are!

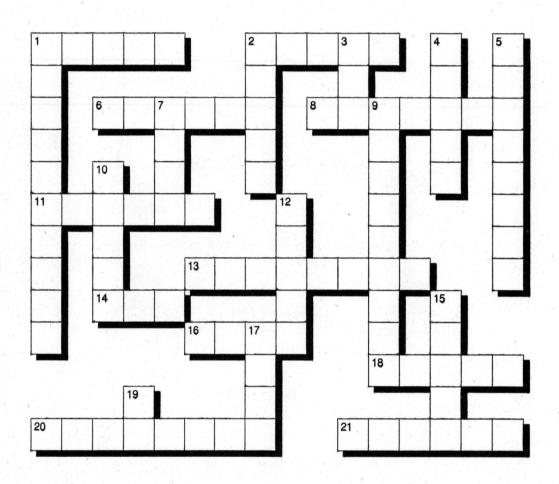

Across

1 #11 Across and _____ up in Christ Jesus (Colossians 2:7)

2 The house of _____ shall take root (2 Kings 19:30)

6 Job described his blessings as having his root spread out by the _____ (Job 29:19)

8 After the death of King Ahaz, Isaiah prophesied that worse things would come out of the root of the _____ (Isaiah 14:29)

11 _____ and grounded in love (Ephesians 3:17)

13 I am the vine; you are the _____ (John 15:5)

14 The promise of Jesus said He was to come as a root out of _____ ground (Isaiah 53:2)

See answer on puzzle answer page 9.

16 If the root be _____ , so are the #13 Across (Romans 11:16)

18 Daniel interpreted Nebuchadnezzar's dream, telling him to leave the _____ of the roots in the earth (Daniel 4:23)

20 Bitter-tasting plant that symbolizes #1 Down _____ (Deuteronomy 29:18)

21 The essential core or heart of something is called the root of the _____ (Job 19:28)

Down

1 Be diligent so _____ does not take root and cause trouble (Hebrews 12:15)

2 The Messiah came out of the root of _____ (Isaiah 11:10)

3 John the Baptist said the _____ is #17 Down to the root of the tree (Matthew 3:10)

4 Before its fall, Egypt was compared to a cedar whose root was by _____ waters (Ezekiel 31:7)

5 Plants without roots, dried up and _____ (Matthew 13:6)

7 To _____ root means to be established (Isaiah 27:6)

9 The root of the _____ yields fruit (Proverbs 12:12)

10 The root of the #9 Down shall not be _____ (Proverbs 12:3)

12 The love of _____ is the root of evil (1 Timothy 6:10)

15 Trees that do not bear _____ are dead, to be pulled out by the roots (Jude 12)

17 The #3 Down is _____ at the root of the tree, to chop it down if it does not bear good fruit (Luke 3:9)

19 Jesus said, "I _____ the root and offspring of David" (Revelation 22:16)

Our Focus

Hidden in the letters below is a message that tells you what God wants from His people. Each word in the message is written backwards. To solve this puzzle and find the message, write each word — from beginning to end — on the blank lines. The first word is done for you.

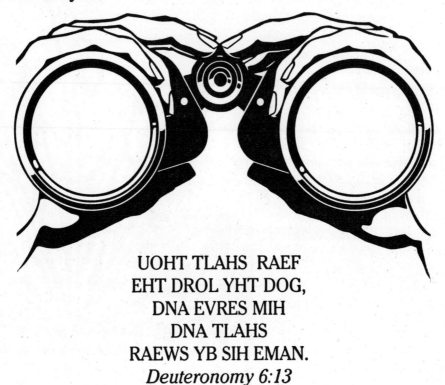

UOHT TLAHS RAEF
EHT DROL YHT DOG,
DNA EVRES MIH
DNA TLAHS
RAEWS YB SIH EMAN.
Deuteronomy 6:13

T H O U ___ ___ ___ ___ ___ ___ ___ ___

___ ___ ___ ___ ___ ___ ___ ___ ___ ___ ___ ___,

___ ___ ___ ___ ___ ___ ___ ___ ___

___ ___ ___ ___ ___ ___ ___ ___ ___

___ ___ ___ ___ ___ ___ ___ ___ ___ ___ ___ ___.

See answer on puzzle answer page 9.

Peter's Decision

After Jesus rose from the tomb, Peter returned to the Sea of Galilee to go fishing. In the city scene below, see how many items you can find that relate to the life of a fisherman.

FISH   FISHING POLE   HOOK   ANCHOR   BOAT   NET   HAND NET

Bible M's

See how many words you can get without looking up the clues shown in the Bible verses in the parentheses.

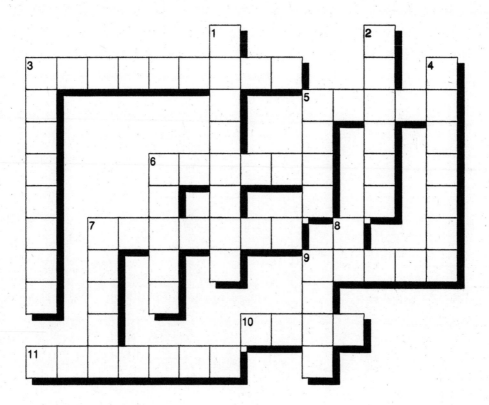

Across

3 Large rock used to grind wheat (Matthew 18:6)

5 Israelites' wilderness food (Exodus 16:15)

6 Mary, the _____ of Jesus (Acts 1:14)

7 Savior, Christ (John 1:41 NKJ)

9 Pity, kindness; His _____ endureth forever (1 Chronicles 16:34)

10 To whom _____ is given, _____ is required (Luke 12:48)

11 Heal the lepers, for example (Mark 9:39)

Down

1 Say to this _____, Be removed (Matthew 17:20)

2 The part of Elijah's robe that fell to Elisha (2 Kings 2:14)

3 To think about or dwell on (1 Timothy 4:15)

4 My soul doth _____ the Lord (Luke 1:46)

5 _____ Magdalene (Matthew 27:56)

6 A harp or trumpet makes _____ (Ecclesiastes 12:4 NKJ)

7 God is the _____ of the earth (Hebrews 11:10)

8 Thou shalt have no other gods before _____ (Exodus 20:3)

9 To make fun of, ridicule (Job 21:3)

See answer on puzzle answer page 9.

On the Road Again

In Numbers 22, in the Old Testament, you can read about Balaam, a man who had an unusual conversation as he was on his way to see Balak, the king of the Moabites. Connect the dots and see who spoke with Balaam.

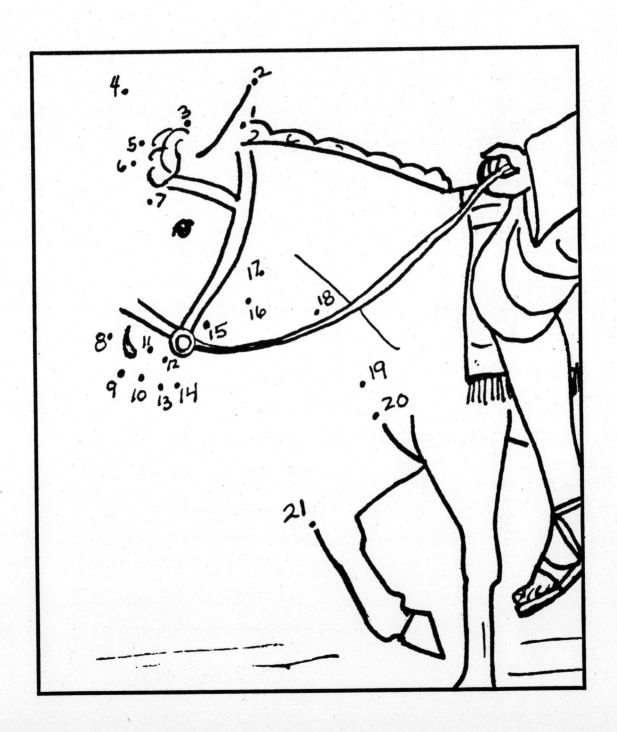

He Loves Us

God has given us the opportunity to be related to Him in a very special way to let us know that He loves us more than anyone else does. Solve the puzzle below to find out who God can be to each person.

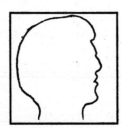 ___ ___ ___ ___ - D = ___ ___ ___

 ___ ___ ___ ___ - O = ___ ___ ___

 ___ ___ ___ ___ - JEL = ___ ___

 ___ ___ ___ ___ ___ ___ - E

= ___ ___ ___ ___ ___ ___

God is our ___ ___ ___ ___ ___ ___ ___

___ ___ ___ ___ ___ ___. *(See Luke 11:13.)*

See answer on puzzle answer page 9.

The Wise Person

Solve the puzzle by using the secret code to find out how you can be wise.

The __ __ __ __ __ of the __ __ __ __ __ __ __ __
       ⊕   ★

is a __ __ __ __ of __ __ __ __; and __ __ that
       ☼   ❦   🚶

__ __ __ __ __ __ __ __ __ __ __
     ★   👥👥

is __ __ __ __. *Proverbs 11:30*
   🎓

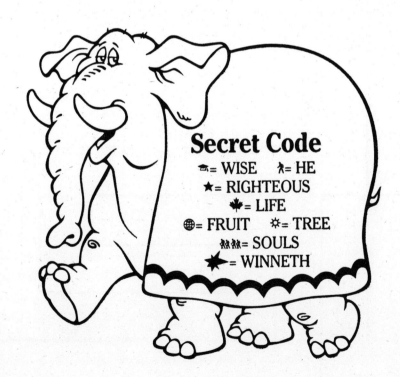

Secret Code
🎓 = WISE   🚶 = HE
★ = RIGHTEOUS
❦ = LIFE
⊕ = FRUIT   ☼ = TREE
👥👥 = SOULS
★ = WINNETH

See answer on puzzle answer page 9.

Return of the Ark

The Bible tells how the Ark of the Covenant once fell into the hands of enemy Philistines. They put the ark in the house of their god, named Dagon, and the next morning, the statue of Dagon had fallen on its face before the ark. This happened twice, and a great plague also fell upon the Philistines. Therefore, the Philistines decided to send the ark away. They built a special cart and yoked two cows to it, and then they put the ark on the cart and sent the cows away. They watched closely to see which way the cows would go. The cows, which had never been linked to a cart before, walked straight toward Beth-shemesh, to the field of a righteous Israelite named Joshua. (You can read about this story in 1 Samuel 5-6.)

Help the cows make their way through the maze below to the Israelites.

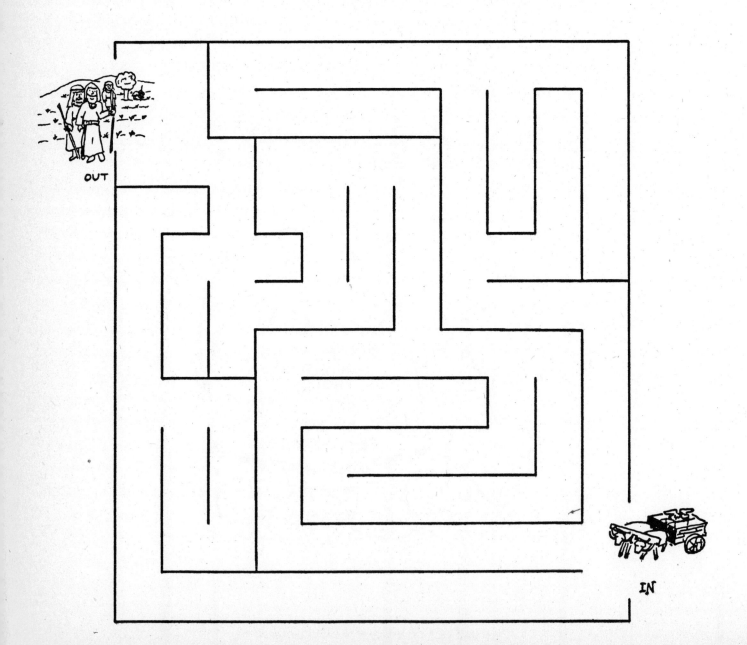

A Bright Shining Place

Unscramble the names of the 12 jewels that will form the foundations of the wall of the New Jerusalem. See how many you can figure out before you refer to Revelation 21 (NKJ).

1 PRASJE __ __ __ __ __ __

2 ARIPHSPE __ __ __ __ __ __ __

3 LOYCHEACND __ __ __ __ __ __ __ __ __

4 MAREDEL __ __ __ __ __ __

5 YADNORXS __ __ __ __ __ __ __

6 DASURIS __ __ __ __ __ __ __

7 ETHOCLSYIR __ __ __ __ __ __ __ __ __

8 REBLY __ __ __ __ __

9 POZAT __ __ __ __ __

10 SHASROYCPER __ __ __ __ __ __ __ __ __ __

11 CAITHNJ __ __ __ __ __ __ __

12 EATYSMHT __ __ __ __ __ __ __ __

What jewel will the 12 gates of the wall be made of? Unscramble the circled letters and see!

__ __ __ __ __ __

See answer on puzzle answer page 9.

Miracles

The clues for this puzzle are all about miracles in the New Testament. When you find the answer, fill in the crossword grid to complete the puzzle.

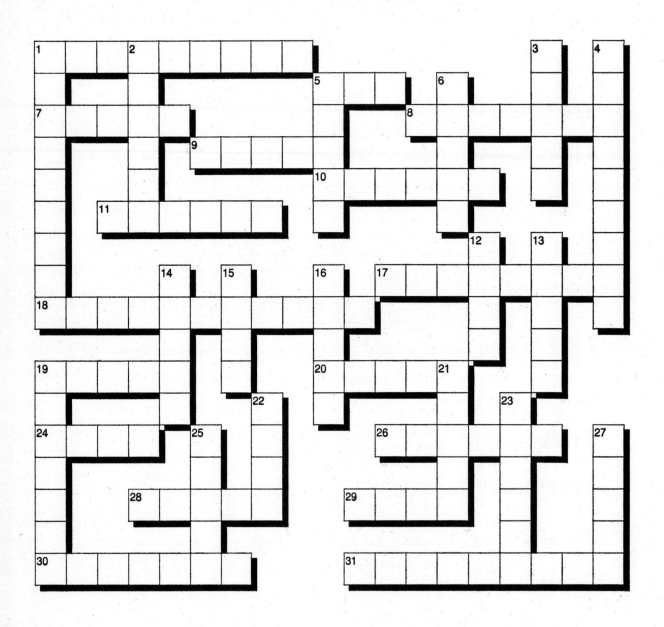

Across

1 The _____ understood #31 Across (Matthew 8:8,9)

5 The _____ reported to John the Baptist that the blind see, the lame walk, lepers are cleansed, the deaf hear, and dead are raised (Luke 7:20-22)

7 _____ had something better than silver or gold (Acts 3:6)

8 The demoniac cried, "_____ me not" (Mark 5:7)

9 One _____ returned to thank Jesus for healing him (Luke 17:12,15,16)

10 The woman asked Jesus for the _____ from the table so her daughter would be healed (Matthew 15:27)

11 Possessed by _____, the swine went over the cliff (Mark 5:13)

17 The nobleman _____ Jesus, and his son was healed (John 4:50)

18 Peter's _____ was healed (Matthew 8:14,15)

19 A man's withered hand was restored _____ (Matthew 12:13)

20 A blind man saw men as _____ #19 Down (Mark 8:24)

24 A possessed man cried in a _____ voice (Mark 5:7)

26 Another word for many (Mark 5:15)

28 Jesus told the Canaanite woman, "_____ is thy faith" (Matthew 15:28)

29 Jesus put _____ on the blind man's eyes (Mark 8:23)

30 Many sick people were made well when they touched the hem of Jesus' _____ (Matthew 14:36)

31 Jesus had _____ over unclean spirits (Mark 1:27)

Down

1 Jesus met #1 Across in _____ (Matthew 8:5)

2 A woman had been ill _____ years when Jesus healed her (Luke 8:43)

3 Jesus said that it wasn't right to toss the children's _____ to the dogs (Matthew 15:26)

4 In _____ a blind man received his sight (Mark 8:22)

5 Blind Bartimaeus asked Jesus to have _____ on him (Mark 10:47)

6 The man with the unclean spirit lived in the _____ (Mark 5:3)

12 Jesus asked, "_____ thou be made whole?" (John 5:6)

13 Jesus laid hands on _____ one of them, and healed them (Luke 4:40)

14 Jesus rebuked the _____ and Peter's #18 Across was healed (Luke 4:39)

15 Jesus healed the _____ (Matthew 14:14)

16 Thy _____ hath made thee whole (Luke 8:48)

19 Men looked like #20 Across _____ to the blind man (Mark 8:24)

21 The blind receive their _____ (Matthew 11:5)

22 Jesus _____ over Lazarus' death (John 11:35)

23 A woman was healed when she touched the _____ of Jesus' #30 Across (Luke 8:44)

25 The leper asked Jesus to make him _____ (Matthew 8:2)

27 Four friends of a man with _____ let him through the roof of a house to be healed by Jesus (Mark 2:3,4)

See answer on puzzle answer page 9.

I AM

Jesus was asked the question, "Who do You think You are?" In the letter grid below
are hidden words that Jesus used in the New Testament that tell us who He is. Find
the words and circle them.

```
R  R  O  O  T  O  F  D  A  V  I  D  Y
E  A  S  O  F  F  S  P  R  I  N  G  E
M  P  H  W  E  R  F  H  A  C  E  W  F
B  R  E  A  D  O  F  L  I  F  E  B  I
I  L  P  T  R  E  S  V  E  R  Y  R  L
O  L  H  B  I  G  W  L  A  T  A  A  H
O  N  E  Z  E  I  N  E  S  G  H  T  T
D  I  R  N  T  I  A  M  E  P  A  S  U
R  O  D  H  I  O  N  M  L  S  E  G  R
U  G  G  W  E  V  O  A  T  R  A  N  T
F  I  G  R  S  A  E  W  O  R  K  I  Y
L  N  O  M  D  S  E  U  B  O  R  N  A
S  O  A  T  E  V  W  E  R  O  O  R  W
D  R  E  S  U  R  R  E  C  T  I  O  N
R  U  I  T  A  T  R  E  Y  A  R  M  D
```

Word Pool

WAY   TRUTH   LIFE   LIGHT OF THE WORLD   BREAD OF LIFE
OFFSPRING AND ROOT OF DAVID   BRIGHT MORNING STAR   DOOR
GOOD SHEPHERD   RESURRECTION   TRUE VINE   ALPHA   OMEGA

See answer on puzzle answer page 9.

Holy Smoke

Complete the puzzle below to reveal the name of a type of incense used by priests in Bible times as a part of worship services. (Hint: It was one of the gifts brought to the baby Jesus by the Wise Men.)

 = (FRENCH) __ __ __ __ __ - IES = __ __

 = (PIGGY)__ __ __ __ - B = __ __ __

 = __ __ __ (WELL) - K = __ __

 = (ONE) __ __ __ __ - T = __ __ __ __

 = __ __ __ __ __ - AL = __ __

The answer is __ __ __ __ __ __ __ __ __ __ __ __ __ .

See answer on puzzle answer page 9.

Heavenly City

Connect the dots below to reveal the skyline of our future home: The New Jerusalem.

Before the Dawn

Connect the dots below to reveal the creature that Jesus mentioned as He talked with Peter in John 13:38.

Angels

This crossword puzzle has many clues related to the nature, appearance, and work of angels. Use the Word Pool or look up the Scripture references for help if you need it.

Across

2 Chief angels

7 "In the beginning, God ___ the heavens and the earth" (Genesis 1:1)

10 Instrument of the sixth angel in Revelation 9:14

11 What the Lord rides on, in Isaiah 19:1

12 Elisha prayed for his servant: "Open his ___ that he may see" the horses and chariots of fire around them (2 Kings 6:17)

15 The chief prince who came to help Daniel (Daniel 10:13)

16 "Our God whom we serve is ___ to deliver us" (Daniel 3:17)

18 Word of praise cried by the seraphim in Isaiah 6:3

19 Words written to the angel of the church in Smyrna: "Be faithful until death, and I will give you the crown of ___" (Revelation 2:10)

20 Angels with six wings as described in Isaiah 6:2

24 "Be not forgetful to entertain strangers: for thereby some have entertained angels _____" (sing.) (Hebrews 13:2, KJV)

26 Mary said after Gabriel's visit: "My ___ magnifies the Lord" (Luke 1:46)

27 One of six that seraphim have

28 One sent with a message; literal meaning of the word *angel*

29 The angel in Revelation 7:3 cried: "Do not harm the earth, the sea, or the trees till we have sealed the ___ of our God"

30 You, in biblical language

Down

1 "For I am persuaded that neither death nor life, nor angels nor ___ nor powers, . . . shall be able to separate us from the love of God" (Romans 8:38–39)

2 Every one

3 "And suddenly there was with the angel a multitude of the heavenly ___" (Luke 2:13)

4 The angel who visited Mary with news of Jesus' birth (Luke 1:26)

5 Gabriel said to Mary: Jesus "will be ___ the Son of the Highest" (Luke 1:32)

6 The angelic host praised God and said, "And on earth ___, goodwill toward men!" (Luke 2:14)

7 Angels who guarded Eden with flaming swords (Genesis 3:24)

8 "Blessed be the LORD God of Israel from everlasting to everlasting! Amen and ___" (Psalm 41:13)

9 Angel who fell from heaven (Isaiah 14:12)

13 Remain

14 The result for Jacob after he wrestled with a heavenly being all night (Genesis 32:25, 31)

17 Biblical greeting; "behold"

18 Ring of light around the head of a holy being

21 Part of the ladder on which Jacob saw angels ascending and descending (Genesis 28:12)

22 Angels' home

23 Angelic message in Luke 2:14: "___ to God in the highest"

25 Location of cherubim at Eden (Genesis 3:24)

26 The victorious in heaven "___ the song of Moses . . . and the song of the Lamb" (Revelation 15:3)

27 Tell Jerusalem her "___fare is ended" (Isaiah 40:2)

Word Pool

ABLE ALL AMEN ARCHANGELS CALLED CHERUBIM CLOUD CREATED EAST EYES GABRIEL GLORY HALO HEAVEN HOLY HOST LAME LIFE LO LUCIFER MESSENGER MICHAEL PEACE PRINCIPALITIES RUNG SERAPHIM SERVANTS SING SOUL STAY TRUMPET UNAWARE WAR WING YE

See answer on puzzle answer page 10.

The Wrong Armor

Before David went out to meet Goliath in battle, King Saul gave him some items that warriors used in those days: a coat of armor, a bronze helmet, and a sword. But David decided not to use them; they were too heavy and awkward for him. Instead, he took his shepherd's staff, a bag with five smooth stones, and his slingshot. In this picture, find the pieces of equipment that Saul originally gave David — the shield, breastplate, helmet, and sword — that David didn't use when he went into battle.

SHIELD   HELMET   SWORD   BREASTPLATE

For the Sick

After Matthew the tax collector decided to follow Jesus, he invited some of his old friends to his house to eat with Jesus and the other disciples. But Jesus and the disciples were criticized for eating with sinners. Solve the puzzle below, to find out what Jesus said to those who thought He shouldn't do that.

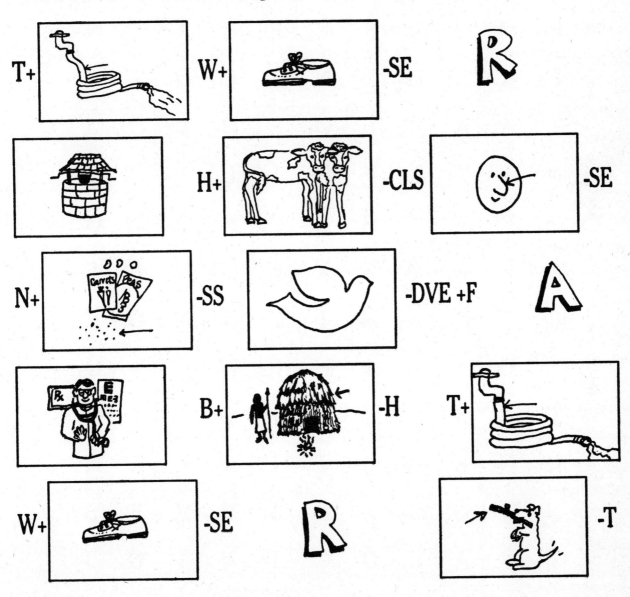

Write out the verse here:

_____

_____

_____

See answer on puzzle answer page 10.

First Deacons

Find the names of the first SEVEN men to be named deacons in the box of letters below. Their names are given in Acts 6:5 and are *among* the names in the Word Pool.

```
R  M  O  L  S  E  P  B  A  S  N
P  R  P  U  T  N  I  C  O  T  I
T  A  A  M  E  O  S  H  P  O  M
N  I  R  C  P  H  I  L  I  P  D
O  P  M  A  H  G  V  B  R  M  O
I  R  E  O  E  X  E  O  U  C  E
C  Y  N  S  N  I  C  A  N  O  R
X  O  A  L  I  H  P  W  K  V  Q
T  R  S  U  O  L  M  C  T  I  O
H  N  E  R  L  T  I  R  B  X  N
U  I  U  Z  N  B  S  P  M  F  S
M  S  A  L  O  C  I  N  I  O  J
```

Word Pool

(Note: Only seven of these men are the names of deacons in Acts 6:5.)

ADOLPHUS   MARCUS   NICANOR   NICOLAS   PARMENAS   PAUL   PHILEMON
PHILIP   PROCHORUS   ROMANUS   SIMEON   STEPHEN   THADDEUS   TIMON

See answer on puzzle answer page 10.

Hard-Rock Promises

In Matthew 16:13–16, Jesus and His disciples are having a conversation. Jesus asks, "Who do men say that I, the Son of Man, am?" After Peter gives his response, Jesus says

FLESH AND BLOOD HAS NOT
9   20   35   25   21

REVEALED THIS TO YOU, BUT MY
5   29   7   34   1

FATHER WHO IS IN HEAVEN. YOU
17   11   28   13   6

ARE PETER, AND ON THIS ROCK
18   12   22   30   2

I WILL BUILD MY CHURCH, AND
27   3   10   8

THE GATES OF HADES SHALL
16   33   24   23   19   4

NOT PREVAIL AGAINST IT.
31   26   32   14   15

Use the numbers under the letters above to
reveal what it was that Peter had said to Jesus.

_ _ _ _ _ _ _ _ _ _ _ _ _ _ _ _ _ _
1   2   3   4   5   6   7   8   9   10   11   12   13   14   15   16   17   18

_ _ _ _ _ _ _ _ _ _ _ _ _ _ _ _ _.
19   20   21   22   23   24   25   26   27   28   29   30   31   32   33   34   35

See answer on puzzle answer page 10.

Bible Es

If you think "E" words, you'll have the answers for most of this crossword.

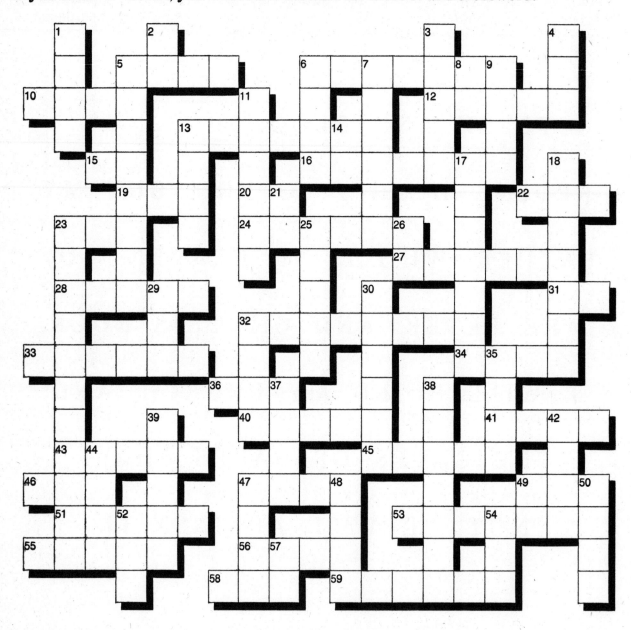

Across

5 Means "red"; another name for Esau (Genesis 25:30)

6 Precious green gemstone; fourth foundation jewel of New Jerusalem (Revelation 21:19)

10 Direction from which the wise men came to worship the young child Jesus (Matthew 2:1)

12 Eagle's nest

13 The direction from which prophets foretell the glory of God will return to Jerusalem (Ezekiel 43:2)

15 Firstborn son of Judah and Shua (Genesis 38:3)

16 Either, or; _____, nor

19 Either, or; neither, _____

20 Opposite of she

22 Large monkey

23 High priest with whom Samuel lived (1 Samuel 1:25)

24 Number of stars that bowed to Joseph in a dream (Genesis 37:9)

27 Jesus' resurrection day

28 Land from which Moses led the children of Israel (Exodus 7:5)

31 Moses' response when God called to him from a burning bush: "Here I ____" (Exodus 3:4)

32 Name of Jesus meaning "God with us" (Matthew 1:23, KJV)

33 Prophet who went to heaven in a whirlwind (2 Kings 2:11)

34 Place with 12 wells of water and 70 palm trees (Exodus 15:27)

36 Job asked: "Is there any taste in the white of an ____?" (Job 6:6)

40 Older one; "rebuke not an ____" (1 Timothy 5:1, KJV)

41 "Whatever a man sows, that he will also ____" (Galatians 6:7)

43 My, mine; thy, ____

45 Linen garment worn by high priests (Exodus 28:4)

46 Central Intelligence Agency (abbr.)

47 Eve's husband

49 Strong drink

51 Opposite of nephew

53 Gets away safely

55 One of King David's wives (2 Samuel 3:5)

56 Name of disputed well in Genesis 26:20

58 "From the ____ of the earth I will cry to You" (Psalm 61:2)

59 Prophet who received a double portion of Elijah's spirit (2 Kings 2:9–15)

Down

1 Mountain on which altar was built in Joshua 8:30

2 Short for editor; also the name of an altar built by the children of Reuben and Gad (Joshua 22:34, KJV)

3 "God created the heavens and the ____" (Genesis 1:1)

4 Jesus said about the bread during the Last Supper with His disciples: "Take, ____" (1 Corinthians 11:24)

5 Forever

6 The garden of ____; Adam and Eve's home

7 Timothy's mother (2 Timothy 1:5)

8 Biblical greeting

9 Entrance to house; Jesus said: "Behold, I stand at the ____ and knock" (Revelation 3:20)

11 Queen who saved her people; 17th book of Old Testament

13 Priest and scribe; 15th book of Old Testament

14 Regarding (abbr.)

17 Another name for a letter in the New Testament

18 One of Joseph's sons (Genesis 41:52)

21 Ancient name for "Lord"

23 Eternal; "the righteous has an ____ foundation" (Proverbs 10:25)

25 Foe; "the last ____ that will be destroyed is death" (1 Corinthians 15:26)

26 Northeast (abbr.)

29 Green soup

30 Last; remain; "They shall fear You as long as the sun and moon ____" (Psalm 72:5)

32 "Escaped the ____ of the sword" (Hebrews 11:34)

35 Master; worship term for Jesus Christ

37 Happy emotion; "a wise son makes a ____ father" (Proverbs 10:1)

38 City of the Ephesians

39 The man who didn't die but who "walked with God" (Genesis 5:24)

42 Capable

44 Salutation; "____, King of the Jews!" (Matthew 27:29)

47 "So be it"; what the four living creatures cry in Revelation 5:14

48 God said, "Let Us ____ man in Our image" (Genesis 1:26)

49 Associated Press (abbr.)

50 Jacob's twin brother (Genesis 25:25)

52 "The ____ of the wise seeks knowledge" (Proverbs 18:15)

54 A good king of Judah; Abijam's son (1 Kings 15:8–11)

57 South Dakota (abbr.)

See answer on puzzle answer page 10.

I Am, You Are

In the New Testament, Jesus used many illustrations to describe who He is as the Son of God, and who we are as His followers. Unscramble the letters under each illustration below and then draw a line to match the word either to Jesus or to us. (You may want to look up the verses in the Scripture Pool for clues.)

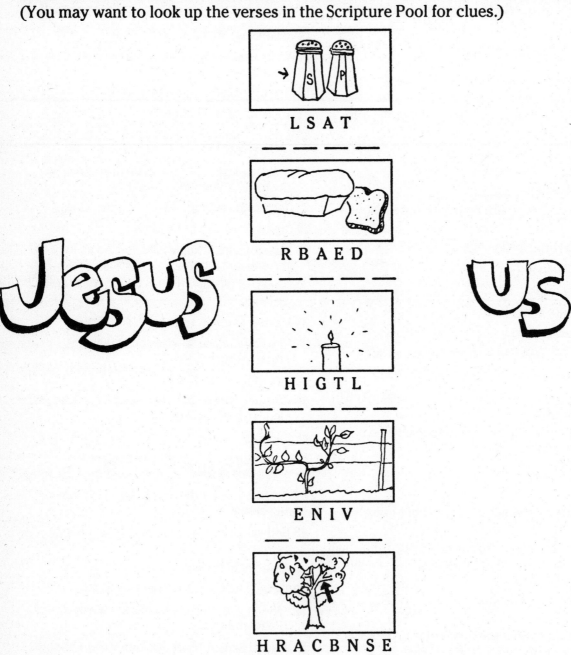

L S A T

R B A E D

H I G T L

E N I V

H R A C B N S E

_ _ _ _ _ _ _ _

Scripture Pool

John 15:5   Matthew 5:13   John 6:35   Matthew 5:14   John 8:12

See answer on puzzle answer page 10.

Wise Words

God gave King Solomon great wisdom, and during his reign, Solomon wrote the Old Testament book of Proverbs — wise sayings. This puzzle contains 10 proverbs. Match the first half of the proverb (column A) with its second half (column B) by drawing a line to connect the two halves. See how many you can match before you look them up in your Bible. After the matching, use the number code to fill in the verse from Proverbs 25:11. Note: Some of the letters are used more than once.

Column A

1. The f e a r of the LORD is the beginning of
4 3

2. Trust in the LORD with all your heart, and

3. In all your w a y s acknowledge Him, and
17 13

4. Do not e n t e r the path of the wicked, and do not
9 14

5. For whoever finds me [wisdom] finds life, and obtains

6. Anxiety in the heart of man causes depression,

7. A faithful witness does not l i e,
6

8. Train up a child in the way he should go,

9. The fruit of the righteous is a tree of life,

10. A man who has friends must himself be friendly,

Column B

A. f a v o r from the LORD. (Proverbs 8:35)
15 10 12

B. and when he is old he will not d e p a r t from it. (Proverbs 22:6)
2   11

C. but a false witness will utter lies. (Proverbs 14:5)

D. wisdom. (Proverbs 9:10)

E. but there is a friend who sticks closer than a brother. (Proverbs 18:24)

F. he shall direct your paths. (Proverbs 3:6)

G. and he who wins souls is wise. (Proverbs 11:30)

H. but a good word makes it g l a d. (Proverbs 12:25)
5   1

I. w a l k in the way of evil. (Proverbs 4:14)
16   8 7

J. lean not on your own understanding. (Proverbs 3:5)

Proverbs 25:11

‾1‾ ‾16‾ ‾10‾ ‾12‾ ‾2‾   ‾4‾ ‾6‾ ‾14‾ ‾8‾ ‾17‾   ‾13‾ ‾11‾ ‾10‾ ‾7‾ ‾3‾ ‾9‾

‾6‾ ‾13‾   ‾8‾ ‾6‾ ‾7‾ ‾3‾   ‾1‾ ‾11‾ ‾11‾ ‾8‾ ‾3‾ ‾13‾   ‾10‾ ‾4‾

‾5‾ ‾10‾ ‾8‾ ‾2‾   ‾6‾ ‾9‾   ‾13‾ ‾3‾ ‾14‾ ‾14‾ ‾6‾   ‾9‾ ‾5‾ ‾13‾

‾10‾ ‾4‾   ‾13‾ ‾6‾ ‾8‾ ‾15‾ ‾3‾ ‾12‾.

See answer on puzzle answer page 10.

The Memorial

After forty years in the wilderness, the children of Israel finally crossed the Jordan River into the promised land. To remember the crossing and God's miracle on behalf of the Israelites, God told Joshua to make a memorial so "all the peoples of the earth may know the hand of the LORD, that it is mighty, that you may fear the LORD your God forever" (Joshua 4:24). Connect the dots to reveal the memorial.

Good Soil

Jesus often spoke in parables, teaching profound truths by means of simple illustrations. In the parable of the good soil, Jesus explains how people are like different types of soil. Answer the clues below and fill in the crossword grid. You can read about the good soil in Mark 4:1-20.

Across

1 One _____ fold is an excellent return

3 Some seed in good soil yields _____ fold

6 The story of the good soil is a _____

7 Some people are like seed sown in stony ground, they have no _____ and wither away when trouble comes

9 The seed represents the _____ of God

10 Jesus taught by the _____

12 The cares of this world and the deceitfulness of _____ choke the Word, making it unfruitful

15 The hot _____ scorched the seed sown in stony ground

16 Those who spent time with Jesus knew the mystery of the _____ of God

17 The _____ that devoured the seed represent Satan who snatches away the Word of God

18 _____ root meant _____ fruit

19 Those who hear the Word and receive it are like _____ soil that brings forth fruit

Down

1 A person who receives the Word of God into his or her _____ bears fruit for the kingdom of God

2 People with shallow roots or no roots lack _____ and fall away in hard times

4 To bring forth, produce

5 The _____ represents the person hearing the Word

8 _____ illustrate anxieties, deceitfulness of wealth, and a desire for other things that choke out the Word, making it unfruitful

9 Seed sown along the _____ side was eaten by the birds

11 The #8 Down grew up and _____ the growing seed

13 Lest their _____ should be forgiven them

14 Where the seed is planted

15 _____ ground had only a thin layer of soil for seed to grow in

See answer on puzzle answer page 10.

Salutation

Circle every third letter below (beginning with the first letter "G") to reveal the way in which the Apostle Paul often greeted the people in the churches to whom he wrote letters (which today we know as the epistles).

```
G A N R B V A Y U C L K E O
P A Q W N J K D D F P A S E Q
P A R I C X O E J L T M C O R
E Y I X O C L U B K F I Q R V
H O Z W M R O G I S O K L D
K W T H A H H G E X W F W K
A M G T G J H I U E O S R Z O
A Y R N F K D S C F U S R V I
O N E M Y T O G E U F V R W
O L I Q O F L R X M D Y S J S
F E S G S H U U J O S P W C B
N H E R R S W I P O S F G T
```

G_ _ _ _ _   _ _ _   _ _ _ _ _ _

_ _   _ _ _   _ _ _ _ _ _

_ _ _   _ _ _   _ _ _   _ _ _

_ _ _ _   _ _ _   _ _ _ _

_ _ _ _ _   _ _ _ _ _ _.

See answer on puzzle answer page 10.

How Old?

The age of Noah when the flood began
(*Genesis 7:6*)

      _____

Minus . . .
The age of Enoch when he walked with God
(*Genesis 5:23*)

−   _____

Minus . . .
The age of Abraham when he left Haran for
the land of promise (*Genesis 12:4*)

−   _____

Minus . . .
The youngest age for men to begin to serve
in the tabernacle (*Numbers 4:3*)

−   _____

Minus . . .
The age of Josiah when he began to reign as
king (*2 Kings 22:1*)

−   _____

Minus . . .
The age of retirement for men who served
in the tabernacle (*Numbers 4:3*)

−   _____

Minus . . .
The age of Isaac when his sons Esau and
Jacob were born (*Genesis 25:26*)

−   _____

Equals . . .
The age of Jesus when He went up to the
temple in Jerusalem with His parents and
lingered behind (*Luke 2:42*)

=   _____

See answer on puzzle answer page 10.

Animal Tamers

Unscramble the names on the left to reveal four Bible heroes. Each of these men had a close encounter with a creature (or creatures) we usually think of as being very dangerous. Match the creature to the name of the Bible hero. Use the Scripture and Word Pools if you need clues!

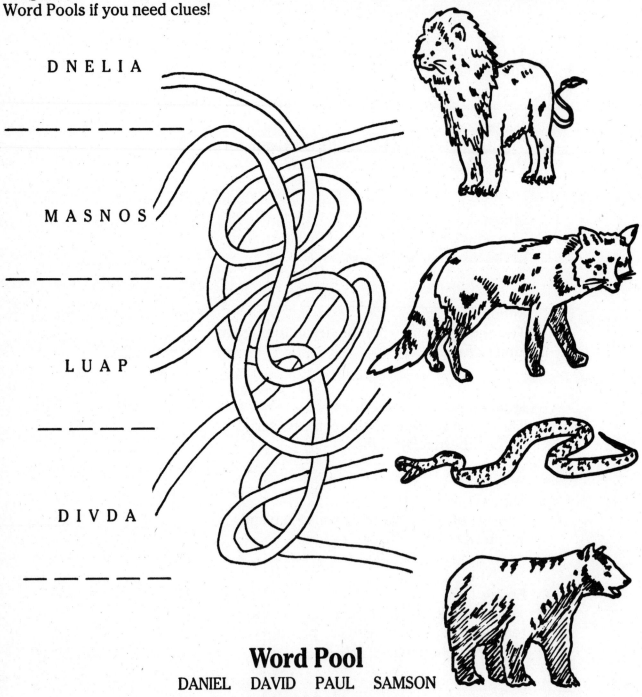

D N E L I A

_ _ _ _ _ _

M A S N O S

_ _ _ _ _ _

L U A P

_ _ _ _

D I V D A

_ _ _ _ _

Word Pool
DANIEL   DAVID   PAUL   SAMSON

Scripture Pool
Daniel 6:10–24   Judges 15:4–8   Acts 28:3–5   1 Samuel 17:34–37

See answer on puzzle answer page 10.

Wilderness Provision

Unscramble the words in the left column to discover some of the things that God provided for the children of Israel as they wandered in the wilderness. (We've provided the position of at least one letter in each word for you!)

WLA   __ __ W

ALIUQ   __ __ __ I __

LILRAP   __ __ L __ __ __

DULCO   __ __ __ __ D

WTAER   __ __ __ E __

BRALTAENCE   __ __ __ __ R __ __ __ __ __

NANAM   __ __ N __ __

REIF   __ __ __ E

LUSERR   __ __ __ __ __ S

MAGNETSR   __ __ __ __ __ __ __ S

Scripture Pool

Exodus 13:21; 15:25; 16:13, 35; 18:25; 24:12; 25:9; Deuteronomy 8:4

See answer on puzzle answer page 10.

Proverbs

All of the references (unless otherwise stated) are from the book of Proverbs.

Across

1 A ____ turns away wrath (2 words; 15:1)

5 A ____ does not love one who reproves him (15:12, KJV)

10 Fools despise ____ and instruction (1:7)

12 Train ____ a child in the way he should go (22:6)

13 Who can find a virtuous wife? For her worth is far above _____ (31:10)

14 Like one who takes away a garment in ____ weather . . . is one who sings songs to a heavy heart (25:20)

17 Proverbs of _____ (1:1)

19 _____ is a little with the fear of the LORD, than great treasure with trouble (15:16)

21 Let your eyes ____ straight ahead (4:25)

22 Keep your _____ with all diligence (4:23)

23 Six things the LORD hates . . . a _____ look (6:16–17)

24 ____ in the LORD with all your heart (3:5)

26 It is easier for ____ [plural] to go through the eye of a needle than for a rich man to enter the kingdom of God (Matthew 19:24)

28 Like one who binds ____ in a sling is he who gives honor to a fool (2 words; 26:8)

31 For the commandment is a lamp, and the law a ____ (6:23)

33 ___ for the upright, he establishes his way (21:29)

34 Do not ____ the bread of a miser (23:6)

35 Three things which are too wonderful for me . . . the way of a ____ on a rock (30:18–19)

37 The ___ of the righteous is choice silver (10:20)

40 Let her own works ___ her in the gates (31:31)

42 For the ____ gives wisdom (2:6)

44 Riches certainly make themselves wings; they fly away like an _____ (23:5)

46 The LORD is the maker of them ____ (22:2)

47 _____ who go to her [evil] return (2:19)

Down

1 As iron sharpens iron, ____ a man sharpens the countenance of his friend (27:17)

2 Go ___ the ant, you sluggard! (6:6)

3 Worthless persons . . . ____ (sing.) discord (6:12,14)

4 He who spares his ___ hates his son (13:24)

6 A ___ rages and is self-confident (14:16)

7 He who receives ____ is prudent (15:5, KJV)

8 By me [wisdom] princes _____ (8:16)

9 Proof of payment made

11 Fools despise wisdom and ____ (1:7)

14 Do not despise the chastening of the LORD, nor detest His _____ (3:11)

15 He who rolls a stone will have it roll back ____ him (26:27)

16 The hand of the ____ makes rich (10:4)

18 Where no ____ are, the trough is clean (14:4)

19 Earnestly desire the ___ gifts (1 Corinthians 12:31)

20 The ___ of the wicked are an abomination to the LORD (15:26)

25 The desire of the righteous is ___ good (11:23)

27 He who deals with a ___ hand becomes poor (10:4, KJV)

29 Will you ____ your eyes on that which is not? (23:5)

30 Wisdom . . . speaks her _____ (1:20–21)

32 Seldom set foot in your neighbor's ____ (25:17)

36 Ask . . . the birds of the air, and they will ____ you (Job 12:7)

37 Wise men ____ away wrath (29:8)

38 Cease, my son, to hear the instruction that causeth to ___ from the words of knowledge (19:27, KJV)

39 Do not ___ your heart be glad when he [your enemy] stumbles (24:17)

41 Deceit is ___ the heart of those who devise evil (12:20)

43 ___ you see a man hasty in his words? There is more hope for a fool than for him (29:20)

45 Do not ___ hastily to court (25:8)

See answer on puzzle answer page 10.

A Place for Us

The letters below spell a message that has been written in reverse! Begin where you see the word START below and then move right to left, from the bottom row to the top to put the letters back into correct order. Break the letters into words to reveal what Jesus said to His followers in John 14:2.

Write Jesus' message here: _____

_____

_____

See answer on puzzle answer page 10.

Anybody Home?

In Revelation 3:20, God gives us a great promise. If we invite Him into our lives and into our hearts, He will come in. God Himself will share not just a meal with us, but everything that matters to us. All we have to do is say, "Come in!"

Fill in all the blanks, and then use the number code to spell a word that describes the love and affection God has for us — and that we should have for Him.

Behold, I s_and at the _oor and k_ock.
1   2   3

If anyon_ hears My _oice and
4   5

opens the do_r, I will come in to him and
6

d_ne with him, and he with Me.
7

___ ___ ___ ___ ___ ___ ___ ___
2   4   5   6   1   7   6   3

See answer on puzzle answer page 10.

Jobs

When you unscramble the letters in the name column and decode the numbers in the profession column, you will know what these Bible characters did as occupations. If you need help, refer to the Scripture Pool.

NAME

PESHOJ __ __ __ __ __ __
         1

RETEP __ __ __ __ __
       2

TWETHAM __ __ __ __ __ __ __
         22   7

KULE __ __ __ __
         20

APUL __ __ __ __
      10   21

DOINGE __ __ __ __ __ __
        16   13

HAHEMINE __ __ __ __ __ __ __ __
               17   18

USAE __ __ __ __
            6

CAJOB __ __ __ __ __
         12   11

LUSTRELUT __ __ __ __ __ __ __ __ __
                  5

SULIUJ __ __ __ __ __ __
        19   4

MOINS __ __ __ __ __
               23

ABODERH __ __ __ __ __ __
         14   3

LIFEX __ __ __ __ __
      15   8

DAILY __ __ __ __ __
          9

VIDAD __ __ __ __ __
            24

PROFESSION

__ __ __ __ __ __ __ __ __
12 10 3 2 14 23 5 14 3

__ __ __ __ __ __ __ __ __
15 18 4 17 14 3 22 10 23

__ __ __ __ __ __ __ __ __ __ __ __
5 10 8 12 1 21 21 14 12 5 1 3

__ __ __ __ __ __ __ __
2 17 9 4 18 12 18 10 23

__ __ __ __ __ __ __ __ __
5 14 23 5 22 10 20 14 3

__ __ __ __ __
11 10 20 14 3

__ __ __ __ __ __ __ __ __
12 6 2 11 14 10 3 14 3

__ __ __ __ __ __
17 6 23 5 14 3

__ __ __ __ __ __ __ __
4 17 14 2 17 14 3 13

__ __ __ __ __ __
1 3 10 5 1 3

__ __ __ __ __ __ __ __ __
12 14 23 5 6 3 18 1 23

__ __ __ __ __ __
5 10 23 23 14 3

__ __ __ __ __
19 6 13 16 14

__ __ __ __ __ __ __ __
16 1 24 14 3 23 1 3

__ __ __ __ __ __ __ __ __ __ __ __
11 6 4 18 23 14 4 4 7 1 22 10 23

__ __ __ __ __ __ __ __ __ __
10 3 22 1 3 11 14 10 3 14 3

Scripture Pool

Genesis 27:1–3; 30:36   Judges 4:4; 6:19   1 Samuel 16:21   Nehemiah 1:11
Matthew 4:18; 10:3; 13:55   Acts 10:6; 16:14; 18:1–3; 23:24; 24:1; 27:1   Colossians 4:14

See answer on puzzle answer page 11.

As the Sands

God told Abraham that his descendants would be as numerous "as the sand which is on the seashore" (Genesis 22:17). How many words with two or more letters can you make up from the letters found in the phrase:

ABRAHAM AND SARAH

More than 30 words — Excellent   20-30 words — Very Good
10-20 words — Good   Fewer than 10 words — Keep Working!

See answer on puzzle answer page 11.

Bible Kids

Many of the clues for this crossword have to do with children in the Bible or what the Bible says about children.

Jesus loves little children. In fact, when the disciples asked Jesus who would be the greatest in the kingdom of heaven, He said unless you become as little children, you won't even enter the kingdom of heaven. Unscramble the circled letters from the crossword to reveal how a person is to be like a child in order to enter His kingdom.

_ _ _ _ _ _ _

Across

1 When people brought the children to Jesus, He _____ them (Mark 10:16)

5 And so forth (abbr.)

8 Petty quarrel

10 Jesus said, "Whoever causes one of these little ones who _____ in Me to sin, it would be better for him if a millstone were hung around his neck, and he were drowned in the depth of the sea" (Matthew 18:6)

13 Rhode Island (abbr.)

14 A young servant girl helped this great army commander to be healed of leprosy (2 Kings 5:3)

16 Children are _____ from the Lord (Genesis 33:5)

18 North Dakota (abbr.)

20 Samuel's tutor (1 Samuel 1:25)

21 As a small boy, Samuel _____ before the Lord (1 Samuel 2:18)

23 Illinois (abbr.)

24 As a child, #22 Down was _____ for salvation (2 Timothy 3:15)

28 As Christians, we are children of God through _____ (Galatians 4:4–5)

29 First child (Genesis 4:1)

31 As a child, he grew strong in spirit (Luke 1:80)

32 Be quiet

33 When children do this, they please the Lord (Colossians 3:20)

34 To listen and pay attention is to give _____ (Psalm 5:1)

Down

1 Piece of equipment used in many games

2 Children suffer the consequences of the sins of their fathers, or put another way, when the fathers eat sour grapes, the "children's teeth are set on _____" (Ezekiel 18:2)

3 At this same hour that the nobleman believed Jesus, his son was healed (John 4:52–53)

4 "_____ not despise one of these little ones . . . their angels always see the face of My Father who is in heaven" (Matthew 18:10)

6 Parents' responsibility to their children (Ephesians 6:4)

7 Some things have been hidden from the wise, but revealed to these people (sing.) (Matthew 11:25)

9 As a young man, Daniel fasted and _____ to the Lord (Daniel 9:4)

11 "Out of the mouth of babes and nursing _____ You [God] have perfected praise" (Matthew 21:16)

12 When Hannah knew her prayers for a child would be answered, she no longer felt this way (1 Samuel 1:18)

15 A heavenly messenger who announced Jesus' birth (Luke 1:30–31)

16 Popular snack item

17 Female sibling (slang)

19 Age when Josiah became king (2 Kings 22:1)

22 As a boy he knew the Scriptures (2 Timothy 3:15)

24 Fathers are to instruct their children, but not provoke them to this (Ephesians 6:4)

25 Each (abbr.)

26 When the young boy gave his loaves and fishes, over 5,000 people _____ and were filled (John 6:1–14)

27 Children are to show "respect" to their parents (Ephesians 6:2)

30 There was a "No Vacancy" sign on this accommodation, so Jesus was born in a stable

31 Junior Achievement (abbr.)

See answer on puzzle answer page 11.

It's a Boy

In Isaiah 9:6, we find some very good news that God gave
His people. He promised to send His Son to them. Use
your Bible to fill in the blanks. Then, unscramble the
letters that are circled to spell the name of Jesus that
means "God with us."

For unto us a __ __ ⃝ __ __ is born,

unto us a __ __ ⃝ is given;

and the __ __ __ __ __ __ ⃝ __ __ __

will be upon His __ __ __ __ ⃝ __ __ __.

And His __ __ ⃝ __ will be called

Wonderful, __ __ ⃝ __ __ __ __ __ __, Mighty God,

Everlasting __ __ __ __ ⃝ __,

Prince of __ __ ⃝ __ __.

Unscrambled letters: __ __ __ __ __ __ __ __

See answer on puzzle answer page 11.

So My Soul

In Psalm 42:1 are the words of the psalmist who wrote that his soul was thirsty for God just as one of God's animals was thirsty for the water brooks. Connect the dots to find out what animal the psalmist was referring to.

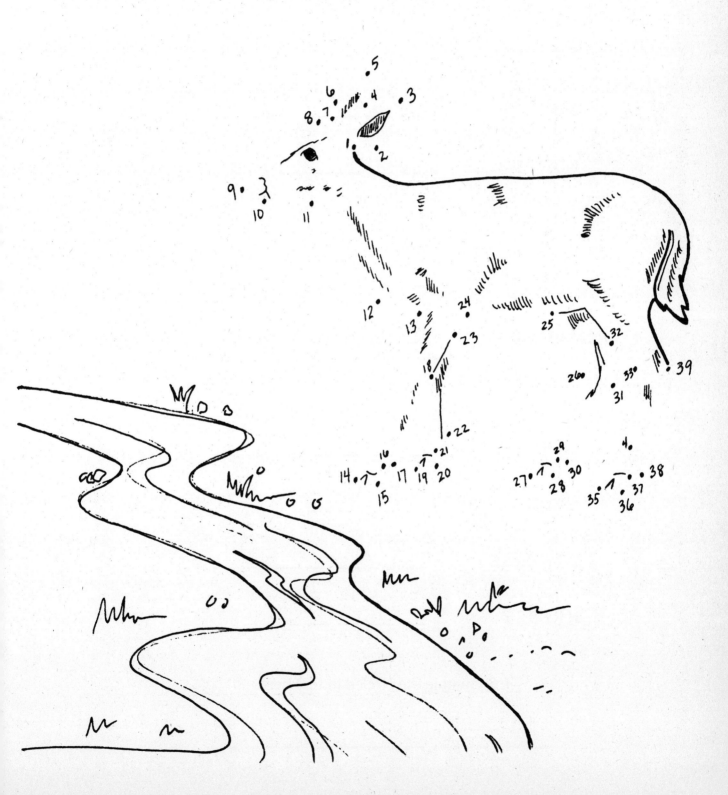

Heroine

Unscramble the words below that are clues to one of the most famous heroines in the Bible. Then unscramble the circled letters to find out what she obtained for her people. You can find these words in the book of Esther.

WJES   _ _ _ _

AHVTSI   Ⓞ _ _ _ _ Ⓞ

EQNEU   _ _ _ _ _

AFTS   _ _ _ _

NAMAH   _ _ _ _ Ⓞ

ASFTE   _ _ Ⓞ _ _

ROEDMACI   _ _ _ ⓄⓄ _ _ _

OLSLGWA   _ _ Ⓞ _ _ _ _

EROB   Ⓞ _ _ _

PTCERSE   _ Ⓞ _ _ _ Ⓞ _

HRESET   _ _ _ _ Ⓞ _

Unscramble the circled letters here:

_ _ _ _ _ _ _ _ _ _ _

See answer on puzzle answer page 11.

Unidentical Twins

Esau and Jacob were twins, but they were different in many ways. (You can read about them in Genesis 25:24–34.) Circle all of the things about Esau and Jacob that are different.

In His Dreams

The Old Testament tells us about five dreams that Joseph interpreted. The first two were dreams that Joseph had. Three were dreams that other people had. The crossword on the next page is based on those dreams. Fill in the blanks to complete the story below, and then use these words to fill in the crossword grid. Some words may be used more than once. (You can read the stories in the Bible in Genesis 37:5–11; 40:5–23; and 41:1–36.)

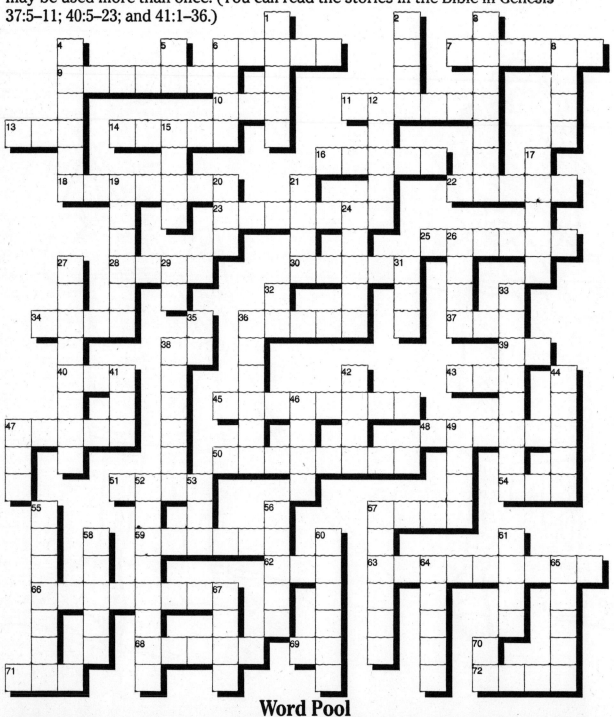

Word Pool

ANGRY   ANSWER   APPOINT   AS   ATE   BAKER   BLOSSOMS   BOTH   BOWED   BRANCHES   BREAD   BROTHERS
BUTLER   COWS   CUP   DAYS   DO   DOWN   EAST   EATEN   EGYPT   ELEVEN   ENVY   FAMINE   FIFTH   FOOD
FORGOT   GAUNT   GOD   GRAPES   HATED   HE   HEAD   HEADS   HIS   LAND   MAGICIANS   ME   MEADOW
NEVER   NIGHT   NO   NOT   OFFICERS   ONE   PERISH   PHARAOH   PLENTY   POOR   RESTORE   RIVER   SEE
SEEN   SENT   SEVEN   SHAVED   SHEAVES   SIR   SO   STORE   SUDDENLY   SUN   THREE   TO   TWO   UGLY   UP
UPRIGHT   VINE   WISE   YET   YOU

Joseph had a dream and he told it to his _____ (27 Down), and they hated him even more. He said, "There we were, binding _____ (18 Across) in the field and behold, my sheaf arose and stood _____ (23 Across) and your sheaves bowed _____ (34 Across) to my sheaf." His brothers _____ (24 Down) him for _____ (40 Across) dream and for his words.

Then Joseph dreamed another dream and said, "This time the _____ (20 Down), the moon, and _____ (19 Down) stars _____ (36 Across) down to _____ (38 Across)." His brothers felt _____ (15 Down) and were _____ (16 Across) with Joseph. They plotted to kill him, but instead, sold him as a slave.

In Egypt, Joseph became the overseer in Potiphar's house, but when Potiphar's wife lied about Joseph, he was put in prison. While in prison, Pharaoh's chief _____ (36 Down) and chief baker were also put in prison. Each of these _____ (47 Down) men came _____ (5 Down) Joseph for an interpretation of their dreams. The chief butler said, "In my dream I saw a _____ (28 Across). It had three _____ (50 Across); and they budded; then _____ (45 Across) shot forth and then clusters of ripe _____ (4 Down) appeared. Pharaoh's _____ (13 Across) was in my hand, and I pressed the grapes into it and gave the cup to _____ (3 Down)."

Joseph said to the _____ (25 Across), "The three branches of the _____ (21 Down) are three _____ (2 Down). In _____ (47 Across) days Pharaoh will _____ (9 Across) you to your place. Remember me and mention me to Pharaoh when that happens."

The chief baker said, "In my dream I had _____ (22 Across) white baskets on my _____ (6 Down). All kinds of _____ (14 Across) was in the top basket and birds _____ (10 Across) of it." Joseph said to the chief _____ (1 Down), "In three days, Pharaoh will hang _____ (37 Across) from a tree." _____ (42 Down) of the events came to pass just _____ (69 Across) Joseph said they would. _____ (54 Across) the butler _____ (59 Across) Joseph.

Two years later Pharaoh had a dream one _____ (12 Down). He saw seven _____ (51 Across) come up out of the _____ (68 Across). They were _____ (26 Down) and gaunt. Pharaoh had _____ (65 Down) _____ (67 Down) such _____ (72 Across) looking cows. While Pharaoh watched, the ugly and _____ (64 Down) cows _____ (71 Across) the seven fat cows that were in the _____ (38 Down). Even after they had _____ (30 Across) the fat cows, they were still thin. Then Pharaoh had a second dream. This time he saw seven _____ (6 Across) of grain, plump and good. Then _____ (17 Down) thin heads, blighted by the _____ (8 Down) wind, _____ (33 Down) sprang _____ (70 Down) and devoured the full heads.

In the morning, Pharaoh called for all the _____ (63 Across) and all of the _____ (61 Down) men in the land of _____ (44 Down). He told them his dreams, but _____ (29 Down) one could interpret them. Then the chief butler remembered Joseph, and he told Pharaoh about him. Pharaoh _____ (46 Down) for Joseph, and Pharaoh's servants brought Joseph out of the dungeon, _____ (7 Across) him, gave him new clothes, and brought him to the court.

After Joseph heard that Pharaoh wanted him to interpret dreams, he said, "It is _____ (31 Down) in me, but _____ (43 Across) will give Pharaoh an _____ (11 Across) of peace." Pharaoh told Joseph his dreams, and Joseph said, "Both the seven good cows and the seven good heads are seven years. The seven thin cows and the seven empty heads are seven years of _____ (57 Down). The famine will deplete the _____ (49 Down). _____ (53 Down), here is what you must _____ (39 Across). You must _____ (55 Down) a wise and discerning man and set him over the land. Let him appoint _____ (66 Across) to collect _____ (62 Across) – _____ (58 Down) of all the produce of the land for the next seven years of _____ (48 Across) and _____ (56 Down) the _____ (57 Across) in the cities. The food gathered by the _____ (52 Down) will be a reserve for the seven years of famine so the land might not _____ (60 Down)."

Pharaoh said to Joseph, "_____ (41 Down), I now set you over all the land of Egypt." Then _____ (35 Down) gave Joseph his signet ring and clothed him in fine linen. _____ (32 Down) Joseph was made the leader over the land.

See answer on puzzle answer page 11.

Call to War

In the Bible we read that "death and life are in the power of the tongue" (Proverbs 18:21). This means that the words we say can make people feel good or make people very angry. It is even possible to start a war by saying the wrong words to the wrong people! In this puzzle, look for Bible words that describe the mouth, tongue, teeth, and lips, and the effects that their actions can have.

```
C R E G A N Y A W H E S T E G L
G S S C U I R J O C O L D Y N A
V S H W L R B R I M E D E R I F
P E F E O U K T X N P F W O R K
S N A W U R I B O O V A I M U M
T D S K D E D T I R L B T Q O D
L E Z B C L S S P E A R S A V E
R K F E I M O W I F C V M S E T
H C D V I N E C N E L O I V D O
P I E R C H N G N K E D E S Y W
A W B N O I T C U R T S E D P C
```

Word Pool

SWORDS   SPEARS   ARROWS   DESTRUCTION   DEVOURING   EVIL   POISON
FIRE   WICKEDNESS   VIOLENCE   BRIMSTONE   DECEIT

Scripture Pool

Psalm 36:3   Psalm 52:1–4   Psalm 55:21   Psalm 57:4   Psalm 59:7
Psalm 64:2–4   Proverbs 10:6   Proverbs 18:7   Isaiah 49:2   Jeremiah 9:8
James 3:5–8   Revelation 9:18

See answer on puzzle answer page 11.

Holy City

Solve the picture puzzle below — which features famous "pairs" — to discover the name of the city that is considered to be the most holy city in the world.

 – LLY = _____

 – B and H = _____

 – S and T = _____

 – H and N = _____

 – OUSE = _____

Now put all the letters together to write the name of the city:

—— —— —— —— —— —— —— —— —— ——

See answer on puzzle answer page 11.

The Owner's Return

Jesus told a story in Matthew 25:14–30 about a man who had to take a trip to a far country. He called his servants together and gave to one servant, five talents; to another, two talents; and to a third, one talent. After a long time, the man began the return trip. Help him find his way back to his home, his servants, and his money!

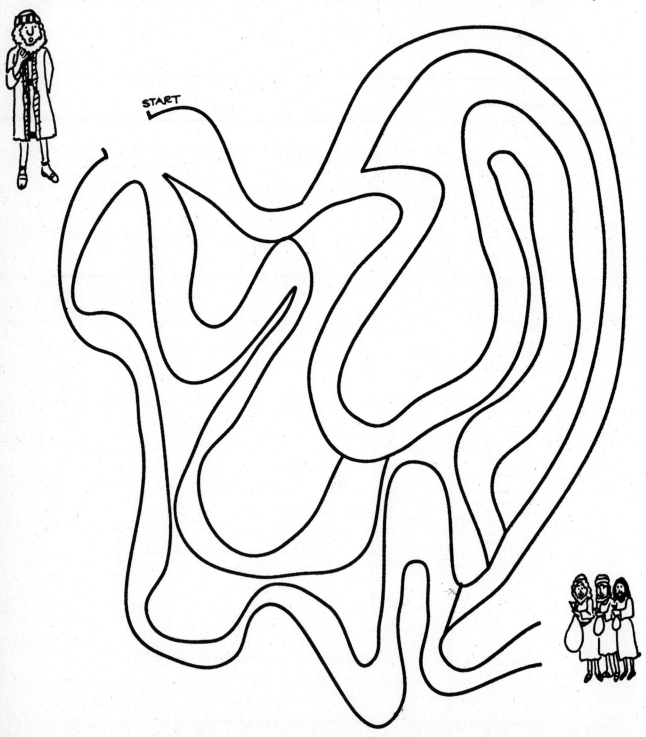

START

What Time Is It?

Match each event to the number on the clock that is related to it. We've made one connection for you! (Use the Scripture Pool for clues.)

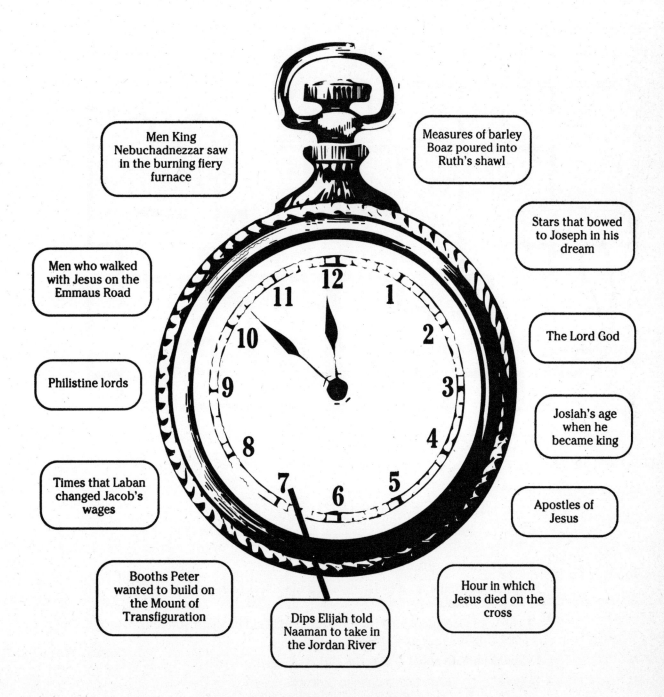

Men King Nebuchadnezzar saw in the burning fiery furnace

Measures of barley Boaz poured into Ruth's shawl

Stars that bowed to Joseph in his dream

Men who walked with Jesus on the Emmaus Road

The Lord God

Philistine lords

Josiah's age when he became king

Times that Laban changed Jacob's wages

Apostles of Jesus

Booths Peter wanted to build on the Mount of Transfiguration

Hour in which Jesus died on the cross

Dips Elijah told Naaman to take in the Jordan River

Scripture Pool

2 Kings 22:1   Mark 15:34   2 Kings 5:10   Genesis 31:7   Joshua 13:3
Genesis 37:9   Deuteronomy 6:4   Ruth 3:15   Luke 24:13
Matthew 10:2   Luke 9:33   Daniel 3:24–25

See answer on puzzle answer page 11.

Bible Ss

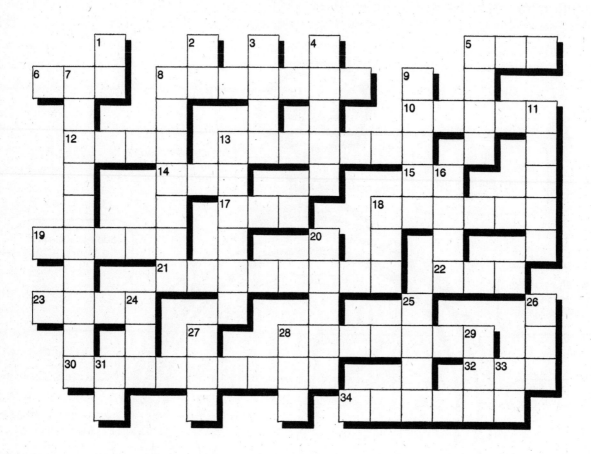

Across

5 "Go and _____ no more" (John 8:11)

6 Bashful; Moses may have appeared this way because he didn't like to speak in public

8 King known for his wise decisions

10 Jesus said that it is an evil generation that "seeks after ___ _____" (2 words; Matthew 12:39)

12 The Lord God kept Israel from invading the land of Moab, Ammon, and Mount _____ (2 Chronicles 20:10)

13 Speak untruth about (Proverbs 10:18)

14 Give ___ ___ shot; take a chance (2 words)

15 "Love your neighbor ___ yourself" (Matthew 19:19)

17 Mr. and _____

18 Location of the house of God in Judges 18:31

19 Viper; serpent

21 Keeper of sheep; David was one

22 The Lord _____; our Heavenly Father

23 Belonging to #13 Down (nickname)

28 One who serves; "whoever desires to become great among you shall be your _____" (Mark 10:43)

30 The high council of Jewish government; Jesus was tried before them

32 Temperature manna couldn't stand; "when the sun became ____, it melted" (Exodus 16:21)

34 Peter said to a lame man: "_____ and gold I do not have, but what I do have I give you" (Acts 3:6)

Down

1 "____ His stripes we are healed" (Isaiah 53:5)

2 "For God ____ loved the world that He gave His only begotten Son" (John 3:16)

3 The eternal part of a human being

4 "Suddenly there came a _____ from heaven, as of a rushing mighty wind" (Acts 2:2)

5 Leprosy is a disease that shows in this part of the body

7 John the Baptist said about Jesus that he was not worthy to carry ____ _____ (2 words; Matthew 3:11)

8 The _____ and Pharisees (Luke 5:30)

9 Abraham's wife

11 When stars shine

13 Hannah's son; he served Eli when he was a little boy (1 Samuel 1)

16 What Paul and Silas did in prison (Acts 16:25)

18 Sorrowful; the reaction of a rich young ruler to the words of Jesus in Mark 10:22

20 Number of days in the creation story

24 Jesus was the only begotten ____ of God (John 3:16)

25 The first king of Israel (1 Samuel 9)

26 "The people who ____ in darkness have seen a great light" (Matthew 4:16)

27 Body of water; the ____ of Galilee

28 The mother of Zebedee's sons asked Jesus: "Grant that these two sons of mine may _____, one on Your right hand and the other on the left, in Your kingdom" (Matthew 20:21)

29 Peter said to Jesus: "You are ____ Christ, the Son of the living God" (Matthew 16:16)

31 "For the LORD does not see ____ man sees" (1 Samuel 16:7)

33 Jesus said, "Which is easier, to say, 'Your sins are forgiven you,' ____ to say, 'Rise up and walk'?" (Luke 5:23)

See answer on puzzle answer page 11.

Noble Wife

The Bible describes a virtuous wife in Proverbs 31. Find the woman below who has become EXACTLY like this noble woman.

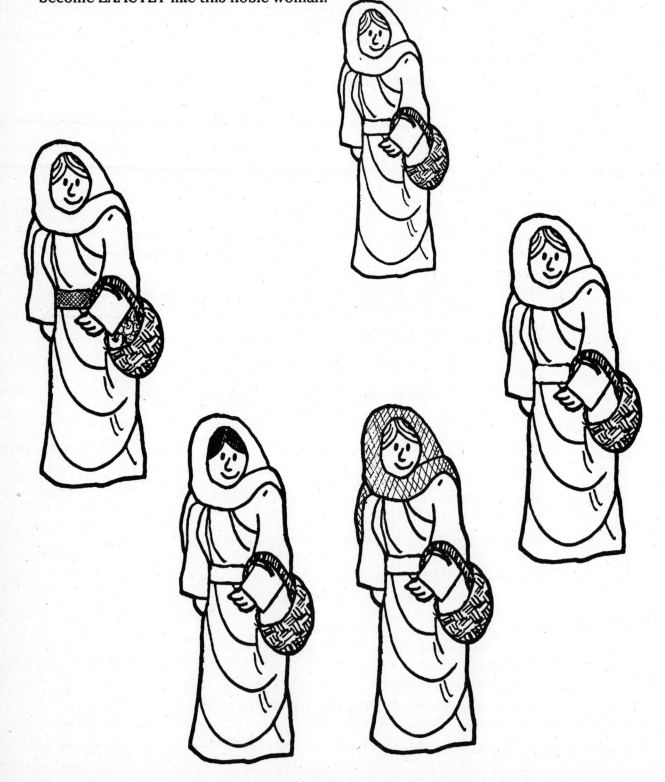

Fifty Days

The word *Pentecost* means "fifty." Pentecost is the Bible feast that comes fifty days after Easter. Try to make up at least fifty words with two or more letters from the letters in the phrase:

PENTECOST SUNDAY

More than 50 words — Excellent (Go for 100!)   40-49 words — Very Good   30-39 words — Good   Under 30 words — Keep Working!

See answer on puzzle answer page 12.

Which Letter Goes Where?

An accident has happened in the Bible Times Post Office, and some very important letters may become lost without your help! Unscramble the names of five of the church groups below to whom the apostle Paul wrote letters. Then match the verse that belongs to each letter to help the postman make his deliveries correctly. You may use the Word Pool for help in unscrambling the church names.

ORME   GLTIAAA   INROCTH

___ ___ ___ ___   ___ ___ ___ ___ ___ ___ ___   ___ ___ ___ ___ ___ ___ ___

EEUPHSS   HIIILPPP

___ ___ ___ ___ ___ ___ ___   ___ ___ ___ ___ ___ ___ ___ ___

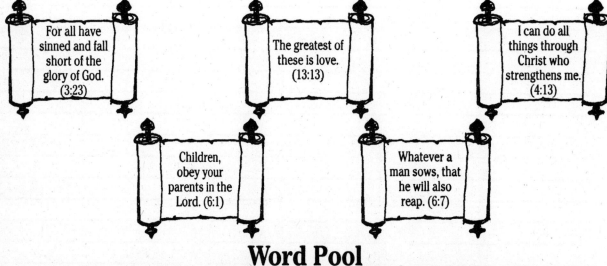

For all have sinned and fall short of the glory of God. (3:23)

The greatest of these is love. (13:13)

I can do all things through Christ who strengthens me. (4:13)

Children, obey your parents in the Lord. (6:1)

Whatever a man sows, that he will also reap. (6:7)

Word Pool
GALATIA   PHILIPPI   ROME   EPHESUS   CORINTH

See answer on puzzle answer page 12.

Bible Plants

Look up the Scriptures below to find the plants that are mentioned in the verses.
Then find the names of the 18 plants hidden in the letter box.

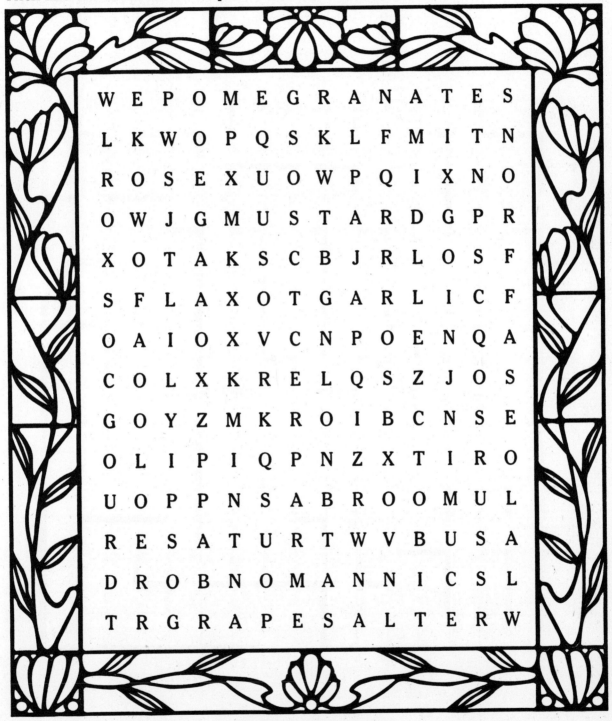

```
W E P O M E G R A N A T E S
L K W O P Q S K L F M I T N
R O S E X U O W P Q I X N O
O W J G M U S T A R D G P R
X O T A K S C B J R L O S F
S F L A X O T G A R L I C F
O A I O X V C N P O E N Q A
C O L X K R E L Q S Z J O S
G O Y Z M K R O I B C N S E
O L I P I Q P N Z X T I R O
U O P P N S A B R O O M U L
R E S A T U R T W V B U S A
D R O B N O M A N N I C S L
T R G R A P E S A L T E R W
```

Scripture Pool

Numbers 11:5; 13:23   Song of Solomon 2:1; 4:14   Matthew 13:31–32; 23:23
2 Kings 4:39   Joshua 2:6   Isaiah 35:1   John 9:39   1 Kings 19:5

See answer on puzzle answer page 12.

The Promised One

Throughout the Old Testament are found prophecies of the coming Savior, the One promised by God from the time of Adam and Eve for the salvation of His people. Fill in the crossword grid with words relating to the these Old Testament prophecies.

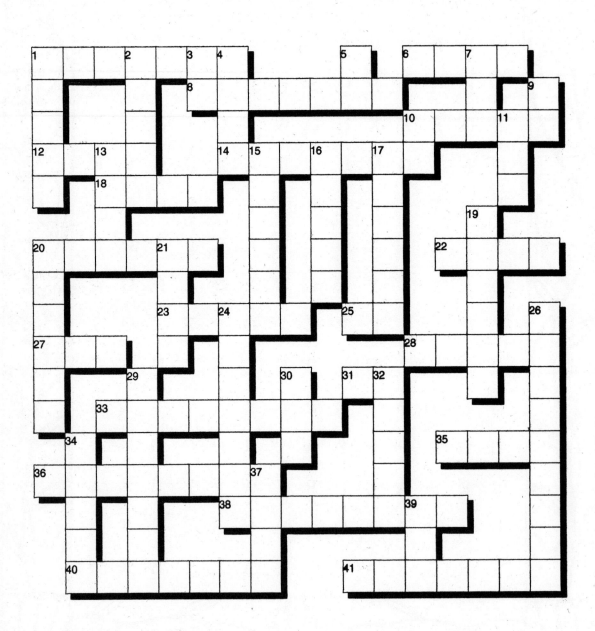

Across

1 In Hebrew, the original language of the Old Testament, this word means "Anointed One" (Daniel 9:25)

6 Righteous; a quality of the Promised One (Zechariah 9:9)

8 "My righteous _____ shall justify many" (Isaiah 53:11)

10 The Scripture prophesies that #1 Across would have no broken _____ (Psalm 34:20)

12 This is what #1 Across will do (Micah 5:2)

14 Freedom; the Anointed One will proclaim this to those who are captive (Isaiah 61:1)

18 The blind will be able to see again, because their eyes will be _____ (Isaiah 42:7)

20 Announce; "_____ good tidings to the poor" (Isaiah 61:1)

22 The prophet declared, "Your _____ is coming to you" (Zechariah 9:9)

23 Humble; a characteristic of Jesus (Zechariah 9:9)

25 "Why have You forsaken _____?" (Psalm 22:1)

27 The increase of His government and #32 Down will not _____ (Isaiah 9:7)

28 Moses told the children of Israel that God would _____ #31 Across a prophet (Deuteronomy 18:15)

31 Opposite of down

33 God's promise to His people (Genesis 17:19)

35 Spirit, life; Jesus poured out His _____ unto death (Isaiah 53:12)

36 Not accepted (Isaiah 53:3)

38 Absence of light; "The people who walked in _____ have seen a great light" (Isaiah 9:2)

40 Jesus was beaten and given these so we might be made whole (Isaiah 53:5)

41 Realm; the Savior will establish this with judgment and justice (Isaiah 9:7)

Down

1 The Christ is anointed to comfort those who "grieve" (Isaiah 61:2)

2 Jesus was silent when He was oppressed and afflicted, like a _____ before its shearers (Isaiah 53:7)

3 "He was led _____ a lamb to the slaughter" (Isaiah 53:7)

4 The Promised One was sent to "_____ the brokenhearted" (Isaiah 61:1)

5 God told Abraham, "_____ you all the families of the earth shall be blessed," a promise that the Christ would be his descendant (Genesis 12:3)

7 "You are My _____, today I have begotten You" (Psalm 2:7)

9 "Unto _____ a Child is born" (Isaiah 9:6)

10 _____ Jesus' suffering we are brought to salvation and wholeness (Isaiah 53:5)

11 There was no reason to hate Jesus, but many people did; the psalmist wrote "Let them not . . . wink with the _____ who hate me without a cause" (Psalm 35:19)

13 The #1 Across will _____ righteousness and hate wickedness (Psalm 45:7)

15 The Christ was prophesied to come from this country (Numbers 24:17)

16 "Out of _____ I called My #7 Down" (Hosea 11:1); a prophecy that was fulfilled when Jesus, Joseph, and Mary fled for their lives shortly after Jesus' birth

17 The promise to David that his _____ would be established for all eternity is fulfilled in the birth of Jesus (2 Samuel 7:16)

19 The birth of the child Jesus by a _____ was a sign from the Lord to His people that this was the One He promised them (Isaiah 7:14)

20 Jesus is described as a _____ after the order of Melchizedek (Psalm 110:4)

21 Jesus' triumphal entry was the fulfillment of the prophecy that the Christ would ride on a _____ of a donkey (Zechariah 9:9)

24 Because of our #39 Down, Jesus was "beaten and bruised" (Isaiah 53:5)

26 The city that Micah prophesied would be the birthplace of the #1 Across (Micah 5:2)

29 Eternal (Psalm 45:6)

30 Out of #26 Down will come the _____ to reign eternally (Micah 5:2)

32 "Shalom" will never end in God's kingdom (Isaiah 9:7)

34 Unit of time: "Your _____ will have no #27 Across" (Psalm 102:27)

37 Through Jesus, the throne of David will endure "as the _____ of heaven" (Psalm 89:29)

39 Jesus was made an offering for our _____ (Isaiah 53:10)

See answer on puzzle answer page 12.

Brothers

Below are four sets of famous brothers in the Bible who have become separated in a forest. First, unscramble the names — use the Word Pool for clues if you need them. Then, draw a line through the maze of trees to connect the brothers. (You may want to use a different color of crayon to match each set of brothers.)

RANOA   NICA

_ _ _ _ _   _ _ _ _

DERAWN   BOJAC

_ _ _ _ _ _   _ _ _ _ _

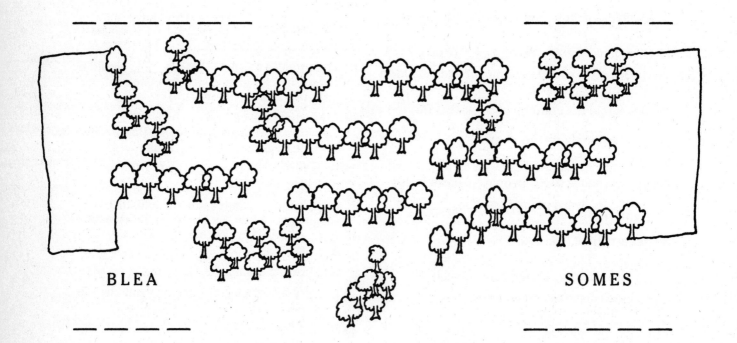

BLEA   SOMES

_ _ _ _   _ _ _ _ _

TEREP   AEUS

_ _ _ _ _   _ _ _ _

Word Pool

AARON   ABEL   ANDREW   CAIN   ESAU   JACOB   MOSES   PETER

See answer on puzzle answer page 12.

Jacob's Grandsons

Jacob had 12 sons. Each of those sons also had children. In the grid below, place the names of the firstborn sons of each of Jacob's sons . . . in other words, Jacob's firstborn grandsons!

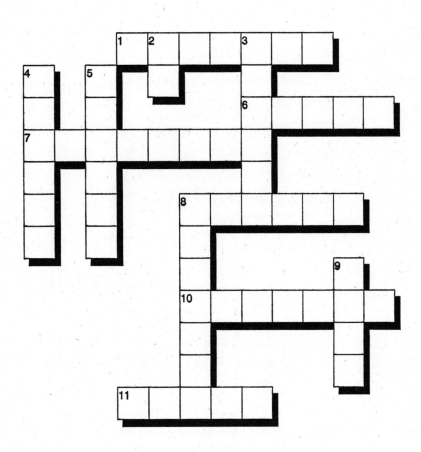

Across

1 Levi's firstborn son (Genesis 46:11)

6 Zebulun's firstborn son (Genesis 46:14)

7 Joseph's firstborn son (Genesis 46:20)

8 Simeon's firstborn son (Genesis 46:10)

10 Gad's firstborn son (Genesis 46:16)

11 Benjamin's firstborn son (Genesis 46:21)

Down

2 Judah's firstborn son (Genesis 46:12)

3 Dan's firstborn son (Genesis 46:23)

4 Asher's firstborn son (Genesis 46:17)

5 Reuben's firstborn son (Genesis 46:9)

8 Naphtali's firstborn son (Genesis 46:24)

9 Issachar's firstborn son (Genesis 46:13)

Word Pool

HANOCH	ER	ZIPHION	BELAH
JEMUEL	TOLA	JIMNAH	HUSHIM
GERSHON	SERED	MANASSEH	JAHZEEL

See answer on puzzle answer page 12.

First Christians

Seven letters of the alphabet are hidden in the picture of a city below. Once you have found all of the letters, unscramble them to reveal the name of the city in which the followers of Jesus Christ were first called Christians.

Put the letters you find here: Now unscramble them to write the city name:

__ __ __ __ __ __ __   __ __ __ __ __ __ __

(See Acts 11:26.)

See answer on puzzle answer page 12.

Old Ages

Some of the people in the Bible lived for hundreds of years! In Genesis, the Bible gives us the ages of some of the first people on the earth at the time they died. The following crossword is based on those ages. Use the Scripture references for the answers. Fill in the grid of this crossword with numbers, rather than letters!

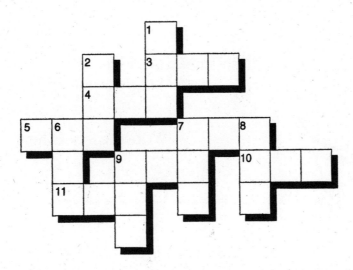

Across

3 Jared (Genesis 5:20)
4 Enoch (Genesis 5:23)
5 Cainan (Genesis 5:14)
7 Methuselah (Genesis 5:27)
9 Joseph (Genesis 50:26)
10 Ishmael (Genesis 25:17)
11 Lamech (Genesis 5:31)

Down

1 Mahalalel (Genesis 5:17)
2 Adam (Genesis 5:5)
6 Sarah (Genesis 23:1)
7 Enosh (Genesis 5:11)
8 Seth (Genesis 5:8)
9 Abraham (Genesis 25:7)

See answer on puzzle answer page 12.

The Lord's Supper

Use the Word Pool to fill in the blanks of the story, and then put the words in the crossword grid where they belong. You may use some words twice. The apostle Paul gives us this teaching about the Lord's Supper in 1 Corinthians 11:23–34.

Unscramble the circled letters in the crossword to get another name for the Lord's Supper:

Write the letters here:

_ _ _ _ _ _ _ _ _ _

Unscramble the letters:

_ _ _ _ _ _ _ _ _ _

On the same _____ in which He was _____, He took _____; and when
13 Down   20 Across   14 Across

He had given thanks, He broke it and said, "_____, _____; this is My _____
                                             5 Down   22 Down   12 Down

which is _____ for you; do this in _____ of Me." In the same manner He
10 Down   11 Across

also took the _____ after supper, saying, "This cup _____ the _____ _____
1 Down   8 Across   18 Across   4 Down

in _____ _____. This do, as _____ as you drink it, in remembrance of Me."
7 Down   14 Down   25 Across

For as often as you _____ this bread _____ drink this cup, you _____ the
21 Down   16 Across   6 Across

Lord's _____ till He _____. Therefore whoever eats this bread or drinks this
28 Across   1 Across

cup of the Lord in an unworthy manner will be _____ of the body and blood of
                                              27 Across

the _____. But _____ a man examine himself, and so let _____ _____
23 Down   19 Across   24 Down   26 Down

of that bread and drink of that cup. For he who eats and drinks in an unworthy

manner eats and drinks _____ to himself, not _____ing the Lord's body.
                       9 Down   3 Down

For this reason many are _____ and sick among you, and many sleep. For if
                         17 Down

_____ would judge ourselves, we would not _____ judged. . . . And the rest I
17 Across   15 Down

will set in _____ when I come.
            2 Across

Word Pool

(Note: One word is used more than once.)

AND   BE   BETRAYED   BLOOD   BODY   BREAD   BROKEN   COMES
COVENANT   CUP   DEATH   DISCERN   EAT   GUILTY   HIM   IS   JUDGMENT
LET   LORD   MY   NEW   NIGHT   OFTEN   ORDER   PROCLAIM
REMEMBRANCE   TAKE   WE   WEAK

See answer on puzzle answer page 12.

O Holy Night

Unscramble these words from the Christmas story (Matthew 1:23; 2:1–12; and Luke 2:1–20). Then unscramble the circled letters to find something you might say to the Lord on Christmas Day.

TRAS   _ _ _ _

SHEOJP   _ _ _ _ _ _

NIN   _ _ _

SEIW EMN   _ _ _ _ _   _ _ _

RAYM   _ _ _ _

DGWSLANID HLSTOC   _ _ _ _ _ _ _ _

    _ _ _ _ _ _ _

VLEAYNEH SHOT   _ _ _ _ _ _ _ _ _   _ _ _ _

LHETBMHEE   _ _ _ _ _ _ _ _ _

NRMAGE   _ _ _ _ _ _

HDSPERSHE   _ _ _ _ _ _ _ _ _

KEFNACNSERNI   _ _ _ _ _ _ _ _ _ _ _ _

LOGD   _ _ _ _

RYHRM   _ _ _ _ _

The phrase: _ _ _ _ _ _ _ _ _ _ _ _ _ !

See answer on puzzle answer page 12.

Mountaintop Experiences

To describe something as a "mountaintop experience" is to say that it was a very significant, possibly even life-changing event. There were characters in the Bible who had experiences like that — on top of real mountains — and the events were so important they were recorded in Scripture. From the Bible references below, unscramble the names of the mountains and the names of the Bible characters. Then follow the paths up the mountain to match the person with his mountaintop where that unforgettable experience took place.

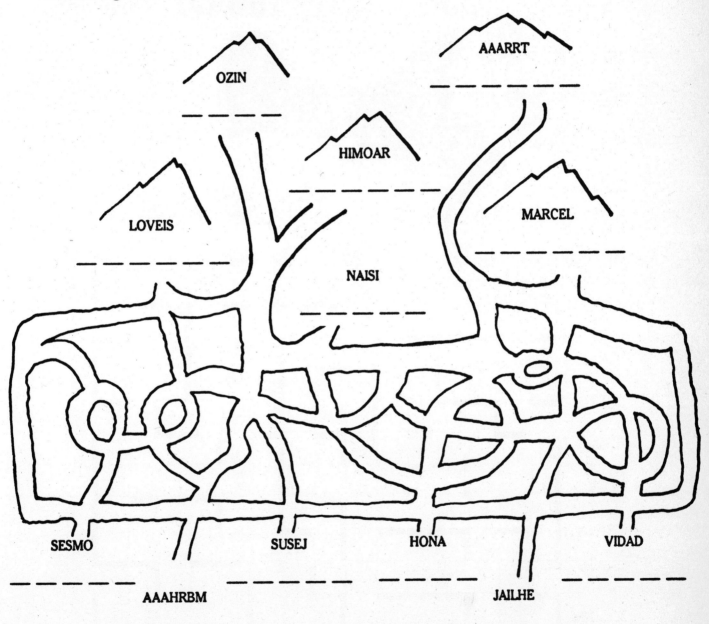

Scripture References

Exodus 19:2–25   Matthew 24:3; 26:30–31   Genesis 22:1–13   1 Kings 18:42   2 Samuel 5:7   Genesis 8:4

See answer on puzzle answer page 12.

Daytime, Nighttime

Did you know that God never sleeps? God is awake and aware of everything that happens to us — 24 hours a day, 7 days a week. He can work in our lives at any hour of the day or night. In this puzzle, you'll learn about some Bible events that took place in the morning or the evening. Some of them even lasted all day or all night! One thing they all have in common: God was always in control.

Across

4 King Saul's son, _____, shot arrows in a field one morning as a signal to David (1 Samuel 20:35)

6 In the evening, they brought to Jesus all who were sick and _____-possessed (Mark 1:32)

7 For Passover, the Israelites killed this animal at twilight and had to eat or burn all of it before morning (Exodus 12:5–11)

9 Moses judged the people from morning till evening, his father-in-law, _____, suggested he get help (Exodus 18:1,13,19–24)

10 Ravens brought this prophet food, day and night (1 Kings 17:1,6)

13 Joshua set _____ thousand men in ambush one morning (Joshua 8:10–12)

17 This priest read the law of Moses from morning till midday (Nehemiah 8:1–3)

18 David sang of God's _____ in the morning (Psalm 59:16)

19 The Levites stood every morning and evening to thank and _____ the Lord (1 Chronicles 23:27–30)

20 Nicodemus, Jesus' nighttime visitor, knew Jesus came from God because He performed "wonders" (John 3:1–2)

22 #24 Across's nighttime vision led him to this country (Acts 16:9–10)

24 The apostle in #22 Across

26 Jesus is the "Bright and Morning _____" (Revelation 22:16)

27 These animals roar after their prey at night (Psalm 104:20–21)

Down

1 This heavenly being freed the apostles from prison (Acts 5:17–19)

2 This apostle swam to shore to meet Jesus one morning (John 21:1–7)

3 A dove brought this man an olive branch one evening (Genesis 8:10–14)

5 The Israelites praised God in this wilderness one morning (2 Chronicles 20:20–21)

7 Jesus fed the 5,000 one evening with two fish and five _____ of bread (Matthew 14:17–21)

8 The princes of Moab stayed with this prophet one night (Numbers 22:7–8)

11 His mother, Mary, went to Jesus' tomb in the morning (Mark 16:1–2)

12 God told the people to "execute _____" in the morning (Jeremiah 21:12)

14 This prophet carried his belongings on his shoulder at twilight (Ezekiel 12:4–6)

15 What you see with (Psalm 119:148)

16 Jesus was taken to Pilate by the elders and chief _____ (Matthew 27:1–2)

21 Those rebuilding the wall of Jerusalem needed a "night watchman" (Nehemiah 4:21–22)

23 Royal leader (2 Chronicles 31:3)

25 With no night in heaven, we won't need one of these (Revelation 22:5)

Word Pool

ANGEL BALAAM DEMON ELIJAH EYES EZEKIEL EZRA
FIVE GUARD JAMES JETHRO JONATHAN JUDGMENT KING LAMB
LAMP LIONS LOAVES MACEDONIA MERCY NOAH PAUL PETER
PRAISE PRIESTS SIGNS STAR TEKOA

See answer on puzzle answer page 12.

The Defense

As Paul's ministry increased so did the number of his enemies. He was taken into custody on false charges and gave his defense before the governor. The account of this incident is in the Book of Acts. Find the answers in the Scripture references at the end of each clue and fill in the crossword grid.

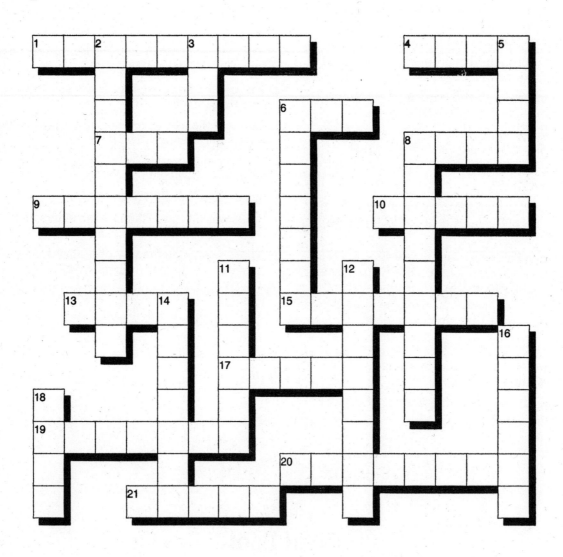

Across

1 Spokesman for Paul's accusers (24:1)

4 Paul brought _____ to the poor (24:17)

6 Another name for Christianity (24:14)

7 Paul's conscience was without #19 Across before _____ and man (24:16)

8 Like his accusers, Paul believed in the resurrection of the #13 Across, both _____ and the un_____ (24:15)

9 Paul was accused of being a _____ of dissension (24:5)

10 Mob; large group of people (24:12)

13 Without life (24:15)

15 It was said Paul tried to _____ the temple (24:6)

17 Paul's enemies were unable to _____their accusations (24:13)

19 A clear conscience is one without _____ (24:16)

20 Paul believed all that was written in the #3 Down and the _____ (24:14)

21 The official who heard the accusations against Paul (23:24)

Down

2 His opponents said Paul was a _____ of the sect of the Nazarenes (24:5)

3 The _____ of Moses is based on God's covenant with the people of Israel (24:14)

5 Paul's accusers called #6 Across a _____ (24:14)

6 To honor and revere (24:14)

8 Paul was arrested in _____ (24:11)

11 Paul denied accusations that he profaned the _____(24:6)

12 Felix was _____ of Judea (23:26)

14 Paul argued his own _____, maintaining his innocence (22:1)

16 Bring charges against (24:13)

18 Paul's _____ was in God (24:15)

See answer on puzzle answer page 13.

What a Blessing

In Matthew 5, Jesus shared with His disciples and with the people some of the Bible's most famous verses: the Beatitudes. Match the first half of these Beatitudes with their correct second half through the maze.

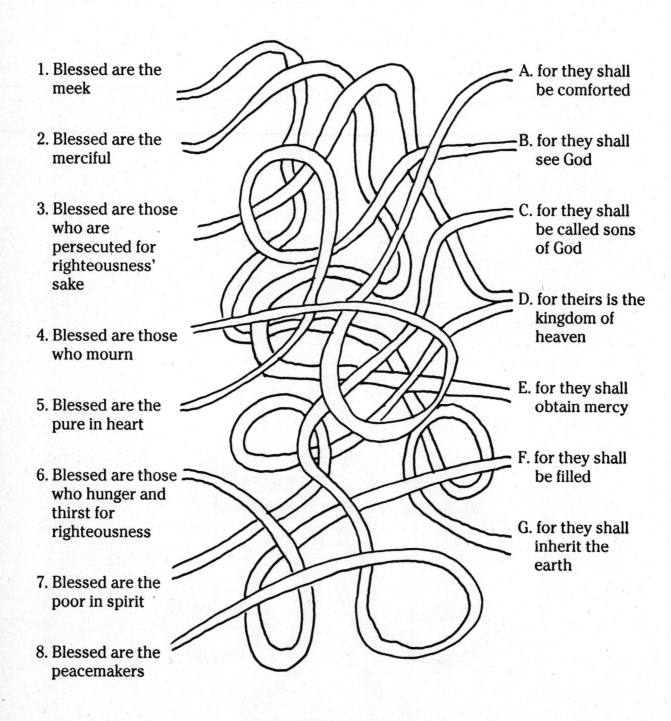

1. Blessed are the meek

2. Blessed are the merciful

3. Blessed are those who are persecuted for righteousness' sake

4. Blessed are those who mourn

5. Blessed are the pure in heart

6. Blessed are those who hunger and thirst for righteousness

7. Blessed are the poor in spirit

8. Blessed are the peacemakers

A. for they shall be comforted

B. for they shall see God

C. for they shall be called sons of God

D. for theirs is the kingdom of heaven

E. for they shall obtain mercy

F. for they shall be filled

G. for they shall inherit the earth

See answer on puzzle answer page 13.

Floating Crib

Moses was born in a time of great persecution of the Jewish people. The Pharaoh had ordered that all newborn boys be thrown into the river to die. But Moses' mother trusted God instead. She made a little ark for her baby — a woven basket covered with pitch to make it watertight. She put the baby Moses in it and hid him by letting him float among the reeds along the river bank. One day Pharaoh's daughter came to wash herself in the river, and she saw the baby in the basket among the reeds. She took Moses home and raised him as her own son. In the puzzle below, help Pharaoh's daughter find the floating crib in which baby Moses was hidden.

Salt

All of the clues in this crossword relate to salt! Use the words in the Word Pool, or look up the Scripture references for help in completing this puzzle. Notes: Several verses are used more than once. And one word is not exactly as it appears in the King James Version.

Across

2 "You shall not allow the salt of the ____ of your God to be lacking from your grain offering" (Leviticus 2:13)

4 "If the salt have lost his savour . . . it is thenceforth good for nothing, but to be ____ out" (Matthew 5:13, KJV)

6 "____ are the salt of the earth" (Matthew 5:13, KJV)

8 King David killed 18,000 enemy soldiers in the _____ of salt (2 Samuel 8:13)

10 When Lot's wife looked back at God's destruction on Sodom and Gomorrah, she became a ____ of salt (Genesis 19:26)

12 Along with salt, wine, and oil — one of the items needed for burnt offerings (Ezra 6:9)

13 King Darius said to give the people whatever they____ for burnt offerings, including salt (Ezra 6:9)

15 "Let your ____ always be with grace, seasoned with salt" (Colossians 4:6)

20 "So can no ____ both yield salt water and fresh" (James 3:12, KJV)

21 "If the salt loses its ____, how shall it be seasoned?" (Matthew 5:13)

22 "Surely Moab shall be like Sodom, . . . Overrun with weeds and salt____" (Zephaniah 2:9)

Down

1 If salt loses its _____, "wherewith will ye season it?" (Mark 9:50, KJV)

3 "Every offering of your grain _____ you shall season with salt" (Leviticus 2:13)

5 The Valley of Siddim is also called the Salt ____ (Genesis 14:3)

7 "Ye are the salt of the ____" (Matthew 5:13, KJV)

9 "The whole ____ is brimstone, salt, and burning" (Deuteronomy 29:23)

11 Along with wheat, salt, and oil — one of the items needed for burnt offerings (Ezra 6:9)

14 "Can flavorless food be ___en without salt?" (Job 6:6)

16 "When you offer them [sin offerings] before the LORD, the ____s shall throw salt on them" (Ezekiel 43:24)

17 In healing the waters, Elisha said, "Bring me a new ____ and put salt therein" (2 Kings 2:20, KJV)

18 The city of Salt is one of the cities of _____ listed in Joshua 15

19 "____ is good" (Mark 9:50)

20 "Every one shall be salted with _____" (Mark 9:49, KJV)

Word Pool

CAST   COVENANT   CRUSE   EARTH   EAT   FIRE   FLAVOR   FOUNTAIN
JUDAH   LAND   NEED   OFFERING   PILLAR   PITS   PRIEST   SALT
SALTINESS   SEA   SPEECH   VALLEY   WHEAT   WINE   YE

See answer on puzzle answer page 13.

Food Messenger

In 1 Kings 17:1–6 we read how God sent food to Elijah in a very special way. Connect the dots to reveal the creature that brought "bread and meat" to the prophet every morning and evening.

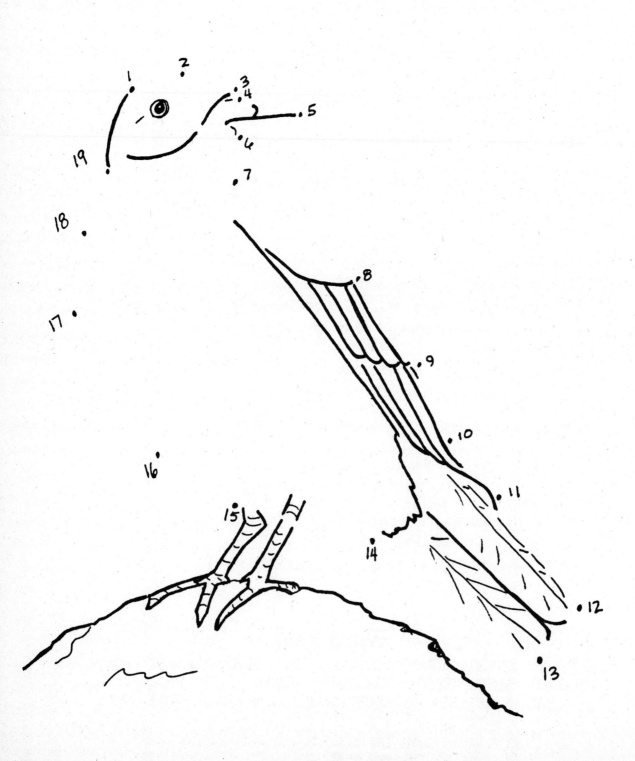

God's Rules

Unscramble the key words below to complete these "rules" that God gave to His people through Moses. You'll find these rules in Exodus 20.

You shall have no other G S D O before Me. __ __ __ (O)

You shall not make for yourself a carved E G A M I; . . . you shall not bow down to them nor serve them. __ (O) __ . . . __

You shall not take the M A E N of the LORD your God in N V A I. __ __ (O) __

__ __ (O) __

Remember the B A S H T A B day, to keep it holy. __ (O) __ __ __ __ __

Honor your R E H T A F and your O T E R H M, that your days may be long upon the land. __ __ __ __ (O) __

__ (O) __ __ __ __

You shall not D R E R U M. (O) __ __ __ __ __

You shall not commit A U T R Y E L D. __ (O) __ __ __ __ __ __

You shall not L A E S T. __ (O) __ __ __

You shall not bear false T E S N I W S against your neighbor. __ __ __ __ (O) __ __

You shall not E T V O C . . . anything that is your neighbor's. (O) __ __ __ __

Write down all of the letters that are circled in the right-hand column here.

__ __ __ __ __ __ __ __ __ __ __

Now unscramble that word to find another word for the word "rules."

__ __ __ __ __ __ __ __ __ __ __

See answer on puzzle answer page 13.

The Serpent's Lie

The following story and crossword puzzle are based on Genesis 3. Use the Word Pool or your Bible for help if you need it. Note: One word is not from the New King James Version.

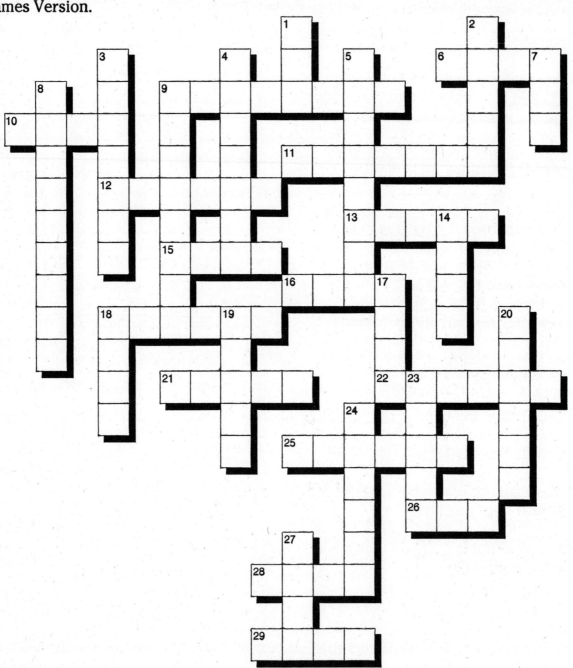

Word Pool

BOTH   BRUISE   CHERUBIM   COOL   COVERINGS   CREATURE   CURSED
DELIGHT   DIE   EAT   EDEN   ENMITY   EVERY   EVIL   EYES   FRUIT
GARDEN   GOOD   HUSBAND   LEAVES   LIFE   NAKED   OPENED   PRESENCE
SEED   SERPENT   SOUND   TOUCH   TREE   WISE   YOU

The _____ was more subtle than any other wild _____ God had made. He said to
4 Down   9 Across

the woman, "Did God say, 'You shall not _____ of any other _____ in the _____'?" She
1 Down   16 Across   12 Across

said, "We may eat of the _____ of _____ tree, but God said, '_____ shall not eat of the
21 Across   23 Down   26 Across

fruit of the tree in the midst of the garden, neither shall you _____ it, lest you _____.'"
19 Down   7 Down

The serpent said, "You will not die. God knows that when you eat of it your _____
18 Down

will be _____ and you will be like God, knowing _____ and _____."
20 Down   6 Across   17 Down

The woman saw that the tree was a _____ to the eyes and to be desired to make
3 Down

one _____, and she took some of its fruit and ate. She also gave some to her _____
27 Down   11 Across

and he ate. Then the eyes of _____ of them were opened, and they knew they were
15 Across

_____. They sewed fig _____ together and made themselves _____.
13 Across   22 Across   8 Down

In the _____ of the day, the man and woman heard the _____ of God walking in the
10 Across   2 Down

garden, and they hid themselves from His _____. God called, "Where are you?" The
5 Down

man said, "When I heard Your voice, I was afraid because I was naked; and I hid

myself." God asked, "Did you eat of the tree of which I commanded You not to eat?"

The man and woman both admitted, "I ate."

The Lord then said to the serpent, "_____ are you. I will put _____ between you and
25 Across   18 Across

the woman, and between your seed and her _____; He shall _____ your head, and you
29 Across   24 Down

shall bruise his heel." Then the Lord God sent the man and woman out of the Garden

of _____, and He placed _____ with flaming swords at the entrance to the garden to
14 Down   9 Down

guard the way to the tree of _____.
28 Across

See answer on puzzle answer page 13.

God's Garden

Shade in all of the segments marked with a /•/ to reveal the name that God gave to His special garden.

The Only Sign

The religious leaders came to Jesus one day and said, "Show us a sign from heaven." Jesus said, "No sign will be given except one." In the signs below find that one sign Jesus said would be given. (See Matthew 16:4.)

See answer on puzzle answer page 13.

Jonah

The story and puzzle below are based on the book of Jonah. Use the Word Pool or your Bible for clues if you need them. Notes: One word is used twice. And a few words are not from the New King James Version.

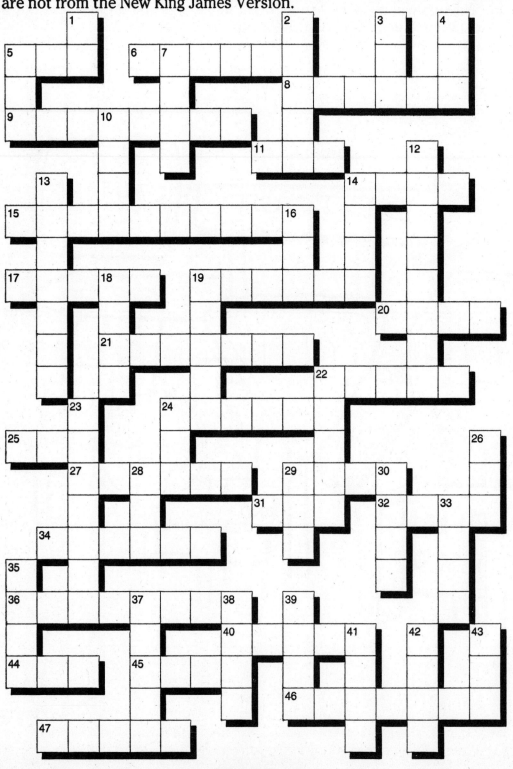

Word Pool

AFRAID ALL ARISE ASLEEP BELLY BLOOD CALLED CAPTAIN CARGO CRY DRY FAST FISH FLEE
GOD HEART HIM HOLY IN INNOCENT KNOW LAND LET LIVE LOT LOTS NINEVEH NOT
OBEYED PAY PERISH PRAYED PRESENCE RAGE REPENT SAIL SAT SEA SHIP SICK SON SPOKE
TARSHISH TEMPEST THEM THREE THROW TIME VOMITED VOW WICKEDNESS WIND WORD

The _____ of the Lord came to Jonah, _____ of Amittai, saying, "_____ , go to _____
      14 Across   5 Across   19 Down   13 Down

and _____ out against it; for their _____ has come up before Me." But Jonah arose to
        26 Down   15 Across

_____ to _____ to escape the presence of the Lord. He boarded a _____ , went into its
42 Down   9 Across   30 Down

lowest parts, and fell fast _____.
                              6 Across

After the ship set _____ for Tarshish, the Lord sent a great _____ on the _____ — a
                      7 Down   14 Down   16 Down

mighty _____. The mariners were _____, and every man _____ out to his god. They
          46 Across   19 Across   34 Across

threw the _____ into the sea. The _____ of the ship awoke Jonah and said, "Call on
            37 Down   23 Down

your _____. Perhaps He will consider us so that we may not _____ but _____."
      4 Down   24 Across   18 Down

Finally the sailors said, "_____ us cast _____ so we may _____ whom to blame for
                            11 Across   29 Across   20 Across

this storm." And as they cast lots, the _____ fell on Jonah. The sailors asked _____,
                                          29 Down   44 Across

"What have you done?" Jonah told them he had fled from the _____ of the Lord.
                                                              12 Down

They said, "What shall we do?" Jonah said, "_____ me into the sea; and it will be calm
                                              22 Down

for you." The men rowed harder, but the sea continued to _____. Then the men
                                                            45 Across

_____, "O Lord, do _____ charge us with _____ _____ ," and they threw Jonah into the
27 Across   43 Down   36 Across 47 Across

sea, and the _____ became calm.
              25 Across

Now the Lord had prepared a great _____ to swallow Jonah, and Jonah was _____
                                    35 Down   1 Down

the _____ of the fish for _____ days and nights. Then Jonah prayed and said, "You
    17 Across   22 Across

cast me into the _____ of the sea. My prayer goes up to You in Your _____ temple. I
                  40 Across   32 Across

will _____ my _____. Salvation is of the LORD."
      24 Down   31 Across

The Lord _____ to the fish, and it became _____ and _____ Jonah onto _____
          2 Down   10 Down   21 Across   3 Down

_____.
33 Down

The word of the Lord came to Jonah a second _____, saying, "Arise, go to Nineveh."
                                              41 Down

This time Jonah _____. When Jonah cried to the people of Nineveh, "Yet forty days,
                  8 Across

and Nineveh shall be overthrown!" the people of Nineveh believed God and

proclaimed a _____. _____ of the people fasted and turned to God. Even the king
              39 Down   28 Down

covered himself with sackcloth and _____ in ashes. God had mercy on _____ and did
                                    5 Down   38 Down

not destroy Nineveh.

See answer on puzzle answer page 13.

Heaven's Citizens

The Bible contains exciting promises of the eternal life in heaven for Christians. In Revelation 3:5 Jesus says that those who overcome will be dressed in white clothes, and that He will "confess his name" to God and His angels. That verse also says there is a special place for the names of those who love Jesus. Connect the dots and then fill in the blanks with letters from the secret code to find out where these names are.

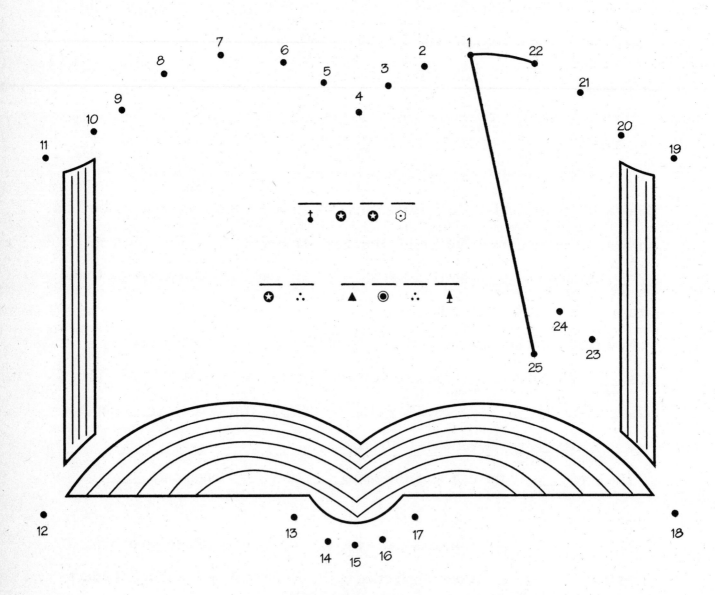

Secret Code

⬡ = K   ▲ = L   ⬦ = B   ∴ = F   ◉ = I   ⬆ = E   ✪ = O

See answer on puzzle answer page 13.

In Pursuit

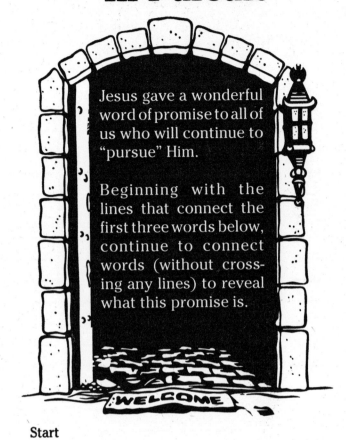

Jesus gave a wonderful word of promise to all of us who will continue to "pursue" Him.

Beginning with the lines that connect the first three words below, continue to connect words (without crossing any lines) to reveal what this promise is.

Start

AND	"ASK,	GIVEN	TO	YOU;
IT	KNOCK,	AND	BE	SEEK,
WILL	FIND;	IT	WILL	AND
BE	OPENED	WILL	YOU	(MATTHEW
TO	YOU,"	SAID	JESUS.	7:7)

See answer on puzzle answer page 13.

The Word of God

The Old Testament portion of the Bible has thirty-nine books. See how many words you can make with two or more letters from the words

OLD TESTAMENT

_____	_____	_____
_____	_____	_____
_____	_____	_____
_____	_____	_____
_____	_____	_____
_____	_____	_____
_____	_____	_____
_____	_____	_____
_____	_____	_____
_____	_____	_____
_____	_____	_____
_____	_____	_____
_____	_____	_____
_____	_____	_____
_____	_____	_____
_____	_____	_____
_____	_____	_____
_____	_____	_____
_____	_____	_____
_____	_____	_____
_____	_____	_____
_____	_____	_____
_____	_____	_____

SUPERIOR: 76 words or more OUTSTANDING: 51-75 words GOOD: 26-50 words KEEP TRYING: 25 words or fewer

See answer on puzzle answer page 13.

The New Covenant

Can you unscramble these books of the Bible?

TAHMETW _ _ _ (_) _ _ _

SAEJM _ _ _ _ _

AKMR (_) _ _ _

MEHOPLIN _ _ _ _ _ _ _

UITST _ _ (_) _ _

OJHN _ _ (_) _

IPSENHAES _ _ _ _ _ _ _ _ _

TIOTHMY _ _ _ _ _ _ _

EPTRE _ (_) _ _ _

LKUE _ _ (_) _

CATS _ _ (_) _

TRNOACIHISN _ _ _ _ (_) _ _ _ _ _ _

ALGTANIAS _ (_) _ _ _ _ _ _ _

ERLVEAITON _ _ _ _ _ _ _ _ _ _

UEJD _ _ _ _

NMROAS _ _ _ _ _ _

EWHESBR _ _ _ _ _ _ _

SSLEHTOANANIS _ _ _ _ _ _ _ _ _ _ _ _ _

SOOCALSINS _ _ _ _ _ _ _ _ _ _

PIHIPAILPNS _ _ _ _ _ _ _ _ _ _ _

Put the circled letters here:

Now unscramble the circled letters to find another name for "covenant":

_ _ _ _ _ _ _ _ _ _ _ _

See answer on puzzle answer page 13.

Where Was Jesus When . . . ?

This crossword's clues relate to places where Jesus was during certain key events and miracles in His life.

Use the Word Pool or the Scripture references for help if you need it.

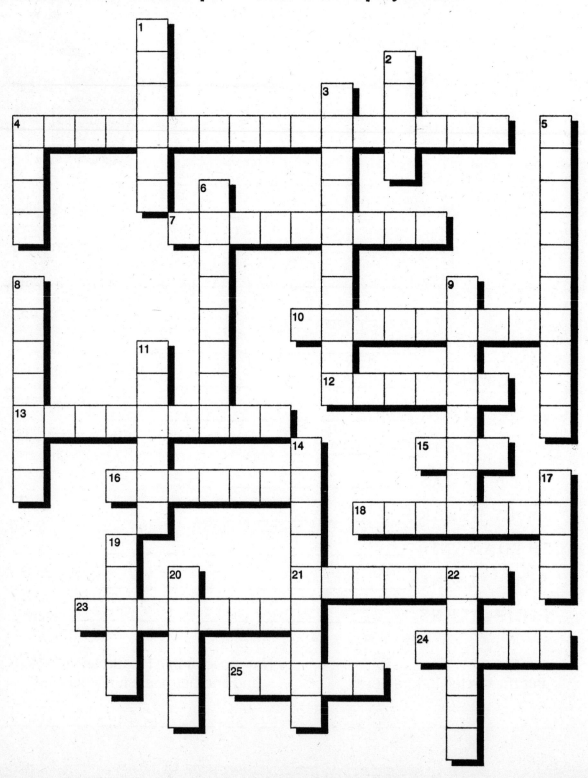

Across

4 Where Jesus asked His disciples, "Who do men say that I am?" (Mark 8:27–29)

7 The town where Jesus was born (Matthew 2:1)

10 The city where Jesus met with the leaders of the temple when He was 12 years old (Luke 2:42–47)

12 The town closest to the place where Jesus talked to a woman at a well and revealed Himself as the One who gives living water (John 4:5–30)

13 The town where a centurion came to Jesus, asking Him to heal his servant (Luke 7:1–10)

15 The place where Jesus was found "walking" — and His disciples thought He was a ghost (Mark 6:47–51)

16 The region in which Jesus preached "throughout" (Mark 1:39)

18 The town in which Jesus raised Lazarus from the dead (John 11:1)

21 The region of the land in which the Bible says Jesus "needed to go through" (John 4:4)

23 The place of the crucifixion, also called "Place of a Skull" (Matthew 27:33)

24 Jesus was in a _____ field when He began to pluck the heads on the Sabbath (Matthew 12:1)

25 Along with Tyre, the area in which Jesus "entered a house and wanted no one to know it, but He could not be hidden" (Mark 7:24)

Down

1 The place where Jesus encountered a demoniac living in the tombs (Mark 5:1–20)

2 The town where Jesus raised a widow's son from the dead (Luke 7:11–15)

3 The place where Jesus was tempted for forty days and forty nights (Matthew 4:1–2)

4 The town in which Jesus turned water into wine (John 4:46)

5 The garden where Jesus prayed before His arrest (Matthew 26:36–46)

6 The pool where Jesus healed a man who had been sick for 38 years (John 5:2–9)

8 The town where Jesus had a meal with Zacchaeus (Luke 19:1–10)

9 The town where the people attempted to throw Jesus over the edge of a cliff (Luke 4:16–30)

11 The river in which Jesus was baptized by John the Baptist (Matthew 3:13)

14 The town where Jesus healed a blind man by touching him twice (Mark 8:22)

17 Along with Sidon, the region in which a woman asked Jesus to heal her daughter, as if receiving "crumbs" from the children's bread (Mark 7:24–30)

19 The place where Jesus Christ made the supreme sacrifice for our sins

20 The land to which Jesus was taken by His parents after Joseph was warned in a dream (Matthew 2:13)

22 The land in which Jesus lived most of His life

Word Pool

BETHANY BETHESDA BETHLEHEM BETHSAIDA CANA CAPERNAUM
CAESAREA PHILIPPI CROSS EGYPT GADARA GALILEE GETHSEMANE
GOLGOTHA GRAIN ISRAEL JERICHO JERUSALEM JORDAN NAIN
NAZARETH SAMARIA SEA SIDON SYCHAR TYRE WILDERNESS

See answer on puzzle answer page 14.

Which Tree?

The Lord God said, "Of every tree of the garden you may freely eat; but of the tree of the knowledge of good and evil you shall not eat" (Genesis 2:16–17). Find the one tree in the garden below that is different from the others.

The Centurion's Mission

A high-ranking Roman soldier once came to Jesus to ask Him to heal his servan (Matthew 8:5–10). Help the centurion find his way to Jesus.

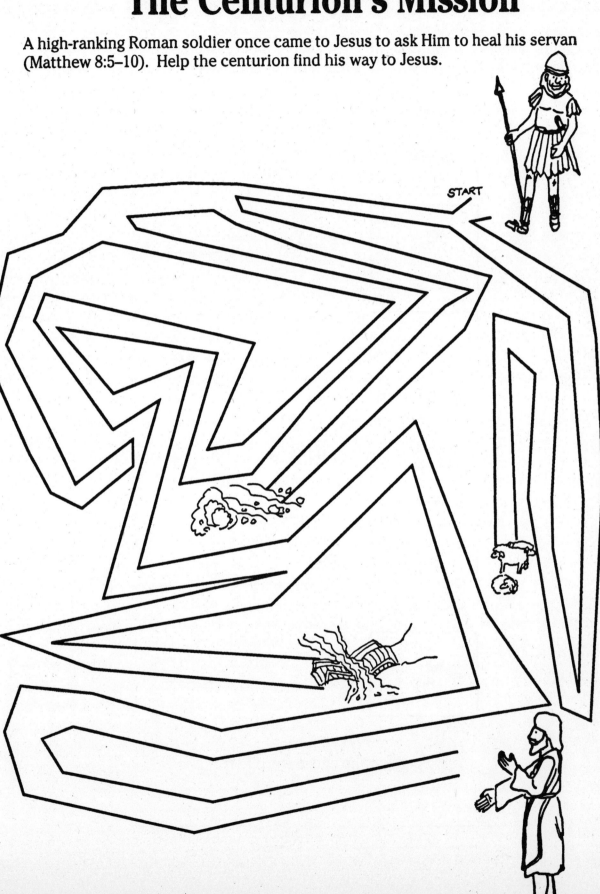

START

To Be Kept

Jesus said that there's something we must keep if we are to abide in His love. Solve the puzzle below to discover what it is that we must keep.

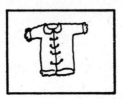 – AT = ___ ___

 – COA = ___ ___

 – H = ___ ___ ___

 – OUSE = ___

 – P = ___ ___ ___

– AN = ___ ___

Spell out the entire word here:

___ ___ ___ ___ ___ ___ ___ ___ ___ ___

(See John 15:10.)

See answer on puzzle answer page 14.

The Right Time

In Ecclesiastes 3:1–8 we read that there is a right time for everything! Use the word pool to fill in this crossword grid. We've given you some letters as clues.

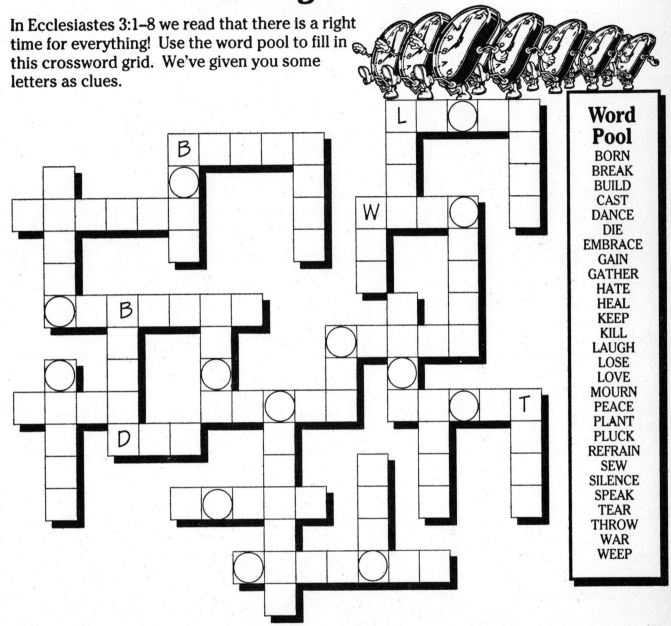

Word Pool

BORN
BREAK
BUILD
CAST
DANCE
DIE
EMBRACE
GAIN
GATHER
HATE
HEAL
KEEP
KILL
LAUGH
LOSE
LOVE
MOURN
PEACE
PLANT
PLUCK
REFRAIN
SEW
SILENCE
SPEAK
TEAR
THROW
WAR
WEEP

Write down all of the circled letters in the crossword puzzle you've just completed:

— — — — — — — — — — — — —

Now unscramble them to find two words that will complete this verse:

To everything there is a __ __ __ __ __ __,

a time for every __ __ __ __ __ __ __ under heaven. *(Ecclesiastes 3:1)*

See answer on puzzle answer page 14.

Oasis

Shade in all of the segments that have a "dot" in them to reveal one of the most welcome sights to a person who is traveling across the desert.

Which Prophet Said It?

In the top row, unscramble the name of each of these three prophets. (Clue: Each one also has a book of the Bible named after him.) Then draw the most direct line you can through the maze to the words he said. (Another clue: The chapter and verse of the book named for the prophet are provided for you.)

_ _ _ _ _ _ _   _ _ _ _ _ _   _ _ _ _ _ _ _
IKELEZE   ASIHAI   HAIMEJER

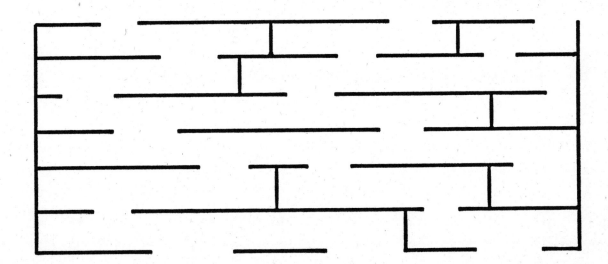

Though your sins are like scarlet, they shall be as white as snow; though they are red like crimson, they shall be as wool. (1:18)

I will put My law in their minds, and write it on their hearts; and I will be their God, and they shall be My people. (31:33)

I will put My Spirit within you and cause you to walk in My statutes, and you will keep My judgments and do them. (36:27)

See answer on puzzle answer page 14.

Moses' Song

The vowels have been left out of this victory song that Moses and the children of Israel sang after they crossed the Red Sea and escaped from the pursuing Egyptian army. Use the secret code to add the vowels to complete the words to this song.

__ W__LL S__NG T__ TH__ L__RD F__R

H__ H__S TR__ __MPH__D GL__R__ __ __SLY!

TH__ H__RS__ __ND __TS R__D__R H__ H__S

THR__WN __NT__ TH__ S__ __! TH__ L__RD __S

MY STR__NGTH __ND S__NG, __ND H__

H__S B__C__M__ MY S__LV__T__ __N;

H__ __S MY G__D, __ND __ W__LL PR__ __S__

H__M; MY F__TH__R'S G__D, __ND __

W__LL __X__LT H__M.

Secret Code

◆ = A   ✱ = E   ♥ = I   ★ = O   ✚ = U

See answer on puzzle answer page 14.

Hidden in Fear

Jesus told a story about a man who went on a trip. Before leaving, he gave sacks of money (called talents) to three of his servants. One of the servants hid the sack of money in a field, rather than risk investing it. Can you help this servant find the hidden talent in this field before his master returns?

FIND THE
HIDDEN
TALENT

They Heard

In Acts 2:5–11, we read about all of the nations and areas represented by the Jews in Jerusalem who heard about "the wonderful works of God" on the day of Pentecost. See how many of these nations and geographical regions you can find in the box of letters below, before using the Word Pool!

```
E M N O P M A P A S I A C
D C A P P A D O C I A I A
I U D E E N E R Y C U D S
J R H P O S E M U J M E C
E A I M A T O P O S E M Y
P G E P O E H N T R L S R
A J E G R R D S U U A C E
R P P A Y A C U D E M A S
T W P G N P T E J O A U E
H E I Y E R T R A P T R M
I A J U P E C H I N E C O
A C T N R O N A O E T O R
N S U C P A M P H Y L I A
```

Word Pool

ASIA CAPPADOCIA CRETE CYRENE
EGYPT ELAM JUDEA MEDIA
MESOPOTAMIA PAMPHYLIA PARTHIA
PHRYGIA PONTUS ROME

See answer on puzzle answer page 14.

The Old Covenant

Unscramble the names of these six Old Testament books, which are sometimes called the "Law" and the "Songs."

ETRNMYODOEU _ _ ◯◯ _ ◯ _ _ _ _

NBMURES _ _ _ _ _ ◯ _

EICSUTIVL ◯ _ _ _ _ _ ◯ _ _

SLAMPS ◯◯ _ _ _ _

ESENGIS _ _ _ _ _ ◯ _

SUDOXE _ _ _ _ _ ◯

Write down the circled letters here:

_ _ _ _ _ _ _ _ _ _

Now unscramble this word to reveal the name that is sometimes used to describe the Bible, especially the Old Testament:

_ _ _ _ _ _ _ _ _ _

See answer on puzzle answer page 14.

Paul's Mission

As God's own "chosen vessel" to take the gospel to the Gentiles, Paul was a tireless traveler. He endured overwhelming suffering and hardship and became the spokesman of the Christian faith in the early church. The clues below all have to do with Paul's life and ministry. Complete the crossword grid with the answers.

Across

1 A _____ left Paul and the other passengers swimming to shore for safety (Acts 27:41, 44)

5 In Jerusalem, an angry _____ sought Paul's life (Acts 22:22–23)

7 _____ is the Hebrew form of the name Paul (Acts 13:9)

9 In _____, Paul and Silas prayed and sang hymns (Acts 16:24–25)

10 A _____ and a voice from heaven caused Saul to fall to the ground (Acts 9:3–4)

12 Paul's hometown (Acts 22:3)

14 By occupation, Paul made _____ (Acts 18:3)

15 Paul was a _____ from Tarsus (Acts 21:39)

16 Paul traveled much, spreading the gospel on his missionary _____ (Romans 15:24)

17 When Paul was bitten by a _____, and he didn't get sick; the people thought he was a god (Acts 28:3–6)

19 Paul preached Christ in the _____ (Acts 9:20)

21 In _____, Saul regained his sight, was converted and baptized (Acts 9:10, 17–19)

Down

1 Before his conversion, Paul consented to the death of _____ by stoning (Acts 7:58–59)

2 Paul was a _____ of the church before his conversion (1 Timothy 1:13)

3 In Antioch, believers were first called _____ (Acts 11:26)

4 Paul's enemies made an oath to _____ him (Acts 23:12)

6 Officials were ordered to _____ Paul and Silas as punishment (Acts 16:22–23)

8 Paul was an _____, which means "one sent" (Romans 1:1)

11 For _____ days Paul was blind (Acts 9:9)

13 The Lord chose Paul to take the gospel to the _____ (Acts 9:15)

16 Paul had opposed the Church, but now he preached boldly in the name of _____ (Acts 9:27)

18 As a citizen of _____, Paul appealed his case to Caesar (Acts 22:27)

20 "To the unknown _____" (Acts 17:23)

See answer on puzzle answer page 14.

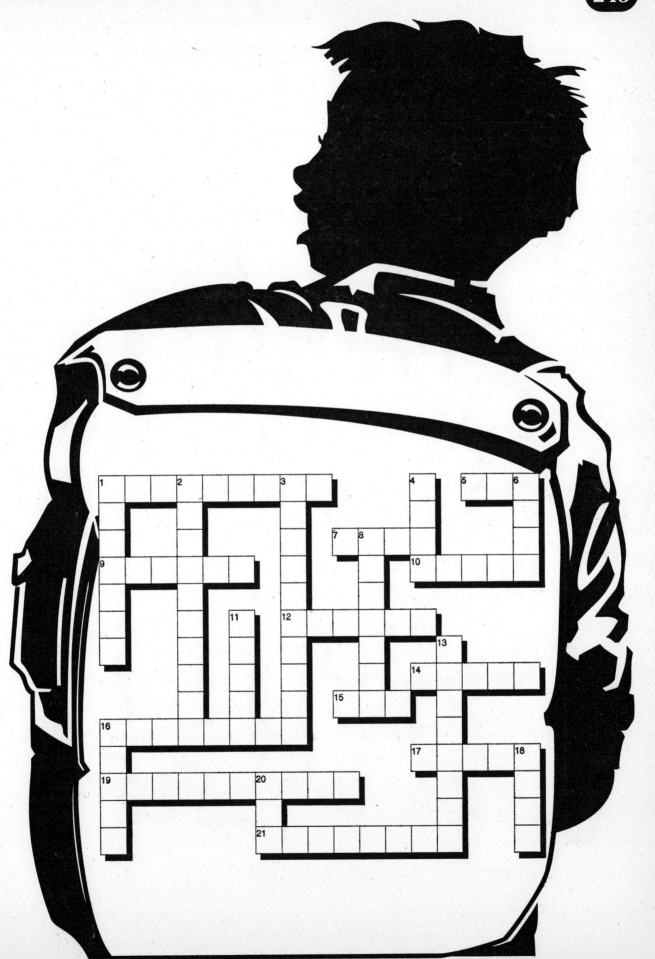

What Does It Mean?

In the New Testament, Jesus sometimes used parables, or stories, to tell the people how important it was to live the kind of life God wanted them to live. Match up the puzzle pieces to connect each of the parables with its meaning. Use the Scripture pool if you need help.

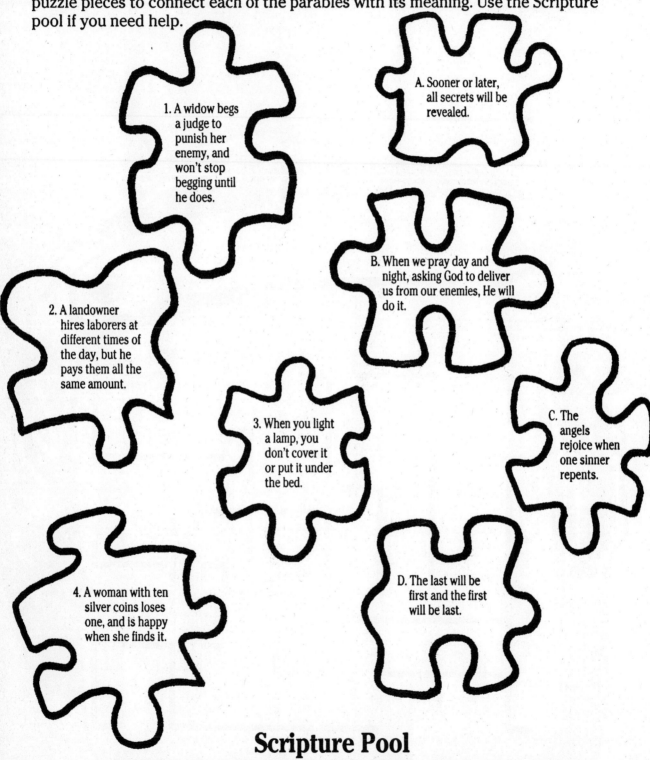

1. A widow begs a judge to punish her enemy, and won't stop begging until he does.

A. Sooner or later, all secrets will be revealed.

B. When we pray day and night, asking God to deliver us from our enemies, He will do it.

2. A landowner hires laborers at different times of the day, but he pays them all the same amount.

3. When you light a lamp, you don't cover it or put it under the bed.

C. The angels rejoice when one sinner repents.

4. A woman with ten silver coins loses one, and is happy when she finds it.

D. The last will be first and the first will be last.

Scripture Pool

Luke 8:16–17   Luke 15:8–10   Luke 18:2–8   Matthew 20:1–16

See answer on puzzle answer page 14.

How Clean?

Jesus warned the Pharisees and scribes about cleaning the outside of something, and then failing to clean the inside of it. Connect the dots to find out what that something is! You can read about it in Matthew 23:25.

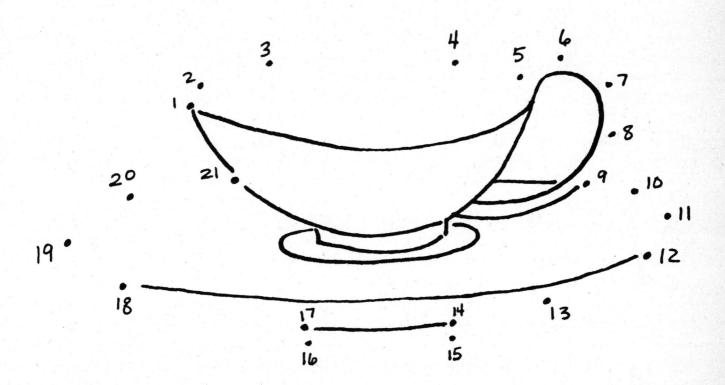

Reprimand

The 25 words below are in scrambled order. Put them in the right order on the lines provided to see what Jesus had to say to some of the religious leaders in His day.

IMPORTANT MESSAGE

Clue:
This puzzle relates to the one on the previous page!

WOE AND FULL SELF-INDULGENCE. AND OF

HYPOCRITES! YOU CLEANSE CUP PHARISEES, TO

SCRIBES FOR OUTSIDE THE BUT OF THEY

EXTORTION INSIDE YOU THE AND DISH, ARE

_____

_____

_____

_____

See answer on puzzle answer page 14.

Going to the Dogs

We think of dogs as man's best friend, but in the Bible, dogs were a little wilder than they are today. When people did evil things, they were sometimes thrown to the dogs — and the dogs weren't too nice.

This puzzle will take you through all the Bible as you solve clues that are all about dogs. Even if you know the answers without checking the verses, read them anyway. Learn a little more about the dog of Bible times.

Across

2 The men who lapped up this liquid like dogs were chosen to fight (Judges 7:5)

4 Interferes in (Proverbs 26:17)

6 Jesus said it wasn't good to take the children's "staff of life" and throw it to the dogs (Matthew 15:26)

7 David's was delivered from the power of the dog (Psalm 22:20)

9 Lazarus sat by this "fence" (Luke 16:20–21)

10 To pull across the ground (Jeremiah 15:3)

12 They washed the king's blood out of this vehicle (1 Kings 22:38)

14 A living dog has this (Ecclesiastes 9:4)

15 Bow-wow (Isaiah 56:10)

18 Bay at the moon (Psalm 59:15)

20 This Philistine hated being treated like a dog (1 Samuel 17:23,43)

Down

1 Not alive (1 Samuel 24:14)

3 Not a dog moved its tongue against the children of _____ (Exodus 11:7)

5 Don't cast pearls before "pigs" (Matthew 7:6)

6 "Watch out for" dogs and evil workers! (Philippians 3:2)

8 The woman from #6 Across had this (Matthew 15:28)

11 The warrior in #2 Across (Judges 7:5)

13 The king in #12 Across (1 Kings 22:37–39)

16 Hazael, a future "royal leader," wondered if Elisha saw him as a dog (2 Kings 8:13)

17 This type of man had to throw torn-up meat to the dogs (Exodus 22:31)

19 Opposite of true; a "dirty" type of prophet (2 Peter 2:1,22)

See answer on puzzle answer page 14.

Which Sack?

When Joseph's brothers prepared to return home after receiving grain and provision in Egypt, Joseph ordered that his silver cup be put in the sack of his youngest brother, Benjamin. Find the sack below that belongs to Benjamin.

The Will of God

When the Apostle Paul wrote to the Thessalonians, he gave them a very important word concerning the will of God for every situation and circumstance. Follow the directions below and find out what he told them.

1. This instruction is written backward. To unscramble it rewrite it from the end to the beginning

S Y A W L A E C I O J E R

2. Circle every third letter

P O P J A R S E A E Z Y W E W S K I B A T A S H W H O T B
U N A T O Y C P I E T E A B A S O W I V Y N O I G

3. Cross out the vowels O and U

O I O U N E O V U E R O Y T O H U I N O G U G O I V U E
O T U H O A N U K O S

(Read 1 Thessalonians 5:16–18.)

1. _ _ _ _ _ _ _   _ _ _ _ _ _

2. _ _ _ _   _ _ _ _ _ _ _

   _ _ _ _ _ _

3. _ _   _ _ _ _ _ _ _ _ _ _ _

   _ _ _ _   _ _ _ _ _

See answer on puzzle answer page 14.

My Shepherd

Psalm 23 says the Lord is our Shepherd. We can trust in Him and enjoy knowing Him and loving Him. Fill in the blanks and then fill in the crossword grid with the words that have been left out.

The _____ is _____
   12 Down   24 Down

_____; I shall not want. He makes me
1 Across

to _____ down in _____
   5 Down   3 Across

_____; He _____ me
6 Down   20 Down

beside the _____ _____. He
          18 Across   26 Across

_____ my _____; He _____ me in the
13 Across   14 Down   20 Down

_____ [singular] of _____ for His name's sake. Yea, though I _____
22 Down   4 Down   21 Across

through the _____ of the _____ of death, I will _____ no _____;
           17 Down   1 Down   15 Across   23 Across

for You are with me; Your _____ and Your staff, they _____ me. You
                         2 Down   7 Down

prepare a _____ before me in the presence of my _____ [singular]; You
         19 Down   25 Across

anoint my _____ with _____; my cup runs over. Surely _____ and
         8 Down   10 Down   9 Across

mercy shall _____ me all the days of my life; and I will _____ in the
           16 Down   11 Across

_____ of the LORD forever.
27 Across

See answer on puzzle answer page 14.

What Kind of Place?

The last book of the Bible, Revelation, was written by "a servant of God" named John. In chapters 2 and 3, Jesus tells John to write to the angels of seven different churches. He has a message for each of them. Can you unscramble the names of the seven churches, and then match them with the correct description?

1. ASRMEOPG __ __ __ __ __ __ __ __

2. RSSDIA __ __ __ __ __ __

3. DAELIACO __ __ __ __ __ __ __ __

4. SEHSUPE __ __ __ __ __ __ __

5. YASMNR __ __ __ __ __ __

6. RATHITAY __ __ __ __ __ __ __ __

7. LAHIDPIHEPLA __ __ __ __ __ __ __ __ __ __ __ __

___ A. I know your works, love, service, faith, and your patience. But you have allowed that woman Jezebel to teach and beguile My servants.

___ B. You hold fast to My name and did not deny My faith. But I have a few things against you, because you have those who hold the doctrine of Balaam.

___ C. You have kept My word, and have not denied My name. Because you have kept My command, I will keep you from the hour of trial which shall come upon the whole world.

___ D. Do not fear those things you are about to suffer. Be faithful until death, and I will give you the crown of life.

___ E. You say you are rich. But you do not know that you are poor, naked, and blind. Buy from Me gold that you may be rich, white garments that you may be clothed, and anoint your eyes with eye salve, that you may see.

___ F. You have a few who have not defiled their garments; and they shall walk with Me in white, for they are worthy. But hold fast and repent. He who overcomes shall be clothed in white garments, and I will not blot out his name from the Book of Life.

___ G. You have labored for My name's sake and have not become weary. But you have left your first love for Me; repent and do the first works.

See answer on puzzle answer page 14.

No Greater Gift

The Bible says that Jesus is the "Author" of something eternal. Solve the puzzle below to find out what it is!

 – CK = ___ ___

 – EAES = ___ ___

 – H = ___ ___

 – BCYCLE = ___

 – CE = ___ ___

Join all of the letters here:

___ ___ ___ ___ ___ ___ ___ ___

(Read Hebrews 5:9.)

See answer on puzzle answer page 14.

Our Riches

Use the secret code to decipher this beatitude.

_____ are the _____ in _____, for _____ is the
    ♦   ⊙   ★   ◪

_____ of _____.
   ♛   ❂

Secret Code

♛ = KINGDOM   ⊙ = POOR   ♦ = BLESSED   ❂ = HEAVEN   ◪ = THEIRS   ★ = SPIRIT

See answer on puzzle answer page 15.

When We Are Sad

Use the secret code to decipher this beatitude.

_____ are _____ who _____, for _____
   ▲   ◓   ✖   ∴

_____ be _____.
   ✹   △

Secret Code

✹ = SHALL   ∴ = THEY   △ = COMFORTED   ✖ = MOURN   ◓ = THOSE
▲ = BLESSED

See answer on puzzle answer page 15.

Puzzle 257

THE BLESSED ONES

Be Nice!

Use the secret code to decipher this beatitude.

__________ are the ______, for
∴ ◉

______ _______ __________ the _______.
⊠ ◩ ⚖ 🌐

Secret Code

⊠ = THEY 🏙 = EARTH 🏛 = INHERIT ◎ = MEEK ∴ = BLESSED ◩ = SHALL

See answer on puzzle answer page 15.

Puzzle 258

THE BLESSED ONES

The Empty

Use the secret code to decipher this beatitude.

_________ are ________ who _________ and _________ for
⊡ ✧ Ⓐ ◉

____________________, for ______ _______ be _________.
◕ ■ ★ ◆

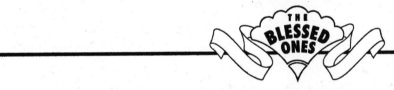

Secret Code

◕ = RIGHTEOUSNESS ⊡ = BLESSED ◎ = THIRST ◆ = FILLED ✧ = THOSE
★ = SHALL Ⓐ = HUNGER ■ = THEY

See answer on puzzle answer page 15.

Be Forgiving

Use the secret code to decipher this beatitude.

_____ are the _____,
       ✖   ⚭

for _____ _____ _____ _____.
    ⚭   ∴   ⚓   ●

Secret Code

⚭ = THEY   ∴ = SHALL   ✖ - BLESSED   ● = MERCY   ⚭ = MERCIFUL   ⚓ = OBTAIN

See answer on puzzle answer page 15.

A Pure Heart

Use the secret code to decipher this beatitude.

_____ are the _____ in _____,
      ✿   🕊   ▱

for _____ _____ _____ ____.
     🚶   ⬡   )(✿

Secret Code

🕊 = PURE   ▱ = HEART   ✿ = GOD   )(= SEE   ⬡ = SHALL
🚶 = THEY   ✿ = BLESSED

See answer on puzzle answer page 15.

THE BLESSED ONES

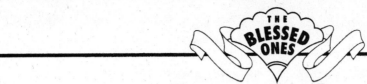

Peacemakers

Use the secret code to decipher this beatitude.

__________ are the ________________, for ______ ________ be
⊙ ● □ △

__________ ______ of _____.
⬡ ▲ ⟁

Secret Code

⟁ = GOD ⬡ = CALLED △ = SHALL □ = THEY ▲ = SONS
● = PEACEMAKERS ⊙ = BLESSED

See answer on puzzle answer page 15.

THE BLESSED ONES

When It Gets Tough

Use the secret code to decipher this beatitude.

__________ are _______ who are ______________ for
▥ ♜ ✉

________________ ______, for ________ is the __________ of _________.
✝ ⬡ ✈ ⚒ 🍁

Secret Code

⬡ = SAKE ▥ = BLESSED 🍁 = HEAVEN ⚒ = KINGDOM ✈ = THEIRS
✉ = PERSECUTED ✝ = RIGHTEOUSNESS ♜ = THOSE

See answer on puzzle answer page 15.

Woe to You!

The clues for this crossword relate to those who were warned by God to repent of their sins and turn from their wicked ways. Use the Word Pool or look up the Scripture references for help to fill in the grid.

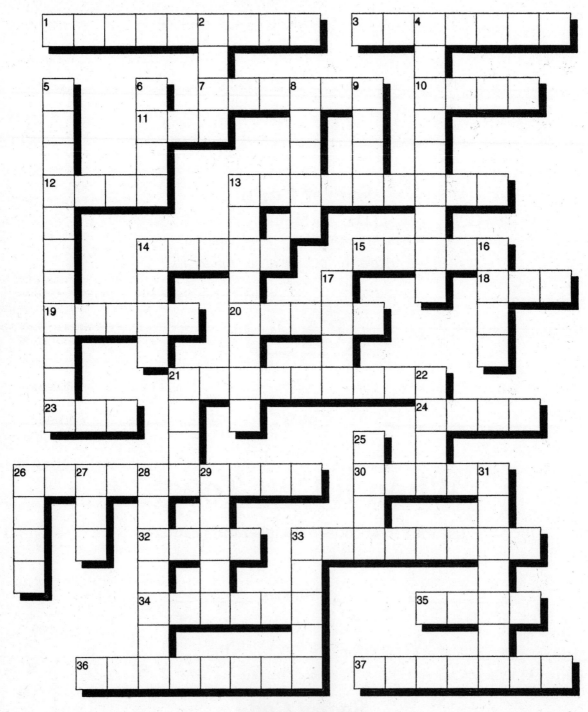

Word Pool

AFRAID   AMMON   ARIEL   AWAY   BABYLON   BETHSAIDA   BIND   BRIMSTONE
CAPERNAUM   CHORAZIN   CRY   DESTRUCTION   DOOM   EDOM   EGYPT   EPHRAIM   FIRE
GLORIFIED   GOMORRAH   HAVE   JUDAH   JUDGMENT   LAID   LIVE   MOAB   NET   NEVER
NINEVEH   OIL   PROPHET   REPENT   SEAT   SIDON   SINS   SODOM   TEAR   THEY   TURNS
TYRE   WICKEDNESS   WIND   WOE

Across

1 I am against you, O Sidon; I will be _____ in your midst (Ezekiel 28:22)

3 Flee from the midst of ____, and every one save his life! (Jeremiah 51:6)

7 Jesus began to upbraid the cities in which most of His mighty works had been done, because they did not ____ (Matthew 11:20)

10 Say to the prince of ____,"Thus says the Lord GOD . . . 'Because you have set your heart as the heart of a god, Behold, therefore, I will bring strangers against you'" (Ezekiel 28:2,6)

11 ____to you, Moab! You have perished, O people of Chemosh! (Numbers 21:29)

12 I will repay Babylon . . . for all the evil ____ have done in Zion in your sight (Jeremiah 51:24)

13 And you, ____, who are exalted to heaven, will be brought down to Hades (Matthew 11:23)

14 Behold, I am against you, O _____; I will be glorified in your midst (Ezekiel 28:22)

15 The punishment of the iniquity of the daughter of my people is greater than the punishment of the sin of ____, which was overthrown in a moment, with no hand to help her! (Lamentations 4:6)

18 I will make . . . their rivers run like _____ (Ezekiel 32:14)

19 While you are looking for light, he ____ it into the shadow of death (Jeremiah 13:16)

20 Woe to ___, to . . . the city where David dwelt! (Isaiah 29:1)

21 Then the LORD rained ____and fire on Sodom and Gomorrah, from the LORD out of the heavens (Genesis 19:24)

23 I will therefore spread My _____ over you with a company of many people (Ezekiel 32:3)

24 For in the day of _____ they shall be against her [Babylon] all around (Jeremiah 51:2)

26 Go to Nineveh . . . and cry out against it; for their _____ has come up before Me (Jonah 1:2)

30 Together they shall plunder the people of the East; . . . and the people of ____ shall obey them (Isaiah 11:14)

32 You ____ become a horror, and shall be no more forever (Ezekiel 28:19)

33 All the nations shall see My ____ which I have executed (Ezekiel 39:21)

34 I am _____ of Your judgments (Psalm 119:120)

35 Seek the LORD and ___, lest He break out like fire (Amos 5:6)

36 Then the LORD rained brimstone and fire on Sodom and _____ (Genesis 19:24)

37 Therefore the anger of the LORD was aroused . . . and He sent him a ____ (2 Chronicles 25:15)

Down

2 I will blow against you with the ____ of My wrath (Ezekiel 21:31)

4 Woe to you, Chorazin! Woe to you, ___! For if the mighty works which were done in you had been done in Tyre and Sidon, they would have repented long ago in sackcloth and ashes (Matthew 11:21)

5 Nor shall you bring an abomination into your house, lest you be doomed to _____ like it (Deuteronomy 7:26)

6 Weep bitterly for him who goes _____, for he shall return no more (Jeremiah 22:10)

8 Take up a lamentation for Pharaoh king of _____ (Ezekiel 32:2)

9 Behold, I am against your magic charms by which you hunt souls there like birds. I will ____ them from your arms (Ezekiel 13:20)

13 Woe to you, ____! Woe to you, Bethsaida! For if the mighty works which were done in you had been done in Tyre and Sidon, they would have repented long ago in sackcloth and ashes (Matthew 11:21)

14 Your wealth and your treasures I will give as plunder without price, because of all your ____ (Jeremiah 15:13)

16 And _____ shall be destroyed as a people, because he has exalted himself against the LORD (Jeremiah 48:42)

17 Because your heart is lifted up, and you say, "I am a god, I sit in the ____ of gods" . . . you shall die the death of the slain in the midst of the seas (Ezekiel 28:2,8)

21 I will . . . _____ up the broken . . . but I will destroy the fat and the strong (Ezekiel 34:16)

22 Egypt shall be a desolation, and ____ a desolate wilderness, because of violence against the people of Judah (Joel 3:19)

25 Her cities shall be in the midst of the cities that are ____ waste (Ezekiel 30:7)

26 Behold, I will raise up against Babylon . . . a destroying ____ (Jeremiah 51:1)

27 The word of the LORD came to Jonah . . . "Arise, go to Nineveh, that great city, and _____ out against it" (Jonah 1:1–2)

28 Woe to the crown of pride, to the drunkards of _____ (Isaiah 28:1)

29 I will bring you down with those who descend into the Pit, . . . so that you may _____ be inhabited (Ezekiel 26:20)

31 Though _____ of old was like a pool of water, now they flee away (Nahum 2:8)

33 Appoint a road for the sword to go to . . . ____, into fortified Jerusalem (Ezekiel 21:20)

See answer on puzzle answer page 15.

Here Am I

Below are three people who heard God calling to them and they responded, "Here am I." Match the people with what the Lord said to them next.

I have surely seen the oppression of My people who are in Egypt, and have heard their cry because of their taskmasters, for I know their sorrows.

Behold, I will do something in Israel at which both ears of everyone who hears it will tingle.

Go, and tell this people: "Keep on hearing, but do not understand; Keep on seeing, but do not perceive. . . .Lest they see with their eyes, and hear with their ears, and understand with their heart, and return and be healed."

Scripture Pool

1 Samuel 3:11   Exodus 3:7   Isaiah 6:9–10

See answer on puzzle answer page 15.

Invitations

First unscramble the names of three people in the Bible who sent out special invitations. Then match those people with the invitations and the people who received them. Consult the Scripture pool if you need help.

ESSUJ   EJALIH   EESRTH

_ _ _ _ _   _ _ _ _ _ _   _ _ _ _ _ _

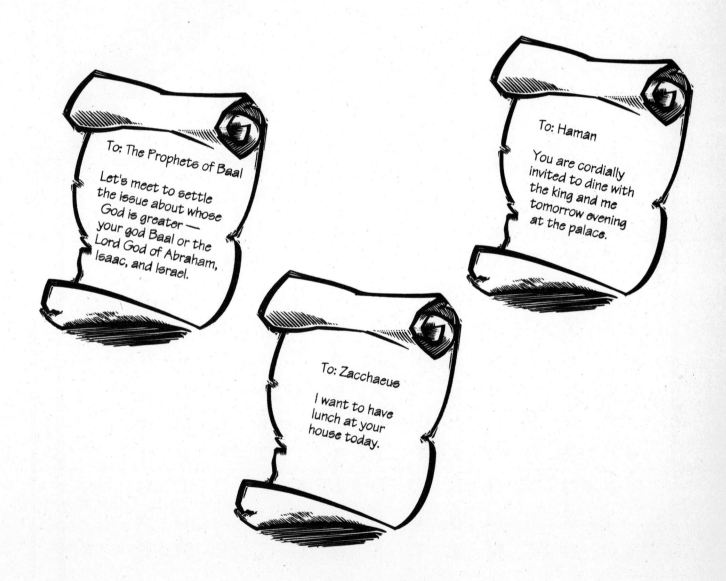

To: The Prophets of Baal

Let's meet to settle the issue about whose God is greater — your god Baal or the Lord God of Abraham, Isaac, and Israel.

To: Haman

You are cordially invited to dine with the king and me tomorrow evening at the palace.

To: Zacchaeus

I want to have lunch at your house today.

Scripture Pool

Esther 5:8   1 Kings 18:21–40   Luke 19:1–10

See answer on puzzle answer page 15.

Spiritual Gifts

The apostle Paul wrote about nine spiritual gifts in his letter to the Corinthians. See how many of them you can find in the letter box below before consulting the Word Pool!

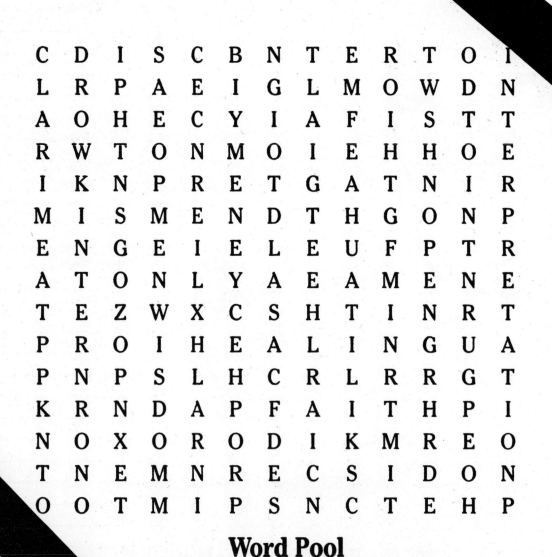

```
C D I S C B N T E R T O I
L R P A E I G L M O W D N
A O H E C Y I A F I S T T
R W T O N M O I E H H O E
I K N P R E T G A T N I R
M I S M E N D T H G O N P
E N G E I E L E U F P T R
A T O N L Y A E A M E N E
T E Z W X C S H T I N R T
P R O I H E A L I N G U A
P N P S L H C R L R R G T
K R N D A P F A I T H P I
N O X O R O D I K M R E O
T N E M N R E C S I D O N
O O T M I P S N C T E H P
```

Word Pool

DISCERNMENT FAITH HEALING INTERPRETATION
KNOWLEDGE MIRACLES PROPHECY TONGUES WISDOM

See answer on puzzle answer page 15.

Evermore

How many words with two or more letters can you make from the letters in the phrase: EVERLASTING LIFE? Read what Jesus said about everlasting life in John 3:16 and John 5:24.

More than 80 words — Truly Superior; 60 - 79 words — Outstanding;
40 - 59 words — Good; Fewer than 40 words — Keep Looking!

See answer on puzzle answer page 15.

Rebuilding the Wall

As you complete the story below using the words in the Word Pool, you will also have the words you need to complete the crossword grid! You can read about this story in Nehemiah 1–6.

Nehemiah was the _____ to the king. One day when he was _____ the king,
      11 Across   9 Down

the king said, "Why are you so_____?" Nehemiah answered, "The _____ of my
               35 Across   16 Across

fathers lies in _____, its _____ destroyed by _____." The king said "What
       26 Across   24 Down   1 Down

do you want to do?" Nehemiah _____ and then said, "If it pleases you, please
                        29 Down

send me to _____ the city." The king _____ what Nehemiah asked. He sent
       19 Across   25 Down

Nehemiah to _____ with official orders to rebuild the city walls. After Nehemiah
       31 Across

had been in Jerusalem for _____ _____, he arose in the _____ to
            10 Across   12 Across   20 Down

_____ out the _____ and gates. Then he said to the people, "Let's _____ up
9 Across   27 Across   30 Down

and _____." The people began to build the gates and walls, even though some
   22 Across

people _____ them. When the wall was rebuilt to _____ its height, _____,
     2 Down   13 Across   28 Across

_____, the _____ and other _____ of the Israelites came together and
32 Across   33 Down   15 Down

_____ against the rebuilding. The people prayed again and set _____ on a
14 Across   18 Down

24-hour-a-day watch. Nehemiah organized the people so that half of them built while

the other half stood _____. Nehemiah _____ the people, saying, "_____
          5 Down   34 Across   36 Across

the _____ and _____ for your families and _____." Every _____ closed
   17 Down   3 Across   4 Down   21 Across

the _____ in the wall that were closest to their homes. So the people were able
   37 Across

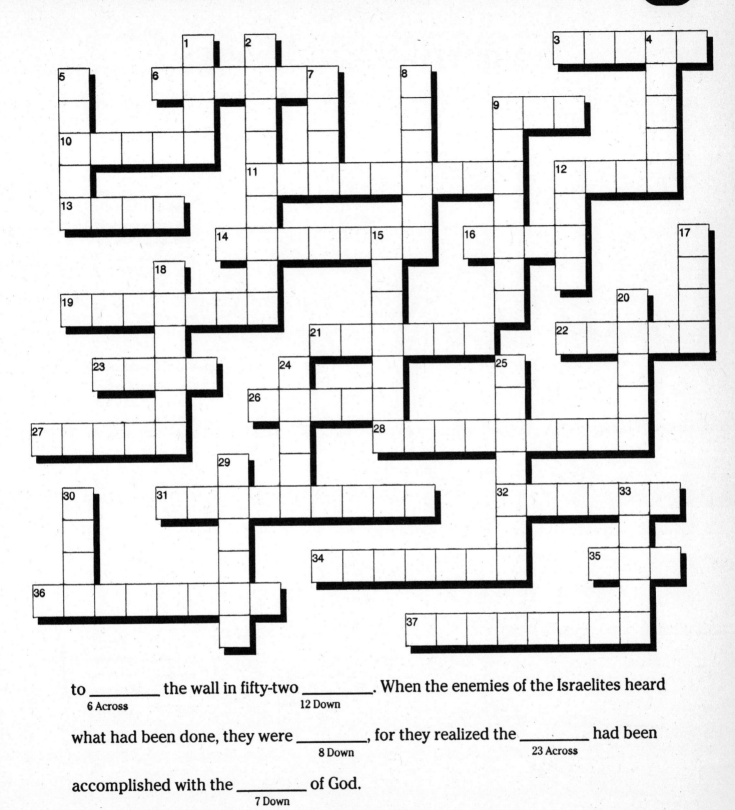

to _____ the wall in fifty-two _____. When the enemies of the Israelites heard

6 Across   12 Down

what had been done, they were _____, for they realized the _____ had been

8 Down   23 Across

accomplished with the _____ of God.

7 Down

Word Pool

AFRAID ARABS BREACHES BUILD CITY CUPBEARER DAYS DAYS ENEMIES FAMILY FIGHT
FINISH FIRE GATES GRANTED GUARDS HALF HELP HOMES JERUSALEM LORD NIGHT
PLOTTED PRAYED RALLIED REBUILD REMEMBER RIDICULED RISE SAD SANBALLAT
SERVING SPY THREE TOBIAH WALLS WASTE WATCH WORK

See answer on puzzle answer page 15.

Songwriters and Songs

The songwriters below have become separated from their song sheets. Match these Bible figures with their songs.

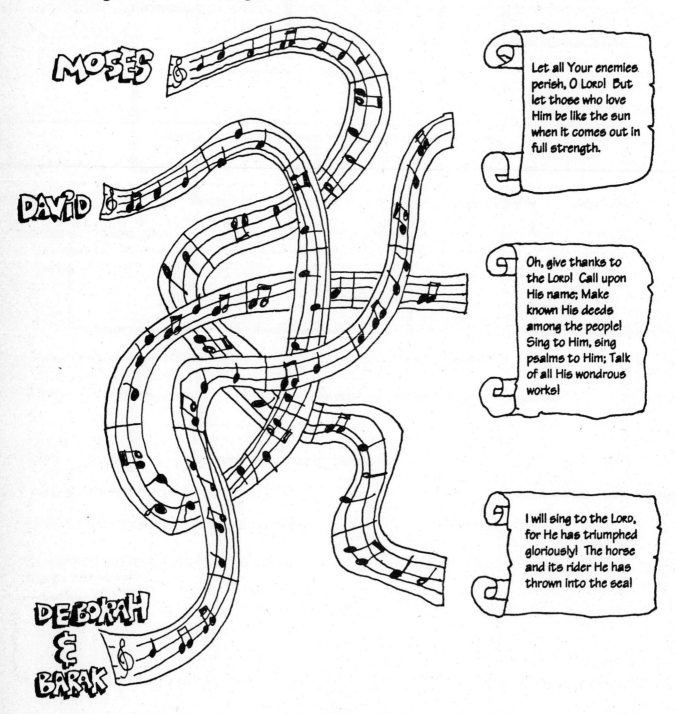

Let all Your enemies perish, O LORD! But let those who love Him be like the sun when it comes out in full strength.

Oh, give thanks to the LORD! Call upon His name; Make known His deeds among the people! Sing to Him, sing psalms to Him; Talk of all His wondrous works!

I will sing to the LORD, for He has triumphed gloriously! The horse and its rider He has thrown into the sea!

You can find these songs in 1 Chronicles 16:7–36; Exodus 15:1–18; and Judges 5:1–31.

See answer on puzzle answer page 15.

Wall Writing

The wicked King Belshazzar had a banquet to which he invited a thousand lords, and he used the sacred gold and silver vessels that had been stolen from the temple in Jerusalem to serve the wine. King Belshazzar made a toast to the gods of gold and silver, bronze and iron, wood and stone as the people drank from these goblets. That same hour, the king saw the fingers of a man's hand appear and write mysterious words opposite the lampstand on the plaster wall of his palace. Decode the message below to see what was written on the wall.

Message

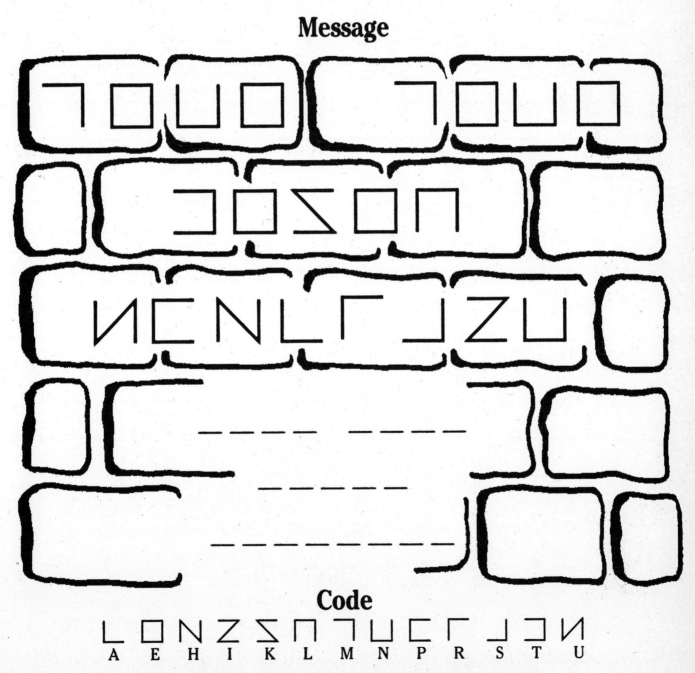

Code

L	∩	N	Z	⊂	⊓	⊓	⊓	⊔	Γ	⊐	⊔	∩
A	E	H	I	K	L	M	N	P	R	S	T	U

Now turn the page to find out what this message meant!

See answer on puzzle answer page 16.

God's Writing

When the words MENE MENE TEKEL UPHARSIN appeared on the wall of King Belshazzar's palace, everyone must have gasped. And then when Daniel told the king what the words meant, the king surely must have been troubled. Decode the message below to discover the meaning of these words.

Message

Mene: ● □ ✧ { ○ △ ▲ ◇

_____

_____

_____

Tekel:) ▽ ■ ✦ ◆ ▌ ▼ △ ✳)

_____

_____

_____

Peres (Upharsin): { ○ □ ◨) △ ◗ ▯ ▌ ♥ △ ♡

_____

_____

_____

Code

△	▼	■	)	▲	✳	)	●	▱
AND	BALANCES	BEEN	DIVIDED	FINISHED	FOUND	GIVEN	GOD	HAS

▽	◆	✧	○	♥	✧	♡	▌	)
HAVE	IN	IT	KINGDOM	MEDES	NUMBERED	PERSIANS	THE	TO

)	✦	)	{
WANTING	WEIGHED	YOU	YOUR

See answer on puzzle answer page 16.

Safe Journey

The word "shalom" in the Bible is a Hebrew word that is often used in place of the words "hello," "good-bye," "God's blessings on you," or "Have a safe journey." Color in the pieces of the stained glass window below that have a /•/ in them to reveal the literal meaning of this word.

Two Brothers

Cain and Abel were very different as brothers. One was a shepherd; the other a farmer. In the field in which they are standing, find three things that belong to Cain, and three things that belong to Abel. Once you have found an item, draw a line to show whether it belongs to Cain or Abel. You can read about Cain and Abel in Genesis 4:1–15.

| BASKET OF GOURDS | HOE | LAMB | EWE | SHEPHERD'S CROOK | SHEAF OF WHEAT |

See answer on puzzle answer page 16.

God's Great Love

Two of the most famous verses in the Bible are these:

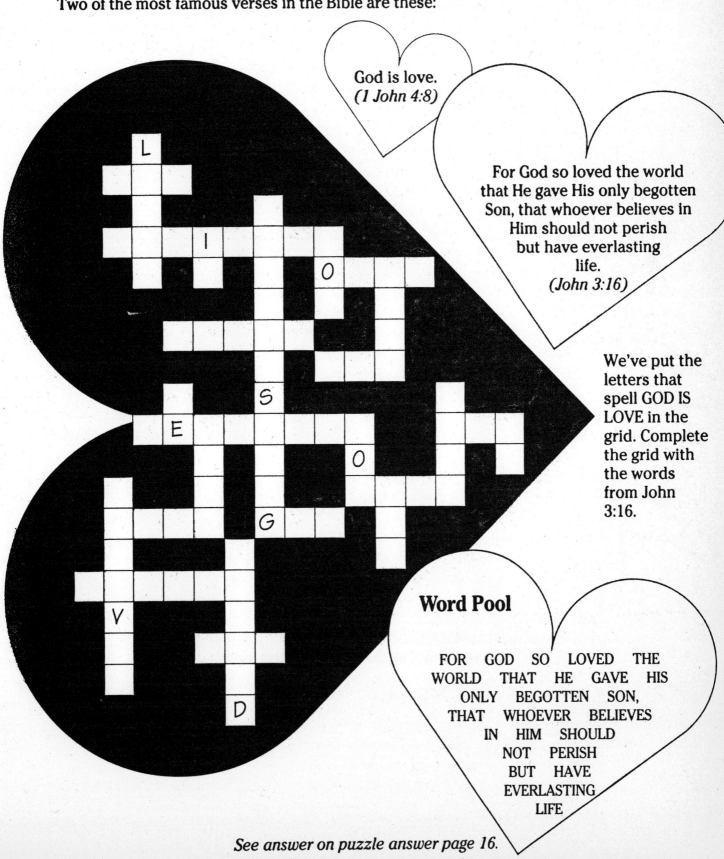

God is love.
(1 John 4:8)

For God so loved the world that He gave His only begotten Son, that whoever believes in Him should not perish but have everlasting life.
(John 3:16)

We've put the letters that spell GOD IS LOVE in the grid. Complete the grid with the words from John 3:16.

Word Pool

FOR GOD SO LOVED THE WORLD THAT HE GAVE HIS ONLY BEGOTTEN SON, THAT WHOEVER BELIEVES IN HIM SHOULD NOT PERISH BUT HAVE EVERLASTING LIFE

See answer on puzzle answer page 16.

My People

God's purpose through all of history — including today — is to have a special people, set apart, to love and serve Him, a people He would call His own. Use the secret code to reveal the relationship God wants with His people.

__ W __ __ __ B __ __ __ __ __ R

G __ D, __ N D __ __ __ __ __ __ __ __

B __ M __ P __ __ P __ __.

Secret Code

◉ = A ✪ = E ✎ = I ↑ = O ■ = U ☻ = Y △ = L ◪ = TH ∴ = SH

Unscramble the letters below to reveal the name of the promise that God made to His people.

Scrambled: NEONVACT

Unscrambled: __ __ __ __ __ __ __ __

See answer on puzzle answer page 16.

Bible Colors

Unscramble the letters in the words below, and then use these words to complete the crossword grid. (You'll have an extra challenge in placing the words on the grid so they fit. Clue: Count the number of letters in the words.)

- Though your sins are like <u>LRAETCS</u>, they shall be as <u>ETIWH</u> as snow; though they are <u>DRE</u> like crimson, they shall be as wool. (Isaiah 1:18)

- I looked, and behold, a <u>KCLAB</u> horse, and he who sat on it had a pair of scales in his hand. (Revelation 6:5)

- I am like a <u>NEREG</u> olive tree in the house of God; I trust in the mercy of God forever and ever. (Psalm 52:8)

- There was a certain rich man who was clothed in <u>PELRUP</u> and fine linen and fared sumptuously every day. (Luke 16:19)

- You shall make the robe of the ephod all of <u>ELUB</u>. . . . And upon its hem you shall make . . . a <u>NEDLOG</u> bell and a pomegranate . . . all around. (Exodus 28:31, 33–34)

See answer on puzzle answer page 16.

It's Possible

Wind, rain, sun, moon, fish, birds and trees . . . all of nature is subject to God's command. At times, God miraculously intervenes through nature to accomplish His purposes. Fill in the grid with answers that relate to miracles in nature found in the Scripture references.

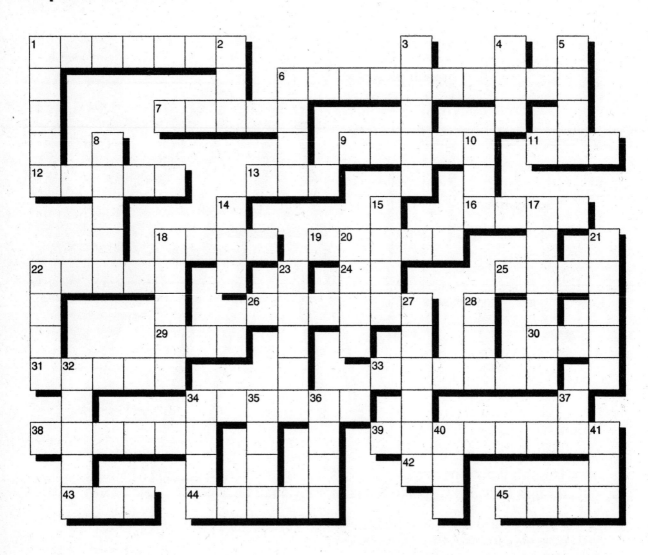

Across

1 One normally uses a boat to get across the water, but Jesus used this method to reach the disciples on the Sea of Galilee (Matthew 14:25)

6 Jesus had _____ for His followers because they had not eaten for three days (Matthew 15:32)

7 God's miraculous provision of food in the wilderness for the children of Israel (Exodus 16:31)

9 This fisherman's belief was not taxed when Jesus told him he would find money in a fish's mouth (Matthew 17:24–27)

11 Because King Ahab "did more to provoke the LORD God of Israel to anger than all the kings of Israel who were before him," there was neither rain nor _____ for years (1 Kings 16:33; 17:1)

12 The #28 Down stood _____ in the sky (Joshua 10:13)

13 There was no _____ like it that the Lord "heeded the voice of a man" (Joshua 10:14)

16 The fishermen had worked all night without success, but Jesus said they would get a catch of fish if they put their nets down here (Luke 5:4)

18 The disciples were filled with _____, not #3 Down, when the storm tossed their boat (Mark 4:40)

19 "This is the _____ which the LORD has given you to eat" (Exodus 16:15)

22 Elijah proved his point with the prophets of Baal when fire consumed the _____-drenched wood and sacrifice (1 Kings 18:33)

24 Peter told Jesus, "_____ Your word I will let down the net" (Luke 5:5)

25 With just two of these, Jesus fed over 5,000 men, women, and children — the people ate and they were all filled (Mark 6:41–42)

26 While Jesus slept, the disciples were afraid they would _____ in the storm (Mark 4:38)

29 The number of waterpots that the servants filled with water at the wedding (John 2:6)

30 Amazement, marvel; a natural response to the miracles of Jesus

31 It was a long trek out of here to the promised land, but God provided time and again for the children of Israel in their wilderness journey (Exodus 12:51)

33 Set forth (Luke 5:4)

34 Stopped; the wind and waves did this at Jesus' command (Mark 4:39)

38 Hebrew leader who led the defeat of the Amorites at Gibeon and eventually led the children of Israel into the promised land (Joshua 10:12)

39 When the Israelites saw what the Lord had done to deliver them from their enemies, they _____ God (Exodus 14:31)

42 When the prophets of Baal called on their god to send fire, there was "_____ voice; _____ one answered, _____ one paid attention" (1 Kings 18:29)

43 Jesus did not want to offend authorities by not paying this money (Matthew 17:24)

44 This prophet witnessed God's miracles in nature — he saw a bush on fire that didn't burn up, a rod turned into a serpent, the Red Sea parted, and food and water miraculously appeared in the desert (Exodus 3:3; 4:3–4; 14:21; 16:15)

45 "Even the wind and the sea _____ Him!" (Mark 4:41)

Down

1 Strong winds caused great _____ that tossed the boat the disciples were in (Mark 4:37)

2 God's greatest miracle of nature, the Creation, is told in this book of the Bible (abbr.)

3 Jesus asked the disciples, "How is it that you have no _____?" (Mark 4:40)

4 Jesus cursed this tree because it did not bear fruit, and the tree dried up (Matthew 21:19)

5 #17 Down put his face between his _____ (sing.) and told his servant to go look toward the sea (1 Kings 18:42)

6 A wedding in this city was where Jesus performed His first miracle (John 2:1)

8 The Israelites would have been literally "in over their heads" had God not provided a way through the _____ of the Red Sea (Exodus 14:16)

10 #44 Across lifted this up and God provided an escape from the enemies of the Israelites (Exodus 14:16)

14 The children of Israel would not die of hunger as they feared, because God miraculously provided bread and meat for them to _____ (Exodus 16:12)

15 When the fishermen obeyed Jesus, these were filled with fish to the point of breaking (Luke 5:6)

17 Years of drought and famine ended when this prophet challenged the prophets of Baal to a showdown (1 Kings 18:21–25)

18 #7 Across looked like _____ on the ground (Exodus 16:14)

20 When fire burned the water-soaked sacrifice, the people proclaimed "The LORD, He is God," and soon the _____ came (1 Kings 18:38–39, 45)

21 Jesus told the disciples to take courage, "be of good _____" (Matthew 14:27)

22 Jesus saved the day for the wedding host by turning water into _____ (John 2:9)

23 His miracles were evidence of His deity (Matthew 14:33)

27 "The LORD said to Moses, 'Behold, I will rain bread from _____ for you' " (Exodus 16:4)

28 This celestial orb did not move for a day (Joshua 10:13)

32 The disciples thought they saw a _____, when they witnessed #1 Across (Matthew 14:26)

34 When Jesus said #37 Down, the stormy sea became _____ (Mark 4:39)

35 The signs and miracles that God did on behalf of the children of Israel (Deuteronomy 11:3)

36 "Your _____ have seen every great act of the LORD which He did" (Deuteronomy 11:7)

37 "Peace, _____ still!" (Mark 4:39)

40 Wood or timber such as Elijah would have used to build the altar of sacrifice

41 The Red Sea parted, and the children of Israel walked across on _____ land (Exodus 14:29)

See answer on puzzle answer page 16.

God's Goodness

Although Joseph was his father's favorite son, he had many reasons to say life had treated him unfairly. He was sold into Egyptian slavery by his jealous brothers and then thrown into prison on false charges. There he could have lived out his days forgotten in a foreign land, but God had other plans for his life. As it turned out, Joseph was the right person in the right place at the right time. (You can read all the details of this story in Genesis 37–50.) How did Joseph respond to his ill treatment? How did he react to his brothers? Decode the message below to find that answer.

There are two verses to this answer. For the first verse, begin with the letter "A" and circle every other letter. Put the circled letters on the blank spaces. To decode the second verse, put a line under every other letter beginning with the letter "Y" and put those letters on the second set of blank spaces.

AYNODUGMOEDASNETNETVMIELBAEG

FAOIRNESYTOMUETBOUPTRGEOSDEMREV

AENATPIOTSFTOERRGIOTOYD.

1. _ _ _   _ _ _   _ _ _ _   _ _

_ _ _ _ _   _ _ _   _ _

_ _ _ _ _ _ _   _

_ _ _ _ _ _ _ _ _ .

2. _ _ _   _ _ _ _   _ _ _ _

_ _ _ _ _ _ _   _ _ _;   _ _ _ _   _ _ _ _

_ _ _ _ _   _ _   _ _ _   _ _ _ _ .

See answer on puzzle answer page 16.

Plagued!

The Pharaoh learned the hard way. God told Moses to tell the Pharaoh, "Let My people go." And that's exactly what He meant. But Pharaoh's stubborn refusal resulted in death and disaster for the people of Egypt. Plagues of blood, frogs, lice, flies, disease, boils, hail, locusts, and darkness all took their toll on the Egyptians. But it was the last one — death of the firstborn — that finally convinced the Pharaoh. In the letter box below, find the names of all ten plagues mentioned above.

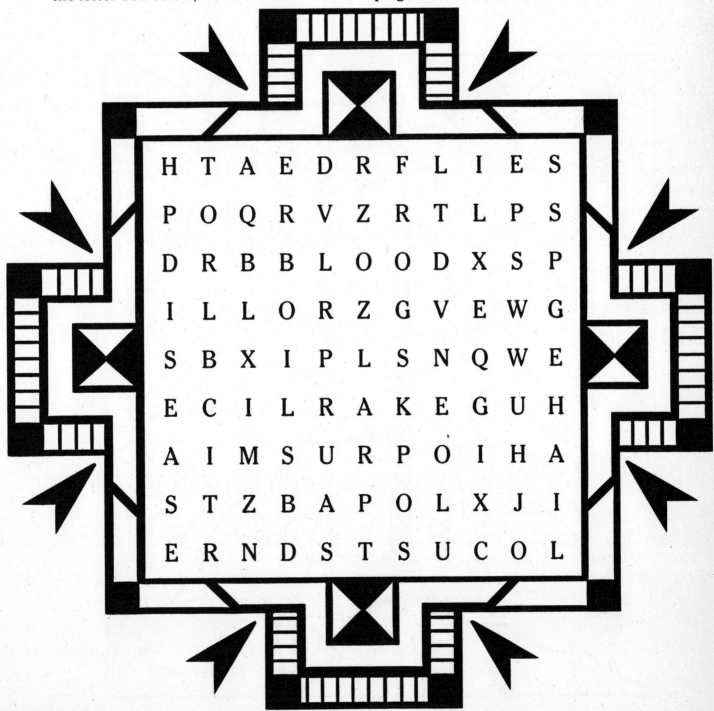

See answer on puzzle answer page 16.

Look At It!

Jesus told a parable about the fig tree. He said that summer is near when the tree has some specific things on it. In the same way, He said there are some specific things to look for to know when the kingdom of God is near. Color in all the areas shaded with a /•/ to find out what Jesus said would be on the tree when summer is near.

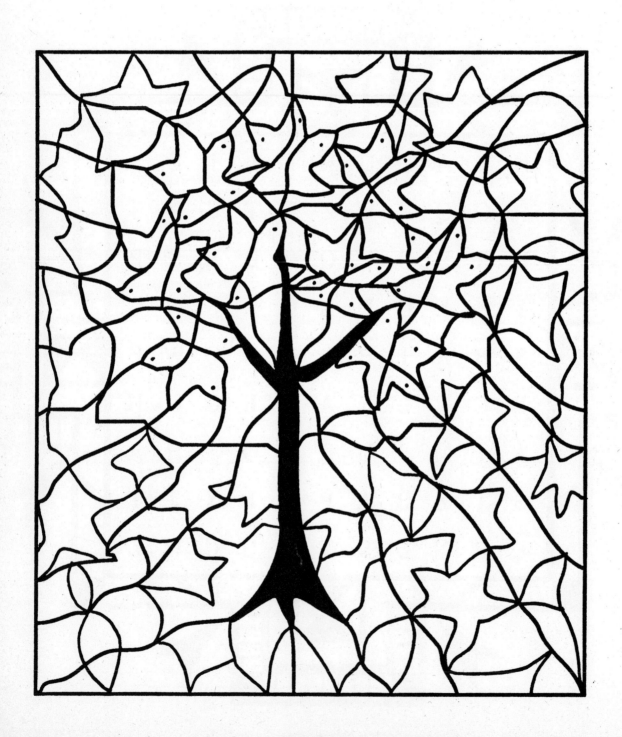

Grace or Works?

The Bible says there is only one way to be saved. Solve the rebus puzzle and find out
— are we saved by good works or by God's grace?

 − EE + Y = __ __

 − PES + CE = __ __ __ __ __

 − NE + UGH = __ __ __ __ __ __ __

 − CE + ITH = __ __ __ __ __

Write all the words here:

__ __   __ __ __ __

__ __ __ __ __ __ __ __ __

See answer on puzzle answer page 16.

Oil and Vinegar

Oil and vinegar were two very important liquids in Bible times. Oil was made from olives. It was used to make bread, and it was used in cereal offerings. It was also used on wounds and to anoint people (such as priests).

Vinegar was also known as sour wine or wine vinegar. It is best known as the drink that was offered to Jesus when He was on the cross.

In solving this puzzle, use the Bible references to help you learn more about the uses of oil and vinegar.

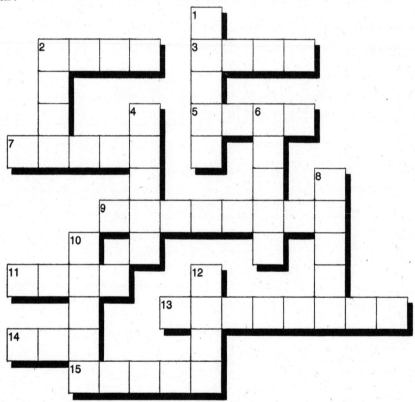

Across

2 The "ill" were anointed with oil (Mark 6:13)

3 God sent "drops of water" from heaven (Deuteronomy 11:14)

5 Taking someone's coat is like putting vinegar on this baking ingredient (Proverbs 25:20)

7 Moses sprinkled anointing oil on this seven times (Leviticus 8:10–11)

9 This type of person couldn't drink vinegar made from wine (Numbers 6:2–3)

11 Talk to God (James 5:14–15)

13 It is "done," Jesus said (John 19:30)

14 You drink tea from this (Psalm 23:5)

15 Oil makes the face "glow" (Psalm 104:15)

Down

1 The psalmist was anointed with _____ oil, not stale (Psalm 92:10)

2 This king's shield wasn't anointed with oil (2 Samuel 1:21)

4 Ruth dipped a "crust" in vinegar (Ruth 2:14)

6 This psalmist's enemies gave him vinegar to drink (Psalm 69:21)

8 You chew with these (Proverbs 10:26)

10 Five foolish virgins didn't have oil for these (Matthew 25:1–3)

12 Not foolish (Proverbs 21:20)

See answer on puzzle answer page 16.

Glory, Glory!

There's a word we all use to express praise, joy, or thanks to God. To find this word, answer all the clues. Then, unscramble the circled letters and put them in the spaces.

God's Son __ __ __ ◯ __   __ __ __ __ __ __

The first book of the New Testament __ ◯ __ __ __ __ __

He built the ark __ __ __ ◯

This son of David was a very wise king __ __ __ ◯ __ __ __ __

This Old Testament queen helped
save the Jews when Haman had
convinced King Ahasuerus to destroy them __ __ __ ◯ __ __

This Old Testament book
comes right after Jeremiah ◯ __ __ __ __ __ __ __ __ __ __

This Old Testament prophet
thought he was too young to serve God well ◯◯ __ __ __ __ __ __

This apostle first met Jesus on the road to Damascus __ __ __ ◯

Jesus used these "stories" to explain the
Kingdom of God to the people
(the mustard seed story is one example) __ __ __ ◯ __ __ __

This Nazirite lost all of his strength when his hair was cut __ ◯ __ __ __ __

Scrambled letters:__ __ __ __ __ __ __ __

Unscrambled letters:__ __ __ __ __ __ __ __

See answer on puzzle answer page 16.

Once Upon a Time . . .

To explain what the kingdom of God is like, Jesus used to tell the people stories, known as parables. Using the Word Pool, can you find all the hidden words and phrases that Jesus used in His parables? (You can read the parables in the New Testament books of Matthew, Mark, and Luke.)

```
S A U L Y O L I V E C S M A R T E F L E
R D K P E E H S T S O L U O F W A S Y R
E T N A V R E S G N I V I G R O F N U U
K U W I C K E D V I N E D R E S S E R S
R K T L S Y U P O F A C S C S O T V K A
O D E A H O B A S T I S P X H N I A N E
W E N T I E W U K Z L G M I R S W E V R
D N V X W H E A T A N D T A R E S L F T
R S I Q D R T R H J R E A R U E N A D N
A E R A E M U S T A R D S E E D W N J E
Y N G T S A E F G N I D D E W E K O B D
E V I G K Z R N R I F O B L H I M E S D
N O N E J O E O W S T N E L A T C G Q I
I A S H A T R V T M W Y I E L A N O M H
V Y E C I R P T A E R G F O L R A E P R
```

Word Pool

SOWER   WHEAT AND TARES   MUSTARD SEED   LEAVEN
HIDDEN TREASURE   PEARL OF GREAT PRICE   DRAGNET
UNFORGIVING SERVANT   LOST SHEEP   VINEYARD WORKERS
TWO SONS   WICKED VINEDRESSERS   WEDDING FEAST   TALENTS
FIG TREE   TEN VIRGINS

See answer on puzzle answer page 16.

A String of Choice

The prophet Isaiah described the coming Messiah as One who would be able to make wise choices. Connect letters below — adding each letter to the phrase as if you were stringing beads together on a string — to see what Isaiah said about the Messiah's ability to choose. See Isaiah 7:16 for help. We've connected the first three letters for you.

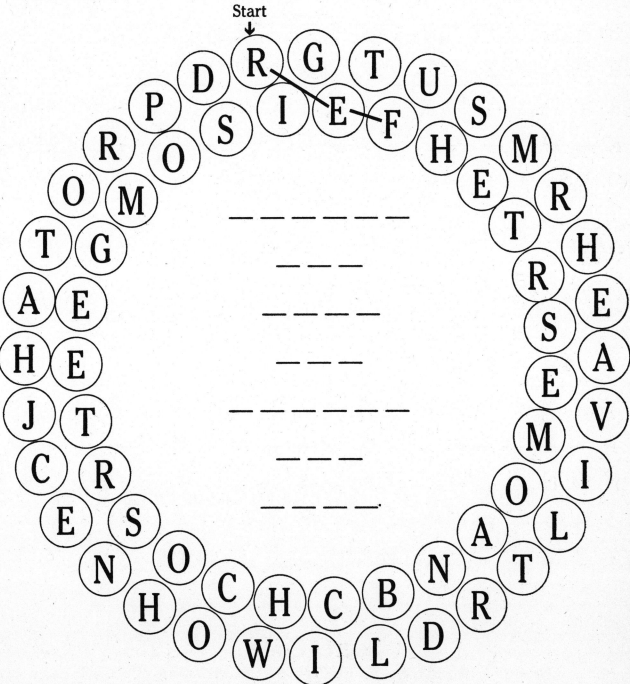

Start

See answer on puzzle answer page 17.

Abraham's Covenant

God made a covenant promise with Abraham for blessing through his descendants through all generations. Decode the cryptogram to read God's covenant with Abraham.

_ _ _ _ _ _ _ _ _ _ _ _ _ A
∴　　⊙　　　　↟　　　⊘

_ _ _ _ NATION; _ _ _ _ _
◧　　　　　　∴　　⊙

_ _ _ _ _ AND _ _ _ YOUR
✪　　　⊘　　　　↟

_ _ _ _ _ _ _; AND _ _ _ SHALL BE A
◔　　◧　　　　　⊘

_ _ _ _ _ING.
✪

_ _ _ _ _ _ _ THOSE WHO
∴　⊙　　　✪

_ _ _ _ _ _ _, AND _ _ _ _ _
✪　　⊘　　　∴　　⊙

_ _ _ _ HIM WHO _ _ _ _S _ _ _;
△　　　　　　△　　　　　⊘

AND IN _ _ _ ALL THE FAMILIES OF THE EARTH
⊘

SHALL BE _ _ _ _ _ED.
✪

Secret Code

✪ = BLESS　　△ = CURSE　　◧ = GREAT　　∴ = I
↟ = MAKE　　◔ = NAME　　⊙ = WILL　　⊘ = YOU

See answer on puzzle answer page 17.

Young or Old?

David was a youth when he defeated Goliath. Abraham and Sarah were very old when their promised son, Isaac, was born. Jesus was 30 when He began His public ministry. As you can see, age doesn't matter much to God. He can use us — and perform miracles in our lives — no matter how young or old we are. All the clues in this puzzle are taken from verses that have to do with being old or young. Use the Bible references to help you find the words.

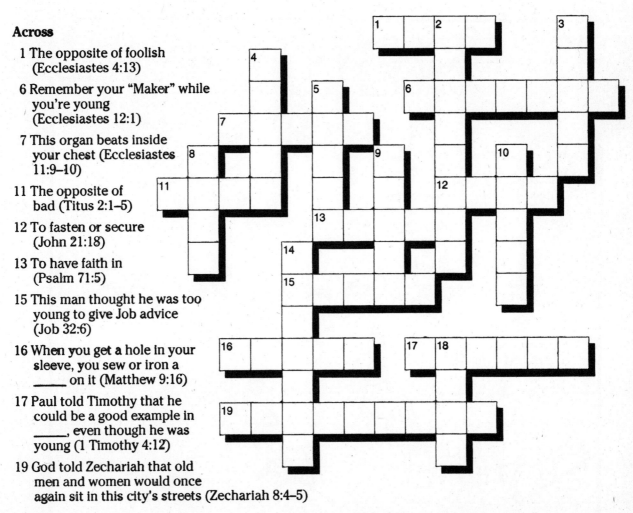

Across

1 The opposite of foolish (Ecclesiastes 4:13)

6 Remember your "Maker" while you're young (Ecclesiastes 12:1)

7 This organ beats inside your chest (Ecclesiastes 11:9–10)

11 The opposite of bad (Titus 2:1–5)

12 To fasten or secure (John 21:18)

13 To have faith in (Psalm 71:5)

15 This man thought he was too young to give Job advice (Job 32:6)

16 When you get a hole in your sleeve, you sew or iron a _____ on it (Matthew 9:16)

17 Paul told Timothy that he could be a good example in _____, even though he was young (1 Timothy 4:12)

19 God told Zechariah that old men and women would once again sit in this city's streets (Zechariah 8:4–5)

Down

2 The glory of young men is their "muscle power" (Proverbs 20:29)

3 The heaven will grow old like a "coat" (Psalm 102:25–26)

4 The psalmist never saw the families of the righteous begging for this food (Psalm 37:25)

5 Apples and bananas are in this "family" (Psalm 92:12–14)

8 Nicodemus wondered how he could be _____ again, since he was old (John 3:4)

9 Jesus replaced our old life with a new life of sincerity and _____ (1 Corinthians 5:7–8)

10 In the last days, old men shall have one of these (sing.) (Acts 2:17)

14 These "written messages" from King Ahasuerus said all the Jews — young and old — should be killed (Esther 3:13)

18 The old lion dies for lack of this (Job 4:11)

See answer on puzzle answer page 17.

Getting to Jesus

One day a sick woman decided that she would get to Jesus and touch the hem of His garment, no matter what it took! Help this woman get through the crowd to Jesus so she can be healed. You can read about this story in Mark 5:24–34.

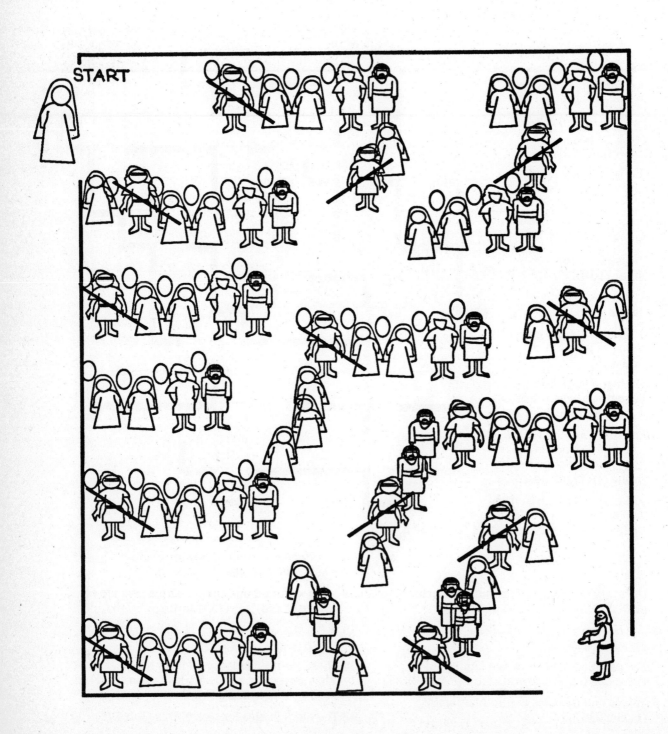

Bible Kin

Unscramble the letters in Column B to find the name of a person related to the person(s) in Column A. When you finish with this acrostic you will discover a word that describes how these people are related.

Column A

1. TAMAR
(*2 Samuel 13:1*)

2. AARON, MOSES
(*1 Chronicles 6:3*)

3. ESAU
(*Genesis 25:26*)

4. RACHEL
(*Genesis 29:16*)

5. ABEL, SETH
(*Genesis 4:25*)

6. JOSEPH
(*Genesis 35:24*)

7. KOHATH, MERARI
(*Genesis 46:11*)

8. MARY, MARTHA
(*John 11:5*)

Column B

1. BALSAMO   _ _ _ _ _ _ _

2. AIRMIM   _ _ _ _ _ _

3. BOCAJ   _ _ _ _ _

4. HEAL   _ _ _ _

5. ICAN   _ _ _ _

6. NINEJAMB   _ _ _ _ _ _ _ _

7. SHONGER   _ _ _ _ _ _ _

8. RUSLAZA _ _ _ _ _ _ _

The people with the same numbers in columns A and B are

_ _ _ _ _ _ _ _ _

See answer on puzzle answer page 17.

The 100th

Jesus said, "If a man has a hundred sheep, and one of them goes astray, does he not leave the ninety-nine and go to the mountains to seek the one that is straying? And if he should find it, assuredly, I say to you, he rejoices more over that sheep than over the ninety-nine that did not go astray" (Matthew 18:12–13). Can you find the lost sheep in the picture below?

Bible Families

Something's missing from each name to keep you from matching up the Bible parents with their children. The missing vowels and the number of times they are missing from each family are given in the last column. Complete each name with the vowels and you will have the names of families in the Bible.

Moms and Dads	Children	Missing Vowels
1. __ BR __ H __ M and S __ R __ H	__ S __ __ C	A – 7, I – 1
2. J __ CH __ B __ D and __ MR __ M	M __ S __ S __ __ R __ N M __ R __ __ M	A – 5, E – 3, I – 2, O – 3
3. M __ S __ S and Z __ PP __ R __ H	G __ RSH __ M __ L __ __ Z __ R	A – 1, E – 5, I – 2, O – 3
4. D __ V __ D and B __ THSH __ B __	S __ L __ M __ N	A – 3, E – 1, I – 1, O – 3
5. R __ TH and B __ __ Z	__ B __ D	A – 1, E – 1, O – 2, U – 1
6. R __ CH __ L and J __ C __ B	J __ S __ PH B __ NJ __ M __ N	A – 3, E – 3, I – 1, O – 2
7. __ L __ Z __ B __ TH and Z __ CH __ R __ __ S	J __ HN	A – 4, E – 2, I – 2, O – 1
8. __ S __ __ C and R __ B __ K __ H	__ S __ __ J __ C __ B	A – 5, E – 3, I – 1, O – 1, U – 1
9. H __ NN __ H and __ LK __ N __ H	S __ M __ __ L	A – 5, E – 2, U – 1
10. N __ __ M __ and __ L __ M __ L __ CH	M __ HL __ N CH __ L __ __ N	A – 2, E – 3, I – 4, O – 3

See answer on puzzle answer page 17.

Bible Authors

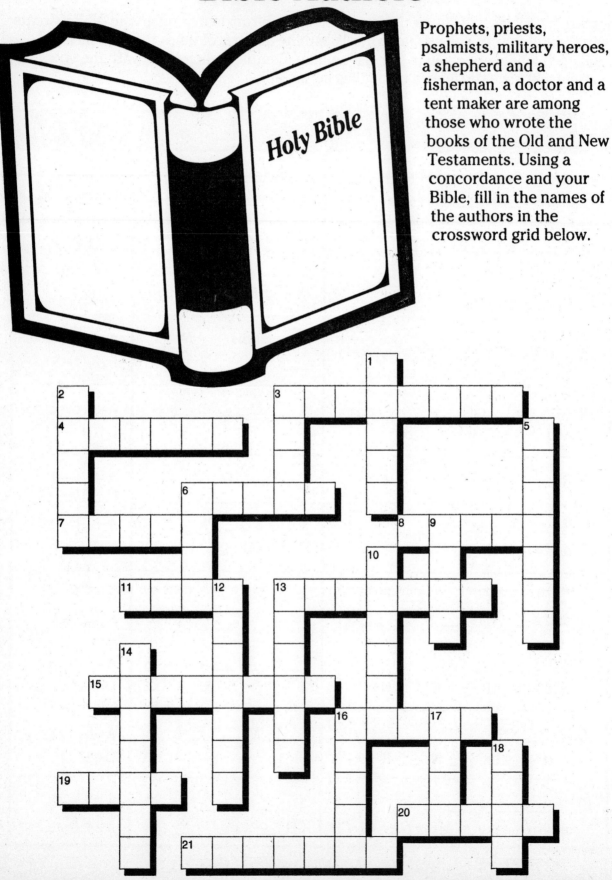

Holy Bible

Prophets, priests, psalmists, military heroes, a shepherd and a fisherman, a doctor and a tent maker are among those who wrote the books of the Old and New Testaments. Using a concordance and your Bible, fill in the names of the authors in the crossword grid below.

Across

3 This Old Testament author, the son of Hilkiah the priest, came from Anathoth; the book that has his name on it says that God set him apart before he was born to be a prophet

4 The book in the Old Testament written by this prophet has the same number of chapters in it as there are books in the Bible

6 Much of the Pentateuch (the first five books of the Bible) is thought to have been written by this Hebrew leader

7 This prophet wrote from heartbreaking experience — his wife, Gomer, was a symbol of Israel's unfaithfulness to God

8 This Bible author had many talents — he was a musician and songwriter, and also a king and mighty warrior; he wrote almost half of the longest book in the Old Testament

11 This author was a physician by profession; he wrote two books in the New Testament

13 Known mostly for his wisdom, this author also wrote many songs; one of his books in the Bible is sometimes called the Song of Songs

15 The book written by this Old Testament prophet ends with the praise that even if the fig trees, olive trees, and the fruit branches did not produce, he would still rejoice in the Lord

16 This New Testament book is about faith and works

19 Four New Testament books bear this name

20 This author was from Elkosh and wrote about the fall of Nineveh

21 The last book of the Old Testament is also the name of its author

Down

1 Jesus gave this New Testament author a name that means "rock" and gave him the keys to the kingdom

2 This prophet of Moresheth condemned the social injustices of Israel and Judah in his book in the Old Testament

3 This short book warns against false teachers

5 The author of the shortest book in the Old Testament wrote a stern word to the inhabitants of Edom

6 This disciple wrote the shortest gospel of Jesus' life

9 A "herdsman and tender of sycamore fruit" from Tekoa preached judgment to Israel

10 Moses' successor wrote the account of the children of Israel's entering, conquering, and settling the promised land

12 This priest-prophet describes his vision of a valley of dry bones in the book named for him

13 Successor to Eli, this author was the last judge and the first prophet of Israel

14 A tax collector by occupation, this man wrote the first gospel in the New Testament

16 This reluctant prophet spent three days reconsidering God's call to take the message of judgment and repentance to Nineveh

17 A scribe and priest, descendant of Hilkiah the high priest, wrote a book of the Old Testament about the rebuilding of the temple

18 The letters of this "apostle to the Gentiles" form much of the New Testament

See answer on puzzle answer page 17.

Yes, Let's

Use the simple code below to help you read these wonderful words from the Bible.

♥ = LOVE

♡ = GOD

BE♥D, LET US ♥ ONE ANOTHER, FOR ♥ IS OF ♡ ;

AND EVERYONE WHO ♥S IS BORN OF ♡ AND KNOWS ♡.

HE WHO DOES NOT ♥ DOES NOT KNOW ♡, FOR ♡ IS ♥.

. . . BE♥D, IF ♡ SO ♥D US, WE ALSO OUGHT TO ♥ ONE

ANOTHER. *(1 John 4:7–8,11)*

Can you write a message below about God, love, and other people,
using the same code?

_____

_____

_____

See answer on puzzle answer page 17.

Sacrifice and Victory

Solve the puzzle below to reveal the name of a place that is both a place of sacrifice and a place of great victory!

 — R = __ __

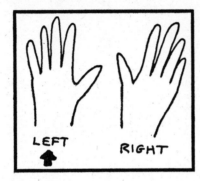 — EFT = __

 — LLEY = __ __

 — A = __ __

Write the word here:

__ __ __ __ __ __

See answer on puzzle answer page 17.

She Was Astonished

When the Queen of Sheba came to visit King Solomon, she was astonished at all she saw! See how many of the things you can find that she admired during her visit — before you use the Word Pool! You can read about this story in 1 Kings 10:1–10.

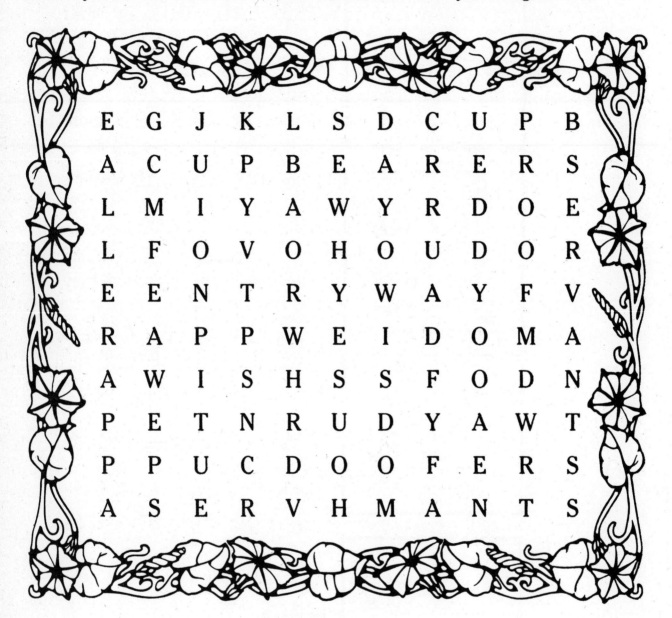

```
E  G  J  K  L  S  D  C  U  P  B
A  C  U  P  B  E  A  R  E  R  S
L  M  I  Y  A  W  Y  R  D  O  E
L  F  O  V  O  H  O  U  D  O  R
E  E  N  T  R  Y  W  A  Y  F  V
R  A  P  P  W  E  I  D  O  M  A
A  W  I  S  H  S  S  F  O  D  N
P  E  T  N  R  U  D  Y  A  W  T
P  P  U  C  D  O  O  F  E  R  S
A  S  E  R  V  H  M  A  N  T  S
```

Word Pool

WISDOM   HOUSE   FOOD
SERVICE of his waiters   APPAREL
CUPBEARERS   Seating of his SERVANTS
ENTRYWAY

See answer on puzzle answer page 17.

Balaam's Problem

The story of Balaam in Numbers 22 has several surprises. See if you can unscramble the letters of the words in bold print in the story below to find out what happened.

Balaam was asked to travel to see the **NGKI** of the **EBOAMTIS**. The **NGKI** needed his advice about how to deal with the Israelites who were moving into his country. But God did not want Balaam to go, even though some really important people begged him to make the trip.

Finally, God told Balaam he could go only if the men asked him one more time, and he was to follow God's strict instructions on what to say and do.

Well, Balaam got in a hurry. He packed up and left early the next morning before the men asked him to go again.

Balaam was riding his **KYDENO.** All of a sudden the animal headed off the **ORAD** and into a **LIEDF.** Balaam tried his best to steer her back on the **ORAD**, but she moved to one side and crushed Balaam's **OTOF** against the wall they were passing.

This made Balaam very angry, and he hit the **KYDENO** with his **FATFS**. But the animal was afraid of something on the **ORAD** that Balaam could not see; it was an **LEGAN.** The **KYDENO** was so afraid that she lay down right in the **ORAD** with Balaam still on her.

And after Balaam hit her again, the most surprising thing happened. The Lord gave the animal the ability to **KEPAS** to Balaam.

To find out what Balaam's animal had to say to him, read Numbers 22:28-31.

NGKI = __ __ __ __

EBOAMTIS = __ __ __ __ __ __ __ __

KYDENO = __ __ __ __ __ __

ORAD = __ __ __ __

LIEDF = __ __ __ __ __

OTOF = __ __ __ __

FATFS = __ __ __ __ __

LEGAN = __ __ __ __ __

KEPAS = __ __ __ __ __

See answer on puzzle answer page 17.

Bible Ts

All of the words in this crossword begin with the letter T! Try to fill in as many blanks as you can before looking up the Bible references or using the Word Pool.

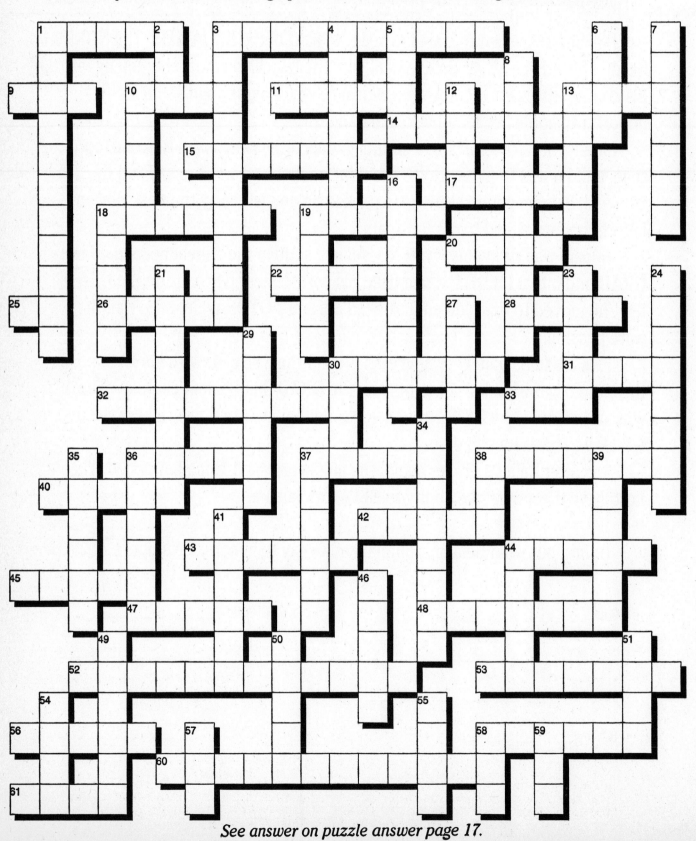

See answer on puzzle answer page 17.

Across

1 _____ and obey

3 Lead us not into it, we pray (Matthew 6:13)

9 Blessed is the _____ that binds our hearts in love

10 Joseph of Arimathea gave his to Jesus (Mark 15:43–46)

11 It is not for us to know these or seasons (Acts 1:7)

13 "Whatever I ___ you in the dark, speak in the light" (Matthew 10:27)

14 Where this is, there your heart is (Matthew 6:21)

15 Father, Son, and Holy Spirit

17 The Lord's fills the temple (Isaiah 6:1)

18 Doubting disciple

19 The Apostle Paul left his cloak there (2 Timothy 4:13)

20 These were made of potter's clay and iron, in Daniel's vision (Daniel 2:41)

22 Judah, for example

25 _____ and fro

26 The number of men cast into Nebuchadnezzar's fiery furnace (Daniel 3:24)

28 The false shepherd will do this to the hooves of his sheep (Zechariah 11:16)

30 Saul's home town (Acts 9:11))

31 _____ shalt not kill (Exodus 20:13, KJV)

32 John was imprisoned on the island of Patmos for this (Revelation 1:9)

33 One of the places where the ram's blood was to be applied (Exodus 29:20)

36 Jesus stood _____ before the Sanhedrin, Herod, or Pilate

37 "Show me Your ways, O Lord; ___ me Your paths" (Psalm 25:4)

38 "The thorn and ___ shall grow on their altars" (Hosea 10:8)

40 "Jesus Christ is the same yesterday, ___, and forever" (Hebrews 13:8)

42 Short for trumpet

43 Where our heavenly Father sits (Revelation 3:21)

44 Jacob and Esau, for example

45 It makes us free (John 8:32)

47 Someday they will all be wiped away by God (Revelation 7:17)

48 The apostle Paul's traveling companion; he also received two letters from Paul (Acts 16:1–4)

52 We are to let our requests to God be made known with this (Philippians 4:6)

53 Jesus said the moneychangers had made the temple a den of ___ (Mark 11:17)

56 The day He arose

58 Abraham gave this (pl.) to Melchizedek (Genesis 14:20)

60 The church in this city received two letters from the apostle Paul

61 We are to do this to the spirits (1 John 4:1)

Down

1 "In the world you will have ___" (John 16:33)

2 The number of days Purim is celebrated (Esther 9:26–27)

3 The one in which Moses conferred with God was named "witness" (Numbers 17:7–8)

4 He came to Jesus in the wilderness (Matthew 4:3)

5 The Lord's "eyelids ___ the sons of men" (Psalm 11:4)

6 Zacchaeus's viewing place (Luke 19:1–4)

7 Better invested than buried (Matthew 25:15)

8 Old and New

10 Adam and Eve were told neither to eat nor ___ the fruit of the tree (Genesis 3:3)

12 Abraham was sitting here when the Lord appeared to him (Genesis 18:1)

13 ___figuration or ___gression

16 The wise woman makes this for herself (Proverbs 31:22)

18 Judah's were called "whiter than milk" (Genesis 49:12)

19 These appeared when the grain sprouted (Matthew 13:26)

21 The place where a poor widow gave two mites (Mark 12:41–42)

23 The way one discovers the Lord is good (Psalm 34:8)

24 Let not your heart be so (John 14:1)

27 He who sat on a white horse was called Faithful and ___ (Revelation 19:11)

29 "Do you not know that you are the ___ of God and that the Spirit of God dwells in you?" (1 Corinthians 3:16)

30 Hiram came from here to do King Solomon's bronze work (1 Kings 7:13)

34 The Lord's are of peace, to give a future and a hope! (Jeremiah 29:11)

35 Every one of these will one day confess Jesus as Lord (Philippians 2:11)

36 What Jesus did when He sat down in the temple (John 8:2)

37 Jesus distributed the loaves after He had given this (John 6:11)

38 The part of Jacob's ladder that reached to heaven (Genesis 28:12)

39 The number of gerahs that make a shekel (Exodus 30:13)

41 Jesus' mock crown was made of this (John 19:5)

44 "Confidence in an unfaithful man in time of trouble is like a bad ___" (Proverbs 25:19)

46 "Touch no unclean ___" (Isaiah 52:11)

49 The Lord said, "I will send a famine on the land, not a famine of bread, nor a ___ for water, but of hearing the words of the Lord" (Amos 8:11)

50 The Apostle Paul's "true son in our common faith" in Crete (Titus 1:4–5)

51 Moses appointed some to be "leaders of ___" (Deuteronomy 1:15)

54 You, in old English

55 "The Lord will make you the head and not the ___" (Deuteronomy 28:13)

57 Jesus said, "I am ___ light of the world" (John 8:12)

58 Zacchaeus and Matthew were both collectors of this

59 The number of lepers who cried to Jesus, "Master, have mercy on us!" (Luke 17:12)

Word Pool

TABERNACLE TAIL TALENTS TAPESTRY TARES TARSUS TASTE TAUGHT TAX TEACH TEAR TEARS TEETH
TELL TEMPLE TEMPTATION TEMPTER TEN TENS TENT TEST TEST TESTAMENTS TESTIMONY
THANKS THANKSGIVING THE THEE THESSALONICA THIEVES THING THIRD THIRST THISTLE THOMAS THORNS
THOU THOUGHTS THREE THRONE TIE TIMES TIMOTHY TITHES TITUS TO TODAY TOE TOES TOMB TONGUE
TOOTH TOP TOUCH TRAIN TRANS TREASURE TREASURY TREE TRIAL TRIBE TRIBULATION TRINITY TROAS
TROUBLED TRUE TRUMP TRUST TRUTH TWENTY TWINS TWO TYRE

True Freedom

Unscramble the letters among the balloons below to find out what truly makes us free. (See John 8:32.)

Unscrambled letters: __ __ __ __ __ __

See answer on puzzle answer page 17.

1 They will lay hands on the sick, and they will _____. *(Mark 16:18)*
    1 Down

2 Send me to Judah, to the city of my fathers' tombs, that I may _____ it. *(Nehemiah 2:5)*
    2 Down

3 You shall go forth from the city. . . . There the LORD will _____ you from the hand of your enemies. *(Micah 4:10)*
    3 Down

4 Learn to do good; seek justice, _____ the oppressor. *(Isaiah 1:17)*
    4 Across

5 For it pleased the Father that in Him [Christ] all the fullness should dwell, and by Him to _____ all things to Himself. *(Colossians 1:19–20)*
    4 Down

6 Those who wait on the LORD shall _____ their strength. *(Isaiah 40:31)*
    8 Across

7 _____ my heart in the LORD. *(Philemon 20)*
    7 Across

8 To the righteous, good shall be _____. *(Proverbs 13:21)*
    8 Down

9 You shall be called the _____ of the Breach. *(Isaiah 58:12)*
    9 Across

10 Though I walk in the midst of trouble, You will _____ me. *(Psalm 138:7)*
    10 Across

11 _____, O LORD, deliver me! Oh, save me for Your mercies' sake! *(Psalm 6:4)*
    6 Across

12 I will _____ to you the years that the swarming locust has eaten. *(Joel 2:25)*
    5 Across

Protection

Connect the dots below to reveal how Jesus said He would like to protect the people of Jerusalem. (See Matthew 23:37.)

Now solve the puzzle on the next page to discover what Jesus said about Jerusalem.

Stones and Eggs

In the pile below, you'll find both stones and eggs. First, separate the stones from the eggs. Then put the "stone" words and the "egg" words into order to show what Jesus said about the city He loved. (See Matthew 23:37.)

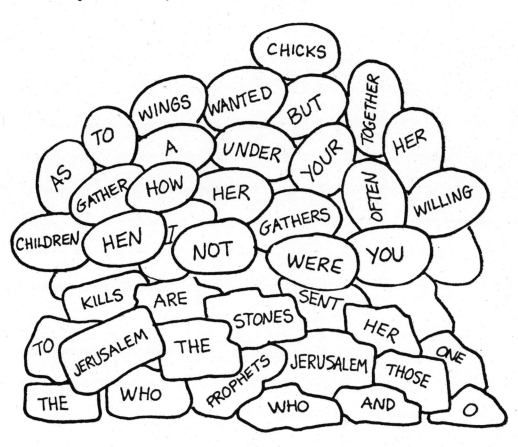

Stone words:

_____

Stone words in order:

_____

Egg words:

_____

Egg words in order:

_____

See answer on puzzle answer page 18.

When We Pray

Jesus taught His disciples how to pray. Fill in the blanks of His prayer below (taken from Matthew 6:9–13) and then use those words to complete the crossword grid.

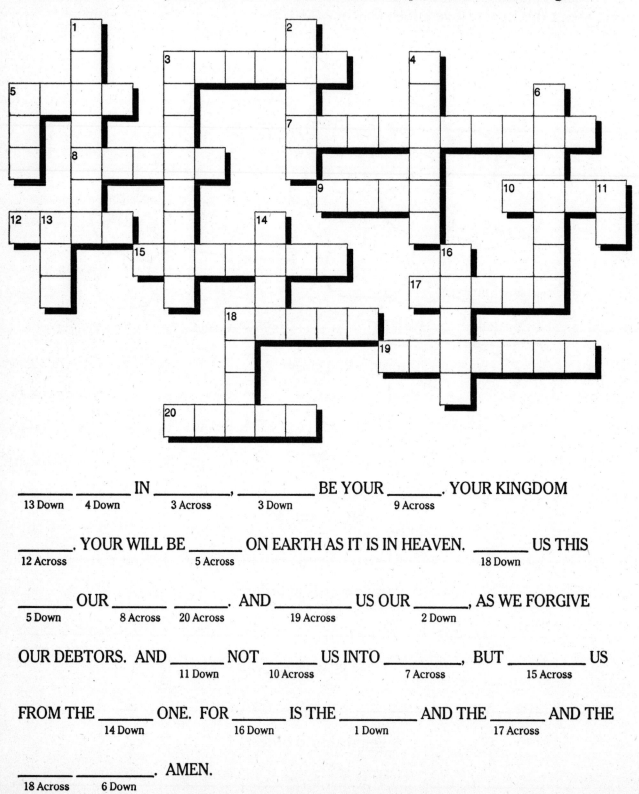

_____ _____ IN _____, _____ BE YOUR _____. YOUR KINGDOM
13 Down   4 Down   3 Across   3 Down   9 Across

_____. YOUR WILL BE _____ ON EARTH AS IT IS IN HEAVEN. _____ US THIS
12 Across   5 Across   18 Down

_____ OUR _____ _____. AND _____ US OUR _____, AS WE FORGIVE
5 Down   8 Across   20 Across   19 Across   2 Down

OUR DEBTORS. AND _____ NOT _____ US INTO _____, BUT _____ US
                 11 Down   10 Across   7 Across   15 Across

FROM THE _____ ONE. FOR _____ IS THE _____ AND THE _____ AND THE
         14 Down   16 Down   1 Down   17 Across

_____ _____. AMEN.
18 Across   6 Down

See answer on puzzle answer page 18.

My Name Is

God spoke to Solomon saying, "Ask! What shall I give you?" and the Scripture says Solomon's reply "pleased the LORD." (See 1 Kings 3.)   First complete the clues below from the book of Proverbs. Then, write your answers in the blanks (the first answer goes in the first line of blanks, and so forth), and you will find out what Solomon asked for that pleased the Lord.

1. I will deliver you from the __ __ __ of evil (2:10–12)

2. I am beyond comparison, better than __ __ __ __ __ __ (8:11)

3. Whoever __ __ __ __ __ me, makes his father rejoice (29:3)

4. Look to the __ __ __ __, and you will find me (2:6)

5. These people despise me: __ __ __ __ __ (1:7)

6. Happy is the __ __ __ who finds me (3:13)

Who am I ?

1. __ __ __ __

2. __ __ __ __ __

3. __ __ __ __ __

4. __ __ __

5. __ __ __

6. __ __ __

See answer on puzzle answer page 18.

Judgment

Christ was very clear about how we are to judge other people.
To find out what He said in John 8:7, use the code box to
decode each letter.

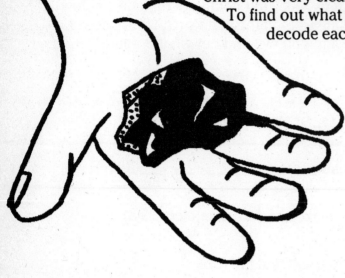

ZD VZG WY

VWPZGLP YWM

UKGMB JGL, NDP

ZWK PZFGV U

YPGMD UP

ZDF AWFYP.

___ ___ ___

___ ___ ___ ___

___ ___ ___ ___,

___ ___ ___

___ ___ ___

___ ___ ___ ___.

Code Box

A = F	B = G	C = Q	D = E	E = P	F = R	G = O
H = D	I = V	J = Y	K = M	L = U	M = N	N = L
O = C	P = T	Q = B	R = K	S = J	T = X	U = A
	V = W	W = I	X = Z	Y = S	Z = H	

See answer on puzzle answer page 18.

All the Day Long

Use your Bible to solve the number equation below:

When the Samaritans had come to Him,
they urged Him to stay with them;
and He stayed there ___ days *(John 4:40)* _____

Please, let us go ___ days' journey into
the wilderness, that we may sacrifice to
the Lord *(Exodus 3:18)*   X   _____

When he [David] had eaten, his strength
came back to him; for he had eaten no
bread nor drunk any water for ___ days
(1 Samuel 30:12)   X   _____

Moses was on the mountain ___ days and
___ nights *(Exodus 24:18)*   +   _____

So they called these days Purim . . . the
Jews established and imposed it . . . that
without fail they should celebrate these
___ days every year *(Esther 9:26–27)*   −   _____

It happened after ___ days that the word
of the Lord came to Jeremiah
(Jeremiah 42:7)   −   _____

You shall march around the city, all you
men of war; you shall go all around the
city once. This you shall do ___ days
(Joshua 6:3)   +   _____

The number of days it took for Nehemiah
and the Israelites to rebuild the walls
of Jerusalem *(Nehemiah 6:15)*   =   _____

See answer on puzzle answer page 18.

Lunch Host

The 10 words below are all clues to the name of a famous person in the Bible. If you know who the person is after unscrambling the first word, give yourself 100 points; if you know the name of the person after two clues, give yourself 90 points, and so on. Color in the number of points you get on the thermometer. (If you need help to unscramble the words, you can read this story in your Bible in Luke 19:1–10.)

100 points
REIJHCO __ __ __ __ __ __ __

90 points
ALSOVATIN __ __ __ __ __ __ __ __ __

80 points
FOFRUOLD __ __ __ __ __ __ __ __

70 points
EATCXOLLOCTR __ __ __

__ __ __ __ __ __ __ __ __ __ (2 words)

60 points
HIRC __ __ __ __

50 points
SNENIR __ __ __ __ __ __

40 points
USEGT __ __ __ __ __

30 points
OEMACYSR __ __ __ __ __ __ __ __

20 points
EMCLIBD __ __ __ __ __ __ __

10 points
HRSOT __ __ __ __ __

100
90
80
70
60
50
40
30
20
10

The name of the person is:

AHACZCSEU __ __ __ __ __ __ __ __ __

See answer on puzzle answer page 18.

Trees

"The LORD God said, 'Behold, the man has become like one of Us, to know good and evil. And now, lest he put out his hand and take also of the tree of life, and eat' . . . therefore the LORD God sent him out . . . to till the ground from which he was taken" (Genesis 3:22–23). The letters that spell out TREE OF LIFE have been placed in the puzzle grid below. Now, fill in the blanks with the names of the other trees in the Word Pool. The circled letters will reveal the place from which man was sent!

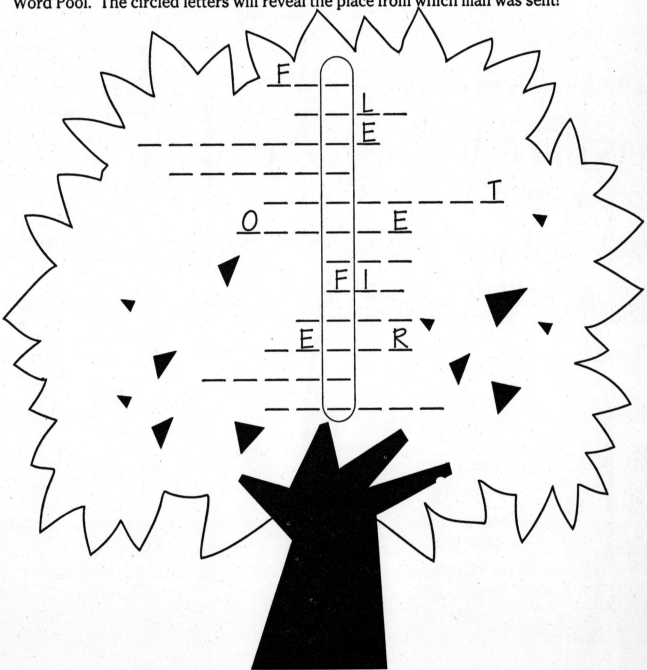

Word Pool
ALMOND APPLE BANANA CEDAR CHESTNUT FIG FIR OAK
ORANGE PALM PEAR SYCAMORE

See answer on puzzle answer page 18.

Remembered

In the Bible, God gave the people many things to help them remember who He is and what He had done for them. Fill in the blanks of these verses with the words from the Word Barrel, and then place the words in their proper place on the crossword grid.

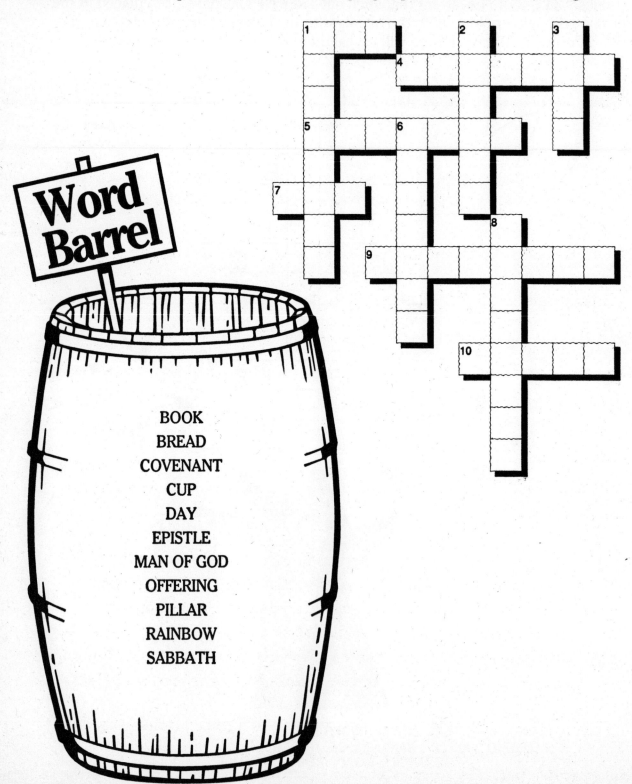

Word Barrel

BOOK

BREAD

COVENANT

CUP

DAY

EPISTLE

MAN OF GOD

OFFERING

PILLAR

RAINBOW

SABBATH

1. The _____ (4 Across) shall be in the cloud, and I will look on it to remember the everlasting covenant between God and every living creature of all flesh that is on the earth *(Genesis 9:16)*

2. God heard their groaning, and God remembered His _____ (1 Down) with Abraham, with Isaac, and with Jacob *(Exodus 2:24)*

3. Moses said to the people, "Remember this _____ (7 Across) in which you went out of Egypt" *(Exodus 13:3)*

4. Remember the _____ (6 Down) day, to keep it holy *(Exodus 20:8)*

5. It is a grain offering of jealousy, an _____ (8 Down) for remembering, for bringing iniquity to remembrance *(Numbers 5:15)*

6. Absalom . . . set up a _____ (2 Down) for himself, which is in the King's Valley. For he said, "I have no son to keep my name in remembrance" *(2 Samuel 18:18)*

7. She said to Elijah, "What have I to do with you, O ___ ___ ___ (9 Across)? Have you come to me to bring my sin to remembrance, and to kill my son?" *(1 Kings 17:18)*
   (3 words)

8. The LORD listened and heard them; so a _____ (3 Down) of remembrance was written before Him for those who fear the LORD and who meditate on His name *(Malachi 3:16)*

9. The Lord Jesus on the same night in which He was betrayed took _____; (10 Across) and when He had given thanks, He broke it and said, "Take, eat; this is My body which is broken for you; do this in remembrance of Me." In the same manner He also took the _____ (1 Across) after supper, saying, "This cup is the new covenant in My blood. This do, as often as you drink it, in remembrance of Me" *(1 Corinthians 11:23–25)*

10. Beloved, I now write to you this second _____ (5 Across) (in both of which I stir up your pure minds by way of reminder) *(2 Peter 3:1)*

See answer on puzzle answer page 18.

The Best

A centurion came to Jesus and said, "Lord, my servant is lying
39   18 47   59   12   53 60   2   46 55 9

at home paralyzed, dreadfully tormented." Jesus said, "I will
      38   37 13   7   29   54   3   32   10

come and heal him." The centurion said,"Lord, I am not worthy
  6   51   43   48   57 24 1   31 21   26

that You should come under my roof. But only speak a word,
42   17   30   28 41   11   5

and my servant will be healed. For I also am a man under
16   22 44   23 45   27 19   52   49

authority, having soldiers under me. I say to one, 'Go,' and he
4   40 20 50   8   33   36

goes; and to another, 'Come,' and he comes."
15   14   25   58   35 34   56

(See Matthew 8:5–10.)

When Jesus heard these words, He marveled. Solve the message below
(using the numbers underneath the letters above) to see what
Jesus said about this man and his faith:

___ ___ ___ ___ ___ ___ ___ ___ ___, ___ ___ ___ ___ ___ ___
 1   2   3   4   5   6   7   8   9   10   11 12 13   14 15

___ ___ ___, ___ ___ ___ ___ ___ ___ ___ ___ ___ ___ ___ ___ ___
16 17 18   19   20 21 22 23   24 25 26   27 28 29 30 31

___ ___ ___ ___ ___ ___ ___ ___ ___ ___ ___ ___ ___ ___, ___ ___ ___
32 33 34 35   36 37 38 39 40   41 42 43 44 45   46 47 48

___ ___ ___ ___ ___ ___ ___ ___ ___ ___ ___ ___ ___!
49 50 51 52   53 54 55   56 57 58 59 60

See answer on puzzle answer page 18.

For the Entry

As Jesus approached Jerusalem, He said to two of His disciples, "Go into the village opposite you, and immediately you will find a donkey tied, and a colt with her. Loose them and bring them to Me" (Matthew 21:2). Help the disciples find the donkey and colt in the city below.

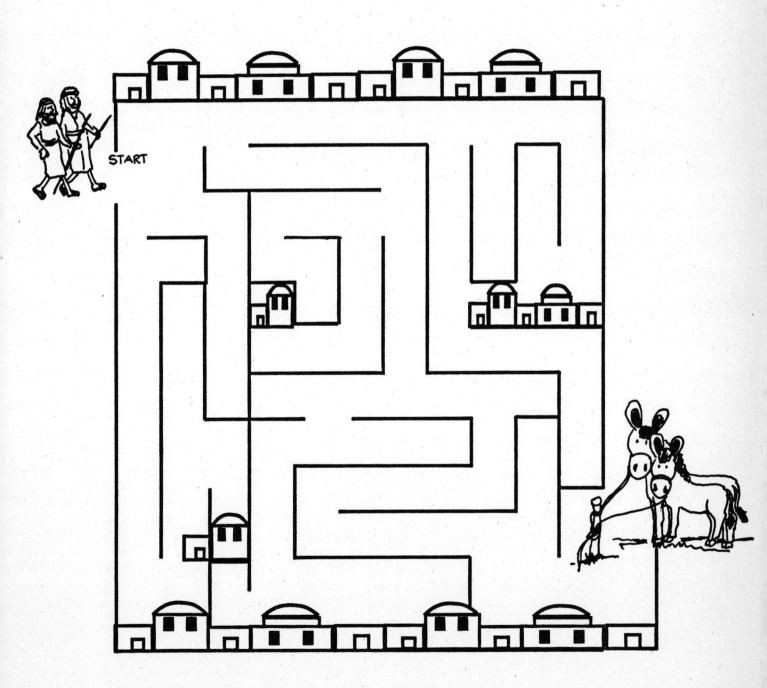

START

What Am I?

One of the most important ways God speaks to us is through what He says in the Bible. There are many different ways to describe the Bible. Look up the references below and you will find what Scripture says about the Bible. When you find the answers to the clues below fill in the blanks, and then you will have what the Bible is to us.

1. The ___ ___ ___ of the LORD *(Psalm 119:1)*

2. Even if some do not ___ ___ ___ ___ the word, they. . . may be won by the conduct of their wives *(1 Peter 3:1)*

3. All of the word is ___ ___ ___ ___ ___ *(Psalm 119:160)*

4. The word ___ ___ ___ ___ ___ ___ ___ forever *(1 Peter 1:25)*

5. The ___ ___ ___ ___ ___ of the Spirit *(Ephesians 6:17)*

6. The law of the LORD is ___ ___ ___ ___ ___ ___ ___ *(Psalm 19:7)*

7. The word is a ___ ___ ___ ___ ___ to my path *(Psalm 119:105)*

8. The word to Jeremiah was the ___ ___ ___ of his heart *(Jeremiah 15:16)*

9. The word is like a ___ ___ ___ ___ *(Luke 8:11)*

1. ___ ___ ___

2. ___ ___ ___ ___

3. ___ ___ ___ ___

4. ___ ___ ___ ___ ___ ___

5. ___ ___ ___ ___

6. ___ ___ ___ ___ ___ ___

7. ___ ___ ___ ___

8. ___ ___ ___

9. ___ ___ ___ ___

The Bible is the ___ ___ ___ ___ ___ ___ ___ ___ ___.

See answer on puzzle answer page 18.

Lessons All Around

The Book of Proverbs gives us many practical rules for living. The writer often uses common everyday things to illustrate his points. See if you can find these items in the picture below.

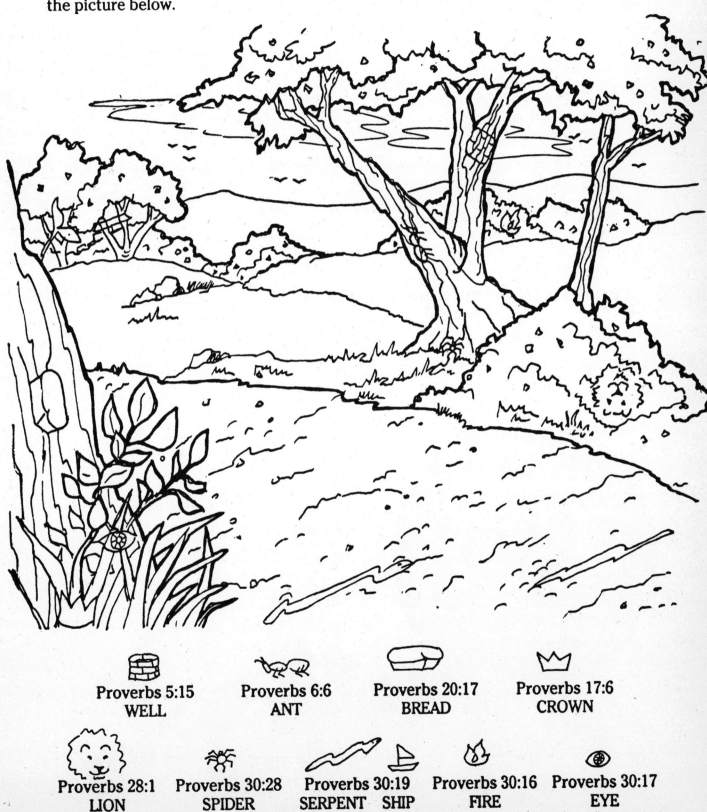

Proverbs 5:15
WELL

Proverbs 6:6
ANT

Proverbs 20:17
BREAD

Proverbs 17:6
CROWN

Proverbs 28:1
LION

Proverbs 30:28
SPIDER

Proverbs 30:19
SERPENT

Proverbs 30:19
SHIP

Proverbs 30:16
FIRE

Proverbs 30:17
EYE

The Sermon

The Sermon on the Mount contains Jesus' teaching on life in God's Kingdom, where He reigns as Lord and King. One answer is already completed for you, the rest of the answers are found in Matthew, chapters 5—7.

Across

3 Don't cast your _____ before swine

7 An _____ for an _____

8 Give your _____ in secret

9 Good #25 Across _____ God

12 There is no reward if you only _____ those who _____ you

13 Give #3 Across, pray, and fast in _____

14 First the _____, then the mote

17 Where Jesus is Lord

22 _____ in the closet, not on the street corner

23 Good trees bear good _____

24 It's impossible to serve _____ masters

25 Deeds done for another's benefit

26 God takes care of the _____, and He will also take care of you

Down

1 _____ not

2 Your _____ is where your treasure is

3 Be _____, as your Father is _____

4 You can _____ if you are persecuted, for your reward is great in Heaven

5 Christians are the _____ of the earth

6 _____ and it shall be given you

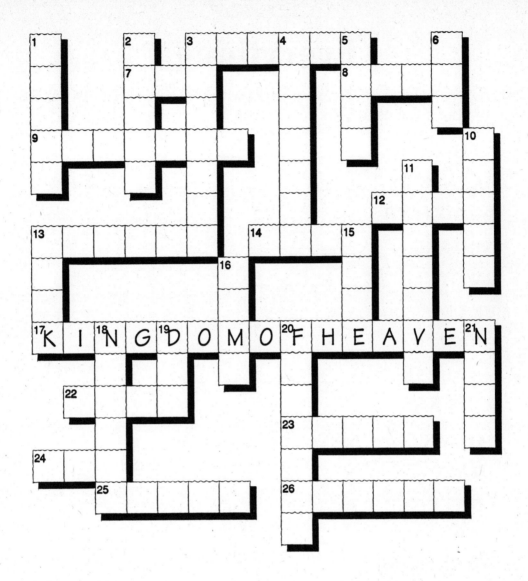

10 Love your _____ (singular)

11 _____ us our debts

13 If you _____ you will find

15 Go the second _____

16 Hallowed be Thy _____

18 The gate is straight and the way is _____

19 Don't worry about tomorrow, each _____ has enough evil

20 Jesus came to _____ the Law and the prophets

21 Your Heavenly Father knows what you _____

See answer on puzzle answer page 18.

Everything

Each of the words below has been associated with the word EVERY in the Bible. Use the Scripture Pool if you need help.

NTIETN   _ _ Ⓞ _ _ _ _
                11

LAFASEWY   Ⓞ _ _ _ _ _ _ _ _ _ (2 words)
           14

DOGOAPTH   _ _ _ _ Ⓞ _ _ _ (2 words)
                   5

NROCRE   Ⓞ _ _ _ _ _
           10

RWOD   _ _ Ⓞ _
              7

ENKE   _ _ _ Ⓞ
                 9

EUGNTO   _ _ _ _ _ _

PROUPSE   _ _ _ Ⓞ _ _ _
                 3

ACLEP   _ _ _ _ _

SIIOVN   _ _ _ Ⓞ _ _
                 2

IMALFY   Ⓞ _ _ _ _ _
           8

SNATI   _ _ _ _ _

NEMA   _ _ Ⓞ _
              6

ODOGROWK   Ⓞ _ _ _ _   _ _ _ _ (2 words)
           1

IEGWHT   _ _ Ⓞ _ _ _
              12

INDARNOCE _ _ Ⓞ _ _ _ _ _ _
              4

RPISIT   _ _ _ Ⓞ _ _
                 13

ERET   Ⓞ _ _ _
           15

Now place the numbered circled letters from above in the matching numbered spaces below to complete this Bible verse:

Every _ _ _ _ gift and every _ _ _ _ _ _ _
      1 2 3 4   5 6 7 8 9 10 11

_ _ _ _ is from above, and comes down from the Father of lights,
12 13 14 15

with whom there is no variation or shadow of turning. *(James 1:17)*

Scripture Pool

Ephesians 1:21   Ezekiel 12:23   Genesis 6:5   Hebrews 12:1   Isaiah 45:23   Jeremiah 51:29   1 John 4:1
Luke 6:44   Malachi 1:11   1 Peter 2:13   Philippians 4:21   Proverbs 2:9   Proverbs 7:12
Proverbs 14:15   Psalm 119:104   2 Timothy 2:21   Zechariah 12:12

See answer on puzzle answer page 19.

Our Whole Armor

In the puzzle below, first unscramble the names of the various types of armor. Then match up the pieces of armor with the spiritual characteristic that the apostle Paul described in Ephesians 6:14–17.

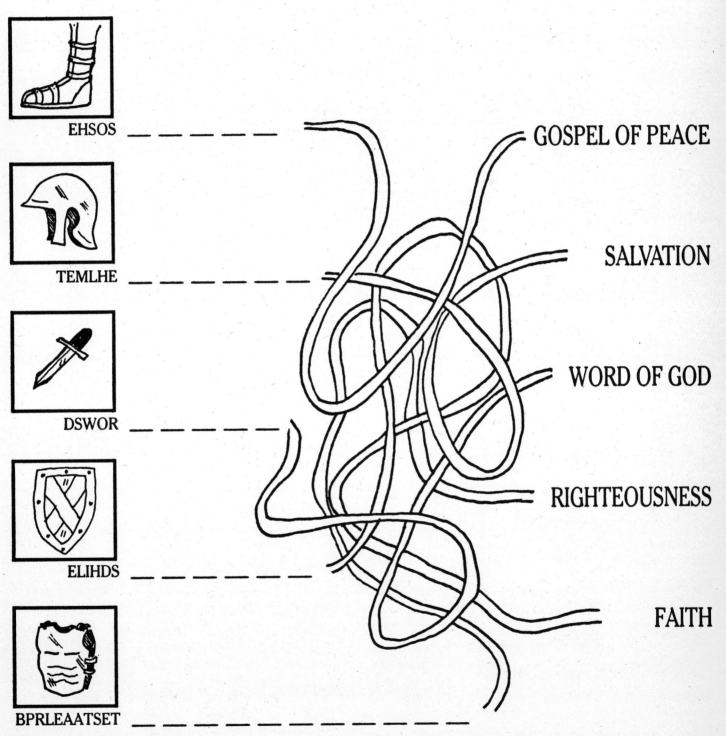

EHSOS _ _ _ _ _

TEMLHE _ _ _ _ _ _

DSWOR _ _ _ _ _

ELIHDS _ _ _ _ _ _

BPRLEAATSET _ _ _ _ _ _ _ _ _ _

GOSPEL OF PEACE

SALVATION

WORD OF GOD

RIGHTEOUSNESS

FAITH

See answer on puzzle answer page 19.

The Work of His Hands

Solve the puzzle below to discover a profession with which Jesus was very familiar. In fact, it was the profession of his earthly father, Joseph.

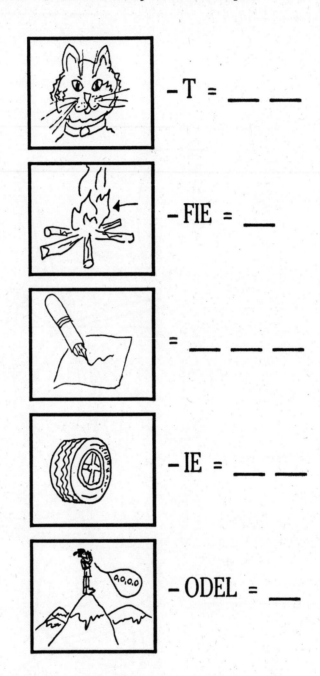

- T = __ __

- FIE = __

= __ __ __

- IE = __ __

- ODEL = __

Write all the letters here:

__ __ __ __ __ __ __ __ __

See answer on puzzle answer page 19.

Love

Use your Bible if you need more clues to solve this crossword puzzle. All the words are found in the "Love" chapter, 1 Corinthians 13.

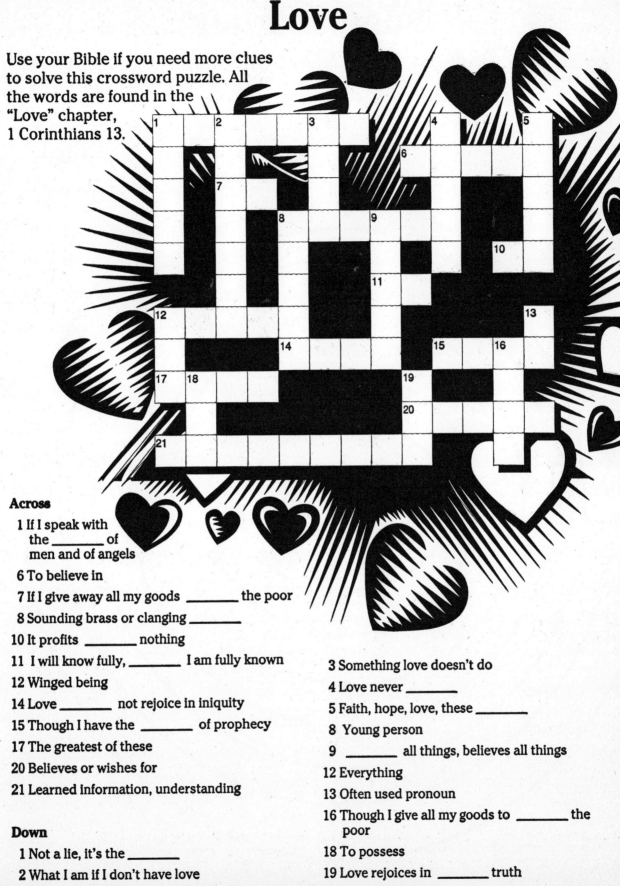

Across

1 If I speak with the _____ of men and of angels

6 To believe in

7 If I give away all my goods _____ the poor

8 Sounding brass or clanging _____

10 It profits _____ nothing

11 I will know fully, _____ I am fully known

12 Winged being

14 Love _____ not rejoice in iniquity

15 Though I have the _____ of prophecy

17 The greatest of these

20 Believes or wishes for

21 Learned information, understanding

Down

1 Not a lie, it's the _____

2 What I am if I don't have love

3 Something love doesn't do

4 Love never _____

5 Faith, hope, love, these _____

8 Young person

9 _____ all things, believes all things

12 Everything

13 Often used pronoun

16 Though I give all my goods to _____ the poor

18 To possess

19 Love rejoices in _____ truth

See answer on puzzle answer page 19.

Blind Journey

While Saul was traveling to Damascus, he was confronted by Jesus in a bright light that left Saul temporarily blind. Saul's fellow travelers had to lead him by the hand to Damascus. Help them find their way . . .

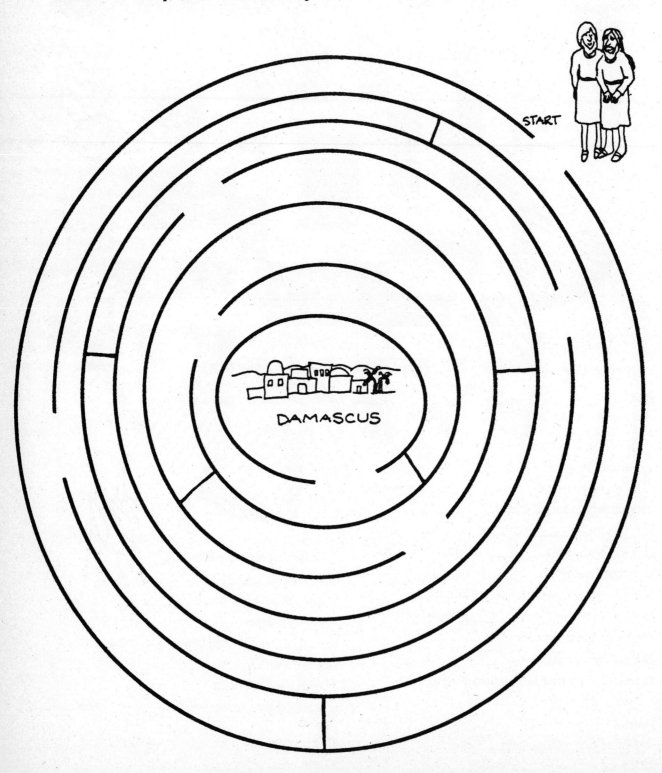

You can read about this story in Acts 9:1–19.

Job's Zoo

All the animals hidden in the picture below are mentioned in the Book of Job. Circle
each one with your pencil when you find it. You can read about these animals in
Job 38–39.

HAWK   LOCUST   LION   RAVEN   HORSE

Fire!

Fire in the Bible is used in many ways including warmth and cooking, and for worshiping God with burnt offerings. All the clues below have to do with fire.

Across

2 The Lord promised to be a "___ of fire" around Jerusalem (Zechariah 2:5)

4 A flaming arrow (Proverbs 26:18)

6 The Lord makes his ministers a "___ of fire" (Hebrews 1:7)

7 According to John, the devil ends up in a "lake of fire and ___" (Revelation 20:10)

9 The apostle John saw a fire that "came down from God out of ___" to devour Satan (Revelation 20:9)

11 The beast and false prophet are cast into a "___ of fire and brimstone" (Revelation 20:10)

12 An altar was to be used for ___ offerings (Exodus 20:24)

13 Elijah's transportation to heaven was "a ___ of fire" in a whirlwind (2 Kings 2:11)

15 One of the plagues that fell on Egypt was "fire mingled with the ___" (Exodus 9:24)

16 "He shall burn all its ___ on the altar, like the ___ of the sacrifice of peace offering" (Leviticus 4:26)

17 "You shall anoint the ___ of the burnt offering and all its utensils" (Exodus 40:10)

19 By night, the Lord led the Israelites in a "___ of fire" (Exodus 13:21)

20 Residue after a fire, often used with sackcloth to show mourning or repentance, as in Jonah 3:6

22 On the Day of Pentecost, "there appeared to them divided ___ as of fire" (Acts 2:3)

23 The Passover lamb was to be "___ in fire" (Exodus 12:9)

24 "Those who dwell in the cities of Israel will go out and set on fire and ___ the weapons . . . and they will make fires with them for seven years" (Ezekiel 39:9)

25 "Death and ___ were cast into the lake of fire" (Revelation 20:14)

26 The lampstand in the tabernacle was made of pure ___ (Exodus 25:31)

27 When Shadrach, Meshach, and Abed-Nego came out of the fiery furnace, "the hair of their head was not ___" (Daniel 3:27)

Down

1 The Lord said to Isaiah, "Do not fear or be fainthearted for the two stubs of ___ firebrands" (Isaiah 7:4)

3 A ___ in the temple was made of pure gold or silver (1 Chronicles 28:15)

5 The type of fire to which the "cursed" are sent in a parable told by Jesus (Matthew 25:41)

6 To add air to flames

7 The angel of the Lord appeared to Moses "in a flame of fire from the midst of a ___" (Exodus 3:2)

8 Pure olive ___ was used in the tabernacle lamps (Exodus 27:20)

9 "God did not spare the angels who sinned, but cast them down to ___" (2 Peter 2:4)

10 "When Moses prayed to the LORD, the fire was ___" (Numbers 11:2)

14 "The chariots come with flaming ___" (Nahum 2:3)

16 Nebuchadnezzar threw Shadrach, Meshach, and Abed-Nego into a ___ heated "seven times more" (Daniel 3:19)

18 Enemy nations are described as a "fire of ___" in Psalm 118:12

21 When Shadrach, Meshach, and Abed-Nego came out of Nebuchadnezzar's furnace, "the ___ of fire was not on them" (Daniel 3:27)

23 The sound of a blazing fire

See answer on puzzle answer page 19.

Great Grapes

The spies that Moses sent to the promised land came to the Valley of Eshcol and there they cut a branch with a very large cluster of grapes. Connect the two sets of dots (1–21 and A–X) to show how they brought the grapes back to Moses. You can read about this in Numbers 13:23.

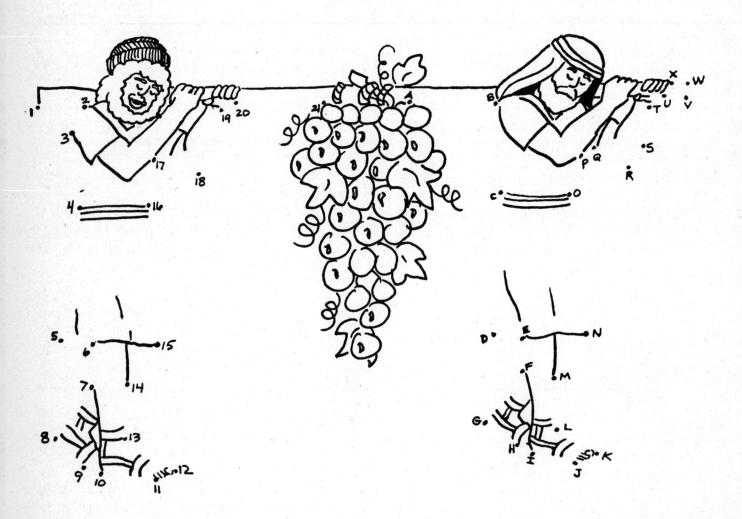

Puzzle 3

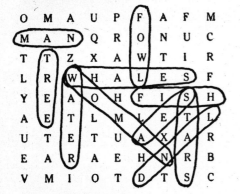

```
O  M  A  U  P  F  A  F  M
M  A  N  Q  R  O  N  U  C
T  T  Z  X  A  W  T  I  R
L  R  W  H  A  L  E  S  F
Y  E  A  O  H  F  I  S  H
A  E  T  L  M  L  E  T  L
U  T  E  T  U  A  X  A  R
E  R  A  E  H  N  R  B  C
V  M  I  O  T  D  T  S  C
```

Puzzle 5

Praise the Lord!
Give thanks to the Lord!
Great is the Lord!
God is our Refuge and Strength!

Puzzle 6

Puzzle 7

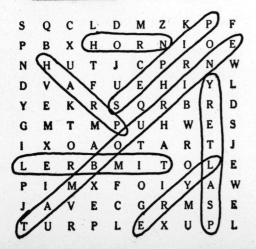

Puzzle 8

JOY
LOVE
PEACE
FAITH

Puzzle 9

Puzzle 10

PALM Exodus 15:27
OLIVE Judges 9:9
FIG Deuteronomy 8:8
CEDAR 1 Kings 10:27

Puzzle 11

Blessed is the man that walketh not in the counsel of the ungodly, nor standeth in the way of sinners, nor sitteth in the seat of the scornful. (Psalm 1:1)

Puzzle 12

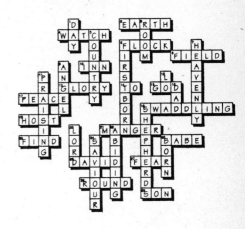

Puzzle 14

```
P  L  R  S  W  I  A  S  H  O  E  R  X  U  M
T  R  H  E  A  D  B  A  N  D  A  N  A  S  K
J  E  L  D  I  F  F  Y  O  L  W  R  K  B  A
A  S  W  E  S  D  C  I  P  M  E  A  C  N  L
H  E  P  Y  T  B  O  H  G  R  O  V  A  E  S
V  E  I  L  T  C  D  E  R  F  L  R  T  S  C  F
K  L  I  C  L  P  A  J  C  E  E  N  C  I  G
S  P  A  O  O  T  R  E  C  A  L  L  A  H  N  M
N  M  E  A  T  V  B  D  A  I  O  U  F  Y  B
R  I  N  G  H  B  M  A  N  T  L  E  R  F  T
S  W  U  T  C  B  I  H  Y  R  N  O  P  E  W
M  N  E  A  I  E  B  L  P  I  D  S  N  C  S
S  W  D  O  H  P  E  M  N  H  R  N  E  O  M
O  S  R  C  H  P  O  W  E  S  O  F  A  P  I
I  R  K  P  F  A  E  N  M  B  A  E  W  T  H
```

Puzzle 15

LET THE CHILDREN COME TO ME, AND DO NOT FORBID THEM, FOR OF SUCH IS THE KINGDOM OF GOD. (LUKE 18:16, NKJ)

Puzzle 17

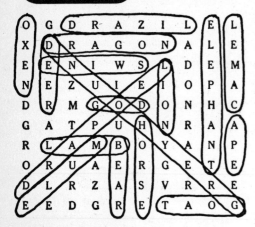

Puzzle 19

1. Zacchaeus, hurry and come down, for today I must stay at your house.

2. Zacchaeus received Jesus joyfully.

Puzzle 20

TABERNACLE

Puzzle 22

Puzzle 23

For God so loved the world that He gave His only begotten Son. (John 3:16)

Puzzle 24

Angel #4 is Gabriel.

Puzzle 26

Trust in the Lord with all your heart, and lean not on your own understanding; In all your ways acknowledge Him, and He shall direct your paths. (Proverbs 3:5-6, NKJ)

Puzzle 27

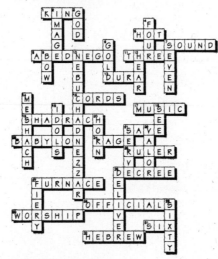

Puzzle 28

PRAY AT ALL TIMES

Puzzle 29

FLOUR (1 Samuel 1:24)
HONEY (Matthew 3:4)
CORN (Genesis 42:25)
FRUITS (2 Kings 19:29)
FISH (Luke 24:42)

Puzzle 30

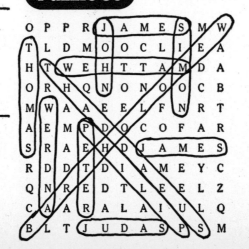

Puzzle 31

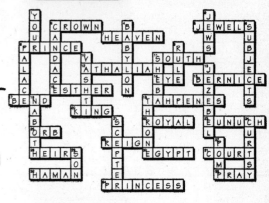

Puzzle 32

LAMB
APE
LION
GOAT
SNAKE
DOG
COW
FOX
MOUSE
RABBIT
OXEN

Circled letters spell MAN AND WOMAN

Puzzle 33

MAN SHALL NOT LIVE BY BREAD ALONE, BUT BY EVERY WORD THAT PROCEEDS OUT OF THE MOUTH OF GOD. (MATTHEW 4:4, NKJ)

Puzzle 35

LOVE ONE ANOTHER.

Puzzle 36

2 x 40 x 10 + 2 + 250 - 600 + 20 = 70

Puzzle 37

Fear not.

Puzzle 38

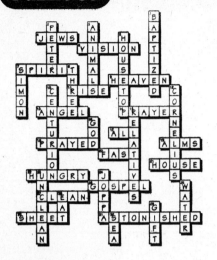

Puzzle 40

DIAMOND
EMERALD
SAPPHIRE
PEARL
RUBY
GOLD
SILVER

Puzzle 42

DESTROY THE TEMPLE

and

REBUILD THE TEMPLE

Puzzle 43

Puzzle 44

JOHN
MATTHEW
MARK
PAUL
LUKE
JUDE
PETER
JAMES

LETTER

Puzzle 45

KINGDOM OF GOD

Puzzle 46

At least 150 words can be created out of the phrase EVERLASTING LIFE:

age, agile, ail, air, aisle, ale, all, alter, are, as, at, ate, eat, elite, eternal, ever, everlasting, fail, fair, fall, falter, far, fast, fasten, fat, fate, fear, feast, feel, feet, fell, fella, fever, fig, file, filet, fill, filler, filter, fir, fire, first, fist, five, flat, flirt, fragile, gale, gall, gate, gave, get, gift, gill(s), gilt, gist, give, if, ill, ire, is, isle, it, lag, lair, last, late, leaf, least, leave, leer, left, liar, lie, life, lift, lifter, list, live, liver, raft, rag, rail, rat, rate, rave, real, rear, reef, reel, rest, rifle, rig, safe, sag, sail, sale, sat, save, sea, seal, sear, see, seel, seer, sell, seller, serf, serge, serve, sieve, sift, sir, sit, site, stag, stale, stall, star, start, steal, steel, steer, stellar, stifle, stile, still, stir, tag, tail, tall, tear, tee, tell, teller, terse, tie, till, tiller, trill, vale, valet, vase, vast, veer, veil, verse, vest, vie, virile, vista

Puzzle 48

Puzzle 49

HOSEA
ISAIAH
OBADIAH
NAHUM
AMOS
JONAH

Puzzle 52

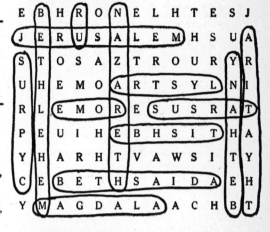

Puzzle 53

Joseph ....Coat of many colors
Moses ....Stone tablets
Adam and Eve ....Apple
Noah ....Rainbow

Puzzle 54

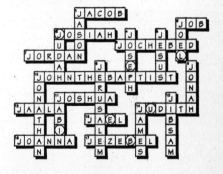

Puzzle 55

JUBILEE

PUZZLE ANSWERS

Puzzle 56

Follow Me, and I will make you fishers of men. (Matthew 4:19, NKJ)

Puzzle 58

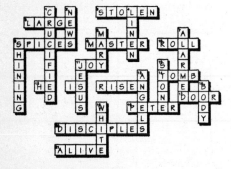

Puzzle 59

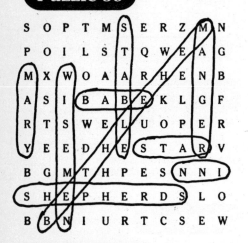

Puzzle 60

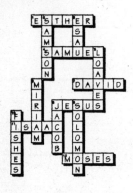

Puzzle 61

MIRIAM
SAMUEL
DAVID
MOSES
JESUS
ISAAC
ESAU
GERSHOM
JACOB
ESTHER
SAMSON

Children are a heritage from the Lord. (Psalm 127:3, NKJ)

Puzzle 62

Let the little children come to Me, and do not forbid them; for of such is the kingdom of heaven. (Matthew 19:14, NKJ)

Puzzle 63

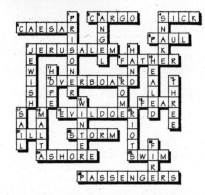

Puzzle 65

The effective, fervent prayer of a righteous man avails much. (James 5:16, NKJ)

Puzzle 66

PATMOS
MALTA
CYPRUS
CAUDA
CRETE

Puzzle 67

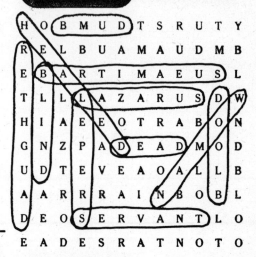

Puzzle 70

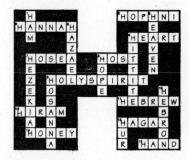

Puzzle 71

If any man will come after me, let him deny himself, and take up his cross and follow me. (Matthew 16:24)

Jesus saith unto him, I am the way, the truth, and the life: no man cometh unto the father, but by me. (John 14:6)

Puzzle 73

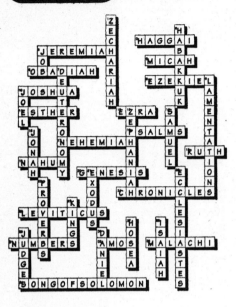

Puzzle 74

Sarah and Abraham
Eve and Adam
Isaac and Rebekah
Boaz and Ruth

Puzzle 75

On that day the priest shall make atonement for you, to cleanse you, that you may be clean from all your sins before the Lord. (Leviticus 16:30, NKJ)

Puzzle 76

Commit your works to the Lord, and your thoughts will be established. (Proverbs 16:3, NKJ)

Puzzle 78

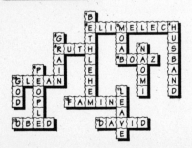

Puzzle 79

This is the King of the Jews

Puzzle 80

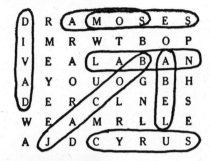

Puzzle 81

13 - 8 x 4 + 41 + 2 + 9 = 7

Puzzle 83

Puzzle 84

At least 75 words can be made from the letters in the word ISRAELITES:

ail, air, aisle, ale, alter, are, ass, asset, ate, elite, is, isle, it, lair, lass, last, late, lease, least, leer, less, lest, let, liar, lie, list, loser, rail, rain, raise, rat, rate, real, reel, rest, rise, riser, sail, sale, sat, sea, seal, sear, seat, see, seer, set, silt, sir, sire, sis, sister, sit, slat, slate, slit, stain, stale, stare, steer, stein, stir, tail, rale, tar, tare, tear, tease, tee, teel, terse, tiara, tie, tile, tire

Puzzle 86

Watch and pray, lest you enter into temptation. The spirit indeed is willing, but the flesh is weak. (Matthew 26:41, NKJ)

Puzzle 87

HOSANNA

Puzzle 88

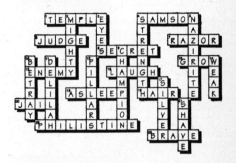

Puzzle 89

David .... Lions' den
Moses .... Rainbow
Noah .... Coat of many colors
Adam and Eve .... The Temple
Jonah .... Angel

Puzzle 90

Abraham
Isaac
Jacob
Judah
Perez
Hezron
Ram
Amminadab
Nahshon
Salmon
Boaz
Obed
Jesse
David

Joseph

Puzzle 91

Puzzle 92

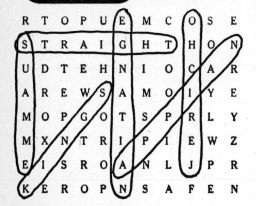

Puzzle 93

Puzzle 96

Puzzle 99

Heaven and earth shall pass away: but my words shall not pass away. (Mark 13:31)

Puzzle 100

YOUNG
MAID
BETROTHED
MOTHER
NAZARETH
JESUS
VIRGIN

MARY

Puzzle 101

CREATION
FRUIT
TREE
SERPENT
GARDEN
ADAM
EVE

EDEN

Puzzle 102

BLINDED
PERSECUTOR
DAMASCUS
PRISONER
MISSIONARY
LETTERS
SAUL

PAUL

Puzzle 103

HOLY FAMILY
JOSEPH
MOSES
PASSOVER
NATION
PLAGUES
PHARAOH

EGYPT

Puzzle 104

ANOINTED
SHEPHERD
KING
VICTORY
PSALMS
SLING
GOLIATH

DAVID

Puzzle 105

DAVID
SLAUGHTER
CENSUS
STAR
WISE MEN
INN
BIRTH

BETHLEHEM

Puzzle 106

CUP
RIVER
SEAS
RAIN
WASH
BAPTISM
BOATS

WATER

Puzzle 107

SLAVERY
PHARAOH
JACOB
FAVORITE
DREAMS
COLORS
COAT

JOSEPH

Puzzle 108

JOY
FEASTS
TEMPLE
HILLS
CRUCIFIXION
CITY
ZION

JERUSALEM

Puzzle 109

BABY
MIRIAM
BASKET
FLOAT
RIVER
RESCUED
LEADER

MOSES

Puzzle 110

BELLS
HOLY PLACE
SACRIFICES
PRIESTS
WORSHIP
WILDERNESS
TENT

TABERNACLE

Puzzle 111

SAINTS
GLORY
PERFECT
FOREVER
ANGELS
THRONE
NEW JERUSALEM

HEAVEN

Puzzle 112

GAP
BATTLE
MIDIANITES
SHOUT
LAMPS
PITCHERS
FLEECES

GIDEON

Puzzle 113

WATER
MIRACLES
STILL
NETS
FISHING
STORM
SEA

GALILEE

Puzzle 114

JESUS
FARMER
FRUIT
ABIDE
BRANCHES
PRUNE
GRAPES

VINE

Puzzle 115

BEAUTIFUL
EASTERN
PEARLY
CITY
GUARD
CLOSED
ENTRY

GATE

Puzzle 116

Puzzle 117

SANHEDRIN

Puzzle 118

$7 \times 2 \times 2 \times 17 + 150 - 40 + 10 + 3 + 4 - 3 = 600$

Puzzle 119

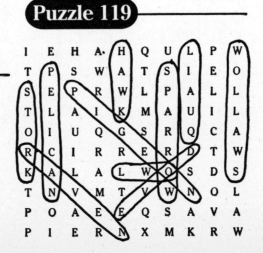

Puzzle 120

THANKSGIVING

aging, ah, akin, an, angst, ankh, ant, as, ash, ask, at, gag, gain, gait, gang, gas, gash, giant, gig, gin, gist, giving, gnash, gnat, ha, hag, hang, hank, has, hat, hating, having, hi, hiking, hinging, hint, his, hit, in, ink, insight, is, it, kin, king, kit, kiting, knight, knit, nag, nigh, night, ninth, sag, saint, sang, sank, sat, saving, shag, shaking, shank, shaving, shin, sigh, sight, sign, sin, sing, sink, sit, siting, skating, ski, skin, skit, snag, snaking, stag, staging, stain, stank, staving, sting, stink, tag, taking, tan, tang, tank, task, than, thank, thin, thing, think, this, tin, ting, vain, van, vast, vat, via, visa, vista

Puzzle 121

MIRIAM
JOCHEBED

EUNICE
LOIS

DINAH
LEAH

LO-RUHAMAH
GOMER

Puzzle 122

For if ye forgive men their trespasses, your heavenly Father will also forgive you. (Matthew 6:14)

Puzzle 123

Puzzle 127

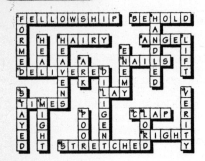

Puzzle 130

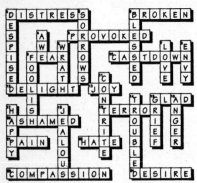

Puzzle 131

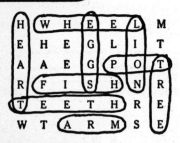

Puzzle 132

Be fruitful and multiply; fill the earth and subdue it; have dominion over the fish of the sea, over the birds of the air, and over every living thing that moves on the earth. (Genesis 1:28, NKJ)

Puzzle 133

Puzzle 134

JERUSALEM
GARMENTS
PALM
BRANCHES
DONKEY
JESUS
KING

HOSANNA

Puzzle 135

MARANATHA

Puzzle 136

OUR LORD COMETH

Puzzle 137

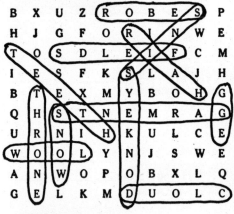

Puzzle 138

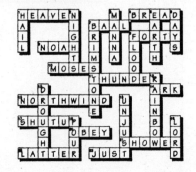

Puzzle 139

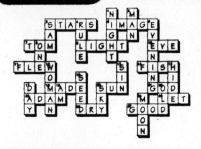

Puzzle 140

Dog
Camel
Lion
Lamb
Dragon
Mouse
Owl
Bear
Horse
Eagle
Cow

Puzzle 141

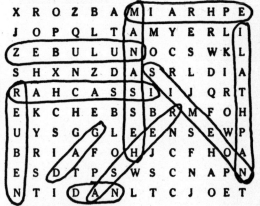

JUDAH, BENJAMIN

Puzzle 143

Abraham (Genesis 15:5)
Joseph (Genesis 37:9)
Wise Men (Matthew 2:2)
Jesus (Luke 21:25)

Puzzle 145

1 G	6 S
2 H	7 R
3 A	8 D
4 O	9 N
5 E	10 T

God has a reason for the seasons.

Puzzle 146

Paul
Mary
Leper
Peter
John
Adulteress
Bartimaeus
Centurion
Demoniac
Woman at Well

BE MADE WHOLE

Puzzle 147

Five of these women appear happy, five sad.

Puzzle 149

The people were all filled with the Holy Spirit.

Puzzle 150

TABERNACLE

abate, able, ace, act, alb, ale, alter, an, ant, antler, arc, arcane, are, art, at, baa, baal, bale, ban, bar, barn, barnacle, bat, be, bean, bear, beat, bee, been, beer, beet, bent, beret, bet, blat, bran, cab, cable, can, cane, canter, car, care, cart, cat, cent, center, clean, clean, clear, cleat, crab, ear, earl, earn, eat, eaten, eater, eel, elect, enable, enabler, enter, lab, lace, lane, late, later, lean, lean, learn, leer, let, nab, near, neat, net, race, ran, rant, rat, rate, react, real, rebel, recant, recent, reclean, reel, rent, tab, table, talc, tale, tan, tar, tare, tea, teal, tear, tee, teen, ten, tenable, tenacle, term

Puzzle 151

12 + 12 - 7 - 3 + 100 - 66 + 3 = 16 and 1 + 6 = 7

Puzzle 154

I AM WHO I AM.

I AM HAS SENT ME TO YOU.

Puzzle 155

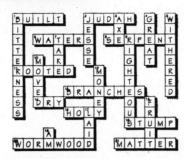

Puzzle 156

THOU SHALT FEAR THE LORD THY GOD, AND SERVE HIM AND SHALT SWEAR BY HIS NAME.

Puzzle 158

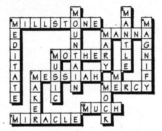

Puzzle 160

Heavenly Father

Puzzle 161

The fruit of the righteous is a tree of life; and he that winneth souls is wise. (Proverbs 11:30)

Puzzle 163

JASPER
SAPPHIRE
CHALCEDONY
EMERALD
SARDONYX
SARDIUS
CHRYSOLITE
BERYL
TOPAZ
CHRYSOPRASE
JACINTH
AMETHYST

PEARL

Puzzle 164

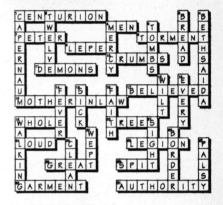

Puzzle 165

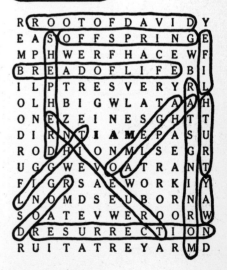

Puzzle 166

Frankincense

Puzzle 171

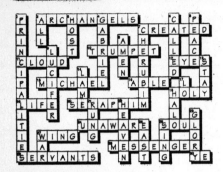

Puzzle 173

Those who are well have no need of a physician, but those who are sick. *(Matthew 9:12)*

Puzzle 174

Puzzle 175

YOU ARE THE CHRIST, THE SON OF THE LIVING GOD. *(Matthew 16:16)*

Puzzle 176

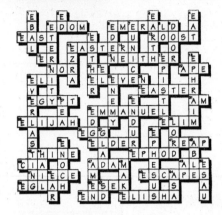

Puzzle 177

SALT - US
BREAD - JESUS
LIGHT - both JESUS and US
VINE - JESUS
BRANCHES - US

Puzzle 178

The matches are: 1-D, 2-J, 3-F, 4-I, 5-A, 6-H, 7-C, 8-B, 9-G, 10-E.

The verse is: A word fitly spoken is like apples of gold in settings of silver.

Puzzle 180

Puzzle 181

GRACE AND PEACE TO YOU FROM GOD THE FATHER AND FROM OUR LORD JESUS CHRIST.

Puzzle 182

600 - 365 - 75 - 30 - 8 - 50 - 60 = 12

Puzzle 183

DANIEL .... LION
SAMSON ....FOX
DAVID .... BEAR (Also a lion)
PAUL .... VIPER

Puzzle 184

LAW
QUAIL
PILLAR
CLOUD
WATER
TABERNACLE
MANNA
FIRE
RULERS
GARMENTS

Puzzle 185

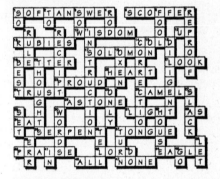

Puzzle 186

IN MY FATHER'S HOUSE ARE MANY MANSIONS. . . . I GO TO PREPARE A PLACE FOR YOU. *(John 14:2)*

Puzzle 187

BEHOLD, I STAND AT THE DOOR AND KNOCK. IF ANYONE HEARS MY VOICE AND OPENS THE DOOR, I WILL COME IN TO HIM AND DINE WITH HIM, AND HE WITH ME. *(Revelation 3:20)*

DEVOTION

Puzzle 188

JOSEPH	CARPENTER
PETER	FISHERMAN
MATTHEW	TAX COLLECTOR
LUKE	PHYSICIAN
PAUL	TENTMAKER
GIDEON	BAKER
NEHEMIAH	CUPBEARER
ESAU	HUNTER
JACOB	SHEPHERD
TERTULLUS	ORATOR
JULIUS	CENTURION
SIMON	TANNER
DEBORAH	JUDGE
FELIX	GOVERNOR
LYDIA	BUSINESSWOMAN
DAVID	ARMORBEARER

Puzzle 190

Puzzle 191

At least 50 words can be made from the letters in the names Abraham and Sarah:

ah, aha, am, an, and, arm, as, baa, bad, bam, ban, band, bar, barn, bash, bra, brahma, brash, dab, dam, damn, darn, dash, dram, ha, had, ham, hand, hard, harm, harsh, has, hash, ma, mad, man, mar, marsh, mash, nab, rad, rah, ram, ran, rand, rash, sad, sand, shah, sham

Puzzle 192

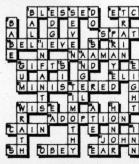

HUMBLE

Puzzle 193

For unto us a Child is born, unto us a Son is given; and the government will be upon His shoulder. And His name will be called Wonderful, Counselor, Mighty God, Everlasting Father, Prince of Peace. *(Isaiah 9:6)*

IMMANUEL

Puzzle 195

JEWS	HAMAN	GALLOWS
VASHTI	FEAST	ROBE
QUEEN	MORDECAI	SCEPTER
FAST		ESTHER

DELIVERANCE

Puzzle 197

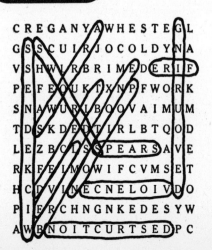

Puzzle 198

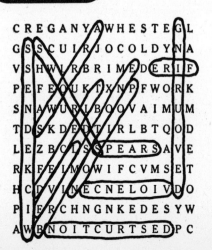

Puzzle 200

The disciples are Peter, James, John, Andrew, Philip, Bartholomew, Matthew, Thomas, James, Thaddaeus, Simon, Judas, and Matthias.

Praise His name!

Puzzle 201

JE
RUS
AL
E
M

JERUSALEM

Puzzle 203

1 The Lord God

2 Men who walked with Jesus on Emmaus Road

3 Booths Peter wanted to build on the Mount of Transfiguration

4 Men King Nebuchadnezzar saw in the burning fiery furnace

5 Philistine lords

6 Measures of barley Boaz poured into Ruth's shawl

7 Dips Elijah told Naaman to take in the Jordan River

8 Josiah's age when he became king

9 Hour in which Jesus died on the cross (3 p.m. is called the "ninth" hour in the Scriptures because the Hebrews start counting the hours of the day at 6 in the morning)

10 Times that Laban changed Jacob's wages

11 Stars that bowed to Joseph in his dream

12 Apostles of Jesus

Puzzle 204

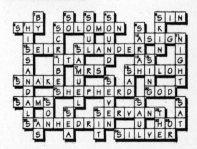

Puzzle 206

At least 150 words can be made from the letters in the phrase PENTECOST SUNDAY:

ace, ad, an, and, ape, as, at, ate, aye, can, cane, cap, cape, case, cast, cat, cease, cent, coast, coat, cod, cone, cop, cost, cot, coupe, cud, cup, cuss, cut, dance, date, daunt, day, den, dense, done, dope, dose, dote, douse, dunce, dune, dupe, dust, dusty, ease, east, eat, enter, eye, nap, nape, nasty, nay, neat, nest, net, no, node, none, nope, nose, not, note, nut, on, once, one, open, pact, pan, pane, pansy, pant, past, paste, pat, patty, pay, peace, peat, peer, pen, pence, pent, pest, pet, petty, pond, pone, pose, posey, posse, post, pot, pout, pun, puss, pussy, sand, sap, sat, say, seat, seen, send, sent, set, so, son, sop, soup, spay, stand, stay, steep, step, stone, stop, sun, Sunday, sunny, tact, tan, tap, tape, taste, taupe, tea, tee, teen, ten, tense, tent, test, to, toast, today, ton, top, tot, tote, tout, toy, Tuesday, tune, yap, ye, yeast, yen, yep, yes, yet, you

Puzzle 207

Churches:
Rome, Corinth, Galatia, Ephesus, Philippi

Letters:

For all have sinned and fall short of the glory of God (Romans 3:23)

The greatest of these is love (1 Corinthians 13:13)

Whatever a man sows, that he will also reap (Galatians 6:7)

Children, obey your parents in the Lord (Ephesians 6:1)

I can do all things through Christ who strengthens me (Philippians 4:13)

Puzzle 208

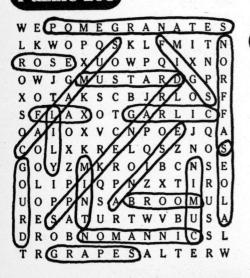

Puzzle 209

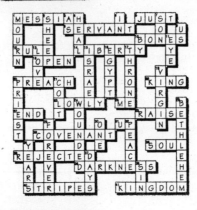

Puzzle 210

ANDREW - PETER
AARON - MOSES
CAIN - ABEL
JACOB - ESAU

Puzzle 211

Puzzle 212

ANTIOCH

Puzzle 213

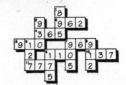

Puzzle 214

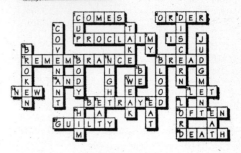

COMMUNION

Puzzle 215

STAR	BETHLEHEM
JOSEPH	MANGER
INN	SHEPHERDS
WISE MEN	FRANKINCENSE
MARY	GOLD
SWADDLING CLOTHS	MYRRH
HEAVENLY HOST	

HAPPY BIRTHDAY!

Puzzle 216

MOSES ....SINAI
JESUS ....OLIVES
ABRAHAM ....MORIAH
NOAH ....ARARAT
DAVID ....ZION
ELIJAH ....CARMEL

Puzzle 217

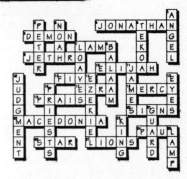

Puzzle 218

Puzzle 219

1-G   5-B
2-E   6-F
3-D   7-D
4-A   8-C

Puzzle 221

Puzzle 223

Puzzle 225

GODS   SABBATH   ADULTERY
IMAGE   FATHER   STEAL
NAME   MOTHER   WITNESS
VAIN   MURDER   COVET

COMMANDMENTS

Puzzle 226

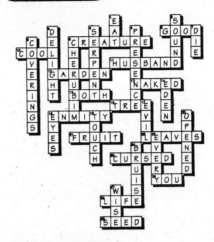

Puzzle 228

Jesus said that only the "sign of Jonah" would be given.

Puzzle 229

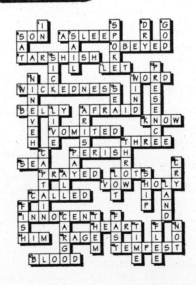

Puzzle 230

Book of Life

Puzzle 231

"ASK AND IT WILL BE GIVEN TO YOU; SEEK, AND YOU WILL FIND; KNOCK, AND IT WILL BE OPENED TO YOU," SAID JESUS. *(Matthew 7:7)*

Puzzle 232

More than 150 words with two or more letters can be made from the letters in the words OLD TESTAMENT:

ad, alms, amen, amend, ant, as, at, dam, dame, damn, date, deal, dean, deem, den, dense, dent, do, doe, dole, dolt, dome, done, dose, dot, dote, ease, eat, eel, elm, eon, lad, lame, land, lane, last, late, latest, lease, least, led, lee, lend, lent, let, lo, load, loam, lode, lose, lost, lot, ma, mad, made, male, man, mane, manse, mantle, mast, mat, mate, me, mead, mean, meat, meet, men, mend, met, metal, moat, mold, most, name, neat, need, net, nettle, no, nod, node, nose, note, oat, ode, old, omen, on, one, sad, same, sand, sea, seal, seam, seat, see, seed, seem, seen, seldom, sent, set, settle, slam, slant, slate, sled, sleet, slot, so, sold, solemn, son, stale, stand, state, steal, steam, steed, steel, stem, stole, stolen, stone, stoned, tame, tan, tat, tea, teal, team, tease, tee, teem, teen, ten, tend, tense, test, testament, to, toad, toast, toes, told, tome, ton, tonal, tot, total, tote, totem

Puzzle 233

MATTHEW   ACTS
JAMES   CORINTHIANS
MARK   GALATIANS
PHILEMON   REVELATION
TITUS   JUDE
JOHN   ROMANS
EPHESIANS   HEBREWS
TIMOTHY   THESSALONIANS
PETER   COLOSSIANS
LUKE   PHILIPPIANS

TESTAMENT

Puzzle 234

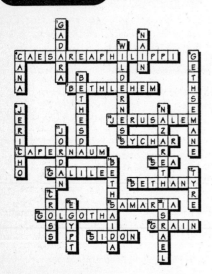

Puzzle·237

CO • MM • AND • M • EN • TS

COMMANDMENTS

Puzzle 238

To everything there is a season, a time for every purpose under heaven. *(Ecclesiastes 3:1)*

Puzzle 240

Ezekiel ....Ezekiel 36:27
Jeremiah ....Jeremiah 31:33
Isaiah ....Isaiah 1:18

Puzzle 241

I will sing to the LORD, for He has triumphed gloriously! The horse and its rider He has thrown into the sea! The LORD is my strength and song, and He has become my salvation; He is my God, and I will praise Him; My Father's God, and I will exalt Him. *(Exodus 15:1–2)*

Puzzle 243

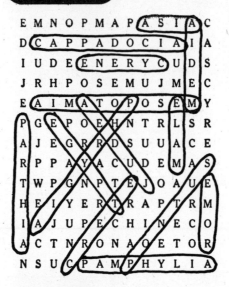

Puzzle 244

DEUTERONOMY
NUMBERS
LEVITICUS

PSALMS
GENESIS
EXODUS

SCRIPTURES

Note: The first five books of the Bible — Genesis, Exodus, Leviticus, Numbers, and Deuteronomy — are called the "Law." The word "Psalms" means "Songs." The Old Testament is referred to as the "Scriptures" by Jesus.

Puzzle 245

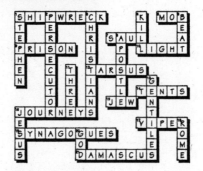

Puzzle 246

1-B 2-D 3-A 4-C

Puzzle 248

Woe to you, scribes and Pharisees, hypocrites! For you cleanse the outside of the cup and dish, but inside they are full of extortion and self-indulgence. *(Matthew 23:25)*

Puzzle 249

Puzzle 251

1. Rejoice always.
2. Pray without ceasing.
3. In everything give thanks.

Puzzle 252

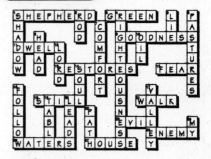

Puzzle 253

The churches are:
   Pergamos, Sardis, Laodicea, Ephesus, Smyrna, Thyatira, and Philadelphia

The matches are:
   1 = B, 2 = F, 3 = E, 4 = G, 5 = D, 6 = A, and 7 = C.

Puzzle 254

SA • LV • AT • I • ON

SALVATION

Puzzle 255

Blessed are the poor in spirit, for theirs is the kingdom of heaven. *(Matthew 5:3)*

Puzzle 256

Blessed are those who mourn, for they shall be comforted. *(Matthew 5:4)*

Puzzle 257

Blessed are the meek, for they shall inherit the earth. *(Matthew 5:5)*

Puzzle 258

Blessed are those who hunger and thirst for righteousness, for they shall be filled. *(Matthew 5:6)*

Puzzle 259

Blessed are the merciful, for they shall obtain mercy. *(Matthew 5:7)*

Puzzle 260

Blessed are the pure in heart, for they shall see God. *(Matthew 5:8)*

Puzzle 261

Blessed are the peacemakers, for they shall be called sons of God. *(Matthew 5:9)*

Puzzle 262

Blessed are those who are persecuted for righteousness' sake, for theirs is the kingdom of heaven. *(Matthew 5:10)*

Puzzle 263

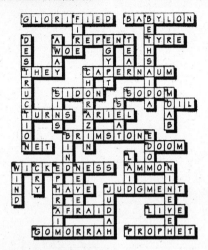

Puzzle 264

SAMUEL .... 1 Samuel 3:11
MOSES .... Exodus 3:7
ISAIAH .... Isaiah 6:9-10

Puzzle 265

ESTHER .... Haman
JESUS .... Zacchaeus
ELIJAH .... Prophets of Baal

Puzzle 266

```
C D I S C B N T E R T O I
L R P A E I G L M O W D N
A O H E C Y I A F I S T T
R W T O N M O I E H H O E
I K N P R E T G A T N I R
M I S M E N D T H G O N P
E N G E I E L E U F P T R
A T O N L Y A E A M E N E
T E Z W X C S H T I N R T
P R O I H E A L I N G U A
P N P S L H C R L R R G T
K R N D A P F A I T H P I
N O X O R O D I K M R E O
T N E M N R E C S I D O N
O O T M I P S N C T E H P
```

Puzzle 267

At least 140 words with two or more letters can be made from the phrase EVERLASTING LIFE:

aft, after, age, agile, ail, air, aisle, ale, all, alter, are, as, at, ate, eat, elite, eternal, ever, everlasting, fail, fair, fall, falter, far, fast, fat, fate, fear, feast, fee, feet, fell, fever, fig, fill, filler, filter, fir, fire, first, fist, five, flat, flirt, fragile, gale, gall, gate, gave, gavel, gear, get, gift, gills, gilt, gist, give, if, ill, ire, is, isle, it, lag, lair, last, late, leaf, least, leave, leer, left, liar, lie, life, lift, lifter, list, live, liver, raft, rag, rail, rate, rave, real, reef, reel, rest, rifle, rig, safe, sag, sail, **sale**, sat, save, sea, seal, sear, seat, see, seel, seer, seige, sell, seller, serf, serge, serve, sieve, sift, sir, sit, site, stag, stair, stall, star, stare, steel, steer, stellar, stifle, stile, still, stir, tag, tail, tale, tall, tear, tea, tee, tell, teller, terse, tie, till, tiller, trill, vale, vase, vast, veer, veil, verse, vest, via, vie, virile, vista

Puzzle 268

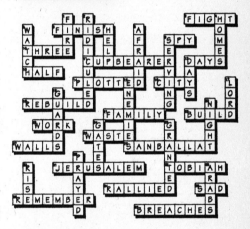

Puzzle 269

Moses — I will sing to the LORD, for He has triumphed gloriously! The horse and its rider He has thrown into the sea! *(Exodus 15:1)*

David — Oh, give thanks to the LORD! Call upon His name; Make known His deeds among the peoples! Sing to Him, sing psalms to Him; talk of all His wondrous works! *(1 Chronicles 16:8–9)*

Deborah & Barak — Let all Your enemies perish, O LORD! But let those who love Him be like the sun when it comes out in full strength. *(Judges 5:31)*

Puzzle 270

MENE MENE TEKEL UPHARSIN

Puzzle 271

MENE: God has numbered your kingdom, and finished it.

TEKEL: You have been weighed in the balances, and found wanting.

PERES (UPHARSIN): Your kingdom has been divided, and given to the Medes and Persians.

Puzzle 273

Cain — the farmer — sheaf of wheat, hoe, and basket of gourds

Abel — the shepherd — a lamb, a ewe, a shepherd's crook

Puzzle 274

Puzzle 275

I will be their God, and they shall be My people. *(Jeremiah 31:33)*

Unscrambled letters: COVENANT

Puzzle 276

Unscrambled words: SCARLET, WHITE, RED, BLACK, GREEN, PURPLE, BLUE, GOLDEN.

Puzzle 277

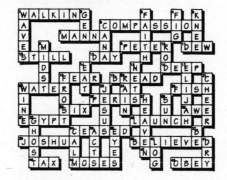

Puzzle 278

1. And God sent me before you to preserve a posterity. *(Genesis 45:7)*

2. You meant evil against me; but God meant it for good. *(Genesis 50:20)*

Puzzle 279

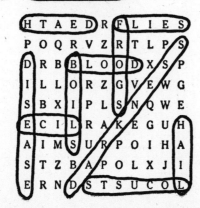

Puzzle 281

BY GRACE THROUGH FAITH (See Ephesians 2:8.)

Puzzle 282

Puzzle 283

The answers to the clues are: Jesus Christ, Matthew, Noah, Solomon, Esther, Lamentations, Jeremiah, Paul, parables, and Samson.

HALLELUJAH is the word used to express praise.

Puzzle 284

Puzzle 285

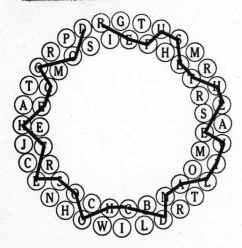

REFUSE THE EVIL AND CHOOSE THE GOOD
(Isaiah 7:16)

Puzzle 286

I WILL MAKE YOU A GREAT NATION;
I WILL BLESS YOU AND MAKE YOUR NAME
GREAT; AND YOU SHALL BE A BLESSING.
I WILL BLESS THOSE WHO BLESS YOU,
AND I WILL CURSE HIM WHO CURSES YOU;
AND IN YOU ALL THE FAMILIES OF THE
EARTH SHALL BE BLESSED. *(Genesis 12:2–3)*

Puzzle 287

Puzzle 289

**Unscrambled names: Absalom, Miriam, Jacob,
Leah, Cain, Benjamin, Gershon, Lazarus**

Siblings

Puzzle 291

1. ABRAHAM AND SARAH; ISAAC
2. JOCHEBED AND AMRAM; MOSES, AARON,
   AND MIRIAM
3. MOSES AND ZIPPORAH; GERSHOM,
   ELIEZER
4. DAVID AND BATHSHEBA; SOLOMON
5. RUTH AND BOAZ; OBED
6. RACHEL AND JACOB; JOSEPH, BENJAMIN
7. ELIZABETH AND ZACHARIAS; JOHN
8. ISAAC AND REBEKAH; ESAU, JACOB
9. HANNAH AND ELKANAH; SAMUEL
10. NAOMI AND ELIMELECH; MAHLON,
    CHILION

Puzzle 292

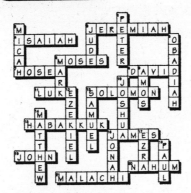

Puzzle 293

Beloved, let us love one another, for love is of
God; and everyone who loves is born of God
and knows God. He who does not love does
not know God, for God is love. . . . Beloved, if
God so loved us, we also ought to love one
another. *(1 John 4:7–8,11)*

Puzzle 294

CAR - R = CA   VALLEY - LLEY = VA
LEFT - EFT = L   RAY - A = RY

CALVARY

Puzzle 295

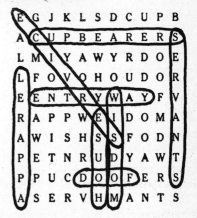

Puzzle 296

NGKI = KING
EBOAMTIS = MOABITES
KYDENO = DONKEY
ORAD = ROAD
LIEDF = FIELD
OTOF = FOOT
FATFS = STAFF
LEGAN = ANGEL
KEPAS = SPEAK

Puzzle 297

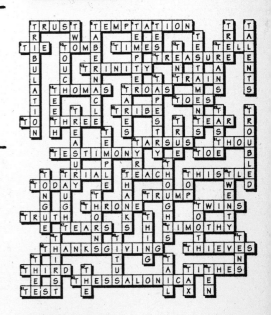

Puzzle 298

TRUTH

PUZZLE ANSWERS

Puzzle 299

If the Son makes you free, you shall be free indeed. *(John 8:36)*

Puzzle 300

RENEW	Isaiah 40:31
RESTORE	Joel 2:25
REBUILD	Nehemiah 2:5
RECONCILE	Colossians 1:19–20
REDEEM	Micah 4:10
REFRESH	Philemon 20
RECOVER	Mark 16:18
REPAID	Proverbs 13:21
REPAIRER	Isaiah 58:12
REVIVE	Psalm 138:7
RETURN	Psalm 6:4
REPROVE	Isaiah 1:17

Puzzle 302

STONES: O JERUSALEM, JERUSALEM, THE ONE WHO KILLS THE PROPHETS AND STONES THOSE WHO ARE SENT TO HER!

EGGS: HOW OFTEN I WANTED TO GATHER YOUR CHILDREN TOGETHER, AS A HEN GATHERS HER CHICKS UNDER HER WINGS, BUT YOU WERE NOT WILLING!

(See Matthew 23:37.)

Puzzle 303

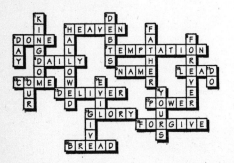

Puzzle 304

WAY
RUBIES
LOVES
LORD
FOOLS
MAN

My name is WISDOM.

Puzzle 305

He who is without sin among you, let him throw a stone at her first. *(John 8:7)*

Puzzle 306

2 x 3 x 3 + 40 - 2 - 10 + 6 = 52

Puzzle 307

JERICHO	SINNER
SALVATION	GUEST
FOURFOLD	SYCAMORE
TAX COLLECTOR	CLIMBED
RICH	SHORT

My name is: ZACCHAEUS

Puzzle 308

FIG
PALM
SYCAMORE
ALMOND
CHESTNUT
ORANGE
OAK
FIR
PEAR
CEDAR
APPLE
BANANA

GARDEN OF EDEN

Puzzle 309

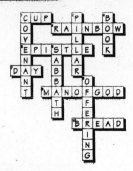

Puzzle 310

ASSUREDLY, I SAY TO YOU, I HAVE NOT FOUND SUCH GREAT FAITH, NOT EVEN IN ISRAEL! *(Matthew 8:10)*

Puzzle 312

LAW
OBEY
TRUTH
ENDURES
SWORD
PERFECT
LIGHT
JOY
SEED

The Bible is the WORD OF GOD.

Puzzle 314

Puzzle 315

INTENT	GENESIS 6:5
FALSE WAY	PSALM 119:104
GOOD PATH	PROVERBS 2:9
CORNER	PROVERBS 7:12
WORD	PROVERBS 14:15
KNEE	ISAIAH 45:23
TONGUE	ISAIAH 45:23
PURPOSE	JEREMIAH 51:29
VISION	EZEKIEL 12:23
FAMILY	ZECHARIAH 12:12
PLACE	MALACHI 1:11
SAINT	PHILIPPIANS 4:21
NAME	EPHESIANS 1:21
GOOD WORK	2 TIMOTHY 2:21
WEIGHT	HEBREWS 12:1
ORDINANCE	1 PETER 2:13
SPIRIT	1 JOHN 4:1
TREE	LUKE 6:44

EVERY GOOD GIFT AND EVERY PERFECT GIFT
IS FROM ABOVE, AND COMES DOWN FROM
THE FATHER OF LIGHTS, WITH WHOM THERE
IS NO VARIATION OR SHADOW OF TURNING.
(James 1:17)

Puzzle 316

BREASTPLATE	RIGHTEOUSNESS
SHIELD	FAITH
SWORD	WORD OF GOD
HELMET	SALVATION
SHOES	GOSPEL OF PEACE

Puzzle 317

CAT - T = CA
FIRE - FIE = R
PEN
TIRE - IE = TR
YODEL - ODEL = Y

CARPENTRY

Puzzle 318

Puzzle 321

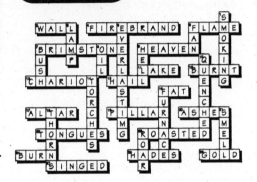

This is to certify that

_____
[child's name]

has successfully completed

_____
[number of puzzles]

puzzles

and is thereby named

Superior Puzzle Worker

on this date

_____
[month, date, and year]

This is to certify that

_____

[child's name]

has successfully completed

_____

[number of puzzles]

puzzles in

Nelson's **GIANT BOOK** of *Bible Activities*

and is thereby named

Superior Puzzle Worker

on this date

_____

[month, day, and year]

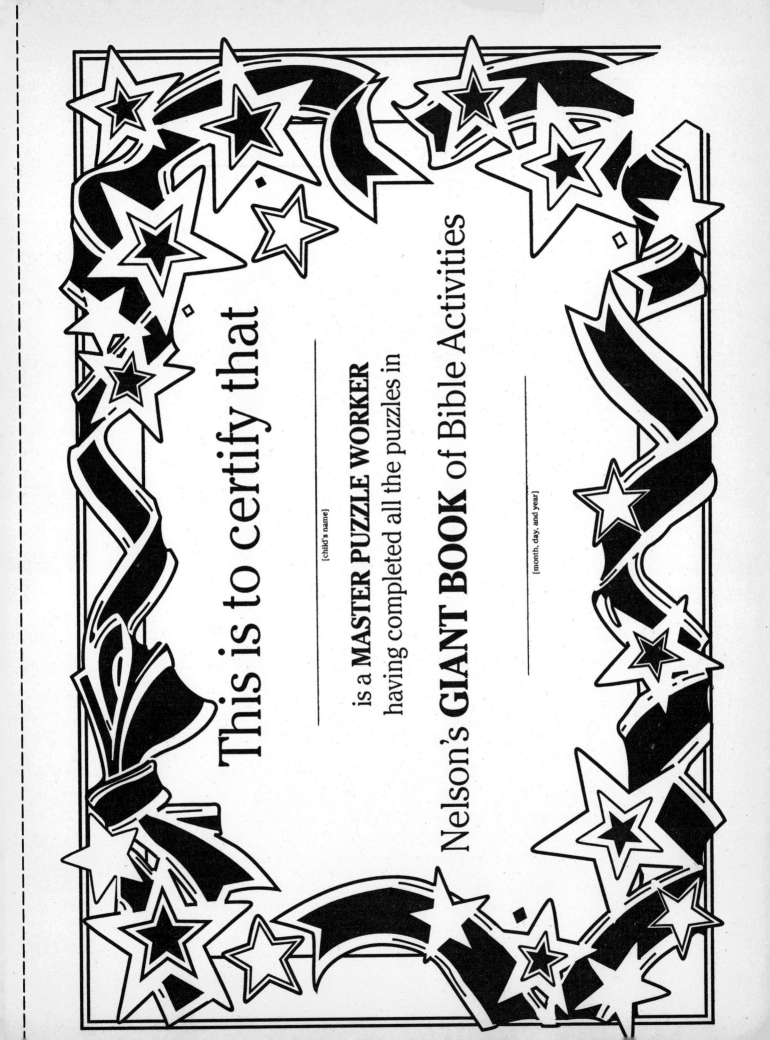

This is to certify that

_____
[child's name]

is a **MASTER PUZZLE WORKER**
having completed all the puzzles in

Nelson's **GIANT BOOK** of Bible Activities

_____
[month, day, and year]